The Curator of Broken Things

Trilogy

Book 2

Escape to the Côte D'Azur

A novel by Corine Gantz

ISBN-13: 978-0-9834366-6-9
ISBN-10: 0-9834366-6-5

To refugees past, present, and future

TABLE OF CONTENTS

Corine Gantz

CHAPTER 1

Ketchup All Over the Place

The early morning light, soft and wintry, entered through the glass pane of Cassie's hotel room window. She lay on her back, the covers up to her chin, wishing she were safely at home in Los Angeles where she belonged and not in Paris where everyone hated her.

Upon arriving four days ago, she had tried to charge her cell phone and laptop by plugging them into a medieval converter, causing them to implode. Now that she was reduced to using public phones like in the eighties, throwing her back into the precise era where she had chosen to get the hell away from her family in the first place, there was the real possibility that she too was about to implode.

She could run away, rush back home on the next flight, but what was there to return to, really? An empty house? A garden in shambles? Motherhood had been her purpose, but Jeanne and Alex were away at their respective colleges, clearly not needing her at all. And was Los Angeles really home? After twenty years, she felt American, but no one let her forget her French accent. She was a foreigner. An immigrant. In Los Angeles, there was work, but her ex's lack of compunction about letting her write his screenplays while he reaped Hollywood's accolades was starting to look a lot like indentured servitude. And the daily witnessing of his matrimonial bliss with Jessica – and by the way Cassie still had not brought Jessica's little gifts to her parents. The perfect little packages were still on the mantle – was beginning to look a lot like masochism.

Peter exploited her. That much she was clear on. But the reason he did, was that she let him. And she let him because five years post-divorce she was still terrified of a life without him.

Damn the mess of her life. Damn the loneliness. There were so many changes she should make, but all of them required bravery and more losses perhaps. The unknown.

Cassie was staring at the ceiling when a faint ray of sun entered the room and hit the crystals that dangled on the chandelier. Blue prisms appeared on the crown molding and swept across the aging wallpaper, briefly transforming the walls of her small hotel room into a kind of fairytale scene. And then, as fast as the enchantment of the light had come, it was gone. She got out of bed and peeked out the window. On the small balcony, the metal table and chairs glistened with dew. Beyond that, shy sunrays bounced off Paris rooftops, and the silhouette of the Eiffel Tower emerged against a pink sky. Beautiful.

She felt a flutter of excitement. Today she had another meeting with Marceline, her father's estranged sister whose existence had been a complete secret until two days ago. Her spry eighty-seven-year-old aunt had already revealed more about her dad than she had known her entire life. And maybe Cassie did have one friend in Paris: Sabine, her younger sister, who did not appear to carry hostility towards her. So, that was something. And there was Hervé, the man with the motorcycle she had met at the Jument Bleue who wanted to have dinner with her, tonight!

She should *never* have said yes to dinner, for so many reasons. Not the least of which was her failure to mention that she lived in the United States and that she was only in Paris for a few more days. She wasn't a monster full of deceit; it's just that it had not come into the conversation. Not that she owed this perfect stranger information about her life. But still, she had flirted, and maybe he had flirted too. Unless he had not; she couldn't be sure. He could as easily be a friendly man (or gay perhaps, or friendly and gay), making amends after their squabble over coveting the same table.

The reasonable thing to do was to cancel dinner, but how? Hervé had not given her his number, and anyway she didn't have a phone. She looked at the clock: seven a.m. He had mentioned that he had breakfast at the Jument Bleue every day before work, so maybe she could catch him there and nip things in the bud nice and clean. It was time she acted like her steady, serious, dependable self. The self that seemed to have gone missing from the moment she had landed in Paris a few days ago. All she needed to do right now was to imagine her twins' reaction to the idea of her having dinner with a stranger to realize how ludicrous it was.

She jumped into her jeans, put on the second-hand red cowboy boots bought the day before, wrapped herself in her grandfather's ill-fitting coat, and ran down the stairs.

At the desk, the elderly proprietor, his bushy white hair and eyebrows uncombed, was trying to button the top collar of his shirt with trembling fingers. "Bonjour, Monsieur!" she called out as she zoomed past him.

"Doucement, doucement," he sighed. "The youth, always rushing."

"I'm forty years old," she called out as she pushed open the door.

"You're a child," the old man responded.

Outside, it was another glorious spring day in Paris: cold, blustery, and wet. She put her purse over her head and, hopping around puddles, hurried toward the Jument Bleue.

The café was loud and filled to capacity with people having their last espresso of the morning (and in some instances their first glass of Beaujolais) before work. Remembering the Open Sesame of all French interactions – something she would have done well to remember the day before when dealing with the creeps at the hospital, Cassie spotted the owner. She called out over the roar of the espresso machine, "Bonjour, Madame. Comment ça va ce matin?"

The patronne, who seemed even more bosomy, pink-cheeked, and small-waisted than the day before, which was remarkable for a woman well into her sixties, looked at Cassie crosswise. But her expression softened somewhat when she recognized her. "Almost no complaints," she said, adding, "a café au lait?" After only two days, Cassie was being treated like one of the regulars, a small reward that made her feel good in a pitiable sort of way.

She took her café au lait and waited with a mix of dread and impatience until 7:30, but Hervé did not appear. "That man," she asked the patronne finally, "the one who comes here all the time, was he here this morning?"

The patronne shrugged. "A hundred men come here every day, Madame."

"The handsome one," Cassie said. "With the motorcycle."

"Ah, oui. You missed him. He left five minutes before you got here."

"Do you know how I could reach him?"

"You can always telephone him," the patronne said.

"Do you have his number?" Cassie asked too eagerly.

The patronne laughed out loud. "Well, like you, the one he gives away is the one to the Jument. It looks like you people have put yourself in a bind."

Back in her hotel room, Cassie mulled over her options. Her meeting with Marceline was not until noon, and hospital visiting hours started after that. After seeing Marceline, she was determined to see her dad, even if that entailed forcing her way into the hospital, wringing her mother's and sister's Hermès-clad necks, and stepping right over their still-warm corpses. She hated, HATED them! It would be a relief, it would be a joy, it would be a gift from heaven never to interact with them again! Ever.

She took a shower standing in the massive bathtub, her thoughts running amok. She had not come all the way to France to be denied access to her own father. She too had feelings, in case they had forgotten. She too was a human being! It was not her fault that her dad had hallucinated when he saw her and thought that she was Marceline. It was not her fault that he hated his sister deeply enough to hide her very existence from his three daughters.

Lost in the comfort of warm water over her body, Cassie rehearsed in her mind all the mean things she might tell her mother and Odile. She then toyed for a few more minutes with morbid images involving strangulation until she changed her mind and decided that her overriding urge was to apologize to them, implore, beg, and crawl on her hands and knees, whatever it took, until they saw how lovable and humble and harmless she was. Sabine did not seem to see her as this formidable opponent. If Sabine did not see her as the enemy, maybe there was hope to get through to Odile and her mother.

She got out of the bathroom and dried her hair with a towel. With the humidity, all hope of looking appropriately polished would need to be abandoned at once. Her hair would look like a cross between lichen and a crow's nest, and that was that. She still had about three hours before going to Marceline's. Maybe in the meantime, she could go to her mom's apartment with the excuse of bringing Jessica's gifts. She would pretend to come with a peace offering and then give her and Odile hell about what they had done. Unless they apologized to her. Or felt guilty. Or something. If they put her name back on the list, she would consider being magnanimous.

****

She stepped out of the hotel and into the street. The rain had stopped. Her parent's apartment was at the corner of Boulevard Barbès and rue Ordener, about a twenty-minute walk from her hotel. She was wondering how in the world she was going to cancel that dinner with Hervé when she walked past the gate of the hospital where her dad was being treated. She stopped to face the building, which looked more like an annex of the Louvre than a hospital, with its stone archways and planted center courtyard. A flurry of people freely came in and out, which was bitterly ironic considering that she was not allowed in and that her father was unable to get out. No good whatsoever would come from going inside she realized. Not only was she banned from her dad's room, but she had alienated the doctors, nurses, and staff with whom she had come into contact. Every interaction at the hospital, whether with the staff, her mother, her sister, or, worse yet, her very ill father, had been an epic disaster. But before she quite realized what she was doing, or why, she was walking through the gate and heading for the intensive care unit.

She knew the way by heart now, loathing every inch of it. She walked through the colonnaded marble walkways alongside the series of tall, arched windows that looked out into the central garden, passing through the peculiar mix of state-of-the-art medical facilities and nineteenth-century architecture. She peeked through the glass of the double doors to the intensive care unit. The waiting room was empty. Only a few nurses and doctors in white coats passed by, busy looking at files or on their cellphones. There was no one behind the reception desk.

She stood by the door, thinking. Two doors down the hallway was her dad, so close and yet so out of reach. She felt a pang of angst. What if she returned to the United States before he awakened? Would their last interaction be one where he screamed at her, mistaking her for someone else? No, she could not bear the thought of this. She had not come to France hoping for a reconciliation, but now she desperately wanted one. Especially now that, thanks to Marceline, she sensed the suffering of his childhood. In the back of her mind, there had always been time to make up with her father.

She thought it would eventually happen when she stopped being angry at him. How ridiculous. He was eighty-five years old. If they did not speak now, if he did not see her and feel her love at long last, if there was not some kind of healing between them now, when would they get the chance?

If she were to go through the door, past the now empty reception desk, she could be by his side in a dozen steps.

She slowly pushed open the door and slithered inside the waiting room. She was alone! She walked toward her dad's room as furtively as she could manage, stepping on the tip of her red cowboy boots in slow motion, cutting through the regulations and interdictions like a knife going through butter. Her hand was on the door to her dad's room when she heard a woman's voice. "You know that's not happening!"

She felt nauseated. It was the odious Mademoiselle Pinçon, the intensive-care unit clerk and obstructionist-in-chief. The woman had her arms crossed on her chest, an expression of outrage on her greenish face. Today she wore her hair pineapple-style, in a fuzzy bun on top of her head.

"What's not happening?" Cassie asked disingenuously.

"You know very well that you're not allowed in that room," Pinçon said.

"I know that," Cassie snapped. "Why do you think I'm showing up here outside of visiting hours?"

Pinçon did not buy this for a second. "Then why are you here?"

"To make an appointment with your Chief of Services. What was his name again?"

"I told you we do not give out names, and I told you that he does not see people."

"And I told you to give him a message that I wanted to meet him regardless. Did you?"

"He's well aware of the entire situation."

"Then let him know that I want to see him and let him decide for himself like a big boy!"

"Madame, there is no reason to raise your voice!"

"You raised yours!"

"You need to leave," Pinçon said. "You aren't welcome here."

Cassie had the urge to grab Pinçon by the bun and shake. "You better tell him about me, or I will go right over your head."

"And what if he won't see you? What will you do then?" Pinçon asked with a smirk.

"Then I'll go right over *his* head. You tell him that. Also tell him that I will fight this with legal means if I have to. But before that, I'll write letters to every journalist, every blogger, every sick person in Paris and expose how this hospital treats its clients."

They were facing each other, both of them breathing hard, both of them overflowing with righteous indignation. In Cassie's peripheral vision, she noticed nurses, interns, a security guard, all looking at her. She turned around toward the exit door and said, "I'll be back today. And by then you better have an appointment time for me."

Outside, she took a huge gulp of fresh morning air to steady her lungs, then hurried away. She needed for Odile and her mother to put her back on the visitor's list and to do that today. Fuming, she hurried up rue Thimonnier. It took her a while to notice the motorcyclist who was driving alongside her, slowing the cars behind him on the narrow, one-way street. There was a honking sound, and she looked in his direction.

"Hervé?"

"Bonjour!" he shouted over the noise of the engine. He still had his helmet on, and she could only see his eyes, which were smiling and so very blue.

She walked faster with the hope that he would not notice how flustered she was. "Ah, hem. Hello," she said.

"What?" he shouted.

"Hello," she shouted back. Behind them, cars began to honk. She trotted faster.

"Do you need a ride somewhere?" he shouted.

"No, I hmm. No. As a matter of fact, I was looking for you this morning," she said, but loud honking of the cars behind Hervé covered her voice.

"What?"

She looked over her shoulder at the cars and angry drivers. "I was looking for you this morning!" she shouted.

"What?" he said.

"I went to the Jument this morning to tell you that I'm busy tonight so I can't—"

"I'm picking you up at the hotel then," he shouted.

"I can't," she shouted back. "I need to cancel."

"D'accord. Around seven p.m."

"No, but—"

"Ok, perfect, see you tonight!" With this, he lowered his visor and drove off.

She stood on the pavement as his motorcycle sped away and turned the corner. "What? No …," she mumbled.

She walked toward her parent's apartment replaying the interaction with Pinçon and the one with Hervé, wondering how they both got mangled so fast and so beyond repair. When she arrived at rue Ordener, the outdoor market was in full swing. The rain was dripping along the sides of awnings, and people in raincoats struggled to fit their umbrellas in the narrow aisles. Merchants called out their prices as people took money from wallets and put groceries in baskets.

Cassie cut through the aisles, the flower shop, the cheese shop, the butcher, the vegetable stands, all so familiar to her, and arrived at the foot of her parent's building, a graceless structure built in the sixties. She buzzed several times without an answer. A woman let herself in and, recognizing Cassie perhaps from years ago, let her enter. In the elevator, Cassie stared at her feet. The woman's straw bag was full of groceries from the market below. There was a baguette in her bag, and from the smell of it, cheese too. But the smell of bread and cheese did not mask the scent of the elevator, so familiar from her childhood. Polish, metal, and perfumes all combined to form a specific alchemy of scents that was like that of no other elevator, in no other street, in no other city. It was the smell of her teenage years, of being bored to tears, of dreaming of escape, of sunlight, of vast expanses of sky.

She knocked on the door to her parent's apartment, but no one answered. Her mother was probably at the market. Cassie felt with her fingers for the key her mother left in a small crack hidden in the wood casing above the door jam and let herself in.

Even in the dark, the smells in the apartment, of her mother's cooking, of that lemony detergent with which she washed everything, the faint scent of mothballs emanating from the coat closet, and her father's lavender aftershave swept her back to childhood, to adolescence, but also back to an underdeveloped, meeker, and more frightened version of herself.

She turned on the light. The entry and living room looked as she remembered it. She inspected the apartment, walking from room to room. The bedroom she once shared with Odile was full of stuffed animals and toys, probably for Odile's children when they came over. Sabine's bedroom had become a laundry hub. There was a drying rack next to the heater, an ironing board in the center of the room, a pile of neatly folded towels on the bed. The rest of the apartment appeared frozen in time. It was dense with her parent's furniture, all in excellent taste, mostly copies but a few authentic eighteenth-century pieces. Her father's rug collection covered the wood floor: Afghan, Turkish, Persian, each precisely in the spot where it had always been. The art on the wall was unimaginative: prints of famous masterpieces, posters of museum exhibitions. Everything was in its place; everything was safe. The throw pillows matched the curtains and what could be in pairs, was: a pair of ceramic owls, a pair of leather armchairs, a pair of candelabra on the mantelpiece. In a corner, the glass cabinet where they displayed their special things. The result was an air of properness, of permanence, of whatever one might call the opposite of free spirit, the opposite of possibilities.

There were so many memories in this apartment or not quite memories – her family was not big on that concept – more like feelings. Not pleasant ones. The feeling of claustrophobia, of starving for daylight. It was the location of the apartment, on the second floor in a narrow street with windows facing north. How many hours had she spent looking out the window staring at the rain, staring at the windows across the street for something interesting to see, never seeing anything? How many hours had she spent at the kitchen table, doodling and procrastinating when she should have been studying? How many hours sitting on that couch, in front of the TV, watching reruns of *Dallas* and *Starsky et Hutch* in a state of apathy so complete and so deep that even going to the bathroom to pee took effort? How many hours, days, years, waiting for her life to begin at last?

In the kitchen, there were the same table and four chairs, same pans lined up on the wall in order of sizes, but now everything had more of a worn look. The stove sported a few permanent stains. The cabinets' paint was chipped in places. The walls had taken on a yellowish hue.

She realized she was hungry. Knowing her mother's clock-like schedule, she was certain Raymonde would soon return with a baguette. But on second thought, Cassie decided that she would look bad for waiting for her mother to feed her like a child. Despite being renowned in the family as a disastrous cook, a label she shook off while in the United States, where every other person was a self-proclaimed disastrous cook, in France that title stuck to her like infamy. But she was perfectly capable of making herself a couple of fried eggs. She opened the refrigerator. There were eggs and, thank goodness, ketchup.

She took a pan from the cupboard, turned on the heat on the stove, added a dollop of butter to the pan, cracked the eggs into it, added salt and pepper. She took the ketchup out of the refrigerator and smiled in spite of herself because it reminded her of how Hervé had teased her about her passion for the condiment. There was only a little bit left at the bottom of the bottle. She shook it, but nothing came to the top. She hoped she would not be thinking about Hervé every time she used ketchup from here on out. She was too old to flirt like that. But it had felt so nice to have a man talk to her. A handsome man. A handsome man who rode a motorcycle like in dumb romance novels.

She contemplated the bottle, shook it more energetically. Still, nothing came to the top. She tapped it against the kitchen table and suddenly, for no reason at all, the top snapped off, and a thick red spray squirted out, volcano-style, onto the table, all over the floor, and even on the kitchen wall. "Merde!" she said. There were no paper towels or dish towels in sight. She stepped over the ketchup spill and zoomed out of the kitchen toward Sabine's room and grabbed a small embroidered towel from the pile of laundry.

She walked through the living room on the way back to the kitchen and stood for a minute in front of the glass cabinet that contained her parents' few precious things: the set of six Baccarat champagne glasses, the silver ice bucket, the Limoges porcelain dishes that were only taken out at Christmas. Christmas: what a joke, what a travesty. Why had her father hidden from his daughters that he was Jewish? What did it matter if he was? These were not the 1930s for heaven sake! No wonder Christmases at her house had always been depressing. It had all been a big lie.

Her father's finial was here, on the shelf, identical to the one his sister Marceline possessed. The finial wasn't much to look at for something he made such a fuss about. In fact, the matching finial in Marceline's Cité des Fleurs house, where everything was so bohemian and bigger than life, had glowed like a precious object imbued with mystery and meaning. But here, in her parents' cramped, puny life, the finial looked insignificant. It was about the size and shape of a toilet paper roll, only made out of some kind of intricately carved metal, hollow in the middle and shaped sort of like a crown with tiny bells dangling here and there.

She opened the cabinet and took the finial out, turning it in her hands. She felt its weight, its fragility, between her fingers. This was not the first time she was looking at it up closely. When she was a child, she had sneaked it out of the cabinet many times when her parents were out of the house, mostly because it was forbidden to open that cabinet. So how could she resist? She was perhaps fifteen or sixteen when she had first paid attention to the inscription inside, engraved in tiny letters: 29 Boulevard Haussmann, Paris. A few days later, she had taken the métro there with romantic notions to uncover powerful family secrets. She had expected to find an antique store at that address, or an art dealer, where some wise old men knew … something. But it was only a Société Générale Bank. She remembered going inside and being struck by the beautiful art deco glass dome, the polished wood counters, the intricate mosaic across the floor. She learned that the bank had been built in the early 1900s and that it was one of the oldest banks in Paris, but she had not known whom to ask about a finial, so she had returned home.

Cassie turned the finial over, looking inside and under it. What part of her had reminded her father of Marceline so strongly, she wondered, that his rage at his sister had spewed out of him like out of a flamethrower the moment he saw her at the hospital? Was it the way she looked? She and Marceline had similar eye color. And Marceline too had black hair in her youth. Was it the way she spoke? The way she moved? And for how long had her father perceived those similarities?

Was it only that day at the hospital, in a morphine haze, or had it been going on for much longer?

And what was that red stuff at her feet on her father's best Kilim rug?

Her heart sank. Was this Ketchup?

She must have accidentally stepped in it in the kitchen, and now it was everywhere! She looked around and could practically retrace her steps. She had tracked ketchup all over the house. On every frigging Persian rug!

At that moment, her mother and sister entered the apartment. What they saw upon entering was the cabinet wide open, ketchup everywhere, and Cassie red-handed with the finial in her hands.

Odile gasped. "Cassandra?"

"Were you taking my finial?" Raymonde asked.

"I – no, of course not. I was just looking at it."

"How did you get in?" Odile said as she snatched the finial out of Cassie's hand and placed it back on the shelf.

Cassie let her do this without resistance. "The key above the door jam," she murmured.

Raymonde rushed to inspect the stain below Cassie's feet. "Oh, mon Dieu! Is this blood?"

"Just ... ketchup."

"Just?" Raymonde bellowed.

"Relax," Cassie said. "I'll wipe it off."

"Not with my best towels you won't," Raymonde said, pulling the embroidered hand towel from Cassie's clutched fingers.

"You can't just barge in here without warning," Odile said.

"I don't see why not. It's my childhood home too. I have as much right to be here as you do," Cassie said, her face hot with embarrassment.

"Why would you want to take the finial and spill ketchup everywhere?" Raymonde said.

"I was not taking it, I—"

"Why did you come here?"

Cassie improvised. "To bring you presents."

"What presents?"

Cassie looked at her hands in the hope that they might magically appear there. "I guess I forgot them at the hotel." Raymonde looked at her with increased suspicion.

"Regardless, you could have called us first," Odile pointed out.

"My cell phone is fried, remember?"

"Which by the way makes no sense at all," Odile said.

"Stop treating me like I'm irresponsible!"

Raymonde sniffed the air, frowning. "What is that smell?" she asked no one in particular.

Odile sniffed, looking around. "Something's burning," she stated.

Cassie's eyes widened. "The eggs!"

All three sprang toward the kitchen and opened the door to a thick black cloud that emanated from a flaming pan. In an instant, Raymonde had put water in the pan and Odile had opened the window and was fanning away the smoke. Cassie stood there feeling horrible.

"I can't believe this. Incroyable!" Odile said.

"I was starving."

"You have a genius for chaos."

"Oh, give me a frigging break, Odile. Like you've never had a pan catch on fire."

"Actually, I don't believe I have."

"Of course, Mademoiselle perfect!"

When the smoke was gone, and they had spent thirty minutes on all fours carefully dabbing at the ketchup stains with damp cloths and baking soda, they sat at the kitchen table. Raymonde put jam, butter, and a baguette in front of Cassie and Odile. She then told them about their dad. She had already spoken to the doctor on the phone this morning. Gustave's status had neither improved nor worsened in the night. The topic of the ignominy of having taken Cassie off the visitors' list was carefully avoided by all.

"I didn't have a phone," Cassie explained, chewing her baguette while Odile and Raymonde sat across from her, observing her like she was a strange animal. "So, I thought I'd stop by. Maman, I met Marceline. I went to her house yesterday."

"The Cité des Fleurs house?" Raymonde asked.

"Have you been there?"

"Your father mentioned it."

"I think I had been there before," Cassie said. "It looked very familiar to me, at least the street, the outside. Do you remember it Odile? I'm pretty sure Papa took us there when we were little."

"I don't," Odile said.

"I don't think I ever went inside, though. I would have remembered. It's pretty grand. Papa grew up there before the war. Marceline lives there now with two adult children from one of her marriages. They take care of her in some ways, but she doesn't seem the kind who likes to be told what to do."

"Was she surprised to meet you? Was she happy?" Odile asked.

"I can't say that she welcomed me with open arms. She did not want to talk at first. Eventually, she warmed to the idea of speaking to me. She told me how they grew up. Marceline is two years older than Papa. Papa's father was from Turkey, believe it or not. He arrived in Paris in the early twenties. His name was Albano. He had a successful rug business for a while."

"Is that why Papa is so into rugs?"

"Must be. Papa's mother was named Lucienne. She was uppity. And they were wealthy."

Odile's face registered doubt. "It's hard to picture Papa with a silver spoon in his mouth."

"Well, believe it," Cassie said. "And there is that other thing." Cassie looked at her sister. When she had broached the subject the day before, it hadn't gone well. "Like the fact that Papa is Jewish," she said tentatively.

Raymonde looked at Cassie, and then at Odile. But Odile was keeping a poker face.

"Apparently, he wanted to hide this," Cassie said. "So much so that he changed his last name,"

Odile tilted her head back in disbelief. "What?"

"Our grandfather's name was Albano Cohen Lombardi. It seems that Papa dropped the "i" at the end, not to mention the Cohen part."

Odile looked genuinely aghast. "Of course not! You're making things up."

"Marceline told me so."

Odile raised her voice. "Well, then *she's* making things up."

Cassie immediately matched Odile's tone. "Someone is making things up, for sure. Me or Marceline. Or Papa. Or Maman. Or you. Someone in this family is lying."

"Maman, is that true?" Odile asked. "Did Papa change his name?" Odile sounded more upset by the thought that their father might have changed his name than by the notion that he had been in the closet regarding religion. Or maybe she had digested that part since learning about it the day before.

"I wouldn't know," Raymonde said. But she was not making eye contact with either of them, which was suspicious.

"If it was true, he would have told me," Odile said with waning assurance.

He had clearly kept Odile in the dark as well, but the reminder that her father and her sister had a privileged relationship hurt Cassie nonetheless. "Would he have? How much do you know about his past? He's not exactly a chatterbox." Raymonde was now going around the kitchen filling the sink with water and putting dirty dishes in it. She was making sure they could not see her expression. "You knew he was Jewish, right Maman?" Cassie said.

Raymonde did not look up from her dishes as Cassie and Odile watched the back of her head. "I did not know about the name change," their mother said at last with a sigh. "But I knew that ... part."

"That he was Jewish," Odile insisted. "He told you?"

"It didn't matter," Raymonde said.

"But he told you that he was Jewish? He said it?" Odile was not about to let Raymonde off the hook. If their father had been present, Odile would not have cross-examined their mother. None of this would have been discussed. But the balance of power was altered by his absence.

"Not exactly," Raymonde mumbled. "He was, hmm ... I just ... knew."

"You guessed it?" Odile insisted.

"There are ... ways to know," Raymonde said mysteriously.

"Papa's circumcised!" Odile exclaimed.

"Don't be crass," Raymonde said.

"Talk about the elephant in the room," Cassie said.

"The *circumcised* elephant," Odile added, and they both giggled.

"Oh, you two are so annoying!" Raymonde said. "When I tell you it did not matter, it did not matter!"

Odile rolled her eyes. "Maman, you can't actually believe this. It was a secret, obviously, some crazy mind trip between the two of you. He was obviously trying to hide it, and you pretended not to know?"

"Did you know he grew up rich?" Cassie asked.

"Kind of," Raymonde said. "Well, yes. That, he told me. But he never wanted a penny from them."

"I'm definitely super curious about that," Odile admitted.

"You want to hear what Marceline told me?" Cassie asked.

"Sure."

"And you Maman? Do you want to know?"

"No sense in stirring up the past," Raymonde said but in a limp way.

"I can just tell Odile another time when you're not here," Cassie said cunningly. "If you prefer that."

Raymonde shrugged. "At this point, it doesn't matter," she said, which was her way of admitting that she burned with curiosity.

As they sat around the small kitchen table, with the not-so-faint smell of burnt eggs and spilled ketchup floating in the air, Cassie repeated to Raymonde and Odile the story that Marceline had told her.

CHAPTER 2

Années Folles

Through her window, Marceline watched Cassandra leave her home that first day. She watched her walk on the gravel path and go through the gate dressed in Albano's coat, and she wondered if she would be coming back.

She sat back in her armchair and rang the bell for Laure to bring her electric blanket. One by one, she removed the bangles on her wrists, the rings, the all-too-heavy loop earrings she had quickly donned when her new-found niece had stunned her with the surprise of a visit. She rubbed her sore earlobes. Gustave's daughter, here in the house, staring at her and speaking with her from across their tea!

All those years, Gustave had shunned her. Four decades of sibling estrangement. All this time, Marceline had been certain that Gustave had dragged her through the mud, that he had told his three daughters all kinds of lies about her. She had inoculated herself from that. But to think he had simply erased her, pretended that she did not exist at all. She did not know what to think of that. It was painful and cruel. Everything that ever happened between them was.

Gustave was incapable of seeing things her way. Incapable of listening even. Albano's death had not been her fault. Or it was Gustave's fault just as much as hers. He knew this, evidently. But it did not fit the narrative where she was the enemy, and he was the victim. That's what she would tell Cassandra when she returned tomorrow. If she returned.

She liked the niece. The young woman – well, not young exactly, but young compared to herself – was dressed every which way. And those red boots were peculiar. But the family resemblance was clear. Lucky for her, Gustave's daughter did not look like him at all. She had gotten the good genes, Albano's genes.

Marceline undid her bun so that her head could rest comfortably against the back of the chair. In the story she would tell Cassandra, where would she start?? What was relevant? But relevant to what? To her relationship to Gustave? To anyone's relationship to Gustave?

Would things have been different between them had they not been children of the war. Gustave was only the end product of the time he grew up in. And so was she.

As a child, Marceline had had the sense of being special. She had been too young to understand that was simply growing up privileged. In the early years of the 1930s, Europe's mounting financial and political troubles had not affected her family. They had a beautiful home and plenty of money. Albano marveled at everything his children did, no matter how lackluster. Her piano playing, for example. Did he realize she was no Beethoven? Truth be told, she did not particularly enjoy artistic pursuits. She perceived it a great injustice to be subjected to tedious ballet, drawing, and penmanship lessons that her brother Gustave did not have to endure because he was a boy. She was athletic. She wanted to ride horses, ski, play table tennis and badminton. She liked to win. Unfortunately, since they were schooled at home and hardly ever in contact with other children, the only person available to compete against was Gustave.

Her mother liked to tell Marceline and Gustave that they had royal blood. Where did she get this idea? Who knows? Lucienne was besotted by the aristocracy. She liked to entertain and had friends, many of them Jewish, some of them not, in government, in the military, at the préfecture. They were magistrates, deputies, politicians, physicians, attorneys, and remnant members of the French aristocracy. The latter you could recognize by the way her mother fretted over them. Lucienne was caught between two worlds: the world of the bourgeoisie and the world of the nobility. She had failed to acquire one of those elusive hyphenated names or titles by marriage, but no matter. No sooner had Marceline been born than she began projecting that dream onto her.

They owned many nice things. The finials were kept in a locked glass cabinet. To Marceline and Gustave, they looked like tiny metal crowns. She had once asked her mother what they were. Her mother said that they were Torah ornaments. "Uncle Moshe brought them back from a trip. They belong to your father's ancestry as a Kohen."

"What is a Kohen?" Gustave asked.

"The singular form of Kohanim. They are from an ancient Jewish priesthood line," her mother answered. "They used to fit on top of an ancient Sefer Torah, which was hidden and brought back from Spain hundreds of years ago."

"Where is the Torah now?"

"A Torah is made of fragile materials and are too bulky to conceal, so there are a number of things that might have happened to it over the years. We don't know. The finials are small and made of metal, and so they are easy to hide and are all that remains."

"Why are there two finials?"

"Each one fits atop the cylinders the Torah is rolled on. They are a pair. They mustn't ever be separated. Gustave will inherit them."

"Why him and not me?" Marceline had asked.

"Gustave is a boy and son of Kohanim, so he is Kohen as well," her mother said.

"Because I have royal ancestors?" Gustave asked.

"You're a Kohanim from your father's side of the family, not from mine. There is an ancient Jewish priesthood line coming through your father, but the royal line comes through me."

Gustave turned to Marceline and exclaimed, "I have royal blood!"

"So do I," Marceline said.

Lucienne laughed that same dismissive laugh she used when Uncle Moshe was mentioned, or when her husband mispronounced a word. "I suppose you both have royal blood," she said. "But Gustave might have gotten the bulk of the Jewish blood."

Perhaps, in retrospect, this could have been a compliment. Only at that time, it had felt like a pronouncement that reverberated within their beings. Marceline had recently understood that a person could be disliked simply for being Jewish. She was old enough to understand that there was such a thing as anti-Jewish sentiment, and here was her mother crowning her brother as the designated Jew of the household. They understood this has something to do with what everyone repeated all the time: that Gustave looked Jewish whereas Marceline didn't.

When Marceline was ten and Gustave eight years old, it was decided that home schooling was no longer sufficient. They were to attend the local private school in the Quartier des Épinettes. Marceline had immediately thrived there, finding in school an outlet for her spirit of competition, as well as something new and thrilling: social intrigue.

Gustave was not so fortunate. He had always been a solitary boy who spent hours alone drawing, carving ships out of balsa wood, or playing with miniature train tracks. He was always bent over lead soldiers, a tiny paintbrush between his fingers. At school, Gustave's quietness was misconstrued as aloofness. He did not know how to make friends. Each morning, he pleaded with their mother to stay home. He said that the other boys hated him. Lucienne dismissed this. Why would anyone hate Gustave, she asked? What was there to hate about a seven-year-old boy? She refused to see that Gustave had been thrown into an environment against which he had no defense. He was exposed to the vitriol of other children not only at a fragile time in his development but at the wrong time in history.

Marceline never believed that there was much wrong with Gustave. Under other circumstances, other boys might have left him alone. But this was a time when the core principles of entire countries were rotting out, when a bizarre, uncontrollable perception shift was sweeping through Europe like a noxious wave. Their mother's generation had not suffered from overt anti-Semitism in France. But in a single generation, everything can be forgotten. Now that the economies of entire countries were sinking, being Jewish, and looking Jewish, started to mean something different. It was to *be* different. Gustave, her sweet and sensitive brother, became the perfect lightening rod for all that is hateful and detestable in other children's natures. He was shy, introverted, and Jewish, attributes that could make a little boy the object of children's cruelty, and this in the context of social hatred that soon permeated everything.

As anti-Semitism grew, Gustave's Jewishness, so to speak, turned into a liability, not only for himself but, Marceline soon started to believe, for the entire family.

When Marceline was born, in 1923, few could have predicted that the political and financial decisions made on an international scale after the Great War, such as the conditions imposed on Germany, for example, or the financial permissiveness that led to the American stock market crash, had already activated the gears of the World War II machine.

The twenties had been the années folles, the roaring twenties, and for a while at least everyone had been determined to be happy and optimistic. The virus of hatred had remained dormant. But give a virus the right environment, allow it to propagate, and it starts spreading. The financial crisis in America had triggered a ripple effect of economic turmoil throughout Europe. In the whispered conversations of the staff, in the headlines of newspapers that she was too young to understand, on the grim faces of teachers, in the long lines of destitute families in front of the soup kitchens that sprouted across Paris, Marceline detected an alarming sense of anomaly.

She remembered one particular dinner in 1934. At eleven years old, she was still told nothing of world politics. Children's questions were brushed off, but this much she knew: France, which had taken pride in weathering the world's economic upheaval, was now on the brink of financial catastrophe. Hundreds of thousands of people were out on the streets without work or shelter as France grew hungry and restless. Adult conversations are the last thing the youth wants to be subjected to, but Marceline was starved for clues as to the workings of the world around her, so she paid attention. That one dinner, in particular, put words to the anxiety she felt.

It was a Shabbat dinner and the guests were gentiles as well as Jews, husbands and wives, all well known to them – although now she could not remember their names – all part of the upper echelon of French society. Shabbat wasn't a religious thing to her family, but rather an excuse to entertain, and the gentile friends lent themselves to the traditions with good humor and gastronomical enthusiasm. She remembered she wore a dress made of burgundy velvet with a white lace collar. She remembered that

Gustave was sitting next to her and that his pockets were filled with marbles and that he was playing with them under the table on his lap, which he was not supposed to do. She remembered that Uncle Moshe was there that night. She loved her uncle, he was so funny and playful, but his presence always irritated her mother.

The prayers were said over the bread and the wine. The candles were lit. Marceline did not remember the meal, what was served or discussed. Everyone seemed in a jolly mood. That was until dessert, when the atmosphere changed. Perhaps it was the arrival of Sandra into the room. Sandra had a great talent for baking. There was a cook but when they entertained, Sandra was asked to make dessert, and then for reasons important to her father, Sandra herself would bring the sweets she had prepared. Marceline thought that her father meant to give Sandra the sense that she was valued, but Sandra, who was a self-effacing woman, only seemed to do it to please him. Lucienne, for her part, felt it a ridiculous and unnecessary charade as Sandra reluctantly became the center of attention, receiving lavish praises for her talent.

That night, Sandra shyly entered the dining room with her tray. The arrival of this foreign-looking woman with a ghastly scar on her face seemed to make some people uncomfortable. Port and brandy helping, voices began to change pitch. It was barely perceptible at first but politeness, along with sobriety, was going out the window.

People began to discuss that little man in Germany. One guest said that he could not help but admire the German man's certainty when France's own politicians were corrupt and ineffectual. "His rise to political power is impressive, you must admit," the guest said.

"If not chilling," someone replied. "In the last two months, he abolished the title of president and declared himself Fuehrer and Reich Chancellor, and eliminated the rivals in his party."

"A purge, you mean," Uncle Moshe pointed out. "A series of murders. And you see what he is doing now, he is rearming Germany, in direct violation of the Treaty of Versailles."

Marceline wondered if Uncle Moshe would mention Hitler's purported ill-treatment of German Jews, but this was not a topic of polite conversation around non-Jewish guests. At home, she heard Uncle Moshe, Baba, and her mother speak about Hitler, but the gentiles did not seem terribly concerned about what happened to the Jews in another country, at a time when France was suffering such economic woes that all it could do was focus on domestic issues.

"Hitler must do what needs to be done," a Jewish guest, a walrus of a man, tall and thick with a white mustache, said. "Our own politicians would be well advised to do the same." He looked at Sandra. "The influx of racially dubious foreigners is out of control." Marceline looked at Sandra, who did not look up. Instead, she set the tray on the table, wiped her hands on her apron, and left the room. Uncle Moshe and Baba looked at each other. Her mother was absorbed in conversation with the woman who sat next to her. "After the war, France essentially no longer had a labor force, and so it made sense to recruit workers," the Walrus continued. "Immigrants were desired, needed, without a doubt. But now, between the political unrest in all those barbaric countries, and the financial crisis, everyone wants to be a political refugee. France is weakened by the arrival in droves of undesirables of every creed and conviction."

In conversations, her father was not one to impose his opinion, so Marceline was surprised when he said, "Refugee does not mean unworthy," he said. "Most are hard-working and capable."

A young man who was not Jewish, and whose polished manners and tall stature Marceline admired, addressed her father conciliatorily. "We needed people like you, Alban," he said. "And look how well you have adapted. You've earned your stripes. You have been here for years. But times are entirely different now. Refugees are draining France. Surely you must agree that immigrants are taking the scarce work there is."

The Walrus stabbed the air with his fork "Precisely! We take on more immigrants than any other country in the world. Even America is second to us. It is madness. Uncontrollable madness."

"Immigrants are also consumers who pay taxes," Baba said. "Are they not contributing as much to the French economy as they are benefiting from it?"

"The depression, Dear Alban, is caused by overproduction, not underconsumption," the young man said. "This is self-evident economics. The last thing France needs is more workers. The more foreigners this country absorbs, the worse the situation."

"However," Baba said, insisting in a way that was uncharacteristic of him, "I believe that there are few more loyal subjects. Who would be more likely to take arms to defend France, should it be threatened by war, than a grateful refugee with nowhere else to go?"

Her father had mentioned war, and now everyone looked upset.

"Would we ever trust them?" interjected one of the guests, a pompous-looking man with reddish skin. "Who is to say that they wouldn't infiltrate our armies with spies and stab us in the back?"

Another guest, a thin, nervous man with a goatee interrupted, "Besides, with France weakened by the present low birth rate, our government thought it beneficial to encourage mixed marriages, but we are all recognizing the mistake that was. We thus not only weakened France, but we weakened French blood and the French race."

Uncle Moshe, usually loud, had taken to gathering crumbs on the tablecloth with the blade of his knife and said nothing. "The French race?" her father wondered out loud.

"When immigrants came from Belgium or Switzerland, it was one thing, but now they come from Italy, Spain, and Portugal. Or worse," the goatee man said. "You must admit that those darker complexions stand out." Marceline's stomach knotted.

The Walrus yelped, "They will never integrate, nor would we want them to! French families don't wish for that kind of mixed-race offspring."

Her eyes met her father's for only an instant, long enough for her to witness the hurt in his eyes. This was not only about Sandra. Her father and Uncle Moshe were foreigners from a country now called Turkey, a country of Muslims, of dark-skinned people.

And the mixed-race offspring were no other than she and Gustave.

At the other end of the table, her mother pretended to hear nothing and breezily instructed a maid to fetch coffee. Gustave was pinching bread dough between his fingers and shaping it into little mice with almond slivers as ears and cherry stems as tails.

Moshe's voice resounded, sharp and clear. "Aren't you concerned that the desire to reject foreigners might extend to people like us?" he asked.

"People like *us*?" the Walrus said with the tone of someone who cannot think of a scenario where a person such as Uncle Moshe and a respectable man like himself could be put into the same basket.

"Jews," Moshe said.

The collective unease grew thick. And Marceline suddenly understood a truth: the Jewish men wanted to convince themselves that they were more similar to the gentiles in the room than to those undesirable foreigners, and Moshe was suggesting that as Jews, they would *all* turn into undesirables.

"Religion has nothing to do with this," the Walrus scoffed. "With all due respect Moshe, we Israelites have integrated into the very fabric of France, generation after generation, each more educated and assimilated than the next. We are doctors and lawyers. We are generals. We are at every echelon of politics. We have never known any language other than the French language. Sir, the Israelites of France are French, have always been and always will be."

The gentile man with the goatee came to the Walrus's rescue. "There is simply no point of making comparisons between foreigners who arrive by the thousands, cause a hemorrhage of values, and tarnish our culture and the French citizens of Israelite conviction," he said.

The Walrus grunted his approval. "To protect the best among us and reject the worst is a natural sentiment."

"Not all instincts that are natural should be encouraged," her father pointed out.

"Plainly said, Dear Alban, we feel justified in wanting France back to the French, and foreigners out," the young Jewish man said.

"Isn't this xenophobia?" her father calmly asked.

"Alban!" Mother exclaimed.

"Not at all," the young man said. "It's economics."

"It's common sense!" the Walrus said.

One of the Jewish wives giggled and said, "If you wish to call it xenophobia, so be it. We have France at heart, and I won't make apologies for it. I think those foreigners have no place here and should be chased away."

"I think like Moshe that from xenophobia to anti-Semitism is not such a wide gap to bridge," her father said.

The thin young man said venomously, "Fear not Alban. What are you so worried about? That we will send you back to your country?"

Terror seized Marceline's heart. Could her father be sent away for being a foreigner?

"I don't have a country to return to," Baba said. "The one I left no longer exists." He paused and added, "But before leaving, I was a witness to how hatred can be used to dismantle governments and break up countries. I saw what hate does once it takes hold in the hearts of men."

Her mother dismissed Baba with a fluttering of her long, thin fingers. "Alban, don't be such a wet blanket. If they ever try to revoke your citizenship, there are at least five men at this table who will vouch for you."

Marceline looked at those red, hostile faces around the table, and one thing was clear to her: should her family ever need these men's help, they would never give it.

****

Gustave came home from school with his first black eye a few weeks later. He had been shoved to the ground and called a dirty Jew.

Sandra was inconsolable. Lucienne only seemed exasperated.

Bullying, which did not even have a name then, was perceived as a failing of the victim. His parents were told that Gustave needed to stand up to the other boys. He needed to learn to get along with others. While at school, Marceline pushed for things to be done her way and would negotiate and cajole and charm everyone into giving her what she wanted. Gustave did not seem to require anything. Gustave did not seem to need friends. He did not need attention, nor did he need to run around and create mischief. Had he been mischievous, all parties would have been greatly reassured. But here he was, quiet, sensitive, or that word never pronounced but on the tip of everyone's tongue: weak. Her father must have blamed himself for not preparing Gustave better. So he immediately enrolled him in boxing classes where poor Gustave was even more miserable.

Following the black eye incident, the mood in the house mirrored that of the rest of the country. The year was 1935. People were losing their jobs in droves. Banks went bankrupt. Factories closed overnight without so much as a sign on their doors. Social panic ensued. Political rhetoric became nonsensical. Desperate people clawed at every scapegoat they could blame for their predicament and, throughout Europe, the mood about foreigners in general, and Jews in particular, morphed into something sinister.

Over the next few years, as Hitler's power grew and the world made its inexorable progression toward the hell that was to become World War II, her father, the Turk, the immigrant, became an undesirable acquaintance, even amongst Jews. If in 1934 there were more dinner parties and salons than could be attended, by 1936, those couples her parents had considered friends all but disappeared. The non-Jews did not want to mingle with a Jewish family, and the Jews did not want to associate with foreigners such as her father and Uncle Moshe. This should come as no surprise to someone familiar with the mechanisms of war. As people try to save their skin, they push to find someone who can be taken in their place. Marceline had witnessed this behavior over the course of her life. She had even recognized it in herself. Righteous people are a rare breed. Heroism usually confines itself to those dearest to us. We will do anything for those we love to survive, even if that comes at the detriment of others.

Xenophobia began to stretch its ugly tentacles within their small family circle. It crept in in subtle ways. Her mother, for whom Baba's lack of belonging to her social class had always been difficult to swallow, began speaking to him with disdain. The core of her wrath was focused on Uncle Moshe, whom she described as a salesman without refinement or manner. But that was not the worst. The pernicious way of thinking toward foreigners crept into Marceline's consciousness. She too wished Uncle Moshe did not look so conspicuously foreign. Now even she could not help but perceive her father differently. He did not speak perfect French, and his accent now shamed her. She began seeing him through the eyes of an entire nation and, with horror, saw what they saw: an immigrant from the wrong side of the world.

She found excuses for him not to take her to school. She stopped inviting friends over. She impatiently corrected his diction. When he spoke in another language to Uncle Moshe, to Sandra, or to a supplier over the telephone, it made her angry. If her father noticed this, he did not mention it.

Her father could not have been more prescient. Within the year, it was no longer about immigrants. Virulent anti-Semitism became acceptable discourse in the press, in the inflamed rhetoric of the intelligentsia, in the work of revered authors such as Robert Brasillach or Louis-Ferdinand Céline. Journalists, thinkers, and politicians began competing for the most extreme anti-Semitic discourse. Anti-Semitism ripened into a noxious fruit. And once racism and anti-Semitism were encouraged in the public discourse, it moved into the streets.

They were powerless as they watched things snowball. The things said about the Jews were absurd, irrational. How could Jews be formidably powerful and, at the very same time, disgustingly weak? They were bloodthirsty warmongers and, at the same time, cowards. Jews were said to steal work away from the proletariat, and in the same breath, accused of controlling and owning everything.

Marceline would awaken in the morning with a ball of anguish in the pit of her stomach, and she would go to bed with it. What she feared exactly was not named, but she needed to look no further than neighboring Germany to populate her nightmares.

Soon, Lucienne was shunned from salons of which she had been the very pulse. She was voted out of her horticultural society chairmanship. A literary salon she had founded and hosted moved elsewhere. A charity for war daughters she presided over stopped receiving funds and withered away. But her mother's torments were mild next to Gustave's. There was not a week when Gustave wasn't called names or beaten. At lunchtime, kids threw things into his food. His books were stolen, his homework destroyed. He would return home from school with his back covered with ink blotches, his study folders torn to bits. Marceline didn't know what she was angrier at: the vicious kids, the system that allowed for these kinds of things to happen, or her brother for being the butt of it all.

In the midst of all this, she turned fourteen. The year was 1937. Her piano playing had improved, thanks to daily lessons and hours of practice, and for her birthday her father bought an Imperial Bösendorfer in utter disproportion to her aptitudes. She remembered feeling guilty about this, as though it made her a fraud. Already, there were signs that she was being treated differently than Gustave whether she deserved to be or not. It was not only happening at home. She looked gentile, but even if people knew she wasn't, she seemed immune to anti-Semitism at school. Boys passed her notes professing their love. If some of the girls hated her for being Jewish, or for any other reason, she had a certain dominance over the group, and none of the kids dared attack her.

One day, her father told her, "You are a beautiful girl and will become a beautiful woman Marceline, but do not let it be the most important thing about you."

"I don't," she protested. "I am learning the piano. I spend hours on it."

"You must also strive to become a mensch."

She thought he was speaking of protecting her brother. "What can I do about Gustave?" she said. "I don't know the boys who mistreat him. Besides, there's a wall eight feet tall that stands between the boys' and girls' buildings."

"I mean that you must look past the social position and physical appearances of others," her father said. She wondered if he could read the content of her soul, how she secretly felt about foreigners, the shameful embarrassment she had begun to experience at being the daughter of one.

"When people appear strong, you must see their fragility," he said. "If they seem fragile, look for their strength. Learn to see past the flaws, even when they seem beyond repair, and know that their suffering is just as valid as your own."

Now she knew he was talking about Gustave. Her father was worried not about how he was treated by other boys at school, but how he was treated at home by her.

That evening, she wrote in her journal that from now on she would strive to be nicer and more tolerant, that she would stand up for her brother at school and fight off anyone who did or said bad things to him. She wrote this perhaps in the hope it would be read. What she did not write in her journal was that she knew popularity to be fickle. She wished she could go to her brother's rescue. But the last thing she wanted was for his Judaism to draw attention to her own.

One day, in the winter of 1938, Gustave returned from school with a bloodied uniform and a broken nose. By the time he arrived home, his nose has swollen to twice its size, and already the space around his eyes had turned purple. They congregated in the bathroom where Gustave sat on the edge of the bathtub holding ice on his face while Sandra helped him out of his blood-stained shirt. He was twelve and growing taller and thinner. Now he even had hair on his armpits. When the undershirt was removed, they all saw the large bruises on his pale body.

"What are those?" her father exclaimed.

Gustave, holding the pack of ice to his nose, glared at them. "No one has ever bothered to know where my bruises came from until now," he said under his breath.

Her father was taken aback, "I ... well. Is it not from the sports you do?"

Sandra dabbed at the dried-up blood with a wet cloth. Her mother, who had been watching with her arms crossed said, "We shall speak to the schoolmaster!"

"You never fight back?" her father asked anxiously. "You are taking boxing. You know how to punch. Isn't that helping?"

"Punch who?" Gustave raged. "They come from behind, several at once; they call me a kike, kick me, push me to the ground."

Her mother sighed, exasperated. "And look at your nose! There are doctors we could hire to repair this, make it look less ... prominent perhaps?"

"If the only thing those savages will understand is violence, then you must hit back," her father said. "You can't just stand there and wait to be punched."

"I've never seen *you* hit anyone!" Gustave snapped. "How easy do you think it is? I wonder what you would do."

Marceline chimed in, "Well, personally, I would hit back."

Gustave threw the ice pack to the ground and shouted, "You're all pretending like I did something, or didn't do something. You're pretending not to see that it's about one thing: it's about the way I look."

They said nothing, but they all knew what Gustave was referring to. There were drawings in the newspapers and on billboards sprouting up all over Paris. They knew the satires, in plays, at the movies, and on the news. Everywhere, the hideous caricature of the loathsome Jew with the hooked nose, the large ears, the pale face, the bags under the eyes. Jews were made to look like sickly vultures. It was all just so confusing and terrifying. Marceline did not recognize this invented beast in herself, but it was impossible not to hate that creature, a creature that could embody humanity's worse qualities, both morally and physically. Was her brother recognizing himself in that terrible fiction?

Her mother said, "Alban, I think it is time we proceeded with what we discussed."

The notion had been floating around for a while. Her mother had gotten herself convinced that Gustave should attend a pensionnat. She loved the idea of boarding schools in general. They were expensive, a sign of good breeding, the clear mark of a superior education. But lately, her reasons were murkier.

Albano turned to her. "Lucienne. I have told you before. We are not doing this."

"I don't want to go to boarding school!" Gustave said with fury. "I don't and I won't!"

"It would be a Jewish boarding school," her mother continued sweetly. "How could you be attacked there? New children, new teachers; with a new attitude, you could make a fresh start. Make friends." She turned to her husband. "His education is suffering, Alban. You know that he needs that fresh start."

"No, Lucienne," her father said.

"But, Alban…."

"The world is going mad again," her father said before leaving the room.

At dinner, Gustave, dressed in a robe like a convalescent, chewed without appetite. Her father was silent and seemed to be churning grave thoughts in his head. They ate wordlessly, oppressed by a sense of foreboding. Her mother broke the silence. "I attended a pensionnat," she said with artificial cheer. "There are clubs and functions, and there are games in the evenings, and on the weekends, you get to go on outings and lovely field trips with your classmates."

"You just want to send me away so that you don't have to deal with me," Gustave said below his breath.

"Lucienne, Dear, let's us have a nice dinner," her father said.

Her mother was not deterred. "It will benefit you. They will keep you safe there."

"How could they?" Gustave nearly shouted.

Her mother gazed around the dining room as though the validation of her thinking might be written somewhere on the walls. "There is more thorough oversight in boarding school," she said in that decisive tone that left no room for questioning. "The children sleep there, so the educators are responsible. They can't very well let the boys hurt one another, or the parents would take them out."

Gustave shrugged, disgusted. "I would be hated there too. Only for more hours of the day. And the nights. And on lovely field trips."

"There is camaraderie," her mother insisted. "Bonds are forged. It isn't like school, I assure you. Not at all."

Tears of rage welled up in Gustave's eyes. He turned to their father. "I don't want to go, Baba. Tell Mother to stop! Please."

"We do not need to be discussing this right now," her father said firmly to everyone at the table.

"I'll make it work at my school," Gustave said imploringly. "I will start getting along."

Her mother had one of her dry laughs. "I'm not certain any of this is within your control, darling."

"Please, Baba, don't send me away!"

That evening Marceline went to Gustave's room. These days he closed his door to her, accusing her of touching his things. To be fair, she did like to touch his things quite a bit. The balsa airplanes dangling from fish lines, the miniature sailboats on shelves, the toy soldiers in formation: it was all so irresistible. And it was fun to move things around or even hide things. That evening Sandra was in Gustave's room, organizing his desk but mostly, Marceline suspected, so that he would not feel alone. She knew that Gustave would be on his best behavior around Sandra. She had a way of looking at you, pained and at the same time believing in you, and neither Marceline nor Gustave wanted to disappoint her.

Marceline sat on his bed where Gustave lay, furious. The area around his eyes was awfully swollen and blue by now.

"Why are you here?" he said. "You are not allowed in my room."

Sandra looked at her with insistence, so Marceline understood that she needed to apologize to Gustave. "You're right," she told him. "I would not know what to do either if people hit me."

Gustave sat up in bed, raging. "Mother says that Paris is the problem, or that the school is the problem, or that the other boys are the problem, or that being Jewish is the problem. But what she means, in fact, is that *I* am the problem. Me."

"You're not the problem," Marceline said, watching the swelling in Gustave's eye nearly shut it closed.

"I am a problem for Mother! That's the truth."

"She has shown me brochures of girls' boarding schools for years. She wants me to go too. You know Mother; she gets fixated."

"Of course, she doesn't want *you* to go to boarding school!" Gustave nearly spat out the words. "She's having too much fun making you her lapdog, and taking you places to show you off."

"I am no one's lapdog, you pest!"

"You see how bored she is now? You're her only activity."

Marceline could have argued that this wasn't the case, but truth be told, it was. "Baba won't let her send you anywhere," she said. "They will go to school tomorrow and ask them to suspend the boys who are attacking you. In fact, they will make sure those boys are kicked out."

"That won't happen," Gustave said as Sandra arranged the pillow behind his head.

Her parents did go to the school, accompanied by Gustave. But the meeting with the school's headmaster did not turn out as hoped. The complaint was that Gustave was a source of conflict and distraction. To her parents' surprise, it was recommended that, for Gustave's safety and the sake of the good functioning of the classroom, he should leave. This was in no way the headmaster kicking a Jewish kid out of school, he unctuously protested. It was a mere suggestion. But he also inferred that they were done defending him. Her mother and father understood the subtext. Gustave, if they chose for him to attend, would do so at his own risk.

Upon their return from their conference with the headmaster, her parents walked straight to the small salon and shut the door behind them. Marceline rushed up the stairs to the library above. She closed the door behind her, lay down on the wooden floor, put her ear to the air vent, and listened.

"I cannot believe Gustave should be the one removed!" her mother said, her voice trembling with outrage.

"Paris is taking a turn for the worse," her father said.

"Can there be no recourse?" her mother asked. "Is there no higher authority? Surely there must be someone we know at the district level, or else at the ministry of education. Perhaps I should speak to Monsieur Hébert. Do you remember him? He is the Minister of Commerce's brother-in-law. He is Jewish."

"Perhaps Gustave should be taught at home for a while," her father said.

"You said it yourself, Alban; you want him to become a man. How will this be accomplished by keeping him sheltered between these four walls? Already, he runs to Sandra at the slightest setback. And he is too old for a nanny anyway. How long do you plan on keeping that woman around?"

"With everything going on, all the negative things being said about Jews, maybe he should indeed be sheltered."

"Would that be to his best interest in the long run? I know you don't want me to speak about this but…."

"What?"

"The Jewish pensionnat, the one I told you about in Rânes. Gustave would not stand out there, but neither would he be overindulged. He would continue his studies in a proper fashion."

My father's answer lacked conviction. "It is the middle of the school year," he said.

"I have enquired," my mother said. "They have room. They will take him."

Marceline was shocked. Her mother had essentially made the arrangements. All she needed now was for her husband to say yes.

"I fear that…." her father began, struggling to find his words. "You know how shy he is … but on the other hand…."

Her mother must have seen in her husband's hesitation that he was waiting for her to persuade him. "You want him to gain strength, but you won't allow him the opportunity," she said shrilly. "If you believe him too weak to cope with life, how will he think anything different? It is by practicing facing his fears that he will master them. You were an orphan. You raised yourself. You had no choice but to become a man."

"But I am different. I am more resilient. Each person is made differently and—"

"Whether they are or aren't is immaterial," her mother interrupted in that clipped, dismissive tone she took with her husband of late. "He might need to learn to be resilient. You are the one who constantly speaks of war. Would you let Gustave face impending war without strengthening him first?"

The mention of war sent the familiar shiver of fear down Marceline's spine. Suddenly, her mother's idea made sense to her. Gustave needed to breathe in some fresh air, grow muscles, make friends. She held her breath, hoping that her father would agree. She realized now that she *needed* Gustave to be sent away from Paris, away from her, so that she could stop worrying about him and the bad feeling in the pit of her stomach could ease.

"Perhaps boarding school would be best," Baba said at last. There was defeat in his voice. "But how shall we tell him?"

"Display strength and resolve, Alban. Lead by example." Marceline did not like her mother's tone, the contempt in it. But she made sense. Baba needed to act firm and tell Gustave about their decision.

"Maybe you are right," her father said.

Gustave was called in to meet alone with their father. Marceline resumed her position, with her ear on the air vent. Her father, who had shown compassion toward Gustave when it was just he and her mother, now forced himself to speak quite coldly to him. He explained that it was for Gustave's best interest so that he could become a man. He would not return to school.

He would be attending Jewish boarding school in Rânes as soon as his wounds healed.

At first, Gustave wept and begged. After a while, he stopped protesting. Marceline imagined him sitting there, trying to swallow his hurt. She imagined him feeling abandoned. For the first time in her life, and this would not be the last, she realized her good fortune to have been born a girl. Being a girl, she got to be as strong as she wanted, but without the pressures men faced. For women, strength came as a bonus. Her generation was the first for which university study was possible. Her mother had been denied that advantage in her days. The bar for women was set low when it came to education, or strength, or intelligence. Women did not have to display them the way men must. Strength was a gift women could use at will but was best concealed. Or else you became like her mother, hard, and no one liked you.

Gustave left for boarding school after the winter break of 1938. Marceline felt lighter at first and wondered if her parents did as well. But in the following weeks, meal after meal, Gustave's absence was like a reproach. Her parents repeated to one another that sending Gustave away had been the correct thing to do, the best thing for him. They said that he would make friends among Jewish boys and that anti-Semitism had been the obstacle. Now he would be protected from the violence of bullies. But she doubted they believed this.

They wrote letters, and Gustave wrote back. Three times between January and June, they visited him. If there were problems, Gustave kept them to himself. His teachers and the boarding school headmaster assured them that he was doing well. But his taut face, his clipped responses to questions, and the tension Marceline sensed in him told a different story. It wasn't until he came back home for the summer that they found out how terribly unhappy he was. They monitor the mail, Gustave told them. One of his letters, where he had spoken of mistreatment by his Latin teacher and some of his schoolmates, had never arrived and probably had been intercepted. A subsequent letter where he complained of loneliness had been read out loud to his class – a much-used technique of intimidation through humiliation. After that, he had stopped writing anything of substance.

That summer, Marceline's attempts at conversations with Gustave led nowhere. Dinner times were tense and fraught with peril. Any little thing she said could set him off. He was angry with all of them. He hated boarding school and begged them not to send him back come September. But there were demonstrations against Jews in Paris and in the streets of France's largest cities. Jews were warned to avoid synagogues. Her parents decided that putting Gustave back in a regular school was not an option. The pensionnat was the correct place to prepare him for the university.

How could they have imagined that within a few years Jewish boys would no longer be allowed to receive higher education?

And so, Gustave was made to return to Rânes. Once there, Gustave stopped writing. His silence weighed heavily on the family. When they sent this fragile, sensitive, lonely boy away, her parents had said they wanted him to turn into a man. What they neglected to consider was the kind of man the experience would turn him into.

While Gustave was in boarding school, the continent unraveled at a pace and with an intensity that baffled them all. Each day came news more worrisome than the next from across Europe. The vitriolic discourse of politicians, journalists, and writers had corroded the general opinion. Even in moderate circles, virulent anti-Semitism and had become commonplace. French Jews, they said, had a personal vendetta against Hitler because of his treatment of Jews in Germany and were manipulating at every echelon of power to push France toward a war against the Fuehrer. Hitler was an expansionist no doubt, but if he wanted Czechoslovakia and Austria, let him have them. What did this have to do with France? And if Hitler had a beef against Jews, who in Europe didn't? The horrors of the Great War were too fresh, the losses too deep. No one wanted to rock the boat with someone as apparently unreasonable and belligerent as Adolf Hitler. It was easier to create a narrative with a villain of manageable power, a villain that, unlike the Reich, could be thwarted. Who better than France's small population of Jews to be that villain?

Everywhere, in the papers, in the schools, on billboards on the streets, Jews were described as moral delinquents, as threats to French racial purity, as warmongers, as enemies of the State. Solutions were suggested, from instating professional quotas, to creating a ministry of race, to purges.

Marceline turned fifteen.

In November, they heard the news of Kristallnacht. The Jews of Germany wound up accused of destroying their own property and were ordered to reimburse the government to the tune of a million Reichsmarks. Following this, German Jews were prohibited from all commercial activities.

Meanwhile, in Paris, the mistrust toward foreigners was ratified by law through a government decree whereby foreigners needed to acquire a special permit to work and could be detained if suspected of being dangerous to the security of the country. Naturalized citizens, such as Albano, could see themselves stripped of their French citizenship and be imprisoned if suspected of behavior harmful to France.

Which one of those events tipped the balance for her father? Following the decree, her parents held a tense discussion behind closed doors. Marceline had rushed to the vent the minute they had shut the door of the small salon behind them, the sign that something important was about to be discussed.

"Moshe and I believe that the time has come to make a change to our business," Albano told Lucienne. "The economy being what it is, rugs aren't selling."

As much as her mother enjoyed their lavish lifestyle, she considered business talk distasteful. Money, to her way of looking at it, was to be spent but not earned or at the very least, not openly pursued. "What is it you should sell, then?" she asked with detachment. "No one has money. Nothing is selling."

"We plan to shift to diamonds," Albano said.

"Alban, Dear, if people cannot afford rugs, how will they afford diamonds?" Lucienne scoffed.

"We don't want to sell diamonds, Lucienne. We want to buy them."

"In heaven's name, why?"

"Moshe and I think that it is time to liquidate."

"Liquidate?" she echoed in an empty voice.

"Sell. Sell everything we own," Albano said. "And buy diamonds with the proceeds. Money can be devalued; banks can go under; assets can be frozen, but diamonds endure."

Marceline naively took what her father was saying at face value. This was a new business venture: rugs to diamonds. But her mother read between the lines. "France will weather the depression," she said aggressively. "And if you think the diamond business is any better than the rug business, so be it, but you're married to a French native. No matter the crisis you will not be affected politically."

"I do not worry about being from Turkey. I worry because we're Jewish."

"Nonsense."

"You see what is happening in Germany," her father said.

"This is precisely the primitive mentality you and Moshe never could shake off. France is a republic. We have laws. We have a government. We have rules. French people are not savages. No one here takes anyone's business away."

"If there is war—"

My mother wanted to stop him from saying what she feared. She raised her voice. "There won't be!"

Undeterred, Albano continued. "And if France loses the war—"

"We won't!" she shouted.

"I am preparing our family for this eventuality," Albano calmly said.

Lucienne fell silent. Marceline would have preferred to hear her scream and yell at her father, telling him that he was an alarmist, that there was nothing to fear, that they were safe. She did not. Marceline imagined her mother, sitting on the sofa, her head in her hands, as she had seen her do so many times in the last few months. "Why not gold?" Lucienne asked in an empty voice. "Everyone is buying gold."

"Too heavy to easily transport," Albano said.

"Why would we want to *transport* diamonds? I don't follow you."

"I know you have little interest in business affairs, Lucienne," Albano said soothingly. Marceline could picture him standing next to her, gently rubbing her shoulder, something he did to each of them when they were upset. "But should the time come to leave the country, we must be prepared."

"You won't leave us, will you?" her mother said, her voice close to panic.

"Of course not," Albano said. "We will *all* leave."

A shockwave of emotions rolled through Marceline's body. Were things that bad?

"All of us?" my mother whimpered. "But how? To go where?"

Where was her mother's certainty? Why was she not reassuring her husband? Why was she not reminding him that they were rich and powerful, that they had friends in high places, that they were immune to the Depression and would be immune to Hitler as well? Marceline felt the crumbling of her safe world. The denial she clung to flew away like straw in the wind.

In the room below, and through the airshaft, there was a long silence. "I think we should sell the house."

"Never!" Lucienne said.

"If that is your wish," Albano said. "I understand. It has been in your family for generations. But know that if we are to leave, there is no telling what will come of it."

"How do you mean?"

"It might be pillaged, burned, who knows."

"Pillaged?" Lucienne laughed angrily, and her anger was a relief to Marceline. "Where do you think we are, Alban? This is not your village in the mountains! Besides, the best way for our things to be stolen is to leave them unattended. I am not leaving this house. You hear me? You can go wherever you wish if you are scared. I shall stay!"

"When it is time to leave, you will leave," Albano said. There was no hesitation. No anger in his voice. No room for arguing.

Surprisingly, this seemed to appease Lucienne. She remained silent for a long minute and then asked, "Where will we go?"

"Away from Paris, see how things are away from the capital."

"And then what?"

"Moshe and I are discussing the options."

"Why is it always Moshe having a say in how we conduct our affairs? Moshe, a man who leads a life of utter depravity and who never even learned to speak decent French!"

"Make a list of what you are willing to sell."

"I shall not sell a thing! If we must go, we'll go. We'll just close down the house for as long as this charade continues."

"If that is your wish, Lucienne. Let me know how I can help you prepare. Meanwhile, Moshe and I will liquidate the business. Also, Moshe is planning a trip to Switzerland. We will put valuables in a Swiss bank: money, gold, diamonds, the finials, and any family heirlooms you would like protected."

"That won't be necessary. My family's heirlooms will wait right here for our return," her mother said.

****

For the next five months, Europe continued to brew, but life for Marceline and her family didn't change. There wasn't any noticeable activity in the house. Nothing was openly being bought or sold, save for a few paintings, and her father continued to go to work every day, until one morning in early April 1939 when her parents summoned her.

"We are going on a journey," her father said while her mother sat beside him, rigid. "You will go to school today, and this will be your last day. Do not tell any of your friends that you will not be returning."

Marceline feigned astonishment. Her heart was pounding. "My exams are next week. Where are we going?"

"We cannot tell you this, ma chérie. Not quite yet."

"But why?"

"Think of it as a holiday," her mother said, but there was no joy on her face.

Marceline was told to pack her schoolbooks, pictures, anything of sentimental value to her. There was a flurry of activity around the house: the furniture was covered with sheets, paintings were taken down and moved to the cellar, crates and suitcases, brought up from the basement, were dusted and filled with belongings. When this was done, the entire staff – save for one as Marceline was soon to learn – was let go and given a month's severance pay. It had all been so sudden, everyone looked as though in a state of shock.

We are going south, her mother told her. And then she admitted, "Your father has convinced himself that Paris is too dangerous for Jews."

"So, Hitler hates Jews. What of it?" Marceline said, echoing the reassuring words that Jews throughout France said to convince themselves and each other. "He doesn't get to decide what happens here."

"Every one of our friends has attempted to explain to your father that there is nothing to fear for Jews," her mother said. "Especially those who have assets and connections in high places. A few months and we'll be back, I'm sure. Your father seems ready to leave at the drop of a hat every time he senses danger, real or imagined. I decided that, rather than fight him, I would go along and let him take us wherever."

"What about my lessons?" Marceline asked, not because she cared but because she needed more information.

"We will find teachers."

"What about my piano?"

"Your piano will be here upon our return, like everything else. Meanwhile, I will make arrangements for one to be rented in the South of France."

"That's where we are going?"

Lucienne rolled her eyes. "Just keep this to yourself, will you?"

"Oh, Mother, please, can it be a baby grand? You know I am ready for one."

Her mother smiled. "We'll see," she said, which usually meant yes.

The South of France? A baby grand? Secrecy? This did not sound so bad. Marceline hoped that maybe there would be interesting boys there. The boys she knew in Paris were tame, and she was bored with them. "What about Gustave?" she asked.

"Gustave will remain in Rânes," her mother said. "The point is to be away from Paris, and that is already the case for him."

The day of the departure, Marceline came down to the breakfast table, where the atmosphere was strained. The maid went from cup to cup, pouring coffee or tea. Marceline could tell from the stiff way her mother brought her cup to her mouth that she was seething. As soon as the maid left the breakfast room, her mother could no longer contain herself. "Why *her*, of all people? How can you make such a decision and just impose it on me, Alban? She would not be my first, second, or even third choice!"

Albano didn't look up from his newspaper. "This is one less person you will have to interview when we get there," he said.

Marceline looked from her father to her mother, trying to understand. What were they talking about?

Lucienne was red in the face. "I just don't see why it is your business to make this decision. I am the one who handles the staff."

Her father said, "She would not find work if we left her behind."

Marceline immediately understood that they were speaking of Sandra, whom her father had wanted to keep even after Gustave had gone away to boarding school. That had been a contentious point between them, her mother wanting to part with Sandra and her father insisting that she stay.

"She is not even Jewish!" her mother exclaimed.

Albano was staring at his newspaper, avoiding to look at his wife. "She will be helpful," he said.

In an instant, Lucienne blew up. "How will a disfigured foreigner be helpful just as we are thrown into a new house in a new city? The help I need is someone whom people can look at without fright."

"Enough," her father said between his teeth.

"You seem blind to the fact that people find her physically repulsive!"

"Enough!" he shouted.

They both looked at him, her mother trembling with rage and Marceline stunned. She was used to her mother's anger, but in her fifteen years had never witnessed her father's. Albano threw his napkin on the table and said, "Get ready to leave," and he exited the room.

All morning, what remained of the staff covered the furniture with sheets and closed the window shutters. It was a cold, blustery day, and from her bedroom window, Marceline watched them load up the two cars in the pouring rain. She gave her bedroom one last look. The bed was stripped of bedding. All the smaller objects had been packed, put into storage, or shipped to the new place. Would she see her bedroom again? She repeated to herself that she would be all right, that a good star had been watching over her and would continue to do so. She wasn't so certain about Gustave. Her brother would now live days away from them by automobile or train.

She slowly put on her coat and gloves, taking in her bed, stripped of bedding and the top of her dresser, now bare. The thought that she might be permanently leaving happiness behind gripped her and she felt ill. What if there were no good star? What if she was, along with all of France, on a descent toward something dark and unnamable?

The staff looked resentful as she stepped outside. Some of them would not make eye contact. She could see how they might feel deserted. There was no work in Paris, and here was her family, off to an extended holiday, or so they perceived. The staff did not see them as a family doing what it could in an uncertain political situation, but as rich Jews.

The Alfa Romeo 2500 and the Renault Juvaquatre were parked in front of the house. Both automobiles were filled to the brim with crates and luggage, with more crates attached to the roofs. Her father took the wheel of the Alfa Romeo. It was not their usual driver in the other car, but one of Uncle Moshe's trusted men.

Sandra came out of the house holding her small cardboard suitcase. She was dressed entirely in black with a peasant skirt and a shawl around her face that made her look much older than she was. Marceline put her arm on Sandra's shoulder to reassure her as she climbed in beside Moshe's man in the Renault.

Lucienne strutted out of the house in her best coat. She refused to look at any of them and walked to the Alfa Romeo. There she waited for Albano to get out of the automobile, come around it and open the door for her to climb in the passenger seat.

Before Marceline climbed in the back of the car, she looked back at Sandra who warmly smiled at her through the window, and suddenly Marceline wasn't sure who was supposed to be reassuring whom.

They drove off, the Renault following their Alfa Romeo. Outside, it was pouring still. In the streets of Paris, Marceline watched men and women, their clothes slick with rain, waiting in long lines outside bakeries. Her mother turned to her and said, "We will drive to Lyon and spend the night there. The following day we will drive to the South of France."

Baba, at the wheel, cleared his throat. "Actually, Lucienne, there is going to be a detour."

"What detour?" Lucienne said in an astonished voice.

"First we will go to Rânes and pick up Gustave."

"But it's on the opposite end of the country!" she exclaimed.

"I know," Albano said.

"It's a fine Jewish establishment. It's in the country. You said it yourself; he will be safe there!"

Her father interrupted her. "I changed my mind."

"And what about me not being given a say?" her mother said shrilly.

"We are not leaving Gustave behind, Lucienne. End of discussion."

Marceline relaxed in her seat. There was something endlessly reassuring about her father's new way of taking charge. Her mother had made all the decisions in the past, and although she continued to say things in that way that tolerated no contradiction, lately she had appeared confused and afraid, and Marceline wasn't sure that her mother had any idea what to do at all.

They arrived, unannounced in the early afternoon, in front of Gustave's boarding school. Gustave was called from his class while she, Baba, and Lucienne waited for him in the schoolmaster's office.

When Gustave entered the room, he blinked at them, not understanding. He looked frail in his uniform. Had he lost weight? She had not seen him in a few months. He had acne now, and he was very pale "What's wrong?" he asked.

"Your parents are here to take you," the headmaster said.

Gustave's eyes widened. "Take me where?"

Her father beamed. "We'll tell you when we're in the car."

"For how long?" Gustave said, his voice shaking.

"You're not coming back here," Albano simply said.

Gustave's eyes filled with tears, and it was too much for all of them. What had they been doing, keeping him away like an outcast? Weren't they all outcasts at this point? There was no sense of pretending to the contrary. Gustave threw himself into his father's arms. "Thank you, Baba," he cried, and they all sobbed, even their mother.

Marceline closed her eyes. This many years later she still could taste the relief, the fear, even the love they all had for each other then. She would not get into all this with Cassandra. How much did the young woman know about her father, when she had not even known that he was Jewish. The abyss of information might prove itself too immense to bridge. However, Cassandra had appeared eager to know the truth. But would she really return, or would she avoid her the way Gustave had?

Marceline wanted Cassandra to return. For the past forty years, she had wanted to tell her side of her story, but everyone who would have cared to listen was either dead or wished to forget.

****

In the kitchen, there was still a whiff of burnt eggs mixed with toast and coffee. Cassie looked at Odile and Raymonde for their reaction to Marceline's story, and they looked at her, waiting for more. "And then what happened?" Odile said.

Cassie shrugged. "That's all Marceline told me. She was tired."

"She's getting up there in years," Raymonde said. "She's must be close to ninety years old."

"She's *really* old," Odile said, emphasizing the word really.

"She's perfectly with it, if that's what you're wondering."

"Something runs in that family. The mother went crazy in old age," Raymonde said.

It was clear to Cassie that they were both looking for ways to invalidate anything Marceline might have said. "How is it possible that Papa never spoke about any of this?" she asked. "He was a Jewish boy, in France, at the most dangerous time in history. And he somehow escaped the Nazis. I mean, wouldn't that be something he would want to tell us about?"

"He wanted to forget," Raymonde said.

"I think he made the best of it," Odile said.

Cassie was walking on thin ice with her questions, but she insisted. "How could it not leave an imprint on him? You know, post-traumatic stress of some kind?"

What they all knew was implied in her comment, was the possibility that Gustave, her father, had a problem, or at least had grown up in a fertile terrain for some psychological scarring.

Raymonde found something to stare at on the floorboards, and Odile ignored Cassie's question and asked, "So how did they survive the Nazis and all?"

"I don't know," Cassie said, omitting to mention that she was meeting Marceline for lunch and that she had every intention to find out.

"Thank goodness," Raymonde chirped. "These kinds of terrible things will never happen again."

"They're still happening, Maman," Odile said coldly. "Only in other countries, to other people, out of sight from you."

Raymonde pouted, upset. "Civilized people have decency now; they have morals."

Odile shrugged. "Until the next economic downturn when the decent, civilized peoples will latch on to the first-power hungry wacko who tells them it's okay to hate."

"That's a gloomy vision of humankind," Cassie said.

"I'm a realist," Odile said. She turned to Raymonde. "Do you know where Papa went? Where he was during the war?"

Raymonde protested, "I was born after the war."

The non sequitur was so classic Raymonde that Cassie and Odile looked at each other as if to say "can you believe it?". Odile was the one who said, "Obviously, you don't have to have lived through it. Papa might have *told* you about it."

"All this is news to me," Raymonde admitted. She shook her head. "He never said a thing about any of this. Not a word."

"What do the two of you speak about?" Odile said, exasperated. "You've been married for over forty years!"

"We talk plenty, I'll have you know," Raymonde said. And with that, she crossed her arms. After a moment of thinking, she said, "He did mention being royalty or something like that. And then there were the finials. They were Jewish he said. The one his sister stole and the one here that Cassandra was about to take."

"I just wanted to look at it!" Cassie exclaimed.

"The finials came from his ancestor," Raymonde said. "Via his father."

"The Jewish Turk?" Odile said.

"He wasn't quite a Turk," Cassie corrected. "He was born in an area that since became Turkey but—"

Odile ignored this and continued grilling Raymonde. "Did Papa ever mention his parents to you?"

"Never his mother, but Gustave was very close to his father. He died long before your dad and I met."

"What did Papa say about him?" Cassie asked.

"Albano? Your father loved his dad. I know that he was a good man, very warm. Other than that, I don't think there was much to say about him," Raymonde said.

CHAPTER 3

Unreasonable Union

Albano had no memory of his rescue, no awareness of the large vessel that floated beside him as he was drowning or of its men who sifted through the sea water, looking for survivors. He had no sense of being scooped up and hoisted into the boat, no recollection of the care that was given to him as he lay barely conscious for days.

As providence would have it, the vessel was a well-equipped British hospital boat. It deposited him and a thousand other wounded refugees in Marseille, where Albano was hospitalized for weeks before he gained awareness of his surroundings. He found himself recovering from an infection on his arm that had nearly cost him his life. He was in a vast room crammed with beds, anonymous among hundreds of men who wailed and moaned day and night. His nights were haunted by terrible nightmares, and when he woke up, it was to discover again and again that reality was far worse. For weeks, Albano could not leave his bed. He needed assistance with the simplest tasks and ignored the hospital workers' attempts at communicating with him in Arabic, Greek, or Armenian, until one morning when he surprised them by asking in French if they would send a cable to his uncle in Paris.

Two days later, Uncle Moshe, who had left Paris immediately upon hearing the news that Albano was alive, was by his side in Marseille.

The doctors explained to Uncle Moshe that Albano refused to leave his bed, hardly spoke, and barely ate. His body was healing. They had been able to save his arm despite the infection, although they feared that permanent nerve damage had occurred. They weren't as optimistic about the state of his mind. Albano's disinterest in food stalled his recovery. Like many of the people rescued from the Smyrna fire, there was little left of him but skin, bones, and a crushed spirit.

Uncle Moshe ordered a wheelchair and had the workers lift Albano onto it. He tucked him in a blanket and wheeled him out of the room and into the sunlight of the manicured hospital grounds.

Outside, Albano saw clouds, thin, swaying palm trees, bougainvillea, and pink laurels and thought that he was back in Smyrna. Uncle Moshe told him that Smyrna was no longer. The city as they knew it had been annihilated by the fire.

Albano wished never to speak of what he had seen, but he owed Uncle Moshe an explanation. Moshe sat on a stone bench under a tree and listened. Albano, with an excruciating economy of words, told him about selling newspapers with Hagop, about how he and Xandra had fallen in love, and about how it had cost them Hagop's friendship. He told him how Hagop was taken by the police when he had left the cave where Albano was hiding him. He told Uncle Moshe about the baby so close to birth when Kemal's army overtook the city. He told Uncle Moshe about trying to find a boat with all the other refugees flooding the quayside. He told him about the carnage in the Armenian quarter, the destruction, the atrocities, the massacre of Xandra's family, how the men set the houses on fire. He told him how he and Xandra were attacked as they tried to escape with the small diamond they possessed, how Albano had given the diamond to a priest in exchange for letting Xandra give birth in the Christian hospital. How he had tried, unsuccessfully, to gain safe passage out of the country. How he had made his way through the burning city and eventually to a hospital reduced to cinders and burnt corpses.

"I killed them both by leaving them there," he said. "I should never have left Xandra's side. I buried Xandra, and I buried our child. Then I went into the water, not to live, but to die." There was a long pause with neither of them speaking. Finally, Albano said, "I never want to speak of this again."

Uncle Moshe listened and wept for Albano who could no longer weep. "Albano," Uncle Moshe said, "you are my family. There is little left of it, and whoever is left would rather pretend that I don't exist. I will care for you if you'll let me. But first answer this question: What do you want your life to be?"

"I don't know life without Xandra. I don't want a life without her."

"Come with me to Paris. You could work with me. Unless you want to resume rabbinical studies. That is possible too."

"I want nothing to do with God."

"You can start life anew in Paris, maybe raise a family one day."

"I can never love again, and I can never again give love."

Uncle Moshe did not contradict him. He stayed in Marseille for two weeks and, through friends, was able to secure Albano a refugee's visa.

When the visa arrived, Uncle Moshe booked two first-class train tickets from Marseille to Paris.

On the train, Albano looked in incomprehension around the cabin. He had never been in such close contact with luxury. The mahogany wood paneling, the polished brass, and copper metalwork, the velvet-covered seating, all so precious and alien to him. At lunchtime, Albano sat facing silver cutlery and porcelain plates, as obsequious waiters poured wine into their crystal glasses and placed menus in their hands and crisp, pressed napkins on their laps. Finally, he asked, "Uncle Moshe, are you rich?"

Uncle Moshe smiled. "Yes, my dear nephew. It appears that I am."

Albano watched how comfortable Uncle Moshe was in these luxurious surroundings and wondered how rapidly one could learn to behave with the confidence brought on by wealth. "I hope you are not wasting your time with me," he told Uncle Moshe. "I'm moving in a fog of memories. I do not take pleasure in things. My memories torment me every instant I'm awake. The happy times and the darkest of times are all I can think of. I worry that I will disappoint you. I have failed so many."

"How have you failed anyone?"

"I brought ruin to those I loved most. Every decision I made was the wrong one. Now I cannot even show you proper gratitude for rescuing me."

"Perhaps it is you who are rescuing me."

"How so?"

"You give me something worthwhile to do. You will be my project."

"I am not even sure I want to survive."

"You will survive nonetheless. I will see to it. Better than survive, you shall thrive. I have my mind set to make a French gentleman out of you."

Albano shook his head at the concept. "How could I ever become a French gentleman?"

"It will be in the way you dress and speak. The company you keep. The way you spend your money."

"I have none."

Uncle Moshe, thrilled like a child who brings his mother a gift, exclaimed, "This also is about to change now that you will work with me!"

Albano recognized in Uncle Moshe's eyes the joy and excitement that came from dreaming up a future for someone else. It was the same joy and excitement he had felt for Xandra at the prospect of giving her a new life in France. But now this very life was offered to him, and it was pointless. He was inclined to tell Uncle Moshe this, but here was this kind man, treating him like a son, and he didn't have it in his heart to disappoint him. "Is it a difficult business to learn?" he asked.

"You who have memorized the Talmud should not have too much difficulty."

****

Uncle Moshe lived in a rooftop apartment on one of Paris's most prestigious streets, Avenue George V. Inside the apartment, Albano walked through the rooms in a state of utter disbelief. It was like a castle, immense, with spacious rooms and tall ceilings and bright with many windows with balconies overlooking Paris. It was on the top floor of a four-story building, with steps to the rooftop, which had a garden on it. There were five bedrooms and as many bathrooms. Uncle Moshe's décor had the feel of Levantine villas. He liked gold-leafed furniture, mosaics, and inlays, statues of

Adonis, red velvet, heavy draperies. In his apartment, there were crystal bowls filled with sweets, lavish flower arrangements, tasseled toss pillows, gilded mirrors, and deep sofas. The art inside the apartment was often scandalous in nature, with many nude sculptures and paintings, most of them men. The herringbone wood floors that ran through the apartment were thick with rare rugs. Uncle Moshe, he soon found out, liked to shop for art, furnishings, and clothes. At home, he wrapped himself in embroidered silk robes belted over his ever-expanding belly. Each morning he groomed himself carefully and dressed in only the finest clothes, shoes, hats, coats, and watches. It was all so extraordinary. All this time, Albano had dreamt of wealth, and yet his dreams, compared to the reality of Moshe's life, had been small and unimaginative.

Uncle Moshe was always in motion and could bear neither stillness nor silence. This was perhaps why his apartment was filled day and night with an endless stream of guests and visitors. Some visitors came and went, and others stayed for weeks or even months at a time. They had little incentive to leave. Uncle Moshe was generous to a fault. His guests were spared no luxury. They were brought breakfast in bed by the maid, and Moshe's cook catered to their eating whims. When they left, at last, it was not because he asked them to, but usually because of an argument or some drama with other guests. Uncle Moshe never passed on an opportunity to throw a party. Beautiful, perfumed men and independent women with their short dresses, cropped hair, and long cigarette holders came there to dance, drink, smoke, play poker, and do many other things that kept a staff of four occupied around the clock. Uncle Moshe was always the first one up and the last one in bed. At work and at play, he was indefatigable.

For a month, Albano did not leave the apartment. Many days he slept the whole day through. There was nothing he could do about it: lethargy overtook him with the first morning light. Consequently, he could not sleep at night. He learned which of the floor's waxed wooden boards creaked so that he could pace without awakening the neighbors below or the guests. For hours he stood at his bedroom window, staring into the night at the falling rain. He observed, disinterested, the loss of the use of his left hand. What was a loss of a limb to a man whose heart had been ripped from his chest? He now was a cripple, like so many men in Paris who were lucky enough to have returned from the Great War. In Paris, it seemed that the majority of men were scarred, missing an eye, an arm, or a leg. Albano ate without appetite. Food no longer had any taste. The alcohol he drank made him forget nothing. Books remained unread on his lap. He found no joy in music. When Uncle Moshe entertained, which was frequently, Albano retreated to his room.

That first month, Uncle Moshe showed no other expectation of his nephew than to remain clean, gain back some weight, and rest. He offered for him to come along on rides through the city, and on occasion, Albano obliged. Uncle Moshe's automobile was a sparkling blue de Dion Bouton Torpedo, a gleaming jewel with a removable top. Dressed in fancy coats with fur collars, they meandered through Paris in the magnificent vehicle driven by a chauffeur. Paris reminded Albano of Smyrna in many ways because his city's architecture had mirrored that of the great capitals of Europe. All of it was familiar, but at the same time, it was alien. The beautiful buildings were there, and the fancy shops, and the restaurants and cafés, but there was no ocean, no camels, no dust; nothing smelled familiar, everything was flat, and rain and cold prevailed even though this was now April. Uncle Moshe was thrilled to show him Paris, but Albano's attention remained focused on the hood ornament, a delicate young woman who appeared to be jumping up, or dancing, her hair in the wind. He imagined it to be Xandra's spirit, preceding him, guiding him happily through the city, as the car glided past the Trocadero area, with its sweeping views of the Seine River and the Eiffel Tower, the Arc de Triomphe, rue de Rivoli, the Louvre Museum. During the day, Albano could imagine Xandra, her smile, her hair, her laugh. He played with imagining that she was alive and marveling at all the extraordinary Parisian sights. But his nights were populated with frantic nightmares in which he was carrying her through a burning Smyrna.

Albano found the strength to read the newspaper clippings Uncle Moshe had kept. In Smyrna, the Armenian, Greek, and Levantine quarters were gone, as was most of the population, who had either perished or found a way to flee. The Turkish quarter had suffered minor damages and, amazingly, the same was true of the Jewish quarter. This is where they should have gone rather than trying to get to the quay with all the refugees, he thought. If I only had listened to Xandra.

He and Uncle Moshe received letters from Uncle Joshua. The family was struggling in the aftermath of the destruction, but they did not plan to leave Smyrna. To go where? Now that the Ottoman Empire had been dissolved, there were no more millets or protection for anyone. Uncle Joshua did not want to attempt taking the family to France. He wanted to stay in the community where he was born and raise his children and future grandchildren there. Uncle Moshe sent them monetary help, but it was nearly useless in a city turned to ashes where little commerce took place, where food was scarce, and water wells polluted. In the end, there was strangely little to gather from the newspapers. It was beyond reason that such a human catastrophe, hundreds of thousands of deaths, the destruction of an entire city would come down to headlines, small articles, footnotes, and everything seen through the lens of the country's political and commercial interests. The alleged neutrality of the ships in the harbor, the failure to act, the indifference, how the captains of those ships obeyed orders rather than consider the human tragedy before them were scarcely mentioned.

"History will sort this out," Uncle Moshe assured him. "One day the destruction of Smyrna will be remembered as one of the most brutal acts of humanity. All through the world, children of future generations will learn of it in schools. You'll see."

When Albano was back to a healthy weight, from the twenty kilos he had lost, Uncle Moshe took him to his tailor. There Albano stood, passive, as they fitted him for a new wardrobe while Moshe fretted over every detail. The shoes, the hats, the jackets, coats, and suits all were custom made for him. "Uncle, I do not need all those beautiful things," Albano protested.

"If you're going to live in France, it can either be in luxury or indigence," Uncle Moshe answered. "For a foreigner from our part of the world, there is practically no in-between. Your attire must convey your importance, or else your race and accent will remind them of your insignificance in their eyes."

Besides enlisting the help of a private tutor to perfect his French and reduce his accent, Uncle Moshe personally handled Albano's lessons in etiquette. He showed him the peculiar ways Europeans ate. He showed him how to hold his fork with his left hand, the knife in the right, only cutting the small bit of food that was about to go into his mouth. He taught him that there were a special fork and knife for fish and how to tell those apart from the regular ones. He taught him how to unfold a napkin onto his lap (Uncle Moshe had a way to do that was full of flourish), how to order wine, how to call for a taxi, how to bend to kiss a lady's hand to varying degrees depending on one's motives. He taught him how to comb his hair parted, how to use pomade. He insisted that Albano wear a monocle he had no use for to appear older, and taught him how to take a handkerchief or a gold watch out of his buttoned-down vest pocket to great effect. Even how to clear his throat knowingly and how to suppress burps. As Uncle Moshe mimicked the behaviors of French gentlemen, Albano was reminded of Hagop's antics. Hagop, who was surely dead now, another life wasted, another heartache too hard to bear. Whatever Hagop had done that last day at the cave before the police took him, hitting Xandra, running away with all the money, the cruel words, were of no importance. He only blamed himself. Hagop had been the victim of society's ills. None of it had been his fault.

Uncle Moshe told him one day at the office where Albano devoted fourteen hours a day learning the rug trade, "You learn fast and you are good with numbers, but it is your good looks that will be the greatest asset to our business. You will make an impression on the ladies and their rich, carpet-buying husbands." In this way Hagop and Uncle Moshe were the same. They had both convinced themselves that Albano had magical powers of persuasion because of the way he looked. When Albano glimpsed himself in the mirror in one of Uncle Moshe's gilded bathrooms, he saw nothing other than sad eyes with an unusual golden hue, and lips that no longer knew how to smile.

Once Albano was suitably attired and better versed in the ways of French society, Uncle Moshe began taking him around town to restaurants, to plays, to the opera, and to the many places where all of Paris danced, drank, seduced, and dined. It was 1923, and Paris was one large celebration. What were the Parisian thinking, Albano wondered? Did they know of a place once called the Ottoman Empire? Did they know anything about his land and its arid summers, its bay with the myriad boats, the caravans of camels? Had they learned of the fire that destroyed Smyrna? Did they care? Parisians did not seem to care about much, other than entertaining themselves.

But it was not fair to resent Paris's apparent insouciance. Although it had emerged victorious, France was devastated by the war. The many crippled men on the streets served as a constant reminder of this. France seemed pulled between two forces: on the one hand the physical and emotional scars of war, and on the other, the youth willing its future into existence with forced joyfulness. Frantic; yes, this was the word that came to him. Paris was frantic. He was arriving in a country in the crux of great change. There was a mad dash toward modernity. Women were becoming emancipated. A cultural and artistic evolution was taking place in the arts, in writing, in plays, in clothes, and political ideas. The notion of what was acceptable behavior was in a state of constant reinvention. Women cropped their hair like boys and dressed garçonne style. They wore fluid, revealing dresses cut at the knee and no corset. They favored bell-shaped hats, long strands of beads; they showed their arms and legs, and in the dancing spots at night, occasionally bared their breasts. The city was looking for absurdist's ways to play. There were carnivals, disguises, parties where men dressed as women, and women as men. And then there was the obsession with racing. There wasn't a week without a new race, sillier than the one before. There were races for café waiters, dressed in their garbs and carrying trays. There were newspaper deliverymen races, chimney sweepers races, boat races on the Seine, even races where legless men raced each other in their wheelchairs, and races of drunken men who had to drink a glass of alcohol every 100 meters. Since the end of the Great War, there was in Paris an almost desperate quest for laughter and enjoyment of life, and Albano was incapable of either.

"Where are the Jews?" Albano had asked Uncle Moshe early on as they rode through Paris. "I do not see any of them in the streets."

"They dress just like French people. Over time they have integrated into French society. They've abandoned many of the customs and ways of our culture. Their children have attended Parisian universities for generations. They are doctors, lawyers, writers, artists, politicians. In fact, they do not feel a kinship with us. They see us as too Jewish. Too ethnic. They see themselves as French, and they see us as foreigners. France might tout itself as the most cosmopolitan place on the planet, but immigrants are still immigrants."

France was what he and Xandra had hoped for: a place where a Sephardic Jew and a Christian Armenian could love each other free of judgment and threat from their respective ethnic groups.

Again and again, the same thought haunted Albano. Why had he decided to stay in Smyrna until *after* the baby was born? They should have left as soon as they had received Uncle Moshe's diamond. Had he done this, they would be together today. A family. It was impossible not to be bitter as he moved around Paris, watching people in wonderment, baffled at the affluence and freedom all around. Why be given the key to this heaven only to be robbed of Xandra, the one person he cared to share it with?

Albano threw himself into his new work. Uncle Moshe's rue des Rosiers store was so successful that it could barely hold enough inventory. Now his uncle entertained the notion of opening an upscale store on rue d'Uzès, one that Albano would run.

Each day they had lunch together at one of the restaurants near the shop. One beautiful June day they walked to a brasserie. The owner hurried toward them, beaming. "Ah, mon cher Monsieur! What a pleasure to see you again. You are bringing a new friend today?"

"This young man is my nephew," Uncle Moshe told her. The woman nodded knowingly.

"Have you ever eaten a choucroute?" Moshe asked.

"What is it?"

"Every part of the pig served on a plate of fermented cabbage."

Uncle Moshe ordered the choucroute. Albano nibbled at the cooked cabbage, careful to avoid everything else on the plate while Moshe dug in with his usual gusto. They discussed work. Uncle Moshe spoke of the bank loans he was securing and the contacts he was making in the diamond trade. He said, "Perhaps we should diversify."

"Diversify?"

"Go into the diamond trade."

"Why do so when the business is doing so well?"

"Rugs are cumbersome," Moshe said.

"Is that a problem?" Albano asked.

"It is not a problem today, but it could become one."

Albano looked at Uncle Moshe, not understanding.

"It's not smart to keep all your eggs in one basket," Uncle Moshe said. "What if there is another war? And don't tell me that we just had the war to end all wars; that's just a fallacy. Wars are only a jumping board to the next war. You saw how it was in the Empire and every empire before that."

"How would we get into the diamond trade?" Albano asked.

"First, we need to learn. Your eye is good and discerning, I have said this before. There is a man I know who could train you. He can teach you how to look through a particular kind of lens and recognize a diamond's quality and flaws even before it's been cut."

Albano said he would learn. But what he was thinking and did not tell Uncle Moshe, was that every glimmer of every diamond would remind him of

Xandra and of the day when he put the diamond in the hand of a priest, and all hope was lost.

They finished lunch and ordered dessert. Around them, gentlemen with curled mustaches, starched collars, and waxed hair sat at tables next to their plump wives. Cups filled with chocolate mousse were set in front of them. Uncle Moshe patted his belly with satisfaction. "France is a good country for us. We must count our blessings that we are here."

"I guess this is a blessing," Albano said, unable to mask his bitterness.

"Don't you think that those who died in Smyrna would have wished a different fate?"

Albano looked away. He already condemned himself for every decision he had made in the last year, and even for failing to die that day in the water. But lately, he also felt shame at his indulging in this deep sadness, at his incapacity to move on. "You are right. They would wish for my fate. I am standing, and of sound mind, and healthy, and I can work, and the work interests me more than any other work I would imagine doing. And the money flows in beyond my wildest imagination. Yet I sink in melancholy."

"That is because work and money won't give meaning to your life," Uncle Moshe said, taking a spoon full of desert into his mouth. "I guess it might be enough for some men, but not for someone with your disposition."

"What is my disposition?"

"You're a man of heart, my dear nephew. You need more than material gains and earthly pleasure. Power does not interest you. What you need is a purpose."

Albano shook his head. "Then I'm at a loss."

Uncle Moshe set down his spoon and stopped eating his chocolate mousse. "I have meant to speak to you about this. I thought about it a great deal. You know how, as part of the rebuilding, France's desperate need for children makes sense. Not only economically, demographically, but also emotionally. France needs to regain strength, hope, and a future."

"True."

"Those happened to be the very things you need."

"I suppose."

"Well, Dear Albano, then you will agree that, like France, the solution is to bring children into your life."

Albano watched his uncle, dumbfounded and amused. "Where am I to find children that will have me?"

"You told me a few months ago that you would never love again. Do you still think this to be true?"

A shadow passed before Albano's eyes. "I am in love still. Only to a person who is no longer."

"You are a loving man and you need a family for which to care and provide."

Albano smiled in spite of himself. "And so, I shall find a family to love? How would you suggest I do that?"

"There are ladies in Paris that will have you, as you must know."

"But I shall not love them."

"But you could care for them! In all the ways women need to be cared for. And they would bear children that you would dearly love."

Albano dismissed the notion with his hand. "But Xandra—"

"This would not be betraying her!" Uncle Moshe interrupted. "Do you think your beloved would have wanted you to spend the rest of your days childless, womanless, and alone?"

Albano was astounded. "You are asking me to marry a French woman I do not love?"

"I am asking you nothing. I'm merely telling you about options you might not have thought about. You could find a nice person and like her enough. Someone with whom you could grow in fondness over time."

"I'm a foreigner, a refugee. Someone who struggles with the language. A crippled man whose heart belongs to a dead woman. No sane French woman would have me even if I wanted her, which I do not."

"You are also a healthy young man, a rare commodity in France these days, and one with a growing business and bank account at that. You are intelligent, hard-working, capable, kind, and caring."

"Please," Albano said, embarrassed. But Uncle Moshe would not be stopped.

"And you are very handsome. Women will line up to marry you." Albano was shaking his head, closing his eyes, rejecting all that Uncle Moshe was saying. Moshe paused and then said, "Think of it as a business arrangement then. One that favors both parties." He added after a longer pause, "Another aspect of marriage not to be dismissed is that it will be your ticket to French naturalization."

"You don't have a wife," Albano pointed out accusatorily.

Uncle Moshe rolled his eyes. "I cannot subject a poor woman to a life of lies."

"But you think *I* should?"

"If you can go to bed with a woman, and provide for her, and treat her kindly, give her children, that's love enough. Together, you can build a life."

Albano dismissed Uncle Moshe's idea that day. But as he walked through Paris over the next several months, watching the trees go bare and then green again, the gaping void in his heart and soul did not fill. Albano had been in France for five months, and he was concluding that his pain might never go away. He began to wonder if Uncle Moshe might be right. What if he could find a French woman? They would have children. Through marriage, he would get respectability and French citizenship. Together, they would create a home life. Uncle Moshe's plan was not just a good solution. If

Albano did not want to turn mad with grief and despair, it was the only solution.

****

In March, he met the woman who would become his wife. He met her at a party Uncle Moshe had thrown at his house. Moshe had brought in a small jazz band, fresh from America. There were a trumpet and two saxophones making a ruckus. The butler could barely keep up with the pace of the flowing wine. Young Parisian men and women, already drunk, for the most part, were dancing, drinking champagne wine, eating caviar canapés, and laughing. Albano made the effort to attend, rather than stay in his room. He stood in a corner, watching the French women. Their appetite for life scared him. How would he be able to give any of them happiness? He was about to retreat to his room when he noticed a serious young woman who stood slightly removed from the scene. The other guests were dancing feverishly, but she just leaned against a door, her arms crossed over her slight chest, and observed the dancers with an air of reproach on her face. She was dressed in the new fashion, her blonde hair cut below her ears. She was not a beautiful woman. Her nose and eyebrows were a bit pronounced, her eyes small and dark, her silhouette angular. But her body lent itself perfectly to the favored tomboy look, which she wore with more elegance than the other, prettier women in the room. As he watched her, he noticed that she had looked at him too. Albano did not for a second think that she was the kind of woman he would want to marry, or who would want to marry him, but he felt that he could speak to her, perhaps because she looked grave, pensive, and maybe upset, emotions he could relate to. He cut through the dancers and came near her. "Do you not enjoy jazz?" he asked.

"Of course, I do." She frowned before adding, "Actually, no, I do not."

"Myself, I don't understand it," Albano said. "Where I come from, melodies are quite different, as are the instruments. My ears must first be trained to recognize all this noise and cadence as music."

"Oh, by all means, tell your ears that there is nothing wrong with them." She was not looking at him as she spoke.

"What music do you enjoy?"

"I'm classically trained, and I intend to remain this way."

"Classical? Aren't you a flapper? An emancipated woman?"

She turned to him for the first time, as though surprised he was still speaking to her. "Not in the sense that I want to dance and drink my life away, only in the sense that I reject the subjugation of corsets."

"I hear that much has changed for French women."

"Is that so? We cannot vote and aren't represented in government. If we want to work, we need the authorization of our husbands or fathers. While our men were at war, we ran the country. We proved that we are so much more than a vehicle for corsets. Most of us do not intend to remain in men's shadows."

Albano had never considered any of this and found himself without an opinion on the subject. "What instrument do you play?" he asked.

"The piano, of course." Albano could see she was happy he was speaking to her, but that she was not trusting, not relaxing. "I have started to give lessons," she said, shrugging.

"I admire women who work."

"Alas, I do not do this by choice. I am unmarried, and I have my mother to support." She seemed bored with speaking about herself. "Where do you come from?" she asked.

"A country they are now trying to rename Turkey."

"Ah! Mustapha Kemal. I hear he is quite the progressive himself."

"That remains to be seen."

"A Muslim country ...," she said. The sentence was unfinished, the question not formulated but he understood.

"I am Jewish," he answered.

"As am I," she said, visibly pleased. "And what are you doing in Paris, Monsieur?"

He bent slightly to take her gloved hand, and brought it to his lips without quite touching it, the way Moshe had taught him. "My name is Albano. I live here now that my country was destroyed."

"Are you a refugee?"

"I am a businessman."

"And what is your business?"

"The oriental rug trade, with my uncle," he said, pointing to Uncle Moshe who stood in the company of two young women. All three were laughing at something or someone.

"Ah ... our dear Moshe," she said. "Quite the character." She peered at him. "He and you are related you say?"

"He and my father were brothers."

"Were?"

"My father passed."

"As has mine," she said.

"The war?"

"It wiped the nation clean of three generations of men. My mother has lost every man she held dear, her father, her husband, and her two sons."

"And so, you have lost them too."

"And so, I have," she said with a sadness devoid of self-pity. "My name is Lucienne," she said, handing him her hand. Having already kissed her hand earlier, he shook it this time, which made her laugh. "Forgive me. I am still learning your customs and your beautiful language."

They walked to the adjoining salon, which was empty, and where the sounds of jazz were muffled, and sat on the sofa. "And what do you intend to do in Paris besides selling rugs?" she asked.

Albano thought of this. "I intend to marry and have a family."

She remained pensive. "I intended to marry as well … but the war has ruined Mother and me, and without a fortune, I seem to hold little appeal."

"You are a distinguished lady, an accomplished pianist, a forward-thinking, intelligent woman. You will find a husband."

She smiled at him. It was clear that she was enjoying his company but was trying hard not to seem too interested. "Oh, but it is too late for me you see. I'm already an old maid."

This was not an expression he was familiar with. "An old maid?" he repeated.

"A woman passed the age when she can find a husband."

"But you are so young!"

"I'm twenty-four. That's the age when the world decides that if no one thought you had anything to offer before, it won't start happening now."

"I am twenty-one years old myself. Am I too late to marry as well?"

"Don't be absurd. Only women's value depreciates with age." She observed him with keen interest. "You look older. I would have said thirty."

"Oh no!" he said playfully. "Do I look that old?"

She laughed. Her serious, almost severe expression vanished. "I'm sorry, I meant it as a compliment. You seem wiser than your years."

Albano was quiet. He thought of Uncle Moshe's advice. Treat her kindly; that's love enough. "I have a question for you. Or rather, a request," he said.

"What is it?"

"Would you accept to have dinner with me?"

This flustered her. "You hardly know me!"

"I am attempting to remedy that."

To mask her pleasure, she took a cigarette out of a thin silver box and brought it to her lips and let him light it for her. "I accept your invitation," she said, taking an elegant small puff out of her cigarette.

****

Lucienne's family, he learned, was of Tsarfati ancestry, but the last few generations had been born and raised in Paris. Several had distinguished themselves for their social, political, and economic achievements. But over the years, the bloodline had not quite replenished, and she and her mother had become its sole remaining members. After the death of Lucienne's grandfather, father, and brothers in the Great War, all that remained of their fortune was a modest military pension and the family house, a three-storied hôtel particulier in the Cité des Fleurs in the seventeenth arrondissement of Paris. Lucienne and her mother were proud women, but they were pragmatic.

The house's upkeep and taxes made it impossible to keep, and soon they would have to find an apartment and sell generations of cherished belongings to make ends meet.

Lucienne had qualities that Albano respected. She was socially confident. She was serious. She was intelligent and had a clear sense of her beliefs and what she wanted in life.

The courtship wasn't a long one. By marrying Albano, Lucienne would save her house and aspire to a comfortable lifestyle. She and her elderly mother would be cared for. She would have to overlook the fact that Albano was foreign-born and of humble roots, but he was Jewish, which mattered to her and her mother very much. Albano, in return, would receive citizenship. And despite Uncle Moshe's opinion that Lucienne was too cold, Albano convinced himself that by choosing a woman for whom he felt neither love nor lust, he would not be betraying Xandra.

They were married at the Synagogue des Tournelles. They were both eager to have children. Marceline was born precisely nine months later, in December 1923. Two years later, in December 1925, they welcomed their boy Gustave.

The children came into the world at a time of tremendous vitality. These were the années folles indeed. The population of France seemed engaged in a frantic effort to forget the austerity and horrors of the war. The mood, forced perhaps, was to lightness, to dancing and drinking, to excesses and indulgences, to modernization and consumption. The economy thrived, as did Albano and Moshe's business.

Uncle Moshe had been correct. Albano immediately fell in love with his children, a deep, all-encompassing love that allowed him to live again. Marceline was a vivacious and self-assured little girl who had inherited his physical features, and unruly black curls, and that strange eye color, neither gold nor green. From her mother, Marceline inherited a strong will and commanding personality.

Gustave was Marceline's opposite. He had dark brown eyes, pale skin, and his mother's aquiline nose. He was a tender soul, fragile and shy, and was easily made nervous by noises and people. Emotions flooded out of him at the slightest upset. Marceline was fearless from an early age and stood her ground unflinchingly before children and adults. Her one soft spot was her little brother, whom she treated as her personal possession. She bossed him around, dressed him like a doll, and rewarded him according to her whim, and Gustave accepted her authority absolutely. Marceline enjoyed her brother's company when he was compliant, but his tears exasperated her.

Albano was concerned about Gustave's gentleness, his vulnerability. Should a boy learn toughness from his sister? Should he not learn it from his father? Albano noted how much more entertaining Marceline was in Lucienne's salons. There, from the earliest age, his daughter's wit and aplomb delighted everyone. In contrast, Gustave would not look people in the eye, and he tended to scamper away the minute he was addressed by a stranger. It was impossible not to compare the two children. Thoughtful, shy Gustave reminded Albano of himself. And lively Marceline, absurdly, reminded him of Hagop.

Lucienne liked to remain active. She found meaning in literary and artistic salons and philanthropy work. She did not tend to the minutiae of the children. This was the function of the nannies, British nannies always since they were, according to Lucienne, the only appropriate choice for French children of high society.

For Lucienne, a good standing in society and the right kind of manners were of utmost importance. This was the way she had grown up and the way she intended to raise her children. Albano, for whom everything in France was a discovery, was blind to many of the subtleties that Lucienne, a well-bred French woman from elite Jewish society, was well attuned to. She could detect in an instant people's good or inferior breeding from the way they moved, spoke, or dressed or from the company they kept. Those she admired most, those at the very top of her personal hierarchy, were the people issued by birth from European aristocracy. Family standing, to Lucienne, meant everything. And although she enjoyed their lifestyle, money – the kind which was not inherited but which she dubbed "nouveau riche" money – was something to be vaguely ashamed of. Albano, for example, learned that in France, all Jews were not equal in the eyes of the French Jewry. He was a Sephardi, and she was Ashkenazi, and for reasons he still could not understand, and according to his wife, the former was inferior to the latter.

Albano did not fit Lucienne's ideal of status and education, and he often sensed that his having been raised in a poor village in another country was embarrassing to her.

For his part, Albano would have preferred if Lucienne showed more tenderness toward the children. But she believed this was not her role, and perhaps she was right.

All in all, they got along well. They did not argue and spoke to each other with civility.

Lucienne's mother lived with them. Grand-mère was a wonderful woman who adored her grandchildren, and since she doted on them from the moment they woke up to the moment they went to bed, the children were never deprived of the warmth of her kind and loving heart.

At the heart of Albano's life were the children. They ate early with the nannies, but at every dinner, Albano sat with them at dessert time. At bedtime, he went into the room they shared and told them stories. Often during the day, he would meet them at the park and play with them or take them to the zoo. Every chance he got, he held them tight and told them how much he adored them. Still, each day, as he watched Marceline and Gustave get tucked into bed, he thought of the baby he and Xandra had lost, and he thought of Xandra and of the life that had not been.

As the years passed, Albano watched Marceline and Gustave become little French children. He observed them inside the nursery, surrounded by stuffed toys bigger than they were, dollhouses, and wooden horses. Marceline's black mane was tamed into polished curls. Gustave was dressed like a miniature gentleman. They knew how to hold their elbows tight against the side of their bodies as they cut their meat with children-size silverware. They said, "Bonjour, Madame," and "Oui, Monsieur," and "s'il vous plaît," and "merci." They did not know a word of Ladino, Arabic, Armenian, or Greek. They would eventually learn Latin and English with tutors, Lucienne said, and when they were old enough, they would attend Hebrew lessons. When the time came, Lucienne planned to send them to boarding school for the best possible education.

As Albano watched his children, dressed in perfect little outfits, practice their piano, or write letters with an ink pen, or color within the lines, he marveled at the difference between their childhoods and his. If Marceline and Gustave had no idea what other children in the world must endure, it was a good thing. His children would forever be safe. They would never lack for anything. Their lives would be perfect.

All too often, Albano found himself dreaming awake about Xandra. Year after year, the daydream continued. Marceline was born, and then Gustave. He and Lucienne celebrated their second anniversary, their third, their fifth, their sixth. Still, it was Xandra he dreamed about. He rose early every morning and went on long walks by himself, but he was not truly alone. He imagined himself with Xandra, walking with her. He dreamed that he showed Xandra the gardens of Paris, the Arc de Triomphe, the banks of the Seine, the Trocadero, the Grand Palais, the bridges. In those dreams, he had conversations with the ghost of Xandra that he could never have had with Lucienne.

He and Lucienne stayed out of each other's affairs and scarcely argued. Alban, as she preferred to call him, aspired to be the most accommodating of husbands. He wanted, above all, to make Lucienne content. He was in charge of their finances, about which she never asked questions, and she handled the details of the house and the children, where to go on holidays, whom to hire and fire, what to wear, whom to see. Over the years, under Lucienne's capable direction and impeccable taste, the house was repaired and modernized with new plumbing, comfortable bathrooms, central heating, and a telephone. They soon owned two automobiles. A full-time chauffeur was hired as well as a cook. Lucienne held salons and dinners and surrounded herself with members of Paris's high bourgeoisie and even the occasional aristocrat. Albano was a bit overwhelmed by the role he was supposed to hold in society, but he was open to meeting new people, and his time living under Moshe's roof had taught him to observe without judgment.

Lucienne became increasingly hard to please, but Albano knew he was to blame for this. He had stopped visiting her bed when she became pregnant with Gustave and had not found it in himself to rejoin her. They now each had their own bedroom in the house. He had moved into his own room on the pretext of insomnia. At first, at bedtime, he would come to sit on her bed and say a few words to her so that she would not feel abandoned. But soon, he could not even make himself do that.

Lucienne grew angry and dismissive. "Don't feel that you need to come here," she said one night after she had worn a new silk nightgown, perhaps in the hope of inciting him, but had only received a kiss on her forehead. "It's obvious that you're only going through the motions."

"I came to bid you good night."

"You clearly loathe to touch me."

"Lucienne!"

"I know you have mistresses."

"I do not."

"You want me to believe that a twenty-eight-year-old man can do without intimate relations?"

He tried his best to reassure her, but this did not calm her jealousy. He felt great guilt at the suffering he had inflicted upon Lucienne by marrying her. She suffered from his lack of social standing, which diminished hers. And now she suffered from his lack of physical engagement. Albano felt alone a lot of the time. But all in all, those were beautiful years watching the children grow up. Still, every day, there was the loss of Xandra, like a feeling of a void in his heart.

****

In the next few years, as Paris continued to lose itself into the general intoxication of the années folles, as Lucienne continued to host dinners and salons, and as his and Moshe's business grew, Albano began to keep a tense, watchful eye on the political situation throughout Europe. He did not like the excitement about National Socialism and its racist theories in Germany, and in Italy, Mussolini's fascism worried him. But when he brought those worries to Moshe, his uncle told him he was only looking for reasons to explain why he was so unhappy, and that he had warned him against marrying Lucienne whom he found cold and snobbish.

In 1929, the world began to unravel. It started with a personal loss. On the night of the New York Stock Market Crash, Grand-mère collapsed of a heart attack. Marceline was six then and Gustave only four. Marceline, being older, was able to grieve and adjust, but Gustave was inconsolable. For months, he had nightmares, and during the day he cried at the smallest frustration.

Albano was pained by Gustave's vulnerability but did not know how to help him. Lucienne felt that Gustave needed more discipline. Lucienne hired and fired more British nannies, capable women trained to be uncompromising. This only made Gustave more anxious. Albano wondered what might become of a boy who seemed to be afraid of his shadow. Life was treacherous as it was, even when faced head-on.

Albano tried not to resent Lucienne for her impatience with Gustave. She was, after all, doing the best she could, frantically going through a new caregiver every few weeks. Why could Gustave not be more like his sister, Lucienne wondered out loud? At six years old, Marceline was a paragon of strength and determination, unsentimental to the point of ruthlessness. Even Lucienne was less unyielding.

This disagreement over how to help Gustave went on for months and created a wedge between Albano and Lucienne. But the hiring and firing of nannies was a new source of tension between them. If the women were pretty, or young, Lucienne would make a scene, accuse Albano of all sorts of evils, and fire them. It wasn't rare for Gustave to awaken with one nanny, and be put to sleep that same night by a different one he'd never seen before.

Immediately following the American Stock Market Crash, Uncle Moshe left for Tripoli, Lebanon, Athens, and Naples to secure arrangements with his suppliers. He would also visit Uncle Joshua and his family in the Jewish quarter in the city now called Izmir.

Uncle Moshe's trip was extended an additional month. Upon his return, he called Albano on the telephone and asked that they meet at the Tuileries Garden the next day. They needed to talk, he said.

As they walked together down the central alley, along the neat hedges of clipped boxwood and chestnut trees, Uncle Moshe was uncharacteristically quiet. "Was your voyage a good one?" Albano asked. "You didn't tell me why you extended it. Is anything the matter?"

"I wanted to speak to you about something. You will want to sit, Albano. What I have to say to you will be difficult."

Albano became worried. "Are you ill, Uncle?"

They sat on one of the stone benches around the garden's large round basin. Little boys sailed their wooden boats, and little girls played with hoops and jump ropes. Mothers and children's nurses sat on chairs, catching the spring sun's timid rays.

"The reason I extended my trip is that I ended up spending much more time in Izmir. The change of name is a good thing. There is little left of the city we loved."

"Please do not speak to me of Smyrna."

"Albano, I must," Uncle Moshe said somberly. "As you know I saw Uncle Joshua."

"Is he not well?"

"The whole family is well and much appreciative of our help. These are trying times for the non-Muslims who stayed, but they are making do. When I saw Uncle Joshua, I could tell there was something he was trying to conceal from me. He was not looking me in the eyes, and I know my brother. He was upset, and when I asked him what was wrong, he would not tell me at first. I pressed him to tell me what was on his mind, and he eventually did." Uncle Moshe hesitated, staring at his round fingers, searching for words. "Uncle Joshua spoke of a visit he had received two years prior. A visit about which he had kept silent."

"What kind of visit?"

"A person came to his door. A woman."

"What kind of woman?"

"A veiled woman. At first, Uncle Joshua found it strange that an unknown Muslim woman would come all the way to the Jewish quarter and ask to speak to him. The woman said she was not Turkish but Armenian."

"Armenian?" Albano became excited. "Had she known Xandra perhaps?"

"Albano, the woman asked about you."

"About me?"

"She wanted to know if you were alive. Uncle Joshua told her that you had escaped the fire and almost died of drowning, but that you had been rescued and moved to France, and that now you were married and had children."

Albano racked his memory for any Armenian woman he might know from the past. Xandra's mother and sisters had perished. There were women he saw at the bakery, but none that knew him by name. "Who was this woman?" he asked.

"She didn't want to say. She thanked your uncle and walked away. Uncle Joshua did not speak of this to anyone. But he ... when he saw me, he felt guilty I guess."

"Guilty of what?"

"He felt you deserved to know, or at least he wanted to place the burden of telling you, or of not telling you, on my shoulders."

Albano was getting impatient. What was Uncle Moshe trying to say? "What burden?"

"Uncle Joshua believed that this woman was, in fact, the same woman he said you left your family and religion for. He believed the woman was Xandra."

Albano shrugged. "Of course not."

"Whoever she was, Joshua felt guilty about keeping that impression to himself. He also said she had asked for your address in France and that he would not give it to her."

"Why not?"

"You had started a new life, and he did not want to be the one to ruin it."

Albano got up from the bench and began pacing. "A childhood friend of Xandra and Hagop perhaps? Who could she be? Uncle Joshua was a fool not to give her my address. This woman obviously wanted to speak to me and had every right to."

"In Uncle Joshua's mind, it would have been uncalled for if this woman was indeed who he convinced himself she was."

"But she was not."

Uncle Moshe hesitated. "There was the complication of her appearance. If this woman was indeed Xandra, she was not the way you remember her."

"Uncle Moshe," Albano said with force. "The woman was not Xandra. Xandra perished in the fire. I buried her."

"Even with a headdress, your Uncle Joshua saw that she was burned," Moshe muttered. "Terribly disfigured by the fire." Uncle Moshe, still sitting on the stone bench, was pale and distraught. He did not look at Albano but still stared down into his lap.

"What are you trying to tell me, Uncle Moshe?"

"You want to know why I spent a month in Smyrna when I was supposed to leave after a week?" Moshe said.

"Why did you?"

Uncle Moshe took in a large breath. He got up from the bench, took Albano by the shoulder, and faced him. "I stayed to look for the woman."

Albano was dumbfounded. "Why would you do that?"

"I needed to know. What if Uncle Joshua had been right? What if the woman was indeed Xandra?"

Albano was angered by this, annoyed by Uncle Moshe's hands on his shoulders. He answered as patiently as he could, "I buried her with my own—"

"I found her," Uncle Moshe interrupted, his eyes filling with tears. "Your Xandra is alive, Albano!"

The two men faced each other. Uncle Moshe strengthened his grip on Albano's shoulders. Neither moved. Albano looked at Uncle Moshe imploringly. There was so much more in Uncle Moshe's expression than the meaning of his words. Moshe seemed both devastated and thrilled. Albano tried to speak, "I ... I don't understand."

"Uncle Joshua was right, Albano. Xandra is alive."

Albano was very pale suddenly. He shook his head vigorously and, freeing himself from Moshe's grip, walked away saying, "It cannot be. It cannot be. I took her in my arms, she and the baby. I carried them to the sand, under the tree, I dug their grave!"

"Your child did perish," Uncle Moshe said gravely. "But the woman you buried was not Xandra. Xandra gave birth to a stillborn child as the fire raged. She was saved! She was evacuated before the hospital burned down. She was carried to safety and was between life and death for weeks. She suffered severe burns, but she lived."

Albano's legs folded under him. He sank onto the park bench. He was panting, nauseated. None of this made sense, but suddenly he had the terrible urge to believe. He did not, could not, believe, but he wanted to. He could not bear to think Uncle Moshe was wrong. He muttered, "How can you know that this is the right person?"

"There isn't the shadow of a doubt. I met her. She and I spoke at length. The cave, Hagop, her parents, the pregnancy, the diamond, the visas, the arrival of Kemal, the fire. She knows everything about you, every small thing. And she looks just like the picture you once sent me."

Albano curled over himself. "I can't have abandoned her!" he muttered. "It's not true! I can't have abandoned her and married another woman. I could not have left her to die alone in childbirth and run away. I have children! With someone else … I forgot her; I tried to forget her. If she were alive, I could never forgive myself. I … she…." He looked up at Uncle Moshe. "But still … It would be the most wonderful gift from God."

Uncle Moshe beamed. "She is alive."

Albano got up from the bench, frantic, speaking loudly. "I am taking a boat. I am leaving today!"

"That won't be necessary."

"I must go to Izmir at once. If this is Xandra—"

"She is here, Albano," Uncle Moshe said.

"Here?"

"Here in Paris. I brought her back with me."

Albano's mouth opened and closed. Words didn't come out. "Xandra is in Paris?" he finally said. His knees buckled again, and he stumbled to the boxwood hedge, bent over, and threw up.

Uncle Moshe patted him on the back. "I debated whether to respect her wish. Although she finally agreed to come to Paris, she made me promise not to tell you a thing."

"But why?" Albano yelled.

"She thought you would be better off not knowing."

Albano was crying now, tears rolling down his face. "How could I be better off?"

"She respects that you are married. She asks for nothing."

And this alone, her demonstration of selflessness, convinced Albano. "That is my Xandra! She is alive!" He was laughing now through his tears.

"Albano, you must know," Uncle Moshe said gravely, "she suffered. She is not the way you remember her. It's been a great many years of grief and physical pain for her."

"Seven years! Seven years later! How will she ever believe I didn't mean to abandon her? How will she ever forgive me?"

"She understands and forgives you."

"That is what she is like!" Albano said, with immense pride. There was on his face enormous hope and excitement. "Where is she?"

"In my apartment."

"Your apartment?" Albano exclaimed.

"She knows that I am here with you now. She hopes for your visit."

"Today?"

"Whenever you are ready. She knows this will be a shock to you, all this. She has known you were alive for a long time. She says to tell you that she understands if you need time or if you prefer not to come at all."

"Let's go right now!"

Uncle Moshe's apartment was only a short drive away. In the back seat of Moshe's automobile, Albano's entire body trembled violently, and he was incapable of a coherent thought. He asked a million questions, but Uncle Moshe said it was better if Xandra explained everything herself. When the driver stopped in front of Moshe's apartment, Albano sprang out into the street, into the building, and up the stairs while Moshe waited for the elevator. Moshe found Albano at the door of the apartment. "I don't know if I can do this. I'm ... I'm so afraid this isn't her."

They entered the salon, which for once was empty. Uncle Moshe had managed to make the houseguests disappear. "I will get her," Uncle Moshe said. "Be courageous. What you are about to see and hear will be difficult."

A few minutes later, there was a rap at the door. Albano rushed to the door, then hesitated, his hand on the doorknob. Finally, he opened it.

Xandra faced him, her grave, beautiful eyes staring unflinchingly. Her long, silky black hair was draped over one side of her face. Albano stood there, his arms alongside his body, his heart pounding, his pulse racing. She did not run to him, and his impulse to run to her was stopped. She was dressed in black. Despite the hair hiding most of her face, he could see the extent of the ravages: the skin pink, crumpled, as though melted. All the right side of her face from her temple and below her eye and all the way down to her neck had suffered a terrible burn. Her hand on that side of her body was burned as well, and he suspected a great deal of her body must also be. She watched him watch her, her eyes overflowing. "Albano," she murmured.

Albano rushed to her, but his legs gave out from under him. He sank to his knees and embraced her at the waist, his arms wrapped around her, burying his face in her skirt. "My Xandra," was all he managed to say. He stayed there a long time, weeping. Then he got up and took her in his arms. She was sobbing too. "My Xandra," he sobbed, "I left you for dead."

She took him by the hand, and they huddled on the couch by the window, crying. Albano took her hands and kissed them a hundred times. When they had cried all the tears in their bodies and could finally speak, Albano, now buoyed by joy, could not stop laughing and smiling, and so Xandra could not help but smile too.

"Are you a dream? You are a dream. Swear to me you aren't a dream!"

"I am real, Albano. You have not changed. You look like a true gentleman."

"You are just the same!" he exclaimed. He moved away slightly so that he could take in her whole appearance. "No. You are better!"

"I am disfigured."

"I believed you dead. I was certain I had buried you. Do you think that I am worried about a scar? Do you think it even matters?" With extreme gentleness, Albano moved the long strands of her hair away from her face and observed the scar carefully. The burn started at the temple, down the eyelid over her right eye, her right cheek, and down her neck.

"All the right side, down to my waist," she said, answering his silent question. "Also, part of my calf and my right foot."

"How you must have suffered," he said, caressing her burned cheek.

"The skin on my foot is the most painful because I have to wear shoes," she said lightly. "One cannot go barefoot in Paris! Moshe failed to tell me this."

"You have found me when I could not find you. I am so sorry. So, so sorry." Albano's words came out rushed and jumbled. "I was hit. Something exploded. I lost consciousness. I returned to the hospital, but it had already burned to the ground. A single wall still stood. There were bodies. Corpses lined against the wall. There was this small, burnt infant … next to a burned body of a woman, and the scarf, it too was burned for the most part, but I recognized it. And I thought … I believed…."

Xandra lowered her eyes. She thought for a long time, putting the pieces of the puzzle together in her mind. "I must tell you what happened. But do not blame yourself, dear, dear Albano. It is all my fault. I can see now how my actions … How you would not have known … You see, already the building had caught on fire as I delivered our child. People were running everywhere. They were trying to evacuate and here I was, pushing our baby out. I pushed. But our son … It must have been the fall when those men attacked us. He never breathed, the poor angel. I saw him. He was beautiful."

"A boy!"

"He looked just like you. I did not know what to do. I wrapped his tiny body in the scarf. I had nothing else. There was no time. The room was hot and filled with dense smoke. A whole side of the building was already in flames. I had to go. They were helping me, but I could not bring the baby.

They would not let me. And I could not leave him alone." She wiped her tears, and then Albano's.

"There was a woman, a kind woman, who had died just a few hours before. She was lying there. I did not want our baby to be alone in the fire, so I placed his small body wrapped in the scarf over hers, and I moved her arms over him so that they would have each other's company. I did this. I don't know why I did it. Then a beam fell, my hair caught on fire, and my dress. People helped me put it out, and then they carried me into a truck, and we were gone."

She shook her head, understanding at last. "I never thought you would come back and see that woman with our baby and think that she was me. I never imagined that both bodies would burn to the point of being unrecognizable. And yet the scarf was not burnt? I thought for all those years, about the reasons why you did not come back, but never once did I think of that."

"I came back and found them. I buried our baby, and this woman, thinking she was you. And then I swam out to sea. I wanted to die. I tried to die."

"Moshe told me this. It was five years after the fire before I had the strength to try to find out what had happened to you. As long as no one told me you were dead, I found reasons to hope. Finally, I had the courage to face the truth. I went to the Jewish quarter. I asked to see your family. People were suspicious. Your aunt chased me away. I left, but I was surprised when a man came after me on the road. He said he was your Uncle Joshua. He told me that you had survived the fire, that you had been rescued from drowning by a British hospital ship. He said that you now lived in Paris.

"This made me so happy. But, at the same time, heartbroken. I could not understand why you had not looked for me, why you had gone to France without me. He asked my name, but I did not want to tell him, I did not know yet if you should think me alive or dead. Your Uncle Joshua had the same thought, I imagine. He felt he was protecting both of us, asking me to move on, by revealing that you had married a Jewish woman in Paris, that you had a beautiful house, and a boy and a girl."

"How was telling you this protecting you?" Albano said. He was furious with Uncle Joshua for attempting to play God and control his future.

"He wanted you to continue your life without the burden of caring about me. Here I was, disfigured. Do not be angry with him Albano. He thought he was giving both of us a chance at happiness, and—"

"I will never forgive him."

"You must," she said, bringing her hands to his cheek as she always had done to soothe him.

"How could you for an instant believe I would just abandon you and our baby? You know I would have searched everywhere."

"Maybe you had looked for me and not found me and believed me dead, or you had learned of our dead child, or you had found out about my wounds. I could hardly expect—"

"Xandra, you know me better than this."

"At first, I was despondent. But over time, I was glad that your dream had come true and that you had found happiness."

"It was never my dream; it was *our* dream!" Albano exclaimed. He added bitterly, "There was no happiness to be found in this dream unless we shared it."

"But you were alive, and that was enough for me," she said. "I accepted this fate. I found comfort in knowing that you had children and that you were well. I could have continued like this for the rest of my life. I felt that imposing myself into your life now would have been cruel. It was your Uncle Moshe who convinced me otherwise." She smiled at the recollection. "One morning, two years after I spoke to your Uncle Joshua, this huge, fancily dressed Jewish man appears in the bakery where I worked, asking to speak to me. I recognized him right away from your description. I was wearing a headdress because I was working in a Muslim shop. The headdress was a good thing. I liked it. I was ceaselessly thankful for it so that I did not have to suffer other's disgust with my appearance. And by protecting my face from the sun, the pain slowly subsided. But when Moshe came, he asked my name and asked to see my face, and he recognized me as the woman he had seen in the one photograph we sent him many years ago. Right away, he asked me to come back to Paris with him."

Albano gently traced the contour of her face with the tip of a finger. "How you must have suffered."

"A part of me welcomed the physical pain. It gave shape to the terrible grief I felt at losing you and our son. Also, I had learned that my whole family had perished. It was hard to find a reason to live. Only my faith stopped me from killing myself. And in time, my faith helped me live. Moshe promised me a better life in Paris, even if I never saw you again. I felt it was what I should do. I agreed to come to France. You see, my life in Izmir was hard. I was bedridden for too long, and I missed the possibility to run away. By the time I was ready, the borders were closed to refugees. The surrounding countries had absorbed too many already. I had no money, no home. I was the poorest of the poor, a crippled woman in a destroyed city." Albano stopped her words by kissing her lips softly. She let him do this, but she continued her story. "The man you gave our diamond to, do you remember him?"

"The priest?"

"Fire was upon us; cinders rained from the sky; we could not breathe. He put a blanket over me to choke out the fire in my hair. After that, he made sure I was carried to safety. We never discussed the diamond, but I believed it save my life. By accepting the diamond, he felt entrusted with my care. There was a time when I should have thanked him, but I cursed him for saving me instead. For forcing me to live."

"What became of him?"

"There was an influenza epidemic. He died. But before that, he found work for me. There was a bakery, a Turkish bakery. They took me in. They were not bad people. They were not good people. I was not mistreated. I took care of the children and worked in the bakery, but I was a pariah in the community. I was not paid. I worked in exchange for food and shelter.

"I explained all this to Moshe, and he said that I was entitled to pay and dignity. He told me that I could find such dignity in France if I followed him. I told him that I had accepted my fate. He told me to then accept my new fate since it had now changed, and my new fate was to live in Paris." Xandra laughed. "What could I respond? He said he would find me work, paid work. That I did not deserve a life of servitude in a dangerous country that had decimated my people. It took him weeks to convince me, but he wouldn't give up and said he would not leave Izmir without me."

"But why hesitate?"

"I was afraid to see you. As long as I did not act, I could still dream. Once you knew about me, then I would have to face the truth."

"What truth?"

She looked at the polished wood floor. "That there is no room for me in your life."

Albano opened his mouth to respond, but she put a finger on his lips. She said, "Moshe stayed and waited. And then I accepted. But I did not want him to tell you about me. Not yet. I was willing to accept the kindness of this stranger. I wasn't yet convinced, though, that I wanted you to know about me. I didn't think that was the right thing to do."

"But, of course, Uncle Moshe told me anyway."

She smiled. "I get the sense that Moshe does whatever he wants."

"He has his own sense of what is right and wrong. He is a man of integrity to his convictions."

"Also, I needed to return these to you," she said. She leaned toward a bag at her feet, took a package out and unwrapped it.

It was the Torah finials. Albano stared at them, speechless. "I thought they were stolen."

"They were with me," she said. Still in a pocket of my skirt.

"But, Xandra, if you had those you could have sold them. I am sure they would have brought you a good sum."

"They are sacred. They belong to your son."

Albano contemplated the Torah ornaments unhappily. They were back in his life at the same time as Xandra. Why should two small artifacts be treated with such deference? Why had he not sold them ages ago? And what did this mean to him? Was it a sign from God that He wanted him to pursue his duty as a Kohen? But the scripture clearly opposed it. He had lost the use of a hand, which made him unsuited for the task according to the sacred text. He had also taken part in a burial and could therefore not be a Jewish priest. But he could see how pleased Xandra was, and to what lengths she had gone to protect the finials, and so he pretended to be overjoyed. And in a way, he was, but only because they were a testimony of her love for him.

"Have you found happiness here?" Xandra asked.

"Now that you're here, sitting beside me, I am happy."

Xandra's eyes filled with tears. "But it's too late now. Much too late."

"Why?"

"The way I look…."

Albano smiled. "I still see the most gorgeous woman in the world, only the most gorgeous woman in the world has a burn on her face."

Tears fell down her cheeks as she said, "And there is your life, your beautiful life here."

"Everything in my life changed the instant I learned you are alive."

Everything had to be told, every torture, every pain, and even – and that was more difficult at times for Albano knowing everything Xandra had endured – all the blessings. Albano had to tell Xandra about Lucienne. Why he had chosen her as a wife, the arrangement of convenience that was their marriage. He tried to explain what his wife was like, even though he was not sure he understood it himself. He described her as a person full of rules and strong ideas, who, much like the Levantines, thought that people must be divided into groups and that to be born in a certain family made you a better person. He told Xandra what it was like to have wealth, to produce wealth, and how it never brought the peace and happiness they both had imagined.

He told her about Gustave, his sweet boy who was five years old now, so wonderfully innocent and fragile, and about Marceline, his spirited seven-year-old daughter. He told her what it had been like to make sense of this life, what it was like to go on living when so many had not. He told her of his guilt about Lucienne, how he no longer would share her bed, and her ensuing suspicion and jealousy.

"How could I tell her that I married her *because* I did not love her? How could I tell her that I didn't desire her then or now, but that I wanted children? How could I tell her that I was in love with a dead woman?" He told Xandra how without Uncle Moshe he would have sunk into despair and madness, and how this family had given him a reason to live. "Yet despite all the richness and joys in my life, despite my love for our children, my thoughts always came back to you, and also to Hagop." He added, "And your family … I felt as though I had let everyone perish and it was unjust that I should be alive."

Xandra listened. And then she asked her question, "That day in Smyrna when I was on the quayside, and you went to the Armenian quarter. Do you remember?" Albano nodded. He knew what Xandra was going to ask. "You said that my parents and my sister had escaped." Albano lowered his eyes. "But you saw them didn't you," she pressed. "You saw that day what had been done to them? You saw them, and then you came back, and you felt you needed to lie to me because you didn't want me to suffer?"

Albano took her hands. "Oh, Xandra, how could I have told you otherwise?"

"I learned of what happened to them from another survivor," she said.

"Our baby, me, and now your entire family. How could you bear such pain, my poor love?"

They wept, holding hands, lost in the brutal memories. Around them was Uncle Moshe's luxurious sitting room, with high ceilings and chandeliers, and silk drapes, and beautiful furniture, all so much more lavish and beautiful than inside the Levantines' houses they used to peek into when they delivered pastries. They were sitting beside the heat of the fireplace. Outside the window, Paris glistened with rain. The trees that lined the street swayed to the force of the wind. But for the moment, they were back in Smyrna, in those fateful days of 1922.

"What about Hagop? Did you learn anything?" Albano asked.

"For years it was chaos and lawlessness. It was impossible to get information. But over the years some people returned, very few of them. They told us who they had seen die, and who they believed might still be alive, who was executed on the spot, who was walked to Syria or sent to forced labor camps. But no one could tell me about Hagop. No one saw him. No one remembered him. I wrote to the Red Cross and the Syrian refugee camps, but no answer came back. And there is not a day when my spirit is not tormented by thoughts of my brother. When I think of the brutal death of my sisters and parents, I can grieve and pray for their souls to rest in peace. But Hagop's mystery is something else. Some days I feel sure he is alive, as though our souls are still connected."

"If he were alive, he would have found a way to return to Smyrna and see about his family."

"What if he is crippled, or blinded, or cannot speak? There are many reasons a man would be unable to call for help." She added, "I had the same thought about you, Dear Albano. I could not help but feel that you were alive. And since I was right about you, maybe there is a chance that I am right about Hagop as well."

"You are proof that miracles exist. I will write to every consulate, every embassy, every government, every church, every office of the Red Cross."

"He could be anywhere. In Syria or Greece, or back in Turkey."

"If he is alive, I will find him. If he is not, I will try to get that confirmed so that we can move on and grieve him properly."

"Do you think that he would still hate us?"

"Not after everything. Not after all these years. If Hagop is found, he will forgive us."

"Oh, Albano. That would be so wonderful."

They spoke for hours and cried until there was not a tear left in them. In the streets of Paris, the rain had subsided, and now they sat by the fire as night fell. Wrapped in each other's arms, they fell asleep with the most profound joy in their hearts.

Albano returned to the Cité des Fleurs house in the early hours. Lucienne wanted to know where he had spent the night, and he told her he had been at his office. She wanted to know why he looked so pale, why his eyes were red, but Albano was not ready to express what had just happened. One day Lucienne would be told, but for the moment he wanted to keep his beautiful secret.

It took Xandra and Albano days to tell each other what had taken place in the eight years since the Smyrna fire. For Albano, Xandra had returned, and it was like she had never left his side. That first week, they spent all of their time together inside Moshe's apartment. He wanted to take her outside and be the one to show her Paris, but that would have to wait. Albano could not take the chance of anyone he knew seeing him with a woman other than Lucienne. He needed to speak to Lucienne first, tell her the truth, but he did not doubt that the truth would destroy her. Each time he thought of this, he felt more incapable of hurting her. Lucienne had done nothing wrong. She did not deserve such cruelty.

After a month, Albano still had not found the right words to tell Lucienne. What could he in good conscience tell her? That the love of his life had returned? That no matter how deep his responsibility and love for his family, his bond to Xandra was deeper? How could he explain to Lucienne that the steel vice that had entrapped his heart for eight painful years, preventing him from experiencing happiness, had vanished the instant he had laid eyes on his beloved? That even the birth of Marceline and Gustave had not felt as miraculous as holding Xandra in his arms again?

Xandra was the antidote to all that had been ailing him. And God, even God, had returned to his life. By bringing Xandra back to him, He had revealed Himself in all of His mystery and glory.

To Xandra, he said, "What can I tell Lucienne? She is innocent. She is a good, decent person. She loves me despite my indifference. I have tried to love her, Xandra. I have tried. She is not unlovable. She is stern and haughty, and difficult at times, but how could she not have become that way when I never let her blossom into the loving marriage she deserved? She gave me two children. Already, she suffers so much that I am in a separate bedroom. And now, to think that I am betraying her this way?"

Xandra said, "In the eyes of God, and in the eyes of the law, she is your wife. I have no claim to you."

"You have every claim!"

"I was first. But she is your wife."

"You are more of a wife to me than she ever could be."

"We have a past. And yes, we love each other. But the covenants of marriage are sacred. I respect your marriage. I would never want to do anything to alienate you from her."

"I will divorce her. People do."

Xandra looked at him. "Not in my religion, Albano."

Albano frowned. "No divorce?"

"I am a Christian woman."

Albano contemplated this. "What are we going to do?"

"I don't know," she said, shaking her head.

"I want you to be the first person I see when I awaken in the morning. I want you to be the last person I see when I close my eyes at night. And when comes that final time I close my eyes, I want you to be the person whose hand I hold."

"I will not be the one who will break up a family. Perhaps we can be friends. The closest of friends."

"I want you in my bed too," he said.

She lowered her eyes and turned pale. "I cannot, Albano. This cannot happen."

Albano looked at her in shock. "But we love each other! I want to hold you in that way."

"We must be strong. God has not spared us to watch us be sinful."

"But we have kissed already? Won't I be able to kiss you?"

"I … I don't know," she said. "I don't know what is right. I need to go to church and ask God."

"We have already missed so many years of happiness!"

"We can be happy. I am happy now. I am so happy that my heart sings."

"I will find a solution so that we can be together every day," he told her. "I don't know what the solution will be. But I will find one."

The crazy idea that Xandra should take care of Gustave and Marceline as their nanny revealed itself to Albano as the perfect solution. She would live with them and take care of the children now that Grand-mère was gone. It all made perfect sense. Lucienne was looking for a nanny able to handle Gustave's broken heart. Albano insisted that Xandra, who he said was a refugee rescued from their home country, be considered. Albano interceded in her favor, telling Lucienne that it was time that a more nurturing woman be hired. When Lucienne protested, he said that Gustave had enough of the circus of uninterested nannies. This time, Albano would choose the nanny, and he was choosing a nurturing woman from his country, someone gentle and loving the way Grand-mère had been. Lucienne, who was always suspicious of other women, was not suspicious this time, only annoyed that she did not have the last word. Because of the way Xandra looked, she did not see her as a threat and ultimately hired her.

Gustave and Marceline quickly bonded with Xandra, who fell in love with them at once. She had much experience taking care of her siblings and, later on, the children of the Muslim family whom she worked for in Izmir after the fire. She was given the nanny's room next to the large nursery the children shared so that she could tend to their needs at night. She bathed them, got them dressed, and put them to sleep. She took her meals with them. She brought them to the park, accompanied them on all their outings. She supervised when tutors and teachers gave them lessons. She played with them, drew with them, helped Marceline make clothes for her dolls, assisted Gustave in creating stories for his stuffed animals. The staff was wary of her at first because of the scars on her face and because she spoke French hesitantly. But they saw that she was helpful and that no task was below her. She was a hard worker, a person who rose early to attend church, someone level-headed who avoided gossip and drama.

Lucienne alone did not warm up to Xandra. She had little affection for her employees in general but displayed a particular impatience for Xandra. The rumor among the employees was that her hiring had been done without Lucienne's consent. Or perhaps she resented that the children had taken to Xandra so rapidly. Also, Lucienne liked to maintain a certain standard of esthetics and propriety. A broken window could be fixed, a drab plant repotted, fading wallpapers replaced. In her house, everything was the very best. But Xandra's appearance was something she could do nothing about. One day she told Albano, "I am sure with our recommendation she would get all the work she wishes."

"What do you mean?"

"There are families in Paris who do not share our standards. She would do well there. But here...."

Albano had shrugged, irritated. "What standards have we?"

"I don't want people to think ... I understand the poor woman did not choose to look this way, but must we be the one family to take her in?"

"She is good for our children. Who cares what people think?"

"Haven't you heard what people are starting to say about Jewish families? The last thing we want to do is fuel gossip. I would prefer to stay completely above the fray."

"And so, you think that a nanny with an unscarred face will ingratiate you with the anti-Semites?"

"I simply want the children to fit in."

"And I want the children to be well cared for."

"I shall never understand your attachment to this woman," Lucienne snapped. "And besides, I am the one who makes these decisions around the house. Since when do you even care who I hire and fire?"

"She is staying," Albano had said, and he left the room.

One night, Albano was enduring one of Lucienne's dinners, with many guests, when the maid arrived with a tray of Oriental desserts. Now that Xandra lived with them, Lucienne's dinners had become famous in Paris for the exotic pastries she served. The compliments guests paid to Xandra's pastries were the only redeeming moments of those insufferable dinners where each guest was more pompous and self-important than the next. Albano loved to listen and later repeat the compliments to Xandra. And so, instead of tuning out the conversation Lucienne was having with a woman in the yellow dress and hat, he listened.

"How extraordinarily delicious!" the woman told Lucienne. "And so unusual. Is this marzipan? Are those pistachios? You must give me the address of your baker."

"We have an unusual situation," Lucienne answered. "My children's nanny happens to be a wonderful baker."

"Oh goodness, don't ever let her slip away. Or else your guests will abandon you one by one."

"My guests will keep coming then," Lucienne said good-naturedly. "She cannot leave us; she has no place else to go. She's a foreign refugee and entirely depends on us for survival."

"How horrid," the woman said. "You must feel trapped, poor darling. Those foreigners have ways of insinuating themselves into every corner of our existence."

Lucienne laughed too loudly. "Well, I did marry one of them, so I should know."

The woman smiled. "Your husband had the common decency of being rich, which puts him into a very different realm."

"Indeed."

"Only make sure that her foreign ways don't rub off on your children."

"I know what you mean. She's a mystery to me. I don't know what she thinks or if she thinks at all. It's quite an irritation."

"Those refugees are masterful at self-preservation," the woman said.

"The children are getting older. I would let her go, but these are hard times, and my husband doesn't have the heart."

"A decent nanny who bakes? She would find employment in no time."

Lucienne lowered her voice. "I'm not certain in her case. She has a tragic appearance. Burned. From head to toe."

"Ghastly!" the woman said as she popped the rest of a pastry into her mouth.

Albano felt disgusted; he was done listening. He tucked his fists into his pockets and went up to the children's bedroom.

Marceline and Gustave were already fast asleep, with warm blankets pulled up to their chins. They were as cozy and warm as birds in a nest. Xandra had dozed off in the armchair, a nearby candle softly lighting her face.

Albano's chest expanded with love for the three of them. What Lucienne said or thought did not matter. Still, though, he would speak to her.

After the guests had departed, Albano tapped at Lucienne's bedroom door. She was sitting at her vanity, removing her jewels. When he entered, he could tell that his arrival into her room flustered her. She began combing her hair. They had not been intimate in years, and this created a terrible chasm between them that was never discussed. If she missed it, she did not say. If she wanted it, she did not ask. Facing her now, he regretted giving her the wrong impression. It felt cruel. But now that he was in her room, he would say what he had meant to say, but he would do it without showing the anger he felt. "I heard you speak of Sandra to that woman."

Lucienne stiffened. She stopped brushing her hair and got up to stand by the window. "And so?" she asked.

"You were denigrating refugees, denigrating Sandra, who is a hard-working, excellent person. Whereas that woman you were speaking with is an arrogant snob."

"An arrogant snob who happens to be the Minister of Agriculture's second cousin."

"Beware of letting the prevalent xenophobia taint your thinking."

"It does not."

"It is an insidious thing, Lucienne. And I want none of it in our house." Lucienne did not answer. "Have a good night," he whispered as he left her room. Again, she did not respond.

Albano saw Xandra during the day, but they had to be careful not to express closeness in public. Albano would meet Xandra and the children at the park or the zoo. There, they would sit on benches side by side as the children played, always cautious not to sit too close or to appear intimate. Sometimes Albano would drive them himself, and they would bring a picnic lunch and eat it at the park, just the four of them, like a regular family. At the children's bedtime, Xandra would sit in the armchair by the fireplace as Albano told stories. Sundays were Xandra's day off. In the morning, she would go to church. In the afternoon, she and Albano met for as many hours as they could manage without raising suspicion. They could not be seen together without the presence of the children, so the only way they could be alone was to meet at Moshe's house. Moshe kept a room just for them and had special meals prepared and deposited in front of their door. Albano and Xandra would spend those Sunday afternoons speaking, eating, listening to music, playing card games, laughing, and kissing. But they would not make love. That had been Xandra's condition. "I will take care of your children, and I will live inside your house, and we have our Sunday afternoons, but I will not be the mistress of a married man," she had told him early on.

"That is because you won't let me leave Lucienne and marry you," he would say.

"You know how I feel about this," she would answer stubbornly.

Again and again, they had the same argument about love and God. She would tell him, "Divorce is a great sin. God saw what we were doing in the cave when we were not married, and He punished us. He did not let our boy live, and He wounded both of us almost mortally. And then He separated us. But then, He had mercy on us and gave us a chance. We are living this chance right now."

Albano did not know how he felt about God, but he felt certain that if God had a hand in the minutiae of humans' daily dealings, He would spare innocents and punish evil. Judging from the state of humanity, it seemed to be the opposite that took place. "I want us to love each other like a proper couple," he would say.

"I do not need that to know that I love you."

"But I do need it. I don't ... but I do...."

She moved her hands toward herself. "Why would you even want this disfigured body."

His eyes lit up when he said, "It is today as it has always been: beautiful."

"We can still kiss."

"Oh, Xandra, what is it you want from me? Please allow me to leave Lucienne so that I can marry you."

"Isn't it enough cruelty that I have stolen her husband's heart? Must she see her family torn to pieces as well?"

"My heart was never hers to steal away, and you know that."

"Yet what crime has she committed that she would deserve to be abandoned?"

"If you do not want me to leave her, at least let us be lovers."

"I cannot be an adulterer," Xandra would say. "When I face my God, and you face yours, it will be with a clear conscience."

"But I want you. I want you just the same as I have always wanted you."

"I want you in that way too. But we both must resist. That is our trial, Albano; please do not put me in the position to deny you."

Albano felt that in this way his relationship to Xandra mirrored his relationship to Lucienne, whom he no longer was intimate with. Thus, he had two wives but no wife at all. Abstinence was his lot. But he was a twenty-eight-year-old man with desires, who got to hold and kiss his beloved but little else. "All I have are the memories of the cave. Maddening memories," he told her.

She would blush. "I have those memories too."

****

One Sunday afternoon, in 1932, when Marceline was nine years old and Gustave seven, Xandra told Albano, "Something ugly happened this week. At the Bois de Vincennes, in the area where they have the wooden horses and the swing sets and slides. There was a group of ten-year-old boys. They came to Gustave and called him names."

"What kinds of names?" Albano asked.

"The kind of bad names they give to the Jews. I did not know what they meant. Marceline explained this to me afterward."

"Were those boys from Gustave's school?"

"They were strangers."

"Marceline and Gustave dress like any other French children. How would those boys know they are Jewish?"

"They looked at Gustave, and they knew."

Albano marveled at this. "In Smyrna, each group dressed differently, so it was easy for people to know. Here they can simply tell?"

"Marceline was angry," Xandra said. "They were targeting her little brother, and you know how fiery she is. She was not about to let that happen. She's had practice defending me when people say things about my face. She rises to her feet and huffs and puffs like a little dragon. And at the park, she faced the boys, and I don't even know what she told them, she was speaking so fast; she just stood tall and told them off. The boys snickered, but they left."

"How about Gustave?"

"He cried at first, but then he was angry at himself for crying. And then he was angry at Marceline for helping him. It humiliated him that a girl would appear stronger than he is."

"He needs to learn from his sister and become more aggressive," Albano said. "That's what Lucienne thinks. She feels that Gustave needs training to be less timid. She also thinks that Marceline would do well to be a little less forceful."

"I don't think Gustave needs to be compared to his sister any more than one should compare a bear to a fish. The bear is perfect at being a bear, and the fish is perfect as it is, being a fish."

Albano shook his head. "But the fish cannot survive on land."

"The fish is not supposed to. If you let Gustave be himself, he will find his own way. That little boy feels deeply. Many things of the world are an aggression to him. He has the talent of being quiet and pensive when others seek distraction and amusement."

"What you see as Gustave's qualities, Lucienne considers weaknesses. Do you think he could become the rabbi I never could be? He is a Kohen after all."

"Or he may become a poet, or a writer, or an artist," Xandra mused.

"He is only seven years old. I supposed he has plenty of time to become more assertive."

"The world is not composed of just one type of man, Albano. There is room for Gustave to be just the way he is."

"Yes, but look at how people have come to think about Jews everywhere across Europe, even in France. And now I learn that even children are acting this out, as you just witnessed. The world is out of balance, and I'm afraid that at the moment it has little use for poets."

"The world precisely needs people like Gustave to return to its balance. He is a wonderful boy. In every way, wonderful."

"But his sister is—"

"Marceline has leadership and emotional strength."

"Marceline needs to learn to become more girlish, just as Gustave must learn to be boyish. She has to learn to tame her dominance. She can be callous, much like her mother."

Xandra smiled teasingly. "Do you want her to have female qualities only?"

"Well, yes." He looked at Xandra and could tell it was not the correct answer. "Why not? Is that not what women aspire to?"

"Perhaps she is a woman destined to greater things."

"Her mother certainly seems to believe so."

"I think Marceline will do greater things than even Lucienne imagines," Xandra said.

Albano returned home on foot from Moshe's apartment. He enjoyed long solitary walks through Paris, which allowed him time to think. He walked briskly from Avenue George V, walked across the eighth arrondissement toward the seventeenth arrondissement and the Cité des Fleurs house, cutting through the Parc Monceau. In the park, the sycamores had lost most of their leaves. Already, the air was crisp. Albano braced himself for another frigid European winter. He had not wanted to alarm Xandra, but the climate against the Jews, throughout Europe, worried him. Now, Parisian children parroted their parent's prejudices all the way to the playground, and Marceline and Gustave were beginning to experience racial hatred. This was the very thing he had sought to protect his children from.

Hagop was once again on his mind. Two years of effort, of letters to consulates and embassies in every country throughout what used to be the Ottoman Empire, had brought no news of Hagop. With each negative response, his hope of finding Hagop alive shrank further. Albano found much to regret about the way he had treated Hagop and much to blame himself for. Had he been straightforward about his love for Xandra when they were young boys, instead of waiting until they were men, had he found the courage to tell Hagop the truth early on, Albano was now convinced that the course of all their lives would have been different. Hagop had learned about Albano and Xandra's love in a time of religious persecutions and political upheaval when the Ottoman Empire's Armenian population was imperiled. Because of this, the thought of Xandra with someone who wasn't Armenian had been intolerable to him. But Hagop, he could see this now, had only meant to control his environment as best he could by hanging on to traditions.

Yet, Albano reasoned, had Hagop given himself some time to cool off, had he not reacted and thus thrown himself into the hands of his enemies, things would have been different. Once again, Albano imagined himself running after Hagop that day on Mount Pagus, and talking him into returning to the cave. Other times, he imagined clubbing Hagop over the head and dragging him unconscious into the cave to keep him protected, against his will if need be. Albano replayed various scenarios in his mind: he and Xandra staying in the cave; Xandra giving birth there instead of in that hospital; both of them leaving for Paris months earlier. If they had done any of those things, the baby might be alive today. He would be ten years old by now. In one scenario, they would not have needed to go to France. He and Xandra would have stayed in the Jewish quarter with Uncle Joshua and his family. In another scenario, they would all have wound up in Paris, and Hagop would be working with him and Moshe. He would never have met Lucienne. He would live in a nice house in Paris with Xandra and their children, although this scenario, which implied that Marceline and Gustave could not have been born, wasn't one he liked to entertain.

Hagop's impulsive nature had been his undoing. He had let his pride rule over his actions. Albano had known all along that Hagop could be reckless, but he had never tried to change him. He had accepted his friend the way he was, even the parts that were flawed. He shouldn't have. He should have reasoned with him, tried to shape him. But he had been afraid to contradict Hagop, afraid to take a stand and say unpleasant things. Now he saw the way Gustave and Marceline were. There was an opportunity to observe them, identify their weaknesses, and mend them while they were still young. He did not need to make the same mistake again of loving without helping, which was not loving at all. Yes, it was easier to accept the other person for whom he or she was. But wasn't to accept people as they were a more selfish act, perhaps a cowardly act? The difficult thing to do, the responsible thing to do, was to help give those you loved the strength to go past their limitations.

And so, Albano began to think that perhaps Lucienne was right, and Xandra was wrong. Gustave might be a fish who would need to be taught how to behave like a bear.

CHAPTER 4

Life in CGI

Cassie left Odile and Raymonde and walked down the street toward the métro station. Had this been progress? Maybe. At least they had listened to her. She had not exactly been the picture of poise and dignity, and she might have reinforced their opinion that she was an unpredictable nut by tracking ketchup throughout the apartment and nearly setting the kitchen on fire.

In the end, she had chickened out of confronting them. She should have demanded that they let her see her dad instead of treating her like she carried the bubonic plague. This was what she did: fight useless battles about insignificant details while what mattered to her festered inside.

In the métro, Parisians were indifferent, half asleep. Most were absorbed by whatever gadget they were holding: smartphones, e-readers, electronic games, and what-have-yous. If hers had not disintegrated, she'd be doing the same thing. She buried her hands into the depth of her father's coat pockets to stop them from craving the immediate gratification of scrolling, swiping, and poking. She was left with no choice but to look around and be with her thoughts, and many of them she did not like.

And she had chickened out of canceling the date with that man too; let's face it.

Maybe she wanted the date?

She got out of the subway at Havre Caumartin and entered the first café she saw. She went to the back and walked down uneven stairs through a narrow, dark corridor looking for the bathroom. She opened the door to the "toilettes" and recoiled in horror: a squat toilet! Nope. Thank you. She turned around to leave but saw the public telephone, and just above it an advertising display for their movie assaulted her. *Women in Black, Part Two*: the title in gold letters this time. It was as though the telephone were beckoning her to call Peter. She swiped her credit card and dialed his cell. From the café above came the sounds of French pop music and the clanking of dishes. A door opened, and a waiter walked past her. She caught a glimpse of the kitchen: a sink, piles of plates and glasses, and a man in a grimy sleeveless shirt, a cigarette at his lips, setting a cast-iron pan on a stove. The phone rang. A rank bathroom odor mingled with the smell of French fries.

"It's me," she said when Peter picked up.

"Cassie!" he exclaimed. "Do you know how frustrating it is not to be able to reach you?"

Cassie felt transported elsewhere. To California, to her house, that haven of calm, the view of the mountain from the porch, hummingbird feeders. "How is everything at home?" she asked.

"Home?" Peter echoed, revealing how absurd her question was. Wherever he was, it was not her home.

"The twins, I mean, how are they? College? Any news?"

"No news is good news," Peter said jovially.

"No news from my children isn't good news to me."

"You're tense for early morning."

"It's not early morning here."

"Did you have your coffee?"

"It's just that...." She hesitated. How could she describe what was happening without starting to blubber like an idiot? She inhaled for strength. "My mom and Odile are not letting me see my dad."

"What?" Peter said with the exact amount of indignation she had hoped from him.

"They took my name off the visitors' list."

"What the hell, Cassie?"

"There was this thing yesterday, this ... hullabaloo. My dad got overwrought or something. When I came to his room, he got into this ... rage. And they are blaming me."

"What did you do?"

"I did nothing of course!"

"I meant what did you do when they said you could not see your dad?" Peter said diplomatically.

"I cried, what else?"

"You're going to take this lying down?"

"You know how I get with them. I get confused."

"Let me unconfuse you. It's always the same shit show with them. You're the black sheep. They always side with Odile."

"If my dad gets dangerously agitated around me, maybe they have a point."

"Trust me; they don't."

This was the type of thing Peter always told her. It was his role to remind her to trust her gut, that she was entitled to feeling offended and outraged, that she must fight for her rights. Except when it came to him. Was Peter correct about any of this? Could he be trusted? He could be self-serving. Maybe it suited him that she remain alienated from her family.

And Peter lied, too. Things he said were layered with omissions and half-truths. She had seen him lie to others, and she had caught him in lies with her. Sometimes she had the energy to ask him to clarify, but most of the time it was easier to let things fly. It was easier not to listen to her intuitions, to that little voice that warned of danger. "So, I went to my parent's apartment to talk to them," she said. "Confront them, you know but I...." She stopped talking. Peter was not listening. He was in a conversation with someone.

"Oh," he said after a moment. "Jessica is telling me to ask you if your parents liked their presents."

Where were they? On the beach? At their house? Were they shopping at Trader Joe's? Had they just had sex? "Tell Jessica Rabbit that this is not about her right now," she said.

She overheard Peter call out to Jessica. "They loved the presents, Honey!"

"Tell Jessica Rabbit that I forgot to give it to them. But I will soon. If I don't kill them first."

Peter called out to Jessica. "Cassie's family says thank you. They say that they hope to meet you one day."

"Lying is truly effortless to you," Cassie marveled.

"It's all smoke and mirrors, darling. Just trying to keep peace and harmony going."

"Okay. So, now I'm in Paris, and I don't know what to do with myself," she said. "Although I'm having lunch with that new aunt I told you about." She did not think it necessary to bring up dates with good-looking French men on motorcycles.

"It would not be such a bad idea to come back early. I'm sensing tension with the studio. Some pressure to rewrite some scenes," Peter said.

"We have plenty of time."

"Ahem ... for the one that's coming out now."

"What? That ship has sailed. They're advertising it here like you would not believe. It's all over the subway, posters, at bus stops, in magazines. I'm staring at one of them right now."

"The studio is thinking of a few added lines, in voice-over."

"To say what?"

"There is a sentiment that perhaps our heroine is all leather and kung fu, but you know how it's the man who saves the day? Well, apparently it might be misconstrued."

"As what?"

"As chauvinistic."

"Not inaccurate. How are they going to pull that off without reshoots?"

"She could speak as we see her from the back, or maybe they could shoot a close-up of her face where she says ... stuff."

"What kind of stuff?"

"They're thinking a sentence or two, something empowering, something feminist. Give the movie more of a girl power sort of thing. Maybe you can think about it, throw around some ideas."

"Why me?"

"You're a woman."

"And that would make me an expert at bullshitting other women?"

"You know the trigger points, what pisses off women, where they take offense."

"I think this conversation just demonstrated that you're the expert at it."

Peter laughed uneasily. "Work your magic, Baby."

"More of that good old smoke and mirrors?" she asked.

"On the plus side, they solved the diversity problem," he said.

"It that still an issue? They should have thought about that at casting."

"No, they're cool with it. They found a way to fix it."

"How?"

"With CGI."

Cassie closed her eyes and groaned, "Don't tell me they're just going to color in the – I'll have to pretend I didn't hear this."

"I'm thinking I should look into changing your ticket."

"Change it to what?"

"To come back earlier. I mean why stay if they're going to treat you this way?"

"You were the one who talked me into coming here in the first place!"

"You were right, love: France is enemy territory for you."

Before she knew why exactly, she saw red. "This realization conveniently coincides with you needing me for work."

"Why do you have to be antagonistic all the time?" Peter exclaimed.

As was the case so often when she was in conversation with Peter, Cassie's mental sharpness blunted, her sense of right and wrong blurred. She could see her own point, the one she was pressing so hard to make, at least in the beginning. And she could see his, but all too often it was the validity of her own point that she began to doubt. She *was* being antagonistic. Perhaps not all the time but a majority of the time. She was being reactive, but reactive to what? She wasn't sure. With Peter, two and two did not always make four. For example, he had professed his love and devotion to her throughout their marriage, so why had she not felt loved? Why did she feel that his devotion to her always took the back seat to his devotion to himself? For example, the affair. He had denied it at first. Or her feelings that he was taking advantage of her professionally. His first line of defense was to say that she *imagined* things, that she was making things up, when he knew that this was precisely what her family said about her, when he knew this was her weak point. And in the face of that, she became confused and harassed and helpless at knowing her mind or trusting the content of her own heart. If Peter could be so casual about her writing credit, then his moral compass was flexible, and everything he said should be looked at through the lens of truth flexibility.

"Maybe that's because you and I have unfinished business," she finally said.

"Such as?"

"Such as you *know* what." She let this hang, and there was a difficult silence.

"Are we still talking about the affair?" he said, in a tone that blended sadness and outrage.

Cassie hesitated. "I'm talking about that and the stuff after that."

"What stuff? There is no stuff!"

"Stuff is everywhere, Peter. It's a euphemism for bullshit!"

On the line, there was the sound of a sharp inhale, and then silence. "I have to go," Peter said at last. "I promised Aidan and Liam to take them to Travel Town, you know, that train thing in Griffith Park? They're breathing down my neck."

It did not sound like Peter's boys were nearby, breathing down his neck or otherwise. "Go where you have to go" she sighed. "Do what you have to do."

"I'll look into changing the return ticket then?" he asked.

"I guess."

She hung up and faced the movie poster. Even the tone-deaf studio saw what she was unable to articulate: her fictional alter ego was no more capable of taking the lead than she was.

She turned away from the poster and tried to calm herself. Maybe she should start small. Try and channel her inner superhero and brave that terrifying bathroom.

She stepped tentatively inside and locked the door. Facing yet another advertising display for *Women in Black, Part Two*, she contorted, pulled down her jeans, bunched up her coat to waist level, held it and her bag tight against her, squatted and tried not to pee on her boots, or touch anything, or breathe.

She left the café. Outside, it was, no surprise, raining. She wrestled her way through hordes of harried shoppers on their way to and from Galeries Lafayette and Le Printemps.

Across from Galeries Lafayette was, interesting coincidence, the beautiful Art Déco Société Générale Bank, the very bank where she had come as a teenager, the address of which was engraved inside her father's finial.

She trudged up Boulevard Haussmann, bumping into people. In this sea of humanity, she noticed everyone and could filter out nothing: not the smells, not the sounds, not the way people looked and dressed. In her frizzy hair, shapeless coat, and cowboy boots, she looked like a garden troll as she walked past Parisian women in trendy winter coats and fabulous shoes. The men were elegant too. Where were the garish baseball caps, the black socks in white sneakers, the T-shirts tucked over beer bellies? Parisian men wore slacks ending at just the right length, polished shoes, and groomed beards. Even the children were nerve-rackingly elegant.

She still had thirty minutes before meeting Marceline. She stood in front of the Galeries Lafayette. Enter or not? A flock of Japanese tourists engulfed her, and before she knew it, she was inside, jolted by the scents of hundreds of designer perfumes.

She walked through the aisles, brushed her fingers against cashmere, leather, silk, cotton, and wool wondering where even to start. The light came through the art nouveau stained glass of the famous Byzantine cupola thirty feet above and shone on the balconies, which looked like suspended gilded alcoves. She was inside the church of fashion. Proper worshippers were able to distinguish what made one sweater, one pair of pants, one shade of lipstick more desirable than another. But no swiftly tied new scarf would make a dent in her disastrous outfit. Cassie would have to start from scratch. She would have to start from the inside out, in fact, since she was at the moment wearing the last of her clean underwear and bras. She laughed to herself, picturing the disaster of a man, say, to name a person at random, handsome Hervé, setting his eyes on the horror of her subpar underwear. She pushed the thought away. She was not letting him go near that. Not at her age, not on the first date. IF this was a date.

In the lingerie department, she hovered around nightgowns, silk negligees, ruffled organza boy shorts, black guêpières, and stopped in front of a lacy bra in a scandalous shade of purple. If she were to, hypothetically, wear such a bra with all that lace, and those half cups, and that wild purple, it might put the wrong thoughts into Hervé's head … or worse, her own!

She charged out of Galeries Lafayette and landed outside in the humid air. Her comfy, 100% cotton high-waist briefs would be an insurance policy against even *wanting* this unsuspecting man to get anywhere near her.

Outside, the rain was pouring down. Cassie's umbrella, bought for ten euros in the street, overturned in seconds in a gust of wind. How was Marceline going to get here, she wondered? She had visions of the ancient lady fighting off the weather, helplessly clambering through the métro. Boulevard Montmartre was a hair-raising nightmare complete with bumper-to-bumper traffic, exhaust fumes, and maniacal honking. Inside their cars, drivers gesticulated, yelled, and hammered their horns as though they were missile launchers.

She waited for Marceline on the sidewalk in front of the exit of the Grévin Wax Museum, where they had agreed to meet. She was stretching her neck for signs of Marceline when the driver of a long, black Mercedes, sleek with rain, swiftly and in a blazing demonstration of hubris, drove right off the pavement, over the curb, and from there proceeded to use the sidewalk as his private driveway. Furious pedestrians yelled and cursed at the car. The Mercedes continued on the sidewalk with the perfect indifference of a black whale through a school of mackerels. When the car got to Cassie's level, it slowed to stop right in front of her. Out of it sprang a hefty man in a black raincoat − a chauffeur, or possibly a bodyguard, judging from his stature − who clicked open a bright red umbrella the size of a parasol, walked around the car, opened the back door, and reached in to assist his passenger out of her seat. To Cassie's astonishment, the passenger was Marceline.

Pedestrians, upset that they had to struggle to walk around the stopped car, hurled insults at the driver and Marceline, but both appeared thoroughly unconcerned. Marceline gingerly put one foot and then the other on the slick pavement and with the driver's help got out of the car. She was the picture of Parisian elegance in black heels, black, lacy pantyhose, orange silk scarf, and long black coat decorated at the top with a large gold brooch. Marceline hooked her arm around her driver's elbow and together, at a snail's pace, they moved toward Cassie who came forward to help. Marceline stopped her with a raised hand. "I'm not crippled! Maurice will get me inside the passage, and then you can take over." To the driver, she said, "Maurice, be here at 1:30 p.m. sharp, will you."

"Oui, Madame la Comtesse," Maurice said.

Inside the passage, Marceline let go of Maurice's arm and stumbled two steps in Cassie's direction, flailing her arms. "Damn Manolos," she said. Cassie took hold of her arm. "No, not like that! I hang on to you, not you to me." She hooked her right arm around Cassie's left, and they walked forward on the marble floor.

"Careful. The floor might be slick."

"This is not my first rainy day, très chère," Marceline grumbled.

Both breathed in relief once they were on dry ground.

Next to the cacophonic street, the Passage Jouffroy was soothingly quiet. Visitors strolled, speaking in hush tones. Grey geometrical mosaics covered the floor, and a diffused, cheerful light flooded the gallery from above through a skylight dome of glass and iron, like a lace glass ceiling. On both sides of the covered alley, there were antique shops, rare books sellers, lithography, old stamps and postcard shops, cafés, and restaurants, all with façades and details restored from an era some 100 years earlier.

"This place is fantastic," Cassie exclaimed.

"You've never been here? It's a Parisian institution. There were over a hundred glass-covered shopping arcades such as this one across the ninth and second arrondissements in the first part of the nineteenth century. Haussmann tore most of them to the ground when he rebuilt Paris. Galerie Vivienne and Passage Jouffroy are two of the nicest that remain." She eyed Cassie. "You're still wearing my father's coat,"

"I forgot to bring a coat to France."

"Nonsense."

"I'd been promised a heat wave."

"Ha!" Marceline croaked. "Here it is. Le Valentin, the tea salon I like."

Le Valentin was an old-fashioned tearoom which opened onto the Passage Jouffroy. The shop windows, framed by green scalloped velvet curtains with dozens of tassels, displayed Easter candies under glass cloches to make it look like terrariums. Pastel marshmallow bunnies, sugar baby chicks, and colorful eggs covered in metallic paper rested on fake grass. There was an assortment of decorated chocolate eggs, jars of confiture, and cake stands of various height displaying pies and pastries.

They entered. "Bonjour, Madame la Comtesse," said the woman behind the counter. Inside, it smelled of liquorice, caramel, and hot chocolate, and maybe a bit like staleness and wax. On the marble shelves and the countertop were glass jars filled with candies from another time, pale guimauve ribbons, and glossy fruits confits. A waitress in a white apron rushed in to help them out of their coats and whispered a greeting in Madame La Comtesse's ear. "They know me here," Marceline said with undisguised satisfaction as she sat down. Over a chic black cardigan, she wore around the neck her bohemian assortment of beaded necklaces, trinkets, old keys, and tassels. "Bring me a Petit Coeur, a Forêt Noire, and a cup of chocolat chaud, ma petite," she told the waitress without even so much as glancing at the menu.

"You're not having lunch?" Cassie asked.

"This is lunch."

"All sweets?"

"Are you worried this might shorten my life expectancy?"

Cassie smiled. "And no guilt?"

"Guilt is a senseless waste of energy. Do what you're going to do, or don't do it. The rest is an exercise in self-mortification."

Cassie laughed. "Maybe we should all follow your diet."

"Try the millefeuille au chocolat and you'll be a centenarian."

Cassie studied her menu. "A chocolat chaud and a millefeuille," she told the waitress. "Doctor's orders."

The smell of chocolate reduced to a thick elixir permeated the air as the waitress filled each of their cups out of a tall ceramic pot.

CHAPTER 5

Côte d'Azur

Marceline took a sip out of her cup and watched Cassandra with curiosity. She had never entertained the idea of having children and, because of Gustave, she had been denied the privilege of knowing her three nieces. So it was a strange feeling to sit across from one of them – a woman she was related to by blood. Marceline could not help but look for, and think she could recognize, something of herself in Cassandra: the tenacity perhaps; the curiosity; a certain form of intrepidness, of contrarianism. "Your father had a difficult time in school before the war," she told her niece. "Children have a way of acting out the pathos around them, and in the year that preceded World War II, Gustave embodied, for lack of a better description, the consummate scapegoat. Something had to be done about it. My parents had no choice but to send him away."

"No choice? There had to be other choices," Cassandra said. "He could have been home-schooled, for example."

Marceline felt irritated by this, by this woman who knew nothing of the details of Marceline's life at the time intent on doing exactly what Gustave had done, which was to point the finger. She had better keep in mind that she was not speaking to a younger, more naïve version of herself and that Cassandra was a different person, one who would not necessarily agree with her, one whom she would need to convince. "You have to see it through the lens of the time. Now boys can be whichever way they want to be. Back then, it was believed that Gustave needed to be fortified, hardened, toughened, or whatnot. He had to be made into the acceptable kind of boy that is ruthless and dominant."

"My dad is as communicative as a doorknob, at least with me, but dominant, no. So, in that sense, sending him away did not work one bit."

Marceline nodded in agreement. "The absurdity, looking back on it, was that society wanted to make Gustave into a leader and me into an artist when, in fact, I was the one with leadership qualities and Gustave was the artist. The fact of the matter is, people can never change the essence of who they are."

"Do you think your mother deserves the blame for sending him away?" Cassandra asked.

"I can't say it was all her doing. If our father was against her plan, he was meek in standing up to her. But our father must have been at a loss. He wanted to do what was right for Gustave, and he listened to those who considered themselves experts. But in the end, I think Gustave resented me the most."

"Why you?"

"He would do nothing but compare my fate to his from that point on. It was a tremendous injustice, seen from his perspective, that I was able to stay with my parents while he was sent away. Gustave got into his mind that our parents favored me. But even if he were right, how must I be blamed for it?"

"Even if it was done with good intentions, it seems a harsh thing to do to a child," Cassie said.

"You must understand that within the context of those years, and the fear and uncertainty that we inhaled with every breath we took, my parents were torn as to what to do." Marceline put her cup down. "Although in hindsight, we might have convinced ourselves that having him in a Jewish boarding school away from Paris was the best thing for him when, in fact, it might have been the best thing for us."

"What do you mean?"

Marceline sighed. It cost her to admit the truth. "Gustave was drawing attention to us – to the fact that we were Jewish. Society was going mad, and perhaps we were going mad too, unable to adjust, unable to understand and accept the new reality of how the Jews were being perceived. We wanted to deny it."

"I can't begin to understand how society would shift just like that."

"Not exactly 'just like that,' but it all happened fast. There was the Great Depression. Well, we did not know what to call it then. No one could imagine an end to it. People were losing everything: work, food, a sense of safety. When people feel out of control, they grasp for causes and solutions to their problems. What they readily find are the wrong causes and the wrong solutions. Powerlessness makes one likelier to embrace the single-minded doctrine of those with the most venom, those who embody the anger people feel within. When given a chance, it is always fear and suspicion that take hold. Hatred is more visceral, easier to access than decency or self-restraint. They began putting Jews into one of two categories: either they were, like our family, among the rich and influential, just when the French population felt increasingly powerless, or they were immigrants and refugees, allegedly stealing whatever little work was available. It was all propaganda-driven. Believe me when I tell you that behaving like a sheep is not just for the impoverished or the uneducated. Propaganda has just as much power over the clever and the rich. Society needed a scapegoat, and who better served that purpose than the Jews?"

"Actually, I don't know why Jews would be so easily pigeonholed into that role," Cassandra said.

Marceline shrugged. "I would guess that it is faster to reignite the collective memory of hatred than to start with a brand-new group of people. At any rate, the whiff of war was too hard to ignore for my father. Everyone else might be in denial, but he wasn't. We children did not quite understand what was happening. All I knew was that one day, I was told to pack my things, and the next, we were sweeping Gustave away from the pensionnat and fleeing Paris." She closed her eyes, let the memories flood in, and began to tell Cassandra about the months before the war.

****

At the Rânes boarding house, Gustave went to his room and gathered his belongings. To the question of where the bill should be sent, my father responded by handing the headmaster a thick envelope filled with francs. No, there would not be a forwarding address, my father told him.

We left Rânes within the hour. My father was at the wheel of the Alpha Romeo. My mother, in her best Chanel suit, sat primly in the front seat. Gustave and I were in back. Following us closely behind was the Renault, driven by Moshe's man, with Sandra and all our luggage.

There was in the air a new strangeness, a trepidation at the unknown. There was dread also. The sense that we were running from a nameless threat. There was at the same time a new closeness with my family, a closeness that is not emotional, but visceral, born from the suspicion that, from this moment forward, we would have nothing and no one but each other.

In Le Mans, we stopped at a charming hotel. For dinner, I remember that we ate the local specialty: buckwheat crêpes and apple cider. We ate in an atmosphere of forced gaiety. Were we trying to fool ourselves, or the people at the hotel, by acting as though things were normal, that we were a regular family on holiday? This gaiety was not our norm. We were just playing a part.

Early in the morning, we left the hotel and drove across France as torrential rain poured. The roads were slick and treacherous. My father's shoulders tensed up under his coat, and his knuckles stiffened on the wheel, and yet I felt relieved. There was comfort in having all those I held dear under one moveable roof, speeding away from Paris, away from our anguishes. War could come and go, I told myself. My father's injury made him unfit for combat, and as for Gustave, he was too young to be drafted. Other men would be sent to die in the trenches. Men I did not care about. If it amused Hitler, he could well knock down our house. We would not be there when he came.

The rain had been omnipresent ever since we left Paris. But as we headed south, past France's mid-point, the curtain of clouds lifted, the downpour stopped, and the landscape turned bright-green. I realized something, which the weather and ominous headlines had made me forget: it was springtime. We drove through large stretches of empty roads, past vast expanses of rolling hills, and beneath clear blue sky, our spirits lifting higher with each turn of the wheel.

Gustave read the map and gave Baba directions. I was in charge of selecting restaurants off the Michelin Guide. In Beaune, we ate Oeufs en Meurettes, a dish of poached eggs and red Bourgogne wine sauce. This time, our father insisted that Sandra and the driver have lunch with us. It was a lovely sentiment that made for a terribly awkward meal.

Past Dijon, the temperature rose noticeably. We rolled down the windows and the scents of wild thyme and sage wafted into the Alpha Romeo. Past Valence, the earth's coloring soon changed to a vibrant red. Oleander bushes as tall as trees lined the side of the road.

On the third day of our journey, we came upon the cobalt blue expanse of the Mediterranean Sea.

"La mer!" Gustave and I exclaimed.

My father, without warning, stopped the car on the side of the road. He got out, and Gustave and I hopped out after him. My father took a few steps toward the cliff that overlooked the sea. He stood there, in his waistcoat and shirtsleeves, his face turned toward the warm sun, his arms slightly open as though they were antennas that allowed him to take in all of that warmth and blue.

"What is it, Baba?" we asked.

"The sea, the smell, even the dirt…. It reminds me of my country." He contemplated the sea that shimmered on the horizon. "Can you hear the wind?" he beamed. "Even the wind sounds the same."

The other car pulled up and parked behind ours. Sandra rolled down her window, and Baba leaned in to speak to her. They said a few words, and both smiled.

Now that he had seen the sea, anxiety seeped out of my father with each kilometer that moved us farther away from Paris. In the car, he became talkative. Now the gaiety was real. My father's joy was communicative. We played charades and twenty questions. Even my mother participated. A nearly tangible weight lifted off me. It was as though we had left blustery Paris sick with worries and had magically stepped into summer and out of the shadow of war.

We drove along the Massif de l'Estérel. Below us, vertiginous cliffs plunged into the foam of the Mediterranean. Cypresses stood like giant swords around ancient stone houses, and the songs of the first cicadas throbbed in our ears. Gustave and I put our faces out of the automobile's windows to smell the unfamiliar fragrances carried by the warm wind that ruffled our hair. Our coats and socks were off by now. Gustave was down to his white sleeveless undershirt, and Mother did not object.

At last, we arrived. We drove past a gate with a sign made of ceramic tile that read "La Bastide." The cars went up a circuitous driveway lined with knobby olive trees until a magnificent house perched on a hill came into view. It was a sprawling villa with a terracotta tile roof, warm ochre stonewalls, and wooden shutters painted blue. A bougainvillea wrapped itself lazily around the side of the house and part of the roof. Cascading ivy and petunias spilled out of dozens of pots. The tires crushed the pebbled driveway, and my father stopped the automobile in front of the house. We got out and took in the scenery. La Bastide had sweeping views of the Bay of Cannes and the Mediterranean. The horizon filled with nothing but blue. The air buzzed with insects, and the pungent smell of rosemary mingled with the perfume of lavender's early blooms.

One by one, the staff selected by the rental agency hurried outside to greet us. With dramatic flair, they stood by the entrance porch as though we were royalty. Be assured that Mother liked that very much. But then an insect zoomed past her face, and she began swatting the air spastically with a copy of her *Vogue* magazine.

Inside, Gustave and I ran from room to room. Light flooded into the house as the staff opened the shutters that had been kept closed to keep the rooms cool. Apparently, in this land of wonders, the sunshine we Parisians were starved for was in such overabundance that they thought nothing of keeping the shutters closed in the middle of the day.

Inside, the décor was sparse but warm. Rather than the moldings seen in Parisian buildings, there were exposed dark beams and white-washed walls typical of the region. Red, hexagonal clay tomettes tiled the floor throughout the house. In the bedrooms, the blankets on the four-poster beds, the curtains, and even the wallpaper were covered with Provençal fabric. "This place swarms with Provençal motives," my mother declared. "There seems to be no running away from it, whether you like it or not." In the dining room, a thick, dark, varnished table with sturdy, graceless legs and matching chairs could have easily seated twenty. There were hutches, and cavernous fireplaces, and nooks and crannies everywhere. "Positively medieval," Mother dropped with a sigh. "I guess it will have to do." But I could tell she was satisfied.

My father smiled a Cheshire cat's grin and gestured toward the living room. He opened the door ceremoniously, revealing not the baby grand I expected but a beautiful Steinway grand piano.

"Baba! Thank you!" I said, jumping at his neck to hug him as my mother and Sandra smiled. Only then did I notice Gustave. My brother stood by the door, looking dour, perhaps stricken. Our eyes met, and he quickly looked at the floor.

A conscience can manifest itself at bizarre times. That day I felt it. At that moment, I felt ashamed of my advantages. I was so catered to, so adored and doted on, that it nearly sickened me. And now, having fetched Gustave as we did, I was reminded of the condemned man's expression on his face each time he had to return to his boarding school after holidays. The brutal coldness of it all now seized me. How had we, for nearly two years, rationalized sending Gustave away? How had this been admissible? I walked to the Steinway and, conscious of Gustave's eyes on me, I brushed my fingers on the keyboard, but I did not play.

We were introduced to the groundskeeper, Monsieur Malou, a Provençal man with a face as gnarly as the pit of a peach. Despite his old age, he had labored on the grounds until they became a veritable Garden of Eden. There were water features with tiny goldfish, lawns that were not mowed with military precision as they were in Paris but allowed to mingle with wildflowers. There was a brook, flowerbeds bursting with lilacs and clematises, an orchard lush with apple, peach, plum, and cherry trees, many of them in bloom. Mr. Malou, in his musical Provençal accent, named the trees and spoke of them with affection. This apricot tree was the sweetest. This peach tree had fruit with yellow flesh. This cherry tree had been a disappointment for the last few seasons, but there was hope for a comeback. On the arid slope below La Bastide stood a small vineyard where buds exploded in tender leaves. We were shown the vegetable garden. Gustave and I had our first experience pulling carrots, onions, and radishes out of the ground, which felt nothing short of miraculous. "We are canning as much as we can," Monsieur Malou told my parents with a knowing look. He added, "We are prepared." I wondered if Gustave understood that he was hinting at the prospect of war.

As we walked back toward the house, my father lifted his nose in the air and took in a big whiff. "Can you smell it?" he said, beaming, "Can you smell the sea?"

"I can't," Gustave said. "Water doesn't have a smell."

"Oh, I can smell it from here," my father said. "I can hear it too! And it is calling our names."

"When can we go to the sea?" Gustave asked.

"We can go now," my father said.

"We haven't got our swimming trunks unpacked," I ventured, hoping this would not stop us from going.

"We'll only take a look," Baba said.

We arrived in front of the house. Sandra was by the automobiles, helping with the unloading and instructing the house staff where to put things.

"We'll go tomorrow," my mother said. "Today we shall get settled."

On a normal day, in a normal world, this would have been the end of it. But to my surprise, my father only shrugged and headed toward the car. "Why delay?" he said. "Let's just go now."

Did my mother's unmitigated ruling of the Paris house have no jurisdiction in the South of France? We looked from my mother to my father. Gustave and I had a quick decision to make, lest we miss the window of opportunity. How we reacted might well set a precedent for the rest of our time here. The decision was whether to go by my mother's boring rules or be free with Baba. It took me but two seconds to run after him. Gustave was perplexed for another few seconds, and then he also piled into the car. My father then turned to my mother. "Come on along, Lucienne, Dear," he said playfully. It will be lovely. I heard the call of the sea, and when the sea calls, we must not be impolite.

"I have had enough driving," my mother said, tight-lipped. "Besides, someone needs to give instructions for the unpacking."

"Please Maman, come," I said. "Don't you want to see the Mediterranean?"

"I shall see it plenty since we must abandon a perfectly good life to bury ourselves here," my mother said.

"As you wish, Dear," Baba said. And then he did a terribly imprudent thing, one that would have lasting repercussions. He turned to Sandra and asked, "Would you like to join us?"

Sandra should have declined and stayed behind to help my mother. That was, in theory, her function here, the reason we were taking her along. But she did not look at my mother. She did not hesitate. She only entered the car. I was surprised by this small act of subversion, quite an uncharacteristic one I might add. But it was enough for my mother to begin resenting her presence even more. My feeling is, she should have sided with my mother. But then again, Sandra was a simple woman who did not perhaps understand the ramifications of her actions.

In the automobile, Baba and Gustave sat in front, Sandra and I in back. We drove down the hill with all the windows open, the warm wind billowing our clothes and ruffling our hair. The colors here were the most vivid. The earth was brick-red, the distant sea emerald green, the sky blue, and everywhere yellow mimosa trees released their powdery scent. The late April sun in the South of France bore no resemblance to the meek Parisian light. It was hot on the skin and quite fierce. It made you want to be reckless.

We arrived in the town of Cannes and drove down the Boulevard de la Croisette. The Croisette was a sight to behold. On one side were luxury boutiques, cafés, restaurants and their terraces, and glamorous hotels painted bright white. We drove past Dior, and Cartier, and countless expensive boutiques. We had to put our faces out the automobile's window to take in the immensity of the Hotel Carlton, a towering palace seven stories high, with twin domes at each corner and a white façade layered with hundreds of small balconies overlooking the sea. To our eyes accustomed to the gray austerity of Haussmannian architecture, Le Martinez hôtel and Le Majestic hôtel took on the air of sugary confections.

The Croisette was all so bright and cheery. At the foot of each hotel, the restaurants' terraces were filled with diners sipping their aperitifs. Servers in black vests and bowties scurried about the terraces carrying tall glasses of pastis and bowls of local olives. Orange and lemon trees in large planters framed the terraces with barrages of fragrant blooms. On the curve, drivers in livery stood by gleaming Rolls Royces and Bentleys, chamois skin in hand.

The sea and the promenade were on the other side with a center divider planted with colorful flowers and palm trees standing between the two. My father turned to Sandra and spoke in a foreign language, which might have been Armenian or Arabic. When my mother was present, Baba only spoke to Sandra in French, but when it was just us around, he used languages she spoke more fluently. He pointed to the palm trees. "Those are trees from our country," he told us. I would soon find that everything in Cannes reminded him of Smyrna: the sea, the beaches, the vegetation, the warmth, the smells, and the gentle, almost inaudible lap of a calm sea on sand beaches.

We could see the sea from the car, but a low parapet hid the sand beach from sight. Baba parked the automobile, and we stepped out onto the promenade. I wished I had come properly dressed. The place was nothing short of a fashion show. Men wore pale summer suits and tipped their hats to the passing ladies. The women protected their complexion from the sun with lacy umbrellas and had the effortless elegance of those for whom mink, cashmere, and pearls were the ordinary. Had Mother not been so stubborn, she would have been perfectly in her element in this setting, she who would never be seen outside without white gloves, even in the scorching heat of summer. In Cannes, everything smelled of money and high class as though this pocket of the world were immune from the blight of the impending war and endless financial depression by which the rest of France and Europe were so alarmingly affected.

We leaned over the parapet to discover the beach below and its many rows of parasols and cushioned chaises, like small beds fit for an Egyptian queen. The Carlton's beach was all yellow and white stripes, the Martinez's, blue and white stripes. In the sand, ladies reclined on chaise lounges. Children in swimming trunks frolicked in and out of the water, carrying metal buckets and shovels. In the distance, the sea, punctuated by sailboats of all sizes, lay like a shimmering sheet beneath the cloudless sky.

I gazed at the sea, at my father's relaxed smile, at his arm draped over my brother's shoulders, at Sandra, whose face looked luminous as she lifted it toward the sun. My anxious thoughts washed away. For that moment, all was right.

No matter what we had promised my mother, all four of us in concert went down the stone steps and made a beeline for the beach. Sandra immediately removed her shoes, bent down, and took a handful of sand that she sifted between her fingers. I removed my shoes too and stuffed my socks in Sandra's bag. The sand was warm and voluptuous under my bare toes. My father stooped, and he too touched the sand. Squatting, he gazed wistfully at the sea. I saw that Sandra's eyes were drowned in tears. My father gave her an indecipherable look. Were those tears of joy or sadness? I did not let myself imagine it could be anything other than the return of happiness to our lives.

Gustave rolled up his pant legs, removed his undershirt, and hopped wildly into the water. "It's glacial!" he screamed.

"It is only April," Baba said. "It will warm up."

We had promised my mother only to look at the water, but no matter;, it was irresistible. I did not care about my clothes and went straight to the sea. I was baptized by Gustave's spray of icy water. "Oh you!" I roared. "I will...." I took water in my cupped hands and hurled it at Gustave, who received it square in the face, surprising us both. He and I began a mad splashing. And now Father joined in. We laughed and screamed and splashed some more while Sandra watched us, hiding her giggles with her hand.

At that moment I felt reconnected with something rare as gold but as necessary as oxygen, something irrepressible: joy. I had been holding my breath for years and not even known it.

My mother, it dawned on me, never would have permitted such freedom. She surely would have forbidden me to remove my shoes and socks in public. And thanks to her absence, Father could be joyful and carefree as well.

My mother's disapproval was always there, whether it was silent or voiced. For sixteen years, my mother had carefully orchestrated my life, my outings, my social circle, and my activities, always with eyes on the future. She had groomed me for a specific life, and because her certainty was absolute, and because I had excelled at meeting her expectations, I had no concept of rebelling. My mother and I, the way I saw it, had a common objective. But at that moment on the beach, it struck me for the first time that I never thought independently from my mother. Her thoughts, her plans, her decisions, her judgment of me and others had a hold on me. Was I even capable of an original thought? Her lapdog, Gustave had called me.

Gustave and I continued frolicking on the beach. When I had enough, I stepped out of the water, drenched, guffawing, my hair wet in my face. I walked into the warm sand. Sandra removed her shawl and offered it to me so that I could dry off. But before I got to her, I saw something that stopped me in my path. Drenched, cold, and disheveled as I was, I stood there and stared, my mouth ajar. The public beach was only separated from Le Carlton hôtel's private beach by a three-foot-tall white fence. There, to my left, under the shade of a Carlton hotel parasol, reclining on a padded lounge chair, was a striking woman in a scandalous, strapless, two-piece white swimsuit. She may have been a French starlet. In my memory, she looked a lot like Betty Grable, the American actress. Her hair was luminescent platinum and coiffed in firm, glossy curls. Her lips were painted incandescent red. Most incredible was how tanned her long legs were. The moment froze into one perfect image: the woman extending her hand toward the iced beverage a server brought on a tray. A cigarette materialized between her fingers. The waiter bent down to light it. She had an enigmatic smile. She brought the cigarette to her red lips, and glamour perfection was achieved.

And to think I had believed myself of this world! I was an awkward little girl in white socks and silly curls without an ounce of glamour to her. In an instant, I knew the kind of woman I wanted to become, and this was it!

I had thus far blindly followed my mother's plan for me. I had understood the goal and worked towards it. But so far, it had been all my mother's goal. What did it have to do with me?

I stormed off the beach, suddenly furious. I ignored Sandra and her shawl and went toward the stairs, hating my hair, my childish dress, my appalling lack of sophistication.

I remember that time of laughing and splashing on the beach as one of the last events of my childhood. I would reappear at the top of the stairs, an adolescent.

We arrived at La Bastide in time for supper. Dinner had been prepared and set on the long Provençal table, but my mother was still pouting and refused to come out of her room. Baba, Gustave, and I ate in awkward silence. Afterward, my father went to my mother's bedroom to smooth things out. The number of hours my father patiently spent trying to make my mother feel better to no avail can probably be counted in years of his life. I'm not sure why he bothered. Some people just seem to want to feel terrible. They want to be cross, and they want to remain that way. My mother, I now realized, was one of those people.

After dinner, Gustave and I stepped into the garden. It was night, and the air pulsated with the songs of crickets. We walked out in the balmy air that smelled of citrus blooms. The huge moon reflected on our skin, giving us an eerie glow.

"Do you think there will be war soon?" I asked Gustave.

"Baba seems to think so," he said.

"But don't you think Mother would know more? She is more French than Baba. Maybe she understands things better?"

"Of course she doesn't," Gustave said, "Mother is hateful and knows nothing."

I was shocked by this outburst. "Mother is not that bad," I said.

Gustave stared ahead, his jaw set. "Yes, she is."

We walked in the moonlight in silence. If Gustave hated Mother now, was it because she had sent him away? I wondered if he held me responsible too.

Perhaps that night was my chance to ask him, but my thoughts were not properly formed in my head yet. Had I acknowledged the injustice, had I asked for his forgiveness, perhaps the course of our relationship would have been different. But words did not come to me. Instead, I spoke of myself. I told him about the woman on the beach, and how horrific my clothes were, and how I was going to become a world-famous concert pianist one day, or an aviator like Amelia Earhart, or the next Vivien Leigh. Gustave listened, as was his habit, nodding, as though he never doubted I would achieve greatness.

A few days later we were having breakfast and making plans for the day when Baba closed his newspaper and slammed it on the table. "Something should have been done about Hitler years ago. And now France and Britain scramble to side with Poland. Can't they see we need to make a pact with the Soviet Union before Germany does?"

My mother had taken to dismissing my father's political opinions, perhaps to reassure us. "The French government knows what it is doing, Alban. France must sign the pact with Poland. That is precisely how we stop Hitler."

My father shook his head somberly. "Hitler will invade Poland. If we sign this pact, we'll have no other choice but to enter the war."

"So, let that hideous little man invade Poland, and let us intervene. What will Hitler do then? It's not like he will attack France if this is what you're worried about."

"If he does invade, France does not have the army to fight him," my father said.

My heart thumped painfully in my chest. Gustave and I looked at each other. My mother blinked in incomprehension. "How so?" she said.

"Our equipment is outdated and insufficient; our generals are set in their ways. Our military won't be able to cope. Not when Hitler has been building his army for years, and certainly not without the Russians by our side."

"So, we could lose the war?" I asked, my throat dry.

My mother shrieked, "You are frightening the children! Besides, you are wrong on all counts. We will hardly need to fight Hitler. He's not stupid enough to risk public humiliation trying to break the Maginot Line."

My father shrugged, "I'm afraid that the Maginot Line is just a line in the sand, Lucienne. If determined armies can invade across oceans, I don't think Hitler will be so easily deterred."

Horrified, we looked at my father. Discrediting the Maginot Line, the impenetrable military fortification along the German and Italian borders, the first line of defense against the enemy, the genius design of our most decorated intelligence: this was tantamount to blasphemy. "The Maginot is unbreakable," Gustave said. "That's what they say in *Le Monde*."

"Oh, but your father needs no Maginot Line," my mother said, putting as much derision in her tone as she could. "He's got himself a fortress up here. Haven't you, Dear?" My father poked at his eggs uncomfortably as my mother went on. "And should the enemies attack, we shall defend ourselves by pelleting them with peach pits, which we'll have plenty to spare come summertime." She laughed and, seeing that no one else did, added, "Alban, when will this silliness end? My friends are mocking us for leaving Paris, and I don't know what to tell them. Frankly, I am beginning to feel embarrassed."

Shortly after that, in May, France and Britain rejected the Soviet Union's proposal for a pact of mutual military assistance, and they agreed to give Poland military help against Hitler. In other words, the opposite of what my father had hoped for. My mother stopped asking to return to Paris, and I willed myself not to think about unpleasant things.

To my disappointment, and in contradiction of the original plan, Gustave and I were not enrolled in school. Instead, tutors came to the house. In what felt like an endless holiday, Gustave and I tended to our studies without much élan, swam in the pool, and ate Provençal food. Madame Malou was a superb cook and treated us to snails with parsley and garlic butter, or boeuf en daube with carrots from the garden, soupe de poisson, and pissaladières. Under her tutelage, Sandra learned to prepare calissons d'aix and lavender-infused ice cream. We competed daily in angry tennis matches that sent Gustave into paroxysms of fury when he did not win, which was almost always. I played the piano and perfected my English with a British boy, red and pimply but with whom I mostly perfected my kissing skills. I was antsy for more excitement and would have loved to meet more people, but my father said that our presence in the South of France needed to be inconspicuous.

"It is only a measure of precaution," my father said during one of our early dinners at La Bastide.

"Baba, our Jewish friends in Paris aren't worried, so why should we be?" Gustave asked, repeating our mother's sentiments.

"It doesn't matter what the greatest number of people think," my father said. "What matters is what we think and what we decide to do."

"But how is one to decide?" I asked.

"The signs are there for those who pay attention," my father answered.

My mother had a little laugh. "Don't you know that your father receives special intelligence from Président Lebrun? Or is it the generals of the Wehrmacht, letting you know their plans before they know it themselves?"

My father stared down at his plate. "I am sorry Lucienne if I am causing you grief."

The next few weeks revealed an upset of the balance of power at home. My mother might have sounded confident, but it seemed to have been an act to reassure Gustave and me. Also, in this new house, and isolated from her friends, she was out of her element and no longer all that mighty. At night, her sleep was fretful, which she blamed on the croaking of hundreds of frogs that emerged out of the pond and onto the lawn at sundown. In the morning, there would often be a few dead ones floating in the pool.

Our mother's poor sleep resulted in cranky moods and lethargy. During the day, she wandered aimlessly around the house, deeming the sun too hot for her disposition. Perhaps there were other reasons for her fading spirit. Maybe she was more afraid of an impending war than she let on. Maybe she knew of Father's plans, still secret to Gustave and me. The thing was, my parents argued now. If they had done it before, it had been discreet, and I had not quite noticed. Before Cannes, there were distractions: Father's work, Mother's charities. Before Cannes, there had been decorum. My future, mapped out by my mother, had seemed a series of straightforward steps. Follow those steps, schooling, manners, a certain attitude, connections, friendships, salons and dinners, the right kind of marriage, and life would follow the desired trajectory. But now my mother was grasping for the way things ought to be while we wandered off course, into uncharted waters. The plan was no longer simple. There were imponderables. There was xenophobia, and there was anti-Semitism, and soon there might be war, terrifying things she could not face, and so she fought Baba instead. Everything seemed to be a reason for her to take offense.

One of the points of contention between my parents was Sandra, whom my mother resented having around.

"Why are you not utilizing Sandra?" I heard my father ask my mother one day.

My mother straightened, "Oh, so she talks behind my back now?"

"She wants to work, and you've given her nothing to do."

"I don't know, Alban," my mother said with lassitude. "This house is fully staffed. Am I to invent things for her to do? Should I have another child so that she can be useful? The children no longer need her, and neither do I."

I felt bad for Sandra, but I was not clear that Sandra felt bad for herself. Her resilience was quite impressive. If my mother yelled at her, which she did quite often, or if she disparaged her, or told her to get 'out of her sight,' Sandra simply lowered her eyes or left the room quietly without appearing upset. Sandra was never one to resist, or take a stand, or even advocate for herself. Instead, she saw what was needed to be done and dove right in without fanfare.

Having known Sandra only in the context of the city life, I had a narrow definition of what she could do. But, apparently, Sandra had no such limitation for herself. She observed the groundskeeper and without being instructed, found things to do in the garden. She weeded and picked vegetables, learned to tend the beehives, picked fruit from trees and bushes, and volunteered for any errands within walking distance. She took it upon herself to drape every bed with fine netting to protect our sleep from mosquitoes. She even did nice things for Mother without being asked. Every evening, she set out to hunt for frogs by flashlight. She collected the little horrors in a large bucket and walked a kilometer to pour them into a nearby pond. No one believed it would make a dent, but it did. Soon there were very few frogs haunting our sleep or polluting our pool.

One day, I saw that Sandra was holding something in her lap. It was yarn, and she was knitting socks by the dozen.

"Do you know how to sew?" I asked her.

"Yes," she said.

I looked at her with renewed interest. "If I were to show you a picture in a magazine, would you know how to make something, such as a dress or a blouse?"

She thought about it. "Yes," she said.

"Mother won't buy the sort of clothes that are fashionable." I went to get the *Marie Claire* magazine on the coffee table and opened the page to a skirt I coveted. "Could you make this if I can find the fabric?"

Sandra gave me a cockeyed look and asked in her disjointed French, "Your mother doesn't want to buy, but you want me to make for you?"

I sat next to her and put my arm around her. "Oh, pretty please, Sandra, could it be our secret?"

"If your mother sees new clothes, she will ask."

"She won't, I promise. I'll never wear any of it when she's around. It's just for me to enjoy. It's just clothes. What harm is there in that? And besides, I don't care if Mother is angry with me."

Sandra frowned, but her lips turned up slightly. "She will be mad at me more than you."

I shrugged, "So, who cares."

Sandra pondered this for a moment. "Get the fabric," she said.

****

I was not the only one whose temperament was expressing itself in new ways. Gustave, too, was changing. Was it the strain of the last few years, his experience at boarding school, or the alchemy of puberty that morphed my sweet, timid, cautious brother into a fourteen-year-old bundle of fury and resentment? The only emotion he willingly expressed with me was brewing anger. Gone was his willingness to resume the role of docile playmate. He seemed to prefer being alone to being in my company. He hardly acknowledged Mother, or me, and when he did, it was through eye rolls, dismissive shrugs, snapping remarks, and slamming of doors. When he did not disappear into his room, he roamed inside the house and out in the garden like a ghostly presence, appearing without being heard, and startling me on purpose. The one person who seemed to find grace in his eyes was our father, to the exclusion of everyone else.

As for our father, he took to going out at night without telling us where or why. He had a telephone installed at the house and made calls behind closed doors. He and Mother argued incessantly, but in whispers. Mostly I could hear my mother's hissing and Father's unflappable reassurance. "Lucienne, I assure you. Lucienne, I promise. Lucienne, please calm your nerves." I began to suspect something. I had never forgotten the words of the servants. My mother was jealous of other women. Could my father have a lover here in Cannes? Could that be the reason he had made us all come here? When those thoughts entered my mind, instead of feeling bad for Mother, I secretly rooted for my father.

The thing was, Baba wasn't going to the office anymore. And so, what was he doing exactly?

"Have you retired, Baba?" I asked him one day.

He laughed. "I am only thirty-eight; I am not an old man yet."

"But you don't go to an office."

"I still do business with Uncle Moshe."

"Where is he?"

"He is abroad," my father said. And that was all the information he would volunteer.

It was good to have Baba to ourselves, at least in theory. It presented some problems, though. For one, he was bored. How else to explain all the time he now spent with Gustave? In Cannes, my brother resumed his carving of little wooden boats for days on end. He'd fine-tune a sail, or a tail, or whatnot and present it to my father to be admired. They had long discussions on the merits of automobiles. They'd visit auto shows. They'd make daylong excursions to neighboring towns to get this locomotive or that miniature forest. They'd construct floating things and test them in the pool. They'd bend over train sets, forgetting the world around them, forgetting I was even in the room.

And me? Well, I was only a girl. Although he was genuinely proud of me, my father understood not one bit about my mastery of the piano, my tennis prowess, or the fact that I could recite Shakespeare with an affected upper-crust British accent. He adored me; this much was clear, but his awkwardness around me grew nevertheless. My new womanly figure was a hindrance to our physical closeness, my breasts a source of embarrassment to us both.

My father now kept me at the respectful distance reserved for people who make you nervous and around whom you're not sure how to behave. Gustave could be wrestled with underwater. Gustave could kick around a soccer ball with him. Together, they could discuss boating and the merits of various train engines. Gustave knew his keel from his rudder, a steam dome from a sand dome. For a while, I tried to be one of the boys, but the appeal of miniature boats was lost on me.

Up until now, my parents had seemed to delight in being my captive audience. But now I was too old to be indulged in such ways. I played the piano, but no one seemed to have much enthusiasm for my nightly recitals. My father was distracted and often would leave the room to take a telephone call. My mother appeared lost in her unhappy thoughts. As for Gustave, in a display of open animosity, he refused to sit and hear my music at all.

So, as Gustave and my father sat side by side in fascination, watching obnoxious little trains make endless figure eights on a plank of wood, I was reduced to the only option left to me, 'turning into a young woman.' My mother and I had different definitions of this. Hers was something out of an 1800s etiquette book. My definition involved boys.

I'm not precisely sure when the resentment between Gustave and me turned to open aggression, but I know when our cold war started. One day in mid-July, Gustave – or I assumed it was he – told Mother that the British boy and I had been kissing. I found out I had been betrayed when my mother, red-faced, her eyes gleaming, burst into my room and slapped me across the face. "Needless to say, you are not to study with this boy anymore."

I held my hand to my burning face. "What did I do?" I shouted.

"You have conducted yourself improperly. Don't you act surprised young lady; you are not fooling me!"

"Who told you? It's Gustave, isn't it? That little brat!"

"Gustave, unlike you, knows the difference between right and wrong."

"If that were the case, he would not tattle."

"How I found out is beside the point, Marceline. Your privileges are revoked starting right this instant."

"What privileges?" I screamed. And with dramatic flair, I added, "What could make my situation here worse than it is already is, with no friends and nothing to do?"

My mother was very upset, and perhaps it was about more than my misbehavior. "The fact that we are here has nothing to do with me," she said. "It is your father who has chosen to isolate us from our social circle, not I. I am as punished as you are."

As it was, Mother seemed more interested in preserving the status quo. My punishment turned out to be a delicate affair because neither of us wanted my father to know what I had done. My father came from a conservative background. I did not want to disappoint him, and I think my mother had an investment in my appearing beyond reproach. Consequently, my punishment was a secret one and tantamount to no punishment at all. For two weeks, I was forbidden to eat ice cream and sweets, and I was not allowed to leave the house.

I bided my time. I read, I swam, I lay by the pool till I turned golden brown. In the privacy of my room and my mirror, I practiced being glamorous, like the woman I had admired on the beach. I stole Mother's cigarettes and smoked them in the orchard when no one was looking. Tutors continued to teach us. As to the matter of learning the English language, my British kissing partner was fired and replaced with an American woman. Gustave and I loved the new accent, which sounded wild and free to us, so we began to pay attention to our lessons. It turned out that by getting that British boy fired, Gustave was instrumental in our properly learning English, a skill that would eventually alter the course of my life. When the need for a translator arose many years later, I was ready for the job.

To be honest, I wasn't certain that Gustave had ratted me out about the British boy. My mother could have found out through Sandra, or Madame Malou, Monsieur Malou, or anyone else on the staff. Still, I stopped trusting my brother with my secrets. When he walked by me or peeped over my shoulder as I wrote, or if he materialized on the same dirt path when I took walks around the property, I accused him of snooping and of being a pest.

One afternoon, my parents were out, and he caught me in the act of practicing in my bedroom mirror the bewitching hand movements of Hedy Lamar in the movie *Algiers*. My lips were red with lipstick, there was an ivory cigarette holder in my hand, and I wore my mother's too-big-for-me Jean Patou black lamé sheath. Gustave opened the door, sneered, and left. I was humiliated. Later on, I cornered him. "You're not allowed in my room anymore," I said.

"You're acting like a fool."

"And stop tattling."

"I don't," he said.

I did not know what to make of this response. "You're the one acting like a fool," I said. "Maybe you should grow up, instead of playing little boy's games."

"Oh, not like you, playing dress-up like a six-year-old?"

"The childish toys you and Baba play with…. You're fourteen years old, Gustave."

"How is it childish, if Baba likes them too?"

"You and Baba are both being childish."

"You're jealous."

"What would I have to be jealous about?" I scoffed. But perhaps he was right.

The other problem with my father not disappearing to the office every day was that with him around, it was harder to ignore the war. One thing about war is that you can pretend it is happening elsewhere and to other people only for so long. It requires vigilance and concentration to remain in the dark. With Baba at home, I could not avoid overhearing troublesome conversations between him and Monsieur Malou. I could not avoid the newspapers left on couches and coffee tables. I could not always turn off the radio when the program I had been listening suddenly made way for a chilling newsbreak. It was on the radio that we all first learned in August that the

Soviet Union and Germany had signed a non-aggression treaty. My father's prophetic worst-case scenario had become reality. What this meant, I was too terrified to imagine. Two strong armies, two aggressive nations, now had an alliance. Where did this leave France?

Following these events, my father's secrecy increased. But he did not seem scared. Rather, he seemed determined. His calm was the only thing that allowed me to sleep at night. If he wasn't worried, he whom Mother called a doomsayer, this meant that things would be all right.

That same month, my father did something extravagant, considering that he lately had been lecturing us on the virtues of thrift. One hot afternoon, promising us a surprise, he took the whole family to the pier, where he parked the automobile. We walked on the dock, admiring the beautiful boats that bobbed over the dark, steely water. I was convinced he had hired one for the afternoon. But when we faced a thirty-foot, pristine fishing boat, named Jolie Fille, my father planted on each of our heads a captain's hat and announced, "I have bought us a fishing boat."

Gustave and I jumped up and down and threw ourselves at our father's neck. "Baba, can we use it now? Do you know how to pilot it?" we asked.

"I have hired a skipper for the month, but soon we shall learn to navigate it ourselves."

"Can we rename it?" I asked.

"What do you want to rename it?" Gustave sneered, "Jolie Marceline?"

The fishing boat was lovely. It had two small, well-decorated bedrooms, each with two sets of bunk beds. It had sleek, varnished wood paneling, handsome naval motifs, a darling kitchen with all elements fitting just so, and a padded chaise lounge out on deck. Mother alone did not appear surprised by the sudden purchase. She narrowed her eyes at the boat, measuring it, as though she were contemplating fate itself.

My father, who had not expressed the slightest interest for boating in the past, now seemed obsessed with learning to pilot his 'toy,' as our mother called it. He practiced taking it in and out of the harbor. He learned to read a compass and maritime maps. Gustave was enthralled by it all. He wanted to be on the boat every day, all day long, if that was an option. Throughout August, he and Baba fished, plunging into the Mediterranean from the boat wearing underwater masks and brandishing thin harpoons. They'd emerge from the water with all manner of loathsome sea creatures, fish, gnarly gray seashells, and small convulsing octopuses that Gustave loved to see wrapped around his wrists. I tried to accompany them at first but soon learned that I was not the type who enjoys staring at the water for hours on end. My brother was in heaven to share yet one more thing with Baba.

On September 1, 1939, the Wehrmacht invaded Poland. Immediately, the French government mobilized its troops. We were listening to the radio when we found out. Everything had pointed in that direction, and yet we had all refused to believe Hitler would be so brazen. For the next few days, we stood by the radio, listening for news.

On September 3rd, France and Great Britain declared war on Germany. Fear swept through me like a million darts attacking my chest, my heart, my belly. War. War with a country whose modern, fanatical army terrified us. My father lowered his head, as in prayer, and Mother just clapped her hands over her heart. Neither found anything reassuring to say.

Over the course of the week, everything my father had said and done up to this point began to make sense. Friends had called him an alarmist and a pessimist when he was in the process of liquidating his assets. They had waited to see what would happen. They had listened to each other's reassurance, and few of them were prepared. Most of our Jewish friends had not planned on the fact that with France entering the war, there would suddenly be no buyers for houses and no takers for businesses. Banks stopped lending. People stopped buying. And no one could liquidate anything.

We sat around the dining room table. There was something my father wanted to discuss. It was a sweltering day without a hint of a breeze, inside the dining room and out.

"With the proceeds from the sale of our business, Uncle Moshe and I bought diamonds," he explained. "Those await us in a Swiss bank."

"Why a Swiss bank?" we asked.

"If France is defeated, French banks won't be safe," he said.

"Do you think that's possible, Baba?" Gustave asked.

My father did not answer. "It is possible that traveling to Switzerland might become impossible, so the bulk of our money will be inaccessible to us."

"Oh, goodness, Alban, what if the war lasts for years?" Mother said.

"I have French and foreign money, several diamonds, and some gold. Those need to last until the end of the war."

"What a disaster!" my mother exclaimed.

"Financially, we are better off than most, Lucienne." He lowered his eyes, reluctant to say more. "On the other hand, children, you are old enough to know that being Jewish puts us at risk." Mother gave him an incendiary look to silence him. My father hesitated but forced himself to speak. "We need to look no further than what is happening in Germany to know what an eventual defeat could mean for Jewish families: frozen assets, confiscation of property, requisitioning, interdictions to practice certain professions, limitations of rights, numerus clausus."

"What is that, Baba?"

"A cap on the number of Jewish students accepted in each school."

There was a lump in my throat. My parents, even Mother, had tried so hard to protect us from the truth, and now Baba was articulating the fear we all felt. There were rumors coming from Germany, at once incomprehensible and terrifying, that Jewish families were being made to leave their homes and forced to congregate in giant prisons.

"What will we do, Baba?" Gustave asked.

"Our most immediate risk is to be dispossessed. This is why I took these financial precautions. As for the rest, I do have plans, but it's too soon to share them with you children." I thought of our friends in Paris. Most of them had dismissed my father as crazy and had no exit strategy. Now I felt grateful for his strength, for the fact that he had a plan at all. "For the time being, remember that a thinking mind is better than a reactive mind," he added.

"Also," Mother said pragmatically, "know that nothing in the newspaper can be trusted from now on. It will be nothing but propaganda; you can be assured of it. That's how it was during the Great War."

****

The French put their faith in the counsel of the old generals who had triumphed in the Great War twenty years prior. What else could we do? To think otherwise would have led to despair. But those old generals, glorious and experienced as they were, could not imagine modern warfare any more than we could. We understood war as it had been in the past: that young men would get foot rot in trenches, that there would be air raids with nights spent in cellars, that there would be pride, patriotism, and, eventually, victory. We were ignorant of modern warfare and unprepared for it. We could not imagine submarines and tanks, the atoms bombs. The few who felt that France was unprepared and anticipated defeat, my father included, still couldn't predict a war without trenches, a war fought for ideology. No one predicted genocide. But all this would come later. For now, there was only clinging to our patriotism and our belief in the powers that be.

For the next eight months, we waited.

There was little military action on French territory, no bombing, no attacks. The people of France did not quite know what to make of it. People began to wonder if perhaps they had worried unnecessarily. Perhaps, they thought, Germany was intimidated by our power and deterred by the Maginot Line. Over those eight months, the French population settled into the new normalcy of the Drôle de Guerre. In this 'phony war,' most everyone in France began to relax. When they ran out of funds, or out of fear, those who had left the larger cities returned. In the end, the place where people want to be is home. It doesn't matter where home is: it is the notion of home, of one's personal things on shelves, of being sheltered under a familiar roof that gives people the illusion of safety. But my father did not relax. He showed no sign of wanting to return to Paris.

In the South of France, temperatures dropped over the winter months. We had not thought of bringing our winter clothes. There were restrictions already, on fuel, on fabric, and Baba mandated that we be more prudent with money. This did not sit so well with me, as it coincided with a time in my life when I wanted to be pretty and meet boys. The inactivity and the waiting were hard on the nerves for everyone. I walked alone around country roads I knew by heart and spent hours reading by the chimney fire, feeling afraid and cold. Anxiety was the only emotion. The only pastime was waiting.

Maybe because we had no control over the world around us, my mother and I engaged in a constant tug of war. She seemed to want to pull me back into childhood, while I pulled to come out of it. She wanted me in smock dresses, Mary Jane shoes, and white socks. I dreamed of nylon stockings and A-shaped skirts. I read *Marie Claire* and *Vogue* magazines, gorged on espionage novels, and the minute my parents were out of the house I'd make a beeline for Mother's makeup, heels, and cigarettes. I discovered in myself a great appetite for disobedience.

Soon enough, Mother's patience with the South of France grew thin. She begged Baba to leave Cannes, and I agreed with her wholeheartedly. Why could we not return home to Paris? Nothing was happening, and it drove us mad.

One late October day at dinner, my father tried to appear casual as he explained that he would be doing business in Nice for a week or so. There was excitement on his face, but that was all he would say. But when the week turned into a month of him going to Nice every day, and often spending the night there, I heard my mother accuse him of seeing another woman. My father insisted that he was only tending to business. "What kind of business has you coming home in the middle of the night reeking of cigarettes and wine?" she asked.

"I neither smoke nor drink as you well know, Lucienne."

"Then why then do I smell it on your clothes?"

"Do you smell women's perfume?" my father asked. "No, you do not. That is because I am not around women."

"Then tell me what it is you do! And please tell me you are doing nothing illegal."

"Of course not."

"Then what is it?"

"An old friend from my country is in town. I am helping him to get acclimated to France. He does not speak the language well."

"Are you helping him with money too?"

My father hesitated. "A little," he said.

"Why am I not surprised?" my mother shrieked. "And is this man the reason I must do without a driver? I scrimp so that you can spend our money on a stranger?"

"He is not a stranger to me," my father said.

"Why the secrecy then? Why not introduce him to me, take him to dinner with the family."

My father hesitated. "In time. For now, he has gone through a lot. He needs to rest."

"Is he troubled?" my mother asked.

"He is a very smart man, and I have faith in him." With this, my father left the room so fast that I barely had time to dart away from the door before he saw me spying.

As the months dragged on, I found myself wanting something to happen: war, violence, bombing, a Nazi invasion, anything to take me out of my torpor. And it wasn't just me being a silly girl. No one could bear the standoff, the terrible latent anguish. Action, of any kind, appeared less intolerable than this state of suspended animation. Perhaps, at a global level, as a nation, we had an intuition of the truth. And the truth was that this period of military standoff wasn't due to Germany's apathy, or German fear, but to the fact that the Germans were preparing how best to devastate us.

Soon it was March. We had been in Cannes for nearly a year, and it had been seven months of non-war when spring began to warm the hills. Spring in the South of France did not creep in slowly the way it did in Paris. It arrived in full fanfare, all the fruit trees bursting with blooms, the sun hot, the very nature of the air festive. For my father, the week of helping his friend had turned into two months, and his excitement must have waned because he now looked pained and preoccupied.

"Why can't we meet your friend," Gustave asked him one day.

"He is a troubled man, my son. He has suffered much and is haunted by too many demons. I am helping him the best I can, but some people are harder to help than others."

"What happened to him?" I asked.

"He is Armenian. Terrible things happened to the Armenian people where I come from."

"Armenian, like Sandra?" I thought of her burn scar and shivered.

"Yes," my father said, a shadow of sadness passing over his face.

"Why would bad things happen to Armenians? What did they do? Who wanted to hurt them?"

"Fanatics did."

"Was it about religion?"

"It was about fanaticism, which needs no other excuse or explanation."

"I don't understand," Gustave said.

"That is because you are a logical person. You want reasons for hatred to exist. You want to justify it in your mind. You want to know if it is about land, or race, or nationality, or politics, or past events, or even religion when, in fact, for the fanatics, butchering and torturing are their own purpose."

"How do people become fanatics?"

"Many are born that way. Just take away the rules that stop them, and it is like unleashing a wild beast."

"Is your friend hurt?" Gustave asked.

"Not physically," my father said. "But his wounds are deep."

"Can he get better?"

My father shook his head with profound sadness. "Once, I loved him like a brother, but he has been changed by his sufferings. Now there is too much violence in him."

"Has he turned into a fanatic?"

My father watched us. I could see in his expression that perhaps he understood something for the first time. "He might have," he said.

After our conversation, I found myself wishing that my father had a secret woman, someone who could comfort him. It pained me to think that he carried so much weight with no help at all from my mother.

In early April, a wealthy Parisian family moved into a nearby house, a quarter of a mile or so from ours. My parents never met the family, but I found myself crossing paths with their only son. He was twenty-two years old and quite attractive. His name was Patrice, and he kept appearing on his bicycle as I walked around the countryside. He had stark, pale-blond hair, smooth as a helmet, which he wore long and combed to one side so that it covered one eye. He dressed in the Zazou style: floppy pants, too long and rolled at the hem, and a plaid sports coat. My father had warned me of the shallowness that can come with good looks, but that wisdom had fallen on deaf ears. I began to stroll the countryside in my best outfits, hoping that sooner or later he would have to stop to speak to me, which did not take long.

"I'm terrifically bored here," he said, his slightly cruel mouth pursed in vague disgust. "But the paterfamilias wants to be here for a while until things settle."

"Aren't you old enough to enlist?"

"Father pulled strings," he said. "A heart murmur purchased at considerable cost from an accommodating physician."

We admitted that neither of us could wait to return to Paris.

"Are you at the university?" I asked.

He flipped his hair back and smiled. "I have done enough schooling for what I intend to do with my life."

"Which is?"

"To enjoy it."

He wasn't Jewish. I did not need to ask to be certain of it. Everything about him screamed Catholic privilege. His parents had wanted to keep a bigger distance between themselves and the German border and had the financial means to do so. Patrice did not ask me if I was Jewish. The question did not occur to him because asking me about myself did not occur to him.

In Paris, he told me, he spent his days recovering from his nights at underground jazz clubs where Negroes played swell tunes, and there was all this dancing, and the place was full of Americans who liked to have a swell time. He was partial to swell American beer. So, yes, he was vain. But in my sixteen-year-old eyes, he was just, well … swell. I knew about sex in some vague, theoretical way. I was innocent enough to think that boys' interests in me mirrored my interest in them: it was all very chaste, a game of seduction that culminated with love professed through written notes and the occasional heated kiss.

We continued to meet 'by accident' that week, and although his conversation was dull, we mostly were looking for hidden corners to kiss. One day he suggested a nighttime rendezvous. It was my idea that we meet in our property's vineyard at midnight. That night, I crept out of my room, after Mother and Baba had gone to bed, and set out. I had put makeup on, and perfume, and my best skirt. He arrived on his bicycle. He had brought wine and a wool blanket, which we laid on the dirt just below the grapevines. It was chilly and the moon cast long shadows in the strange darkness. Silly cow that I was, I thought it was romantic. I did not know much about the risks. I did not know that men could turn to beasts. Oh, it was sweet enough at first. One kiss led to the next, and soon he was overheated and rough. I told him to stop. I told him to back off and that he was hurting me. He did not stop.

By the time I understood what was happening, I yelled and raged for him to stop; I tried to shout, but he pressed his hand on my mouth. I bit his palm as hard as I could and tasted blood. I felt a roughness between my legs, and then an acute pain that felt as though it were breaking me in half. I turned my face, freed my mouth, and bit again. I spat in his face. But already he was pulling away.

He came off me, and I curled upon myself, reached around, struggled to gather my torn panties. An immediate sense of shame overpowered every other emotion. Whatever had just happened to me, I already sensed that no one should ever find out about it.

He was up on his feet above me, pulling his pants up.

At that moment, a silhouette emerged from between the rows of trees. It was Gustave. Had he heard us? Had he seen us? My brother was younger than I, but his time in boarding school must have informed him that something was awry. He was only a few feet away. I was still on the ground. Gustave said nothing, threw a rock at Patrice, and, in the dark, missed him. Patrice faced him menacingly. Gustave turned on his heels and began to run toward the house. Patrice started after him but his pants were still unbuttoned, and it was dark, and the ground was uneven. Patrice made three steps; his arms flailed, and he fell flat on his stomach with a thump. He let out a muffled shout and sat up, cursing. I was up on my feet now, my shame replaced by immense fury. I grabbed a large rock at my feet. Not feeling its weight, I raised it above my head and threw it hard at Patrice's face. It made a terrible sound. He screamed in pain and was knocked unconscious. I saw blackness spread on his face in the moonlight. Blood. His nose was smashed flat against his face. Had I killed him? I didn't know. I was drunk with rage, and at that moment, I truly hoped that I had.

I hobbled back home, unable to fully comprehend what had just happened to my body. In silence, I searched the sleeping house for Gustave, my blood laced with adrenaline, the sound of my pulse pounding in my head. All I knew was that Gustave was going to tell on me, and he needed to be stopped. Mother would send me to a convent in the mountains or a home for lost girls. But mostly I thought about my father. He would never again see me as his princess. Whatever I had just become through this terrible act, I was not sure, but I knew it to be something vile and shameful.

When I found Gustave in the dark hallway, Sandra was behind him. What particular kindness or calculation prevented Gustave from telling Mother and alerting Sandra instead? Did he believe, as I did, the offense unforgivable? He disappeared into his room as Sandra wordlessly took my arm and guided me to the bathroom at the farthest end of the house where my parents could not hear us.

In the bathroom, Sandra turned on the light, a look of anguish on her face. "A boy touched you?" she whispered as soon as I entered. "Did he hurt you?"

"Leave me alone!" I whispered back, furious.

"Did he hurt you?" she pressed, caressing my cheek. "Are you hurt anywhere?"

"What kinds of filthy lies did Gustave tell you?" I said. Sandra looked into my eyes and caressed my hair. Something in my chest burst open. I began to sob, and for a while, I could not stop. "Something happened," I told her at last. "The boy. He did something to me." I looked down at my body. "Down there."

She looked at me with profound sadness. "You will wash," she said. "And then you will drink something I will make for you. And then you will sleep and forget what this boy did."

"I don't even know what happened," I wept. "We were kissing and ... we were only kissing...."

She searched deep down into my soul with her melancholy eyes. "You promise me. You forget this boy. All that he did to you."

Sandra helped me wash. She brought me a glass of an awful black concoction, some remedy from the old country, or what have you. She said nothing other than, "This will stop babies from coming." No lectures, admonition, or judgment, bless her heart.

The following day was April 9, 1940. I had slept fretfully, waking up a dozen times, each time to be reminded of what had happened. And in the morning, I had a new anguish: what if Patrice was dead? What would become of me if they found out I had killed him? Would I be made to confess to what he had done to me? I came down to the breakfast table, where my father and mother were reading the paper. "Are you quite all right, my lovely," my father asked. "Sandra said you were ill last night?"

"Food poisoning, I think," I muttered.

Mother lifted her eyes from the newspaper. "I hope it wasn't that dessert she made. We all had it." "She" and "her" were how my mother referred to Sandra. Ever since we arrived in Cannes, Mother was determined not to call her by her name.

Gustave pretended I was not in the room. He had his ear close to the radio as he adjusted the antenna and turned knobs to hear more clearly the news bulletins on Radio Sud-Ouest.

"How horrific," Mother said, reading from the local pages. "Madame Malou said that there was a brutal attack in the neighborhood last night. A young man was savagely assaulted less than a mile from our house." Gustave and I didn't look at each other as our mother went on. Gustave resumed his position, ear glued to the radio, fiddling with the knobs. "Two men attacked him, she said. They hit him with rocks, and bit him."

My father raised an eyebrow. "Beat him?" he asked.

"Bit him," Mother said, gnashing her teeth to demonstrate.

My father laughed. "Are you sure his vicious attacker wasn't a squirrel?"

"Children, stay near the house until they catch these men. Speaking of men," my mother continued, "what about that purported friend of yours, the one draining our resources?"

"Don't concern yourself with this," my father said. His good mood was gone.

"I know you see yourself as the defender of the orphan and the oppressed. First her, and now him. I'm only surprised you haven't moved him in to live with us as well."

"Let's not discuss this now," my father said.

"As if there isn't enough unknown in our life as it is," my mother said. "And of all places, why must we go there?"

I perked up, curious. "Go where?" I asked.

"Not now, Lucienne, please," my father said.

"Shhh, everybody" Gustave said. "They're saying something on the radio."

"You cannot insist on dictating what I can and cannot tell my friends," Mother told Father.

"Tell them what?" I asked.

"Shh!" Gustave commanded.

My mother switched gears, pointing to Gustave. "And besides, you are neglecting your son."

My father gazed up from his newspaper in disbelief. Although it was true that my father's visits to his friend resulted in him all but stopping his outings with Gustave, my mother's concern was entirely self-serving.

This is when we all saw Gustave rise from his position near the radio and look at us, all the color drained from his face.

"What is it?" Mother asked.

"The Germans attacked Denmark and Norway."

"The th ... what? Gustave, darling, this is impossible," Mother said. "These countries are neutral."

"Denmark has already surrendered," Gustave said in a hollow voice. "within six hours of the attack."

The telephone began to ring, and we knew this was true.

To me, that morning remained engraved in my memory as the turning point for the rest of our lives. I will never know if my father had lied about having a friend he was helping in Nice. Perhaps it was all a cover for everything else he and Moshe were doing at that time and which I only found out about after the war.

From that point on, things went fast. Throughout April we anxiously followed the naval combats between the British and the Germans, our hopes soaring and plunging with news of the fighting. We attended a Passover service in the Grande Synagogue de Nice. I think we went to get a sense of what people in the community were saying. They seemed mostly concerned about friends and relatives in other parts of Europe. They felt safe in France. I heard that years later, in 1943, local French people had rounded up Jewish families in that very synagogue before they deported them.

In early May, the Germans attacked the Netherlands, Belgium, and Luxembourg.

A few days later, my father announced that we would be spending the night on our boat. We had done this before, so it was not particularly unusual. The house was being fumigated, and Mother and Sandra were coming as well, he informed us. That should have triggered suspicion as it was unlike my mother to spend the night on a boat when the Hotel Miramar was only a stone's throw away. Also, I had seen no sign of bugs.

After dinner, we drove down to the dock. Sandra brought a large basket of food, which also was unusual. Why not eat at a restaurant near the pier or anywhere on the Croisette? On the drive, Mother and Baba were tense, but again, I did not think much of it, as used to their fights as I was.

The boat was safely moored in the Bay of Cannes, among hundreds of others. We climbed into our respective bunks for the night. Gustave and I bunked in one cabin with Sandra. Our parents were in the other cabin.

I fell asleep quickly. I had a scary dream. Gustave's toy tanks were coming up our driveway in procession, but as they got closer, they turned out to be massive Nazi tanks, so loud that the ground shook, and the house began to crumble. I woke up in a fright, my heart pounding. The noise was real. The boat's engine was on. In fact, we were moving. Why would that be? This was the middle of the night? Why would we be leaving the dock? I leaned down. Gustave was sound asleep in the bunk below, but Sandra wasn't in the cabin. I slipped a warm sweater over my nightgown and walked up on deck. I looked for city lights, but it was pitch black. We were nowhere near the pier. I don't know how long we had been at sea. I turned around and saw Mother and Sandra. They were fully dressed. They were holding lanterns and had life jackets on. Their faces were strained. "What's the matter?" I said. "Why are we at sea?"

My mother handed me a lantern. "Wake your brother and the two of you get dressed."

That's when I saw our luggage neatly stacked on the deck. All the suitcases and hat boxes we had brought with us from Paris had miraculously materialized on the boat. How had Sandra packed all this without my seeing anything? My heart began beating faster. "What are we doing? Why would the boat—"

"Not right now, Marceline. Do as I say."

"But, Mother—"

"Go!"

I ran down the metal steps and shone the lantern in Gustave's eyes. "Wake up, Gustave; you're missing everything," I said.

"Are we sinking?" he asked through his yawn.

"Probably."

We dressed in a hurry and came up on deck. Sandra, inscrutable, fitted us with life jackets. We saw that my father was absorbed in piloting the boat, going from his compass to his map. He did not even look at us.

"Mother, are we really sinking?" Gustave asked.

"We're not sinking," I said, exhilarated. "We're going somewhere!"

My mother opened her mouth to speak. Words had trouble getting out. "Your father believes it's best to leave France. Immediately."

Leave I could understand, but leave France? "Where are we going?"

"I, um, we shall tell you later. Now please, be quiet. This is stressful enough without a barrage of questions."

I gave Sandra an interrogative look, but her face registered nothing I could read.

"Maybe we're going to Italy," I whispered to Gustave. "Or Spain."

"The boat doesn't carry enough fuel to go that far," he said. "Corsica or Sardinia maybe."

Gustave and I sat on the deck in our life jackets and waited. The night was moonless, and the sea flat as oil. Above us, the number of stars was dizzying, and I had a vertiginous sense of how insignificant we were. After about an hour, Baba abruptly stopped the engine. We were plunged into an immense silence. "Turn off the lanterns," my father ordered. We did. With the remaining one, he began signaling in a rhythmic pattern. Soon across the sea appeared a light that shone intermittently. "They're here," he said. Mother and Sandra sighed in relief.

Ten minutes later, we heard the approaching flapping sound of oars scooping water. Baba shone his light on two wooden dinghies, which were heading toward us. In them, two strange-looking men in turbans and loose white shirts rowed silently. The dinghies touched our boat. My father threw down ropes, then the ladder.

"All three of you go on the larger dinghy," my father said. "First you, Gustave, then Marceline, and then Lucienne."

"Goodness gracious, those things are flimsy! How are you expecting me to do this, Alban?" my mother said. She sounded terrified.

"Come down the steps and climb on board."

"I'll go first," Gustave said.

Gustave easily descended the short ladder and climbed aboard the dinghy. I came down the thin ladder. The dinghy moved quite a bit as I came on board. The man in the turban offered me his hand, and I tightened my grip on his as I made my way to the back. When came my mother's turn, she looked down at the ladder and recoiled. After a while, she did manage to put her legs overboard and her feet on the ladder, but then she froze. She lifted her foot off the ladder, dipped it one inch down, and promptly put it back on the ladder as though she had just been bitten by an invisible creature. The man with the turban tried to help her but seemed hesitant to grab hold of her.

"Mother, come down already," I called from below.

"It's easy. It's only a few steps down," Gustave said.

"Alban!" she whimpered. "Alban, I'm afraid I shall not be able to do this!"

"You can do it," my father said. "Just put one foot below the other, and the man will set it in the right place on the ladder; just don't look down."

"I don't want this stranger's hand on my foot. What if he pulls me?"

But the man seemed just as unwilling to touch her foot as she was to give it to him. She managed to go down two steps, but the boat swayed, and she went right back up the ladder.

"Mother!" I urged her. "Just come on down. It took me seconds."

"I shall not make it," she said, near hysterics.

The men in their turbans sat in each boat, their faces masks of forbearance. I looked up at Gustave and saw that he was trying not to laugh.

Baba realized he needed to change tactics. He came down the ladder, and from below guided her down by gently moving her feet on each step. "Come on down, Lucienne. That's good. One more, just bring your other foot down. No, Lucienne, not up, no, no, down, that's right, good … almost there, that's it."

"I'll fall," she wailed.

"If you fall, I'll catch you."

Hearing those words, our mother inexplicably let go of the ladder, flailed her arms, and fell backward, down onto Father. Both of them collapsed to the bottom of the dinghy, Baba mashed under, and Mother sitting confusedly on top of him. Looking down from our boat, Sandra covered her mouth to hide her smile. Despite the tension of the moment, Gustave and I began laughing, and we were powerless to stop.

Baba extricated himself from under Mother and came back up the ladder and onto the boat. The rest proceeded without further trouble. My father went back up. The suitcases were lowered into the dinghy, and then he and Sandra came down and sat together in the second dinghy.

"Are we leaving our boat in the middle of the sea?" Gustave asked. "Isn't it too deep to anchor? Won't it drift?"

"Shh," my father said.

The turbaned men secured our luggage and began rowing effortlessly on the flat sea. There was no wind and only the sounds of oars touching the water. We moved, guided by the dim light of a structure in the distance. Next to me, my mother trembled violently.

To find oneself on a small floating device in the middle of the sea, imagining the depth below, was terrifying. We were alone with infinite blackness above and infinite blackness below. When the dinghy holding my father and Sandra moved ahead of ours and we could no longer see them, Mother sobbed helplessly.

Minutes later, we were beside the metal hull of a large vessel. It was a large commercial fishing boat, rusty and slick with grime. We had to climb a ladder at least fifteen feet up. Thankfully, Mother was able to go up better than she had fared going down.

The boat stank of fish and unwashed men. My mother, usually the picture of strength, now looked as vulnerable as a small girl. Sandra put her arm around Gustave. I tried to ignore the looks of the dark men on board. A man came out and spoke to my father in an unknown, guttural language. To my amazement, my father answered in the same language, a language I had never heard him speak before. The two spoke in low tones for a few minutes. My father was handed a pistol. Without so much as looking at it, he casually slipped the weapon into his belt.

Two of the men returned to one of the dinghies and headed out toward our boat, which could not have been more than a few hundred yards away, but that we could not see in the deep night. "What are they doing?" Gustave whispered. There was light on our boat, and then a brighter light. He understood before I did. "Holy mackerel," he said.

In a matter of minutes, our boat was in flames. As soon as the two men returned, the fishing boat started its engine and cut through the water away from our boat. The blaze, close at first, diminished into the distance until it disappeared from our sight.

It's not that I wasn't afraid. I was. But along with the fear came a new form of exhilaration. I knew then that it was my first time feeling truly alive. By alive, I mean that there was no thinking, and worrying, and being self-conscious. There was no past, and there was no future. There was only action, instinct, my racing pulse. While Mother, Sandra, and Gustave were understandably petrified with fright, I felt ready to jump up and grab one of those pistols and shoot at any pirate or anyone who would be mad enough to stand in our way.

We spent the next three days hidden on board the fishing boat. There we learned of our parents' plan as the mysterious boat took us away and we sat, all five us in a cramped cabin, on terrible mats set on metal bunks. "We're heading for North Africa," my father explained. "We are going to be living in Algeria. Everything there is arranged for our arrival."

"But why did we leave in the middle of the night?" Gustave asked.

"Because there is nothing to lose by being prudent. If the Germans do invade France—"

"Which is unlikely," my mother interrupted, but I could tell she was only trying to convince herself.

"And in case they start to detain foreign Jews, as this has happened elsewhere, I feel it is better not to leave a trail. And so, we will have false papers in Algeria, a new identity. New names."

"Is that why you bought the boat and learned to pilot it all those months ago, Baba," Gustave asked. "Did you already know we would do this?"

My father nodded, "Yes."

Inside the fishing boat's cabin, things creaked and clanged from every direction. The rocking of the sea compelled us to hold on to the cots and walls. The news that we would live under a false identity in a strange country swept through me like a shockwave of confusion, dread, and something resembling excitement. You have to understand that up until that moment war had been theoretical and vague to me. There had been words in newspapers and on the radio, gleaned fragments of conversations. We had no capacity to measure it against anything known to us. To Gustave, war was strategy. War was play. To me, it was an unpleasant state of affairs I carefully avoided thinking about. And for neither of us did there seem to be direct implications for our family. Sure, we had left Paris to humor my father, but this was something else entirely. We were fleeing. We were in danger. "This is an industrial fishing boat," my father said. "It is monitored by the authorities. It has to do its work and bring its catch to port, so as not to raise suspicion. These men will fish, and we will wait until they are done, at which point they will take us to Algiers. We'll arrive early in the morning so that there won't be too many people in the streets."

"Where will we live?" I asked.

"In an apartment Uncle Moshe found for us," my father said.

An apartment in Algiers. The word apartment sounded like an adventure in itself. I had no frame of reference. My father could have just as well suggested a yurt in the plains of China.

"What about the new name? What are we supposed to call each other?" Gustave asked.

"The thing is, children," my father said, "we want to make it harder for authorities to find us, should the authorities be … German. And so we won't let anyone know where we are going. We will stop all communication with anyone we know in Paris or the South of France."

"No letters to friends?" I asked, astonished. "No calling people on the telephone? Won't they wonder where we went?"

"It needs to remain an absolute secret for the time being."

"What if they think us dead?"

"That is a risk your father is more than willing to take," Mother said bitterly. "Since he hates all my friends."

"I do not hate them, but neither do I trust them," my father said.

"But, Baba," Gustave pointed out, "Algeria is still part of France. If you're worried about the Germans winning the war, would they not rule Algeria, too?"

"Indeed, Gustave, but although Algeria is French territory, the Germans are quite a bit farther away. It buys us time and distance."

"Why did you and Moshe choose Algeria, Baba?" I asked.

"Because it is open to the entire continent of Africa. And we know people there."

"What kind of people?"

"Friends of Moshe," my father said. "From this point forward, you must remember only to trust Jews. And even then, not all Jews. Moshe will give us our identity papers when we arrive. We will keep our first name but will use a different last name."

"But even if Germany wins the war, things will return to normal at some point, won't they, Baba?" Gustave asked. "We won the Great War, and we did not make the Germans abandon their language and start speaking French."

My father looked at him gravely. "The world has gone mad, my son, and it is getting worse. Even reasonable people are speaking nonsense. You've seen anti-Semitism, how it took hold in France. The more insane the hatred and the accusations, the more willing people are to embrace them. I saw this happen in my country as well. I have seen with my own eyes madness taking hold in the hearts of men. I am not worried about the kind of war fought between soldiers. Those are the wars of history books, which speak in numbers and offensives, as though war is fought by masses that move as one without feelings. In actuality, war is about the suffering of individuals. You are my family, and I will do everything to protect you. In this war, there will only be us. We will be the only people who matter."

"But we can't very well run away indefinitely," my mother said weepily.

"If what we must do to get away from the Nazis is to circle the globe one hundred times, that is what I plan to do," Baba responded.

I felt as though I were seeing my father for the first time. My soft-spoken father was, in fact, a man who plotted and planned, a man able to orchestrate secret missions to save his family. He was in his element on this strange boat, among these scary men, speaking their mysterious language. And Mother, the dragon that she usually was, was listening to him, expecting him to have answers. My purportedly meek father was decisive and assertive, while the pompous loudmouths who had disparaged him in Paris scrambled. It was the most exciting event of my life, and my father was at the center of it.

We stayed at sea for two whole days while the men caught fish. None of us could get much sleep on those metal bunks covered with dirty burlap mattresses. Sandra's basket of food did not last, and we were fed inedible things. The latrine was impossible to stomach. My father discouraged us from going up on deck unless it was nighttime. By the second day, we reeked of fish and were desperate for a bath and a decent bed. Making things worse for them, Mother, Sandra, and Gustave were seasick. By the second day, they had a hollowed and exhausted look in their eyes. Sandra and Gustave were stoic about it, but my mother was at her wit's end.

I was the opposite. Although I did not sleep or eat much either, I felt vibrant with energy.

In the early morning of the third day, we crept up on deck to glimpse the strange new land ahead of us. The dawn was barely breaking over a white city that appeared to climb the flank of a mountain. As our fishing boat neared the bay, it was daybreak, and the sun peeked slightly over the mountain, its rays reflecting against the minarets of many mosques. At the top of the hill, overlooking the Bay of Algiers, was what I later learned was the beautiful Basilique Notre-Dame d'Afrique, which to my Parisian eyes resembled the Sacré Coeur. Below the city, the vast bay was breathtaking. My father turned to Sandra and said a few words to her in Armenian. Sandra nodded, her eyes flooded with tears.

"What is it, Baba?"

"This looks like the Bay of Smyrna. Before the fire. That was our land."

"Where Sandra got her burn, and your arm was hurt?" Gustave said.

"Yes," my father said darkly. "It is said that over three hundred thousand people perished in the flames."

"You and Sandra were the lucky ones then?"

My father nodded. "Indeed, we were."

****

Marceline took a sip of her hot chocolate. It had turned cold. She called the waitress and asked her for a fresh pot. "For the better and for the worse, Africa changed my life," Marceline told Cassandra. Inexplicably, her eyes clouded with tears, and she lowered her gaze, hoping her niece had not noticed. This was such an infuriating aspect of old age: one could forget essential things, but emotions one spent a lifetime keeping at bay could helplessly resurface without warning.

"Perhaps this is a good time to stop," she said. "Maurice will be here momentarily, and I'm feeling a bit wan." This was not the truth. She did not feel tired or weak but profoundly overwhelmed. Now she would have to tell Cassandra about Algiers. About Fernand. About Khaled. About all the events that had precipitated the terrible things that had driven her and Gustave apart.

"How did you recover from the assault?" Cassandra asked.

"The assault?"

"That boy," Cassandra said. "The one in the orchard."

Marceline waved away the question. "There is no point in raging and lamenting about it. What would dwelling on it accomplish?"

"I don't know how people recover from those sorts of things."

"One just does."

"It's that simple?"

The waitress arrived with the fresh pot of hot chocolate and poured the thick liquid into their cups. The rich, velvety aroma rose to their nostrils. Marceline waited for the waitress to leave and asked Cassandra. "Why does it sound as though you are not angry at the rapist, but at me, the victim, for not appearing to suffer enough?"

"Oh no, absolutely not but—"

"Women get on because they have to. Name a woman who was not violated in one form or another."

"I wasn't," Cassie said.

"Perhaps you think that you did something right? That you deserved not to be? Or perhaps you believe that you've earned the right to a peaceful, predictable life? Well, that isn't the case, my dear. You had the good fortune not to cross paths with a predator; that is all."

"I was only saying that you've earned the right to feel sorry for yourself."

"All that does is rob people of their strength." She looked at Cassandra, who appeared distraught. She looked at the doorway. "Maurice is here," she said. "I guess this means nap time for me."

Cassie did not hide her disappointment. "You need to leave? I really was hoping to learn what happened to your family."

"This is *your* family, in fact," Marceline pointed out. "Your ancestors. Your bloodline." Marceline looked at Cassandra. "I have an idea," she said. "Maybe it's time for me to write that memoir, you know. So many good stories, and my fair share of horrible ones."

"Oh, you should definitely do it," Cassie said enthusiastically.

"Perhaps I am too old," Marceline said, shaking her head with apparent discouragement.

"There is really nothing to it. Set an hour every day," Cassandra assured her. "Step by step and day by day. Writing is more about being consistent than anything else."

Marceline marveled briefly at her niece's innocence. "Alas, my eyes and fingers are weak," she said. "Books used to be my greatest joy. Now I must hold a magnifying glass to the page, which is tiresome. My fingers betray me when it comes to turning pages, let alone hold a pen."

"I can see how that would be difficult," Cassie said.

"So, you'll do it then?" Marceline said.

"Do what?"

"Write it down."

"What?"

Marceline rolled her eyes with impatience. "Well, my memoir, evidently."

"But I don't … I … I mean I'm only in Paris for another week.…"

"And so?"

"I don't think you realize, but it would be a momentous undertaking."

"Bah! I tell you the gist of it, you jot it down and find the right words later when you're back in America. How hard can it be? Be consistent is all. You're a writer. Isn't that what writers do?" She sensed that Cassandra was about to try and explain the months, if not years, of work this would entail. But for some reason, Cassie decided not to. Instead, she sighed heavily and shrugged. "Don't you own one of those nifty portable typing machines people have?" Marceline asked.

"A laptop?"

"That's it."

"Mine's in repair."

"So, that's a yes! Wonderful."

"But I …," Cassandra protested feebly.

Maurice was beside them now, helping Marceline out of her chair. How infuriating it was to require help for the slightest things. She pointed to the notepad. "You stay and write down what we just talked about while it's still fresh in your mind. I don't want you forgetting things. You really ought to have recorded our conversation. That would have been the professional thing to do."

"But I – you only asked me today," Cassandra objected. Marceline concealed her smile. What an excellent idea. A memoir. Why had she not thought of it earlier? And now she had the perfect person to do it. "It's settled then. Meet me at the Fontaine Médicis at eight in the morning. Do you know where it is?"

"Inside the Jardin du Luxembourg."

"Correct. You will be punctual, I hope?"

"To a fault."

Marceline gripped Maurice's arm and left Cassie, the tearoom, and the bill without looking back.

CHAPTER 6

A Menagerie

Cassie settled back into her chair. On either side of her, French women, young and old, sipped tea. Marceline had expressed real tenderness toward Gustave. They had both grown up under the menace of war and the looming shadow of the Holocaust, but it seemed like Marceline had enough empathy to paint a clear picture of her dad's unique hardship. Sent away to boarding school because he was conspicuously Jewish, he must have felt rejected by his family and loathed by all of Europe. Cassie could detect in Marceline's account of those years the seeds of resentment, but nothing that could explain a mutual hatred followed by a complete rupture. Something must have occurred. Something ugly.

She ordered a coke and wrote furiously everything she could remember about what Marceline had told her. Three hours later, she put her pen down. Le Valentin was almost empty except for a table with four elderly ladies who giggled like schoolgirls. One of them said something that, if she heard it correctly, included the word penis, and they guffawed.

It was too late for visiting hours now, which conveniently postponed the fight that awaited her at the hospital. She'd have to call Sabine for news.

She left Le Valentin and walked around the covered passage. There were antique booksellers, merchants of old posters and records. How could such a place make money long enough to justify its existence, Cassie wondered? In the United States, a prime retail location such as this one would have been filled with Jamba Juices and nail salons. She stopped in front of a collectible postcards shop, and after a moment, she entered. The place had the mildewed scent of old papers. A man with a Cossack mustache and black sweater vest was sitting behind a counter, looking down at a series of old documents with a magnifying glass. Behind him were rows of wooden shelves, carefully numbered. He lifted his face, in all appearance, none too pleased to have to deal with a customer.

"Do you have anything from the South of France?" she asked.

After a brooding, awkward moment the man barked. "Time period?" She had again forgotten to say bonjour.

"Late 1930s. Before World War II," she said, and hurried to add, "s'il vous plaît, Monsieur."

Grumbling but somewhat pacified, the man got up and pushed a stool up to the shelving. He climbed, reached above him on one of the shelves, and pulled out a box which he placed on the counter in front of her. "Merci!" she trumpeted.

She foraged through the box. The Riviera that Marceline had described came to life between Cassie's fingers, on yellowing postcards heavily stamped: Hôtel Le Negresco, Hôtel Carlton, men and women at the terraces of cafés, smiling for the photographer, palm trees and long antique cars, and little children knee-deep in seawater. She dug through the box, which was well organized by cities and dates: Cannes, Juan Les Pins, Saint-Jean-Cap-Ferrat. This was such a finite number of postcards; thirty of them in the stack she was going through, maybe forty. Was that all that was left of that era? In the future, there would be an infinity of images, now that everyone was a photographer, so many in fact as to render them meaningless. Or perhaps it was the opposite. The pictures we took nowadays were on hard drives that could self-destruct in an instant, as her experience with her cell phone and laptop had proved. But no, she reasoned, digital photos could be recovered. Most were safely stored in The Cloud. The Cloud, whatever that meant. But what if The Cloud was as tenuous as its namesake? An illusion. A delusion, more likely. A single fiber-optic glitch, a satellite hack, and all might vanish in an instant: recordings of and by an entire era of humanity, gone poof! into thin air. Come to think of it, digital photos had even less physical substance than thin air. What were they even made of? Neutrons, atoms, Higgs Bosons particles? She stared at a postcard of three women on a beach in hats and bathing suits, showing some skin and looking playfully at the camera. "How much for that one?" she asked.

"Twenty-five euros."

"Twenty-five euros? For an old postcard?"

"Twenty-five euros for a one-of-a-kind remnant of history, Madame," the shopkeeper answered glacially.

She bought the postcard and left the shop. She walked past more shops selling antique postcards, stamps, posters, and books. She realized that she was thinking about her father. Her father as a small boy. Her father as a young man. Her understanding of him was shifting so rapidly that even her memories seemed altered by what she had learned: her feeling of closeness to him in childhood as well as her sense that he had drifted away from her emotionally as she got older. Her subsequent disappointment and eventual resentment could not be reassessed fast enough. Already, she was losing her old notions of him and would never recover them, which was maybe a positive thing. But in a way, the more she found out about her dad, the more elusive he became. She starved for the real him, but the closer she got to the story, the more secretive she realized he had been, the less she felt she knew him. She longed for her father, for his truth, his voice, his emotion, for a window into the depth and hurt she suspected in him but that he never expressed. What trauma, what pain turned a child into a man so closed-up and protected, so unwilling to tell his story? What made a man turn away from his own sister, his own mother and father? This morning, at her parent's apartment, when she had suggested his past experiences might not have been digested, what she had meant to intimate was the possibility that pathos had affected his relationships. Specifically, his relationship to her. What made a man turn away from his own daughter?

Growing up, she had stuck out like a sore thumb, always. She had been talkative, opinionated, even as she tried to be perfect to gain his approval. Was her craving for his attention a particular turn-off? Her father had called her a know-it-all, a motormouth. He had told her she should not be so bossy, pushy. He had called her *harsh*. Over time, she had learned to smother her exuberant self into something more acceptable, something more lovable. Keeping that bubbly part of her alive had ultimately not felt worth the risk. Adapt, accommodate, or die.

Marceline was *harsh* too. She was bossy to a nearly military level. She was intimidating even in old age. Cassie did everything she could to appear unintimidating. She wanted to be perceived as nice, as accommodating. And if she wasn't feeling so nice or accommodating, she tried to hide it as though it was something shameful. Her anger eventually came out the other end, and she would end up blowing up at the wrong time and making a mess of things.

She headed back to the hotel to face the inevitable. The date or non-date, with Hervé. She would explain to him that she lived in another country. She'd make that clear from the moment he picked her up.

Her stomach churned with anxiety on her way to the métro station as she hurried past the Galeries Lafayette. What would Marceline do, she wondered? Young, fearless Marceline of 1942 seemed no more a slave to convention than old Marceline was. Young Marceline would welcome the adventure in every sense of the word. Young Marceline would say not a single peep about living in another country, and she would most definitely have bought that purple bra.

****

Cassie stepped down from Hervé's motorcycle, steadied her legs, and removed her helmet.

"Your hair is fluffy," Hervé observed.

"Pure music to a woman's ears," she said, loosening the wool scarf he had lent her.

He peered at her. "Are you all right? You're a little green."

"This was my first time on a motorcycle."

"Vraiment? Did you like it?"

"Is hanging on while shutting your eyes the same thing as liking it?"

"I see," he said. "You must be one of those adrenaline junkies."

"Believe me, I have already reached my adrenaline quota for the week."

They had parked in a public garage. On their way up the street, Cassie groaned under her breath as they walked past walls covered with dozens of *Women in Black, Part Two* posters glued side by side. They walked a few more steps and emerged into the street. Outside, it was cold and humid and so quiet that it felt as though she were screaming her thoughts. I'm on a date! With a handsome man! I'm going to lose my lunch!

And there it was again, at the bus stop, a six-feet-tall incarnation, the title in giant red letters this time: *Women in Black, Part Two*. Hervé shook his head at the posters. "What *is* this crap?" he said.

"Beats me," she said.

They crossed the street, and now they were above the quays, facing the Seine. The sun was setting, giving an orange glow to the surrounding buildings. Hervé led her down the stairs and onto the quays. As they walked on the uneven cobblestone, the river's water was just a few feet below, grey and reflecting the orange hues of the sky. "Our reservation is in ten minutes," he said, taking her elbow gallantly. "So, tell me, what is the matter with you?" She looked at him interrogatively. He clarified: "the adrenaline?"

"Where to start. My week was traumatic," she said. "I moved into a crappy hotel thinking I had made a reservation at a much better one."

"It happens."

"To me, mostly. But it's for the best. I was supposed to stay at Hôtel de la Seine, but the people there were awful."

"Ah yes, a friend of mine works there, at the reception desk."

"The mean blonde who comes to the Jument?"

"She's only mean to people she doesn't know."

"Would that not be everyone finding themselves before a reception desk?"

"You have a point."

"People like her are the reason foreigners find French people rude, you know."

He seemed genuinely surprised by this. "Foreigners think French people are rude?"

"Americans do." Cassie had already walked into her own trap. She added, "Supposedly…."

"Americans should know," Hervé said. "They happen to be the world's authority on what is rude and what isn't."

"The hotel where I ended up turned out to be lovely. Once you've climbed the two hundred stairs, you're rewarded with the prettiest view of the Eiffel Tower."

"I'd love to see it."

Under his leather jacket, he wore a sweater that matched his eye color, lagoon blue. "Any time you want," she said glibly.

"Tonight?"

"Of course," she said and regretted that immediately.

"And so, the adrenaline?"

It was not that she intended to *mislead* him about where she lived, but she had this nebulous sense that if he had a shred of interest in her, she wanted to find out. At that moment, she did not feel like pushing him away with something as annoying as the truth. It was an overwhelming impulse not to rock the boat. So, she said nothing about her dad being hospitalized and told him instead how her father had only just admitted that he had a sister, how she had met her, and how she was only now discovering her father's past. "It turns out my grandfather was a Jew from Turkey who came to France after the first war and made quite a bit of money selling rugs. The crazy thing is, my father never told us anything about him, or about growing up wealthy, let alone Jewish. This is all brand new to me."

"When was your father born?"

"1925."

Hervé made a quick mental calculation. "Let see. He must have been fourteen when World War Two started. How did his family survive the Holocaust?"

Cassie felt a chill, a sense of dread. Why had this never gone through her mind? "They went to the South of France?" she said, involuntarily making her sentence sound like a question.

"How would that protect them? Jews were no safer in the free zone, especially after 1942 when Germany changed its mind and rolled their tanks right over it. At that point, the Jews of the South of France were rounded up and sent to death camps, just as terribly as anywhere else throughout most of Europe."

"Apparently, they were able to go to North Africa. I'll know more tomorrow. She's agreed to meet every day until I have the full story."

"It must be a pretty long story."

"She goes into details. And we have to cut it into chunks. She's very old."

"And you don't want to ask your dad, rather than get the information second-hand from his sister?"

Well, there *was* the coma thing. "He refuses to speak about it," she said, which was not a lie. "He went about his life without telling us a thing."

"What is he like?"

"Worked dutifully all his adult life, but not a day past retirement. He raised three daughters, kept the same wife."

"Is that all there is to say about him?"

"He's not a chatterbox, but he's a decent man. He doesn't have a big ego. He is quiet. He is nice enough to people." As she said this, she realized that this was actually true. And so, what sick point was there in her looking for anything else, especially now, if he had indeed survived the Holocaust? So what if he was not the warmest to her? A part of him was damaged or unresolved, that was all. How many people turned into a mess after far less than that? "I would think that he was intent on rebuilding and forgetting," she said. "He didn't dwell."

They arrived at the restaurant, which was at the level of the river. They were given a table that overlooked the Seine and Paris in the setting sun. They looked at the river in silence. There was music in the background, a woman's voice singing "Le Tourbillon de la Vie." The waiter came in, and they ordered each a glass of wine.

"So, what about you?" she asked.

"What about me?"

"For one, I have to ask how come you spend so much time at the Jument."

"I work close by, and I go there to cool off when I can't stand my job, which is increasingly often."

"You said the other day that your life was complicated?"

"I have recently ended a two-year relationship, yes."

"With a woman?" she asked.

He shrugged questioningly. "As opposed to what? A possum?" He looked at her. She quickly looked away. He scowled. "You don't think I'm gay, do you?"

She swallowed. "Do *I* think you're gay?"

"You obviously think I am," he said.

"Not at all. Absolutely not!"

He frowned. "Is that why you accepted to go out with me tonight?"

"Why would I accept to go out with you if I thought you were gay?" she said breezily. "Because it would feel *safer* or something?"

"Well. Good," he said, looking upset.

"You don't give out a gay vibe whatsoever."

"I knew I shouldn't have worn this stupid cologne."

"I assure you—"

"Okay, fine, fine."

"So, tell me about your work," she said, desperate to change the subject.

"I am not my job," he said glumly. "It does not define me, my dreams, or even my daily thoughts."

"Have I offended you twice in thirty seconds?"

"I'm a physician. Was. I made a few choices that cost me my license for five years."

"Such as?"

"Nothing I would not do again in a heartbeat. It's all very noble you see. I was on a mission for Doctors Without Borders and, well, I saw a need, a need for vaccines. But there was red tape. So, I took it upon myself to smuggle them into the country."

"Yikes."

"Another year and my license will be returned to me."

"What will you do then?"

"Probably get in trouble again."

"You're lucky they didn't put you in jail."

"Oh, but they did worse: they put me in charge. That was a pact with the devil if I ever heard of one. Now I work in administration. All I do is administrate. I don't like the people I work for, the people I work with, or the people I work around."

"Why not quit?"

"That is the irony. My marriage was ruined because my ex-wife resented the fact that I traveled too much. She begged me for years to take a position that would keep me in Paris. Apparently, she wanted an actual marriage, a man able to be a parent to our kids. I would have none of it. I needed to feel free, if you know what I mean. I do give her credit: she put up with my beautiful idealism for quite a long time. But in the end, she left. Met someone. The kids were still young enough that my taking a desk job ultimately was better for them. Interesting to note that I'm now the embodiment of the perfect man, with the type of desk job she always wanted me to have. But, you see, back then I could not be fenced in."

"And now?"

"Now I'm fenced in."

"It doesn't seem worth it, spending all those hours doing something you loathe."

"I've become quite philosophical about it. How about you, your writing work, do you like it?"

"I made my own pact with the devil. I work with my ex. We've been divorced for years. But yes, I like my work."

"You're both ghostwriters?"

She laughed. "Hard to explain, but let's say he's the writer and I'm the ghost. Well, I'm his 'editor' according to the divorce settlement. I guess it would be more accurate to say that I like *his* work. I'm good at it."

"Do the two of you get along?"

"We used to bicker like a couple, and now we bicker like a brother and sister."

"What kind of writing do you do?"

How could she tell him about the screenplays without telling him she was American, living in California? "Oh well, things here and there. That kind of stuff...." Just as she said this, a huge billboard of the movie floated by on a specially chartered péniche. When the studio decided to put its back into a promotional event, it was shameless. Nothing was off limits, not even the Seine River, not the sky, not the moon. "But work does not define who we are, does it?" she said, eager to bring this conversation to a close. "By the way, the Jument's patronne said you don't have a cell phone? Is that true?"

"You tried to call me? To cancel, I bet."

Was she going to insult him again? "Not at all," she said, bringing her list of lies to a stratospheric height. "So, why no cell phone?"

"Do you remember ever needing one before those were invented?"

"No, but—"

"Me neither. I have not felt the need to join in the madness since."

"How Zen of you. I've been feeling crazy in the head ever since mine broke."

"Of course, you do. Our society has an addiction to convenience. After a few days of pain and withdrawal, you might find that you get on better without one."

"I doubt that. No one can reach me; I can't reach anybody."

"Perfect. Technology shackles you, and now you are set free. Allow some time for re-insertion into sanity. But notice how freeing it is not to have to give everyone a minute-by-minute account of your whereabouts. Also, you no longer have to interrupt your train of thought constantly and substitute your thinking with theirs."

"Although it's nice to stay connected, don't you think?"

"What connection? Only sound bites. Noise. Faux relationships. Heavily curated faux experiences that slowly turn our species into subhumans."

"I guess I better not ask you how you feel about social media."

"Just the fact that those two words were put together without irony whatsoever should raise some red flag."

"All right. But cell phones aren't that bad. Of all the evils of society, cell phones don't top the list."

"Quite the opposite; evil is precisely what cell phones are. Evil in a sleek metal suit that fits into the palm of your hand. Nobody is where they are, you see. People might be with you in one spot, but they are also carrying on all kinds of emotional and intellectual relationships in another spot."

"Hmm ...," she said, unconvinced.

"Look, you're having an experience, you're at dinner with a very polite gentleman, and suddenly you get that buzz in your pocket, and it's your ghost husband telling you to pick up some ectoplasm on your way home. Now your mind and attention have been hijacked into being subjected to the caller's experience. And there is no running away."

"You can run away. Just don't answer. We have free will."

"Was there free will when we rushed to purchase the phones, like sheep? And there is no such thing as not answering, by the way. Everyone always answers. They're addicted to that. And as soon as we pick up that call, or answer that text, or check out that notification, we forget where we are. We forget with whom we are. We shift our focus to where we aren't and who we aren't with. Reality disappears. The moment is missed. That ringing is like a jolt, a reminder that we do not belong to ourselves. The devil's way of keeping us on a tight leash."

"Okay …," she said, trying not to smile at how passionate he was about the whole thing.

"For example," he insisted, "had your cell worked, would we have met?"

"I don't see why not."

"You would have been head down, developing sciatica and carpal tunnel typing on one of those tiny keyboards. Or someone would have called you: that ghost ex-husband of yours. You might have rushed across town to help him perhaps. Only once there, you would have found him on his phone carrying on a conversation with yet another person."

"You might have a point."

"Also, would you have stayed at the Jument, waiting for a call."

"How did you know I was receiving phone calls at the Jument?"

"I asked."

"What did you ask exactly? And who answered?"

"I asked the patronne why an unknown woman was being given my table, and why she seemed to be there at all hours. The patronne responded that you were waiting for calls because you didn't have a cell phone either. She saw it as a sign that the two of us were meant for each other."

Cassie laughed. "Doesn't she think that relationships should be based on more solid ground?"

"They rarely are." He looked at her, and she felt herself blush. A few days ago, she was slashing through bougainvilleas like an unhinged jungle woman, and tonight she sat at a beautiful Parisian restaurant at sunset across from a charming man. "Why don't you get a new telephone if you love them so much?" he asked.

"Mine is in repair," she lied.

She ordered a sole meunière, and he asked for a lotte au fenouil. He chose the wine, a Meursault, and they watched in silence as boats glided along the Seine, illuminating the façade of buildings. Down on the quay, lovers walked hand in hand. She found it hard to look at him as she tried to calm her thoughts.

"Why don't you tell me your story," Hervé said.

"I have a story?"

"You arrive out of nowhere. You move into a hotel. No computer, no telephone, not even paper to write on. Like you've been picked clean. What happened?"

He wasn't being nosy she could tell. He was giving her the opportunity to unburden herself. She felt a slight tightening of the throat. Picked clean. Yes, that was exactly how she felt. She took in a breath and dared say it: "I'll give you the short version. My son and daughter have left the nest. My ex is remarried, with little kids and a baby on the way. The fuller all of their lives get, the emptier mine feels. Meanwhile, I'm in this horrible fight with my parents and at least one of my sisters over some old gripes." Of course, there was all that she was leaving out. Not lying exactly, but omitting.

"What's your ex like?" Hervé asked.

"Warm and friendly, at least on the surface. Likable, but self-serving. Selfish for the most part."

"What animal would he be?"

She halted her fork in mid-air. "What do you mean?"

"You know, like you: you would be a cat."

"Me? A cat?"

He looked at her intently. "Your eyes are yellow like a cat."

"I prefer gold if you don't mind."

"And you have a funny way to eat, with little bites, where you bring your fork up to your mouth and lap it up really fast."

Cassie looked at her plate, her fork. "I did not know that about myself." She thought about Peter as an animal. "He would be a fox, quick and calculating. I always wonder what he wants from me. If there is an agenda. I get bogged down by his small offenses and can't always see the forest for the tree. Same with my father. I feel that there is a bigger picture. Something I must have missed."

"What kind of animal?" Hervé asked.

"Uh?"

"Your dad."

She thought about it. How inscrutable her dad was. "I guess, an owl would do."

"And your mother and sister?"

Cassie made a rodent face. "A wallowing wombat and a honey badger."

He laughed. "You're getting good at this. See, now I can picture them perfectly. And me? What animal?" he asked.

"I don't know you well enough to tell."

He changed the subject. "What does your family reproach you?"

"I dig, I ask questions. They consider it a betrayal that I am getting to know my aunt. They punch. I counterpunch. I'm reactive. They're intense. They push me away; I set their house on fire." Hervé raised an interrogative eyebrow. "A mishap in the kitchen," she explained. "You'd be amazed at the inordinate number of things and relationships I've bungled in the last few days."

"Is that why you moved into a hotel? A bungled relationship?"

She was circling around her lies. But if she told him the truth, why she was here, for how long, would he lose interest? She did not want him to lose interest. "What about you?" she asked. "What about that complicated home life of yours?"

Hervé shook his head. "I love women, don't get me wrong...." His voice trailed off.

Cassie laughed. "You know that is a terrible pickup line."

He smiled. "Maybe I'm getting older. I don't need the validation the way I used to. And the chase, well that's exhausting. Often it's more trouble than it's worth."

She had no idea where he was going with this. All this candidness unnerved her. "I'm curious. What usually happens when you have to explain to a woman that you can't give away your cell number because you don't own one?"

"Usually, she thinks I'm lying."

"And then you give a lengthy explanation about the devil and his leash."

"And she runs the other way."

"She thinks you're trying to get rid of her."

"And she would be correct about that."

Cassie stepped back mentally. She was sitting in an incredibly romantic restaurant in an incredibly romantic city across from a very seductive man. She had many conflicting emotions to reconcile, and she was in no shape to reconcile anything. The key now was to calm the hell down, appear cool and collected, whatever that looked like. She changed the subject. "Your notebook has come in handy. My newfound aunt asked me to take notes as she is telling me our family's history. I wrote for two hours this morning, with a pen, mind you. It was exhausting. I'm so used to typing."

"Exactly! We've come to rely on technology so much that we're devolving."

"I prefer to devolve."

"You can't even write using your hands without risking physical exhaustion. That should tell you something."

"You certainly have unique ideas about things."

"More of a life's philosophy," Hervé said. "And you must be thinking, a man with a life's philosophy most likely makes little room for someone else's." He smiled an apologetic smile. "But I am consistently amending it."

Chill, she told herself. This is just a dinner. "So, what are the latest amendments?"

"I've been dabbling in simplicity," he said. "You know, slowing down, using less. Needing less."

"No electronics?"

"It goes beyond that. But I'm still figuring it out. Take coffee for example. People buy complicated machines to brew coffee. But would you not agree that it's better to put expensive coffee in a ten-euro coffee maker than cheap coffee in a thousand-euro machine?"

"I ... guess."

"And pasta. People buy pasta already made; this is madness. All you need to make pasta is flour and water and eggs."

"And time."

He lifted his finger. "And time!" he declared. "That is the true currency. People with money are those who miss out the most. They delegate all that is fun for someone else to do. They pay someone to walk their dogs, to take care of their children, to drive their cars, to wash their hair."

"Wash their hair? Come on...."

"How many hair salons do you count on a single street?"

She laughed. "Touché."

They were interrupted by the arrival of their plates. Outside, the city's monuments were lit up. "The rich pay people to cook their food," Hervé continued, unfolding his napkin and setting it on his lap. "I'm surprised they have not found people to eat their food for them."

"That's a fantastic business idea."

"Or at least to chew it for them."

"That already exists," she assured him. "It's called purée."

"Speaking of which!" Hervé foraged in his pockets and retrieved a tiny bottle of ketchup. "This is for you."

She turned the bottle between her fingers, touched that he had thought of it, touched that he had gone out of his way for her. "They're not going to kick me out of this restaurant for drenching their fancy food in ketchup?"

"You'll have to do it when the waiter's back is turned. As a matter of fact, even eggs are optional."

"Eggs?"

"In pasta-making. Would you like to make fresh pasta together one day?"

"*You* can make pasta, and I can watch you do it," she said.

As night fell over the river, they spoke about their children, about what it was like to be parents, about marriage and divorce, about their exes, about books and music. Hervé was interested in everything and jumped from science to psychology to art. Not in a pedantic way, but with child-like enthusiasm and curiosity. By the time dessert came, Cassie was picking the crunchy caramel off his île flottante, and he had his fork in her chocolate cake. "I hope you don't think I'm selfish," he said out of nowhere.

"Selfish?"

"The whole table debacle – I must apologize about that – And having a life philosophy. The fact that I don't want people to interrupt my precious thinking with phone calls. I worry it all makes me appear self-centered."

"You don't fit the profile of the selfish person."

"What profile is that?"

"The little bottle of ketchup, the notebook, the scarf you brought because I might get cold on the ride here. You anticipated my need."

"There must be a different definition of selfish then because I clearly recollect being called that by quite a few women."

As the dinner progressed, she forgot to be self-conscious. There was a masculine earthiness to him, something genuine, and gruff. No mind games. He was at the same time eager to please, and terrible at altering himself to be liked. He was intelligent, educated, and attentive but had an uncomplicated straightforwardness that was unexpected, unsettling even. Peter was a charmer, someone who would manipulate you into what he wanted, and you could not even be mad at him once you realized you had been manipulated. Hervé was charming not because he tried to be, but almost in spite of himself.

On the way back, the thunderous roar of Hervé's motorcycle vibrated up her spine. She opened her eyes this time, because now — and the delicious Meursault was partly to thank for this — she was in the moment and did not want to miss an instant of it. Hervé rode steadily this time, mindful of her comfort. Paris was all glittering lights and sumptuous architecture as they rode along the Quay des Tuileries, passing the Musée de l'Orangerie, the Louvre, and the Pont Neuf, veering left at l'Île de la Cité and then up Boulevard de Sébastopol. Each turn of the wheels drained her mind of thoughts. She did not feel the cold and drizzle. It was as though she were sitting on a carousel of colors and lights. She pressed herself against Hervé's back, wrapped her arms around him, and let Paris unfold around them.

At the foot of her hotel, she hopped off the motorcycle, composed the grin on her face into something dignified, removed the helmet he had brought for her, unwrapped his scarf from around her neck, and handed it to him. "Keep the scarf," he said as he turned off the engine, removed his helmet, and hopped off his motorcycle. "For next time."

Next time? "If you were an animal, I think you'd be a bear," she said.

"A bear?"

"A bear likes his little habits. He likes his alone time, in his cave, making egg-less pasta and good coffee in lousy pots."

He thought about it and nodded. "I do like honey. Although I've had terrible luck catching salmon upstream with my bare claws."

"I'm not judging you. I'm increasingly turning into a bear myself."

"Thank goodness you don't smell like one," he said, stepping closer and leaning toward her cheek sniffing in a bear-like fashion. "You smell very good." He sniffed some more, along her cheek and then silently, as she froze in wonderment, her neck.

"It's the coat," she said, flustered. "I think there must have been lavender sachets in the pockets or something."

He shook his head. "It's not lavender."

"What is it?"

"Bear men lack the vocabulary to describe."

She too had noticed his scent, an amalgam of unknown things: cologne, leather, pipe tobacco, diesel fuel, and a mysterious something else. Something that made her want to burrow her face in his neck. "Well, thank you so much for dinner," she said. But to her dismay, Hervé was busy moving the motorcycle to the sidewalk. What is he doing? He rolled the heavy machine closer to the bus stop where a light box was shining with a poster of *Women in Back, Part Two*, like her good fairy's bitchy way of reminding her that this moment was an aberration and not her actual life. Hervé nodded in the direction of the film poster. "This merde is everywhere," he noted.

He crouched to lock the motorcycle. "You … are you parking your bike?" she asked. There was perhaps a hint of panic in her voice.

He lifted his head above the seat and raised an eyebrow. "You invited me to see the view, remember?"

"But that was when you were gay!"

He laughed, a contagious, unbridled laugh. "Is the Eiffel Tower canceled over such a trivial detail?"

"I can't even offer you a drink," she said. "The only liquid I have up there is a bottle of Scope." *Oops,* she through. In her manic attempts at deflecting her panic with humor, she had put her foot in it: French people didn't know what Scope was. It was an American product: an invented American need. What else was scattered around the room that would give away that teeny-tiny white lie large enough to fit fifty states? She needed to tell him that he could not, absolutely not, come up to her room. View of the Eiffel Tower or not.

And that was when she realized that there was no way in hell she was going up without him. She wanted him to come up to her room more than she remembered wanting anything else in her life. "I'm warning you," she said, in a voice she did not even recognize as her own, "my room's way up, and no elevator."

He followed her inside the hotel. The old hotelier wasn't there. She began up the stairs with Hervé following. Halfway up the first set of stairs, realizing that she'd rather not have him stare at her butt for five sets of stairs she stopped and said, "Would you mind climbing ahead of me?"

"Are there ghouls hiding in the recesses of the stairwell?" Hervé asked.

When they arrived at her door, he doubled over to catch his breath and looked at her. "Either I'm totally out of shape, or you're a triathlon athlete."

"I just do a lot of laundry," she said. "It keeps me fit." Maybe she had not lost her breath, but her heart pounded loud enough to be heard from another arrondissement. They entered the room, and she turned on the light. Hervé looked around. "That's rare, a hotel that has not been remodeled to look generic." He pointed to Jessica's four little packages, which were still on the bed. "Isn't it early for Christmas?"

"Ha, those," she said. "They're gifts for my parents and sisters. They're not from me. They're from my ex-husband's new wife. I don't know why she is giving them anything, come to think of it."

Hervé picked up one of the packages, held it between two fingers, and made a disgusted grimace. "They're horrible."

"What are you saying? They're adorable. You don't like bows and glitter."

"I mistrust a gift that is too well wrapped. Good presents come in ugly packages."

"You do have theories about everything."

"This wrapping forces you to fuss much more about the gifts than the gifts deserve. The person guilty of this wrapping job is a phony. And where does she get off sucking up to your family at a time you're struggling with them?"

"You might be reading too much into this."

"Well, I don't know how you can stand to look at them."

Cassie stared at the four glittery boxes. "I *can't* stand to look at them," she admitted. "They're reminders of all my failures."

"Well, I think that was precisely her objective," Hervé said.

She looked at him. "I'm not even sure why you're here," she mumbled.

"I'm here for the view. And to try a glass of that Scope you told me about. It's that liquor from Norway made with gooseberries, right?"

"Scope? I, hmm … I don't think you'd enjoy it."

She opened the French window, and they stepped outside on the balcony. The Eiffel Tower sparkled and shimmered. They looked in silence, leaning over the balustrade. If the air was cold, she wasn't feeling it.

"Beautiful, isn't it?" she asked in a small voice.

"Mesmerizing," he said. She felt his eyes on her. She did not dare to turn to look at him. By now her heartbeat was thunderous, and her entire body was on high alert. He came closer to her, leaned, and ever so slowly went to kiss her. For one second, she wondered what in the world was happening, the next, she was melting into his kiss, and he had his arms around her.

Now they were not on the balcony, somehow, but on her bed. Jessica's presents had been kicked off to the floor; her coat was off, and so was his jacket, and he was brushing his lips up and down her neck, moving down her clavicle and sending shivers of expectation through her body. "I am not …," she muttered. "I did not think—"

He kissed her lips. "I have condoms," he said.

"No, I mean, I can't … I don't—"

"Do you want me to leave?" he whispered, still kissing her. "I'll leave. I'm a gentleman."

"You did climb so many sets of stairs …," she said, breathless.

"If you ask me to leave, I'll go. No need for stairs. I'll throw myself out the window." Saying this, he kissed her again, and her body turned to mush.

He made love to her in the most luscious ways. She was hungry for this. Hungry for him. She had a hunger in her she did not know possible.

Later, they rested side by side, naked in bed, her head on his chest, her brain incapable of a single thought. How easy this all was. How simple. A one-night stand. Just like a grown-up. How wonderful.

"You really were only going to show me the view," he said.

"I told you I was."

"Now I believe you."

"Why?"

"Your panties."

"What about them?"

"My granny would not wear those. A woman who did not mean it about the view would have worn pretty lingerie. That's how I know."

She opened her mouth, and then closed it, speechless. Then she said, "I am speechless."

"It proves my point that the best gifts don't come in the best packages."

"Hmm ... I'm not sure if this is a compliment or...."

He lifted himself on his elbow and looked at her. He caressed her body with a finger. "It's very much a compliment."

"Well, I'm pretty certain you did not come up just to see the view."

"How did you guess? My underwear was mute as to my intentions."

"But not your jeans pockets, which were filled to the brim with condoms."

"I have no idea how they got there," he said, kissing her stomach. Then he lifted her like a rag doll and moved her on top of him.

CHAPTER 7

The Refugee

There had been so much Lucienne needed her to organize at the Cannes house that it was an entire month before Xandra was allowed a day off. War was brewing, of that Moshe and Albano were convinced. They had liquidated their assets, sold the business, opened bank accounts in Switzerland. Moshe had left Paris and gone directly to Algiers. Albano thought that the South of France would be less traumatic on Lucienne.

So now, without Moshe's apartment to meet at on Sundays, he and Xandra needed to find other ways to see each other in private.

Albano told Lucienne that he had business to tend to in Nice and that he'd drop off Sandra in town. Instead, he and Xandra were now driving in the direction of Théoule-sur-Mer, and then to Fréjus, where he had a plan for them to spend the day.

It was the last Sunday of May 1939. The tourist season was near, but for now, the roads and villages still had the quietness of wintertime. The cold winds had all but subsided. With each passing day, the sun shone longer and warmer, and the smells and feel of the air resembled Smyrna's climate a little bit more. Across the Côte d'Azur, roses bloomed in every garden, birds chirped, and cicadas began their vibrating songs. The inexorable descent into another worldwide war, the uncertainty, the fear, the folly of men had no effect whatever on nature. As he drove, Albano watched Xandra from the corner of his eye. She was sitting very straight and nervous, so he took her hand. She smiled. In the South of France, they knew no one. All they needed to do was to drive a few miles from the house to experience freedom. And so, today they would authorize themselves some happiness. They drove following the coast along the jagged volcanic cliffs that plunged into the foam of the sea, past the coves and beaches, and the twisted pines shaped by the mistral, the tree roots that clung powerfully to the red earth. They drove past small restaurants by the sea, and medieval towns, and harbors filled with boats. In Agay, they parked the automobile in the street and, for the very first time since they had met as children, Xandra and Albano were able to sit on the terrace of a restaurant, together in plain sight.

It was as though by leaving Paris they had flown away from judgment and even from their own limitations. He was thirty-seven years old, and so was Xandra, but they were giddy like children at the novelty of sitting across from each other at a restaurant table, their forearms resting on the red-and-white checkered tablecloth, their fingers entwined. After lunch, they walked down to the cove and stepped on the empty beach. They found a nook under the shade of pine trees and set a blanket on the sand. They lay down on the blanket and looked up at the white clouds in the azure sky. Before them was the Mediterranean Sea. Behind them, as if standing guard to protect them, was the bright red Massif de L'Estérel. They spoke about Marceline and Gustave as if they were the children they had had together, expressing pride and concern the way loving parents would. When Albano and Lucienne spoke of the children, it was usually about logistics, the need for money to tend to this or that, or informing each other about a new tutor or some event that needed attending. Xandra told him of little things, a funny comment that one of the children had said, a good grade, or even something sad she had noticed. Xandra sat in the sand and Albano lay on his back, his head on her lap. She was passing her fingers through his hair when he announced, "Marceline is growing up!"

"And you only see this now, my love? She is sixteen years old and has been a young lady for quite some time."

"Men look at her," Albano said worriedly. "Why do men have any business looking at my daughter? It will be good for her to be away from Paris. With all the distractions of the city, the silly functions her mother organizes for her."

"You know how Marceline thrives on being active and meeting people. It is isolated up at La Bastide. She can't walk into the streets the way she could in Paris."

Albano shrugged. "And so, she must learn to do without."

"A young woman her age wants romance."

"And should not get it! I see no need to anticipate such a thing."

"You might have to. So that you can prepare."

"If there is something she is unhappy about, she will tell us. Marceline is a practical person. In fact, I wish Gustave were as easy to understand."

"Are you concerned about him?"

"If only he told me how he felt," Albano said, "I could give him guidance. But since he doesn't, the advice I give him feels awkward or unwelcome."

"Continue to speak to him. Do not mistake his quietness for a desire to be left alone," Xandra said.

"I have been preoccupied the last few years, with our business, and with preparing to come here, and looking for Hagop, and seeing you on Sundays, and with all the things Moshe and I plan to do if the war comes."

"You have more time now. Maybe you should spend it with Gustave."

"I might have lost his trust by sending him to boarding school. I listened to his mother again and again, about the boxing, and boarding school, when I should have listened to you. Gustave has suffered. I do not want him feeling fearful and untrusting toward the world, no matter how treacherous it has become."

"But he has also watched you be a loving father and a capable man, and he will, in turn, know how to become a wonderful man. He is a good boy, a big-hearted boy who wants to please you and impress you."

Albano sat up. "This is what I shall do! I shall make time for him. I shall strive to become a better father."

"Only make sure Marceline isn't left out."

"I do not worry about Marceline. When she needs attention, she knows how to ask for it."

"And what about Lucienne?" Xandra asked quietly. "Should we not worry about her?"

Albano tensed up. "This is such a beautiful day. Must we spoil it?" He seldom wanted to discuss Lucienne, as though she were a permanent houseguest, a relative whose presence one must endure.

Xandra looked at her fingers and pursed her lips. "We must discuss her at some point."

Albano sighed. There was no subject he could avoid if Xandra had her heart set on bringing it up. "All right then, what of her?"

"Her entire life has changed, Albano. The politics in Paris, the alienation from her social circle, and leaving her home to come here against her wishes—"

Albano interrupted. "It is hard for me to feel empathy for her when she has so little for you."

"She suffers that you do not tend to her happiness."

"When Paris is under attack, she will come to her senses and see that all I ever intended was to save her."

"She senses our closeness."

"I doubt she does. She lives in a world of her own."

"When you brought me here, you proved to her what she suspected: that you cared about my well-being. And at the same time, she feels that you do not care for hers."

"And so, what choice do I have?" Albano said, agitated. "With all that is happening and the threat of war, divorcing her is out of the question, even if you finally allowed it. I could never leave the mother of my children to fend for herself now. It's too late; I missed my chance. I should have asked her for a divorce the very day you returned. Perhaps she would have understood then. And she was still young. She could have remarried. But now, after nine years of your living with us, it would be just terrible." Albano closed his eyes and shook his head. "I don't want to think of all the mistakes I've made."

"We made a choice that kept your family intact," Xandra said. "We did the right thing."

"And so, given the circumstances, I am taking care of her the best I can. I treat her kindly. I give her all she desires."

"Except for your love, Albano. None of this is Lucienne's fault," Xandra said, and the fact that she used Lucienne's name turned her into a full human being, with feelings and wounds. "The French turning on the Jews is not her fault. Neither is our story or the feelings you cannot have for her. She is hurt and does not deserve to be. Lucienne is not well. The way she holds her body, her new way of stooping, or sitting in a chair and not speaking, and the way she looks at the horizon without really seeing. She is troubled and sad, and the children are impatient with her."

"How can you be so kind, so empathetic, when Lucienne has done nothing to deserve it?" He took her hand and kissed it. "What am I to do to make you happy? Tell me, and I will do it."

"If you cannot see her as your wife, then perhaps you should see her as one of the children. She is a little girl again. She is sad and needs your care."

Albano sat up and kissed Xandra on the mouth in broad daylight, and they both laughed at the novelty of this. "And so, it is that you and I are raising yet another child together," he said.

****

The letter addressed to Albano bore the stamp of the Red Cross refugee camp in Aleppo Syria. It had been sent to the house in Paris and then forwarded to La Bastide. Xandra was the one who took the mail from the postman and turned it back and forth between her fingers. The letter had been mailed from Syria a full month ago. She hid it in her pocket and waited all day for Albano to return. He opened it and read it.

Dear Mr. Cohen Lombardi,

We think we have found the person you have been looking for. As the old refugee camps are dismantled, we're able to conduct a more thorough survey of each camp's population. The chief humanitarian preoccupation of the League of Nations' workers in the field has been the children. Adults can often be more elusive to identify, especially when there are no known relatives, or they do not come forward. Our research indicates that an individual responding to the name of Hagop Katsukyan might still be living in proximity to the camp. It is unclear if the individual is of sound mind, but he appears relatively healthy. Records show that he arrived at the camp around the dates you mentioned. He appears to be about the correct age, although he says he does not remember how old he is. We have attached a photograph. Please advise if this person might be the relative in question. In the hope of hearing from you soon to resolve the matter.

Salutations,

Mlle. Durant, Secretary of Mr. Pontou
Office of the Red Cross
Aleppo, Syria

The photograph was of a frail, stooping, bearded man wrapped in something that resembled a frayed blanket. He was barefoot in galoshes, and his ankles appeared swollen and covered in scabs. How could this old man be Hagop? No. It was impossible. But there was something so familiar in the man's stance. Those eyes, defiantly staring at the camera. The mouth. The striking resemblance to Xandra. Albano was so shaken that he nearly dropped the picture. Hagop! Was it really him? Albano realized he had been holding his breath, and a warm feeling enveloped him. He had to be sure. He could not let Xandra hope. But she was waiting on the other side of the door, and he would have to tell her the truth.

When he handed her the photograph, she stared at the man and made the sign of the cross. "It is him," she said gravely. "My brother is alive!"

The next few months were a whirlwind during which worries of an impending war with Germany were eclipsed by the efforts put in place to rescue Hagop. Albano hired a man who spoke Armenian to find Hagop in Aleppo with instructions to locate him inside the refugee camp, facilitate his departure out of Syria, and secure his safe passage to France. The man, Monsieur Perrin, a broad Alsatian in his sixties, was a retired official from the League of Nations who came highly recommended and would not be intimidated by the task at hand.

Upon finding Hagop, Monsieur Perrin had described him in his letter as reluctant to communicate, covered in vermin and scabs, dressed in rags, and grossly underfed. Such were the conditions of the encampment where so many other Armenian refugees languished. With Albano's instructions via telegraph, the man had taken Hagop to a doctor to be deloused and given medication for his various ailments. He was also put up in a decent hotel room and was bathed, fed, and clothed. According to Monsieur Perrin, Hagop hardly spoke but was amenable. He had accepted to be taken out of the country and showed deep gratitude at the things presently offered to him. He had suffered trauma to be sure and appeared confused and disoriented at times, but he was responding well to being cared for. His appetite was excellent, and already he had regained a few kilos.

More telegraphs were exchanged. Monsieur Perrin helped procure the necessary papers. It took months to obtain consent from the French government, but, finally, Albano had procured an authorization for a temporary visa. Eager to avoid a perilous journey across Europe where conflicts were making the crossing of borders uncertain, Monsieur Perrin suggested that he would bring Hagop to France on a specially chartered boat.

The ship would sail across the Mediterranean, leaving the Syrian coast to reach Cyprus, with stops in Malta and Corsica, and at last, arrive in Nice.

In September 1939, six months after Albano and his family had left Paris, France declared war on Germany. Borders began closing one by one. In November, Hagop was on a boat making its way to the southern coast of France.

On the day of Hagop's arrival, Albano paced the length of Nice's harbor with tremendous excitement, but also something else. As he peered at the horizon for the chartered boat, an emotion he had pushed aside until that moment surfaced. Facilitating Hagop's exit out of Syria had been of all-consuming complexity, but now, walking up and down the harbor, a conversation with Xandra, one he had dismissed at the time, nagged at him. When they first learned that Hagop was alive, Albano had instantly made up his mind to bring him to France. "Hagop's struggle will end," he had told her. "It will be a wonderful thing to bring him here. His life will be changed."

But Xandra had said, "I wonder how it might affect us."

"What do you mean?"

"I wonder what kind of man he is now."

"What kind of man would he be?"

"He was taken in 1919, never to be heard from or seen. Twenty years have passed."

"And what do you suggest we do?" Albano had teased her, "leave him to rot in a refugee camp when I have the financial means and the wherewithal to rescue him?"

"What will you tell him about us?"

"There is nothing to tell him. We are doing nothing wrong. We have only to make sure he does not tell Lucienne that you and I knew each other before we came to France."

"But will he listen?"

"He will. We are rescuing him. He will be in our debt."

At first, Albano had planned on Hagop's living with them at La Bastide, at least until he was healthy and could find work and begin his own life. But Xandra had warned him against it. "Before you let him meet the children, you must be certain that he is who he says he is, and that he is of sound mind and a positive mindset toward us."

To soothe Xandra, Albano had rented a room with a view at Le Negresco hôtel and arranged every detail: fresh flowers, plenty of towels, iced champagne, and food to be brought the minute Hagop arrived. Xandra would not be there. As much as she wanted to see her brother, she said she preferred to wait a few days. The closer to Hagop's arrival, the more anxious she had been. Albano's happiness could barely be contained. He remembered so vividly the day when Moshe had rescued him in Marseille when he was sick of body and soul. When all hope was lost, Moshe had been his guardian angel. Through patience, support, and good humor, he had offered him a key to a new life and given him a future. Now, and the thought thrilled him, Albano was about to do the same for Hagop!

They predicted a harsh winter throughout Europe. But the Mediterranean climate, the sea, the pier, the palm trees would, he hoped, make Hagop feel more at home.

Standing in the chilly November wind, which could be cutting even in the South of France, Albano watched French soldiers walk by. It was possible to think himself back in 1914 on Smyrna's quayside when he and Hagop had watched soldiers from every nation, mobilized for war, gather on the dock to return to their respective countries. The French soldiers were dressed in khaki color instead of indigo as they had in the last war. But in other ways, the French uniform appeared recycled from the Great War: the suspenders, the belts, the laced boots designed for trench warfare, the golf pants, the haversacks, the standard Adrian helmet, even the Lebel rifles looked as though they were taken out of mildewed storage bins. The German army, in comparison, seemed to be marching in from the future with modern weapons, well-cut uniforms, and a steely discipline that was frightening to witness.

For now, his family would not see any of this. Albano's infirmity made him unfit for combat. As for Gustave, he was only fourteen, young enough that he might avoid combat altogether if the war was short-lived. Albano forced himself not to think of it. There was no point in worrying about things he had no control over. What he needed to focus on were the things he could control. He and Moshe were making plans, not only for themselves but with larger context in mind. Their plan was broader than their temporary safety. Germany had to be stopped, or else there would soon be no safe place in Europe for Jews. He and Moshe were operating from the standpoint of a worst-case scenario. A military defeat. If this happened, there would be an underground popular movement. The time to plan and put things in place was now while they were free to roam and communicate, when borders were still porous, when railroads and telephone lines were up and running, when the news was still mostly uncensored. And this was what they were doing, through a network of connections. They were creating a matrix of communication. There were codes, routes, fields for drop-offs, banks to channel monies, houses for hiding and gathering. For the last few years, he had felt the frustration of not succeeding in warning others to prepare. It was as though his personal experience was useless to others. What he had seen happen in Smyrna could take place anywhere. He recognized the signs. He recognized the discourse. This war would not be like the Great War because it wasn't about politics, this time around, but ideology. In this war, the Germans would not be obedient soldiers, but fanaticized ones. Yesterday, the Armenians. Tomorrow, the Jews.

The French Jews were extremely worried, yet he and Moshe had not convinced anyone they knew in Paris to act. Lucienne especially dismissed it all. But he was the husband and father, and so she followed him with the children, and in the end, that was all that mattered. What he had not quite admitted to Lucienne was that, to him, the principal appeal of the South of France wasn't the pretty house, or the climate, or the distance from the capital. It was its location, a boat ride away from another continent. Moshe was the principal architect of their plan. He had crisscrossed the world enough times to have a broader view of the geography and politics of various nations. He had left France without a forwarding address, hidden his and Albano's assets in Swiss accounts, and was at the moment making connections throughout France's colonies in North Africa, in Morocco, Tunisia, and Algeria.

Albano looked out over the water. He had made sure to dress simply. He had left his gold watch and leather shoes at home and was wearing an old suit. He did not want to make his old friend feel embarrassed by his appearance after he had spent weeks at sea in less than luxurious conditions. He did not know Hagop's particular sufferings, but he was familiar with the state of shock brought on by a rapid change in circumstances. After a long time of dejection, the human mind grew so callused that it could not easily switch back to happiness. Depression was common, as was anxiety. He was prepared to find Hagop changed.

"What if he is still angry with us?" Xandra had wondered.

"We were young and impulsive. Twenty years is a lifetime. Years change a man."

"But not always for the better," Xandra worried. "There was always a brash side to him."

Albano recognized the name of the boat that made its way toward the dock. This was it! His heart pounded as men threw ropes and the boat moored.

As if by enchantment, the cold wind stopped. The façades of the hotels shone in the soft light of late fall. In a moment, he would see his friend, lost for twenty years. Life was full of miracles.

He recognized Monsieur Perrin who was walking down the ramp toward him. But the man who walked next to him was an old, toothless man with an ashen face and a hesitant gait, a man much too old to possibly be Hagop.

Albano stood in place, dejected. Had he helped a stranger who would now be at his charge? And that would mean that Hagop was still lost. What would he tell Xandra?

Now the old man was next to him and murmuring in Armenian, "Albano. My brother."

Albano, shocked to recognize the voice looked into the old man's eyes. What he saw in them nearly brought him to his knees. "Hagop! It is you!" Albano's voice broke into a sob of relief and sadness at witnessing his friend's terrible state. They fell in each other's arms. At first, they could only cry and hold each other. Hagop was emaciated; he who had been taller than Albano by a head, now was so hunchbacked that he was noticeably shorter. His teeth were rotten, most of his front teeth missing, his movements difficult, as though every one of his bones suffered from rust. "I am so happy you are here," was all Albano could say.

He could scarcely pay attention as Monsieur Perrin gave him all the paperwork for Hagop's entrance into the country, his visa and his application for immigration as a political refugee. Albano gave him an envelope with the rest of the fee he owed. As Monsieur Perrin spoke, Albano and Hagop just looked at each other, Albano grinning and crying, Hagop red-eyed, confused. When Monsieur Perrin was gone, Albano said, "You are so thin."

"And you are so young," Hagop said. "And as good-looking as when you were a boy." He tried to smile, but it looked more like a grimace of pain.

"How was your voyage?"

"It was terrible," Hagop said. His voice was low, monotone. "My temperament did not agree with the sea. All the weight I had gained is lost again."

"I will not be done with you until you are plump as a baby," Albano said, putting his arm around Hagop.

"No hell was worse than the one you just put me through, bringing me here on a boat," Hagop said. "Why could you not have me come here by train instead?"

Albano was taken aback by the acerbity in Hagop's voice. "The frontiers are closing," he answered. "The railroads are insecure. There were fewer chances of being stopped at sea. I was not sure your papers would withstand the scrutiny of frontier agents, especially now that France is at war."

"You speak Armenian well, my brother. Where did you learn? You did not speak so well years back."

Albano smiled. He could not wait to tell him all about Xandra, but they were still standing in the harbor, and Hagop needed to rest, eat. They had so much to tell one another, but all would be shared in due time. "I had a good teacher," he only said.

Upon entering the lobby of Le Negresco hotel, where doormen stood in their blue and red coats and black hats, Hagop removed his cap and crumpled it between his hands, lowering his head. Albano thought back to the time when he too was first introduced to wealth. He had felt insignificant but also mystified and awed. This time of war and uncertainty called for frugality; already he had tried to broach the subject with Lucienne, and it had not gone well. But for the next few days with Hagop, he wanted to be extravagant.

Inside the hotel room, Hagop looked around and clucked his tongue in appreciation. Albano was thrilled like a child. "This is one of the best rooms in this hotel, and it is one of the best hotels in Nice. Look at the bathroom! You must be eager to take a bath. Are you hungry? You can order food, and they will bring it right up." Hagop did not seem eager to take a bath, although he smelled quite bad. He said he would eat.

Albano took the telephone and ordered breakfast. He was aware of Hagop's eyes on him as he spoke French. After seventeen years in France, he had become accustomed to giving orders with the confidence that comes from having money and thought nothing of it. But it must look strange, even extraordinary to his friend.

A waiter came to the room to set a table on the balcony, which overlooked the Bay of Nice. Breakfast was brought up. Hagop dove upon the food, eating without decorum, throwing himself at the croissants, the jam, the eggs, the orange juice. Albano watched him eat and worried. Something in the way Hagop ate ran deeper than hunger. It resembled despair. As he ate, Albano asked him questions, but Hagop was too focused on the food to respond, and Albano did not insist.

As he waited for Hagop to finish, he forced himself to take in the startling deterioration of Hagop's physical body. If his friend's life had been dire enough to impact his body so dramatically, what might have happened to his soul? He would have to prepare Xandra for this. In many ways, Hagop's appearance was more shocking to him than Xandra's disfigurement had been. It was not only that the body was different. He kept looking for signs of the Hagop he knew, the easy laugh, the cunning, the gusto, the life force, but the man who grabbed food and thrust it into his mouth, swallowing it without being able to chew, appeared to be someone new entirely. Albano closed his eyes to fight the onslaught of emotions. I will heal you, he thought. I will glue you back together, all the broken pieces, just like Moshe did for me.

At last, Hagop leaned back into his chair away from the table. There were crumbs and bits of eggs around his mouth. He belched loudly. Now there was a spark of contentment in his eyes as he asked, "How did you come upon such good fortune, Albano? Your letter said you are married and you have a boy and a girl, and now you work for your uncle. Does he live here too, that fat one?"

"He's in North Africa at the moment."

"Where?"

"Algiers."

"Still, how did this happen?" Hagop asked. "How did you come to escape the Smyrna blaze without a scratch on you?"

Albano presented his arm. "There are a few scratches. Four fingers of my hand are paralyzed, but I got used to it, and I make do." He regretted saying this immediately. It was obscene to compare his hand to what Hagop must have endured. He wondered how Hagop knew that he had escaped the blaze rather than left Smyrna long before the fire, or for that matter, years later.

But Hagop continued with his questions. "And how did you get so wealthy that I am now brought to France at your expense?"

Albano felt that these answers demanded lengthy responses, but first, he asked a question about a mystery he wanted to understand. "After Monsieur Perrin found you in Aleppo, I sent you many letters," he said. "I know you received them, and the man read them to you. But you did not write back. You agreed to come here, but the only news I received was through him."

"I see I have offended you," Hagop answered in a plaintive voice. "Do not be angry at your poor old friend."

"I am not offended or mad," Albano said. "I am only curious."

"Oh, please forgive me. Look at me, and look at you. You look like a prince, and I'm like a bum twice your age. I am not educated the way you are. I was never so good with reading, and writing even less. And my eyesight is impaired." He thought about it and added, "Also, it was hard for me. How could I hear about your good luck when my life has been so miserable?"

Albano remembered Moshe's words from years ago, and told Hagop with a smile, "My good fortune is now your good fortune, dear friend."

"And will my good fortune extend to a few more of those pastries, or is this all I am allowed to eat?"

Albano ordered more food and said, "Speak to me Hagop. Tell me how you survived."

"My parents and sisters were killed when Kemal's army arrived," Hagop said. "Do you know this?"

Albano nodded. There would be time to tell him the details and reveal that Xandra was alive. He had a sense that first, he needed to know more about Hagop, about what the years might have done to him. "I want to tell you about all this, but please first tell me what happened to you?" he insisted.

Hagop shrugged impatiently. "You think you want to hear. But perhaps it is better if you don't."

"I want to know."

"There were maybe thirty of us arrested that day, the day I left with the money after we had that fight in the cave. Do you remember?"

"I shall never forget that terrible day," Albano said somberly.

"You remember that man who had come once to the Armenian quarter when we were children? The survivor? You and I listened to his tale."

"I remember him."

"Remember how we could not believe him at the time?" Hagop stared at Albano who nodded. "Everything he said was true. Those stories we were fed of displacements, of wanting the Armenians to be moved elsewhere. Those were lies. They didn't want us moved out of the country. What they wanted to do with us is wipe us from the surface of the Earth."

Albano sat down at the table and listened to Hagop's story.

"The first groups of men they took out of the Armenian quarter they took further up the mountains to be shot dead," Hagop said. "By the time they arrested me, their tactics had changed. They had been disorderly about burying the bodies. Too many cadavers of Armenians found rotting on the outskirts of town. The government wanted things done more discreetly. Important people from around the world had eyes and ears in Smyrna. This is why the Armenians of Smyrna were not experiencing the same fate as villagers throughout the Empire. But eventually, they began to take the men of the Armenian quarter, inventing lies to do it. They started with men they thought were community leaders. You see, they are the ones who organize others. You start with the leaders, those who make decisions, and suddenly no one knows what to do."

"This is why they took your father?"

"This is the reason they took me! They knew I was the son of Silas, the baker. They recognized in me things I myself was not yet aware of: my natural leadership and my gift." He tapped his finger to the side of his head to illustrate. "My superior intelligence. They took me, beat me, and they stole all my money."

"The satchels?" Albano asked. The satchels were filled with the money they had both earned from years of selling newspapers in the streets of Smyrna. For Hagop to refer to it as his money was simply inaccurate. That day in the cave he had been furious at Xandra and Albano because he had discovered their love. He had beaten Xandra, and he and Albano had gotten into a fistfight. Hagop had then left the cave, taking with him all the money, his share and the half that belonged to Albano. But this was water under the bridge.

Hagop's eyes flashed with anger at the memory. "They did this quietly. They were waiting right outside the Armenian quarter. Everything they did in Smyrna, they did in secret."

"They?"

"The police."

"It was easier to take us out of town one by one, and then do with us as they pleased. And what pleased them was to make us die slowly of thirst and hunger, of despair, of exhaustion, of physical and mental torture." Hagop felt in his pocket and retrieved a pouch of tobacco. For a moment he was engrossed in the task of rolling a cigarette. His fingers trembled as he did. The result was uneven. He put the misshapen cigarette between his lips and lit it. His middle finger and index were yellow from tobacco, almost orange.

"They took me and others into the Syrian Desert," he said, inhaling. "At first, they had many gendarmes surrounding us, later on, less so. Still, I should have attempted to escape when I still had the strength, in those first few days, before the dehydration rendered me as weak as a little girl. Whatever food the villagers had brought with them ran out quickly. It did not take long before the first of us died from thirst. The first to die were the children too old to be nursed, the old folks, the pregnant women. Then, everybody else."

Hagop stopped and looked at Albano, as though he was observing the effect his account had on him. Albano had nothing to say. What could he say to this? Hagop went on. "Each time we stopped for the night some of us did not wake up. Our caravan moved forward. At that time, you could almost believe they were trying to take us someplace. But then, when we were far enough from the city, the gendarmes got the help of blood-thirsty mad men full of hatred. They were armed, and they began to rape and beat all those defenseless people." Hagop crushed the cigarette into an ashtray. His chin trembled. "Those who rebelled they just attacked with bayonets. There was nothing we could do. By then we were very weak, all of us were. Any rebellion meant instant death. So, we huddled and hoped we wouldn't be next, at least those of us who still had the will to live."

There was a rap at the room's door, and a hotel server entered with a basket full of chocolate croissants and brioches. The crumbs on the white tablecloth were removed, the pot of coffee refreshed. Hagop eyed the basket the entire time. When the server was gone Hagop began to take the pastries out of the basket, but he was no longer hungry, and so he took one bite of this one, one bite of the next, putting the pastries down on the table until he had taken a few bites of each. His fingers and face were covered in crumbs.

"This continued for what seemed like weeks," he said. "So many died, and yet there were always more villagers joining our caravan, and so there were always more people to kill. The gendarmes grew tired of this. It was taking too long. We weren't dying as cooperatively as they wished. They too were thirsty, and hungry, and tired, and wanted to go home. And yet there were so many of us still. I think that they had instructions that not one of us would make it to Syria alive, and they were trying to complete the task. They needed ways to kill us faster. Now they became frantic about it. They made us remove all our clothes so we would have no protection from the burning sun and icy nights. They made us walk on the ledges of mountains. When there were cliffs, they pushed the children down to their deaths, knowing that many of the women would jump after them, which they did."

"By God! Hagop. I—"

"Certain women, they would get rid of their children and keep them alive to do what they wished with them until they were tired of them or the women turned insane." Hagop shook his head in disgust. "When there were rivers, they would throw us in the water to drown and then shoot at us if we seemed able to reach the bank. If you lagged behind, you were beaten to death. If you could not go on, you were left to die."

Albano was sickened and astounded. Not only did Hagop's story echo that of the man who had spoken to the Armenian men back in Smyrna, but the way he described those horrors in a tone detached to the point of numbness sounded almost identical. "How did you survive?" he asked.

"I don't know how long we walked, perhaps weeks, perhaps months. I made sure I was never in sight, never noticed, always in the center of the crowd. I made myself invisible. I had no one I loved to watch die either. That made a difference. Despair killed people faster than any other method they used. Also, I had a strong body and the endurance of youth."

"You had strength of spirit."

Hagop dismissed the notion with an impatient motion of his hand. "I was like cattle. Unthinking. I just moved. Put one foot in front of the other, waiting to die I suppose, only I did not. In the end, it was not those who deserved to live who did. Not the loving mothers, not the children, not the old people, not the pretty faces who incited their lust, but those of us who were like sturdy goats, people that nothing can quite kill, not starvation, not thirst, not humiliation." Hagop had a small laugh. "You will see, Albano. One day you will want to kill me, but hard as you might try, you won't be able to, that's how tough I am."

Albano shook his head at the absurd notion. "You must be tough indeed to survive such atrocities."

"Humans survive. Cattle just exist. By the time we arrived at the refugee camp, there was no one left that was not destroyed by despair in one way or another. Including me."

Albano thought of his despair when he had hoped to drown off the coast of Smyrna. "How did you recover your will to live?"

Hagop shrugged angrily. "What makes you think I have? What keeps me standing is this body, which refuses to entirely fall apart. And also rage." He peered at Albano, as though measuring his words' impact on his friend's face. "Yes. Often I can make it through a day on rage alone."

"Your rage is understandable," Albano said.

"As this was happening, and in the years of hunger and agony that followed, all I thought about was how others in the world ate and drank and lived in abundance, people who rejoiced and had children and wives, with lives that were nothing but bliss. Yes, that injustice fueled me with enough rage to power me like coal does a steam engine. Why did I suffer so? I asked myself again and again, while others have all the luck. The opportunists, the sweet-talkers, the greedy and conniving, they did not only survive; they profited. They thrived."

Albano swallowed. He hoped it wasn't blame he heard in Hagop's words. Of all the horrors in Hagop's account, the idea of survival with rage as the sole motivator seemed to Albano the epitome of hopelessness. "And so, after this, you did not want to return home? You stayed in Syria."

"What home? My country was gone, and it had betrayed me. My family was gone. I had no reason to return. But life in the refugee camp was grim. There was no work. Little food. Everyone was ill. Everyone had to contend with their losses."

"You did not marry?"

"I've had women," Hagop said. "None of them fit to marry. Not a single one left still a virgin and most of them crazy by then. And outside the refugee camp, the Syrian women wanted nothing to do with Armenian men."

Albano wondered how virginity had relevance when one sought someone to give and receive comfort, someone to share a burden. "What was it like inside the camp?" he asked.

"Searching trash for something to eat? What was that like?" Hagop hissed. He then smiled thinly. "I guess now that you have spared no expense to rescue me you want your money's worth. You want to hear all the details of my misery. You want to know every one of the indignities I suffered." This was said in jest, but Albano did not think it funny. "Well, my brother," Hagop continued, "let me tell you about a life where you are eaten by scabies so much so that there isn't an inch of skin that doesn't render you mad. I was sick a lot. Typhus, even cholera, both of which I miraculously survived. I tell you I am like a scorpion. I can live in a crack in a wall for years without sustenance. My eyesight was damaged by the desert sun and poor nutrition. My hearing is bad. I had broken bones that did not reset properly, and so my limbs are crooked and gnarled like tree branches. The few teeth I have left are of no use. My body is nothing but pain."

"I will take you to the best doctors."

Hagop emitted a roaring laughter. "Listen to yourself: the best doctors, the best hotel, the best boat, a man hired just to pay my bills, procure my papers, and whisk me out of a place where all others have been left to die. You are a powerful man, Albano."

Albano laughed too, but uneasily. In the compliment was the kind of teasing that was Hagop's alone. He remembered how he used to both love and fear the cleverness of the spunky little boy Hagop used to be. He had been a boy full of mirth, ready to challenge everything that was serious and turn it into a joke. Hagop had been a grabber of opportunities, a jester, and also someone who told truths that were sometimes unpleasant to hear. "I am so happy to have found you at last," he said.

Hagop beamed his near toothless smile and said, "Not as happy as I!" He tore some bread and put it into his mouth. Instead of swallowing, he let it stay in his mouth as he spoke defiantly, almost angrily. "Here is something you don't know perhaps," he said. "Xandra is alive."

Albano was taken aback by Hagop's tone as much as by the news itself. "I … when did you learn this?"

Hagop shrugged. "She left a message at the Armenian Prelacy in Aleppo maybe ten years ago." Albano tried to reconcile this. Xandra told him she had looked for Hagop for years. There had been much more than one letter. "Do you know she was burnt in the fire?" Hagop said, with no more emotion than if he was speaking about a stranger. "Disfigured. Now she's a slave of sorts to a Muslim family in Izmir. She thought you might still be alive; she said so in a letter. She said she looked for you. She went to the Jewish quarter where they treated her like a dog. They wanted to keep your secret, those smart Jews. Yes, Albano, fate has treated you more kindly than the rest of us. I can see how with your new life you would have little use for her."

I found her! Albano wanted to say. But he stopped himself because of the callousness of Hagop's words. Also because of the way Hagop had already returned to eating, putting his fingers in the butter and jam dishes and wiping those clean with a great smacking of his lips. His long-lost sister, the last remaining member of his family who he knew to be injured and practically enslaved, was already gone from his mind. "And so, you did not look for her?" he asked uneasily.

Hagop laughed, and now his laugh sounded different to Albano. Not full of mirth, but bitter. "What I needed was a rich, powerful man such as yourself. Not a woman more downtrodden than I was."

Albano got up from the breakfast table and came to stand by the window. A cold breeze from the sea cooled his face. Xandra, at this moment, was at La Bastide, waiting expectantly for his return. How would he explain that in the years she had relentlessly searched for her brother, Hagop had known she was alive and had not cared? Hagop was avidly pouring leftover coffee into his glass and topping it off with all the milk and sugar that was left. The task absorbed him fully, reminding Albano of the way little children and very old people engrossed themselves in a treat. It was possible that years of suffering in solitude had made Hagop unable to think past his own survival. He would need to prepare Xandra for Hagop as much as he would need to prepare Hagop for Xandra.

He left Hagop at the hotel at the end of the day and told him he would return in the morning. He showed him how to use the telephone to order food and drove back to La Bastide.

Back at the house, Albano waited past midnight for Lucienne and the children to be asleep and met Xandra in the orchard. He told her about Hagop's distressed appearance, his tale of capture, his agony through the desert, and the hopeless stagnation in the refugee camp.

"Many have left the camp and started anew. Why didn't he?" Xandra asked. "The camp was a terrible place no doubt, but he wasn't imprisoned."

"It is as though he was put in a hole and forgotten there. He will need time to come out of the hole, like a man who was deprived of daylight and is made to face the sun. All he can do at the moment is eat," he said. And be angry, he thought.

"What did you tell him about us?"

Albano scratched his face, uneasy. "I had planned to tell him so many things, Xandra, but Hagop did not act curious, or even interested in any part of my life. It is too soon. By the look of things, it will take time for him to expand himself any further than the next meal."

Xandra asked in a small voice. "You didn't tell him about us?"

"He was overjoyed to learn that you were alive," he lied. "But … I did not get a chance to tell him that you were here in Cannes, let alone living with me."

"Where did you tell him I was?"

"He did not ask," Albano said. This admission spoke volume. They were both quiet for a few minutes. "It might take time before you can be reunited. When he sees you are here, questions will surface. You were right that I should not bring him to La Bastide. It is too soon. You and I struggled with the moral ramifications of the choice we made. It is a choice that few people besides Moshe can understand."

Xandra lowered her eyes in sadness. "I will wait to see my brother since you think it is best," she said.

"I should have thought of all this before. In my eagerness to bring him here, I did not think of all this."

"Had you anticipated it, you would have wanted to rescue him all the more," she said. "He is alive, and he is here. That is all that matters."

Albano had encouraged Hagop to enjoy a long, hot bath, have a good night's sleep, and order as much food and wine to the room as he liked. But when he knocked on the hotel room's door the next morning, there was no answer. Thinking that Hagop must have gone on a walk, Albano let himself in with his hotel key. Overnight, the pristine room had turned to a pigsty. Hagop was not inside the bed but on the floor, snoring loudly. He had moved most of the bedding and pillows around him like a sort of nest, which was surrounded by toppled glasses, ice buckets, plates of leftover food, and empty wine bottles. By the smell of things, he still had not bathed. More worrisome were the broken chair and a cracked mirror, the shattered wine bottle on the floor, and the red splatter on the wall, as though, at some point in the night, Hagop had been in the throes of a fit of rage. But now he slept like a puppy that looked contented and unrepentant amongst the ruins he had created. Albano went around the room and picked up trash. He placed the empty dishes and bottles on a tray outside the door and tidied up the room the best he could. When Hagop woke up an hour later, his first words were, "When will we be on our way?"

"On our way to where?" Albano asked.

"Do you live far away? Will we take a train or an automobile?" Hagop yawned and stretched. "I hope not a boat. Do you remember how we used to admire the Levantine's wealth, their palaces and the way they dressed, and their many servants? Now you are just like them. Better than them!" He laughed like a child on Christmas morning. "Your fortune has changed and now mine has too!" Hagop reached around him. Lifting covers and pillows and finding nothing he asked, "Can you call for more wine?"

"It is only eight in the morning," Albano said. He hesitated. "What happened here last night? Were you all right?"

"Does your palace have a cellar full of wine bottles?"

"I will disappoint you, I'm afraid, dear friend. I do not have a palace, or anything resembling the ways of the Levantines. Tell me, do you always drink this much?"

"I am only celebrating my freedom. So? When are we going?"

If Albano had any notion of introducing Hagop into his life, those thoughts vanished the moment he had entered the chaos of the hotel room. He did not know what to tell Hagop, and so he improvised. "I thought that for the time being you would be comfortable living here, while you gain strength."

"Why would I be made to stay in a hotel rather than one of the many rooms of your palace?"

"I don't have a palace."

Hagop continued; he was chatty, in a great mood. "Do you have servants, and cars, and many rooms, and a cook?"

"I, eh, yes, but … I want to take you to see a doctor, heal some of that vermin, and get some health back into you, and then when I have fattened you up a bit, I shall buy you clothes that befit you."

Hagop found a bottle under his pillow and drank from it. "God is good to me at last. I have found my savior!" Albano could not decide if Hagop was speaking of him or the wine.

"How about we run you a nice bath," Albano suggested. Hagop finally took his bath, but Albano had to undress him and coax him for an hour into stepping into the water. Hagop mistrusted the whole thing, only accepting a small amount of water at the very bottom of the tub, as though drowning was a very real possibility. He pushed away soap and washcloths angrily as if they were instruments of torture. Perhaps this was natural. Hagop's body had the frailty of a near skeleton. He was wobbly on his feet. His skin was nothing but sores and scabs. His filth was such that all the grime could not come off. Albano hoped to do a better job on subsequent baths, but for today it was a victory.

After Hagop's second night in Nice, Albano arrived to find him still drunk. To his relief, nothing in the room was broken. The repairs of the night before were sure to cost him considerably. Hagop asked to see Albano's palace again, and so Albano took a deep breath and said, "If you do not like this hotel I can find you a place of your own."

Hagop asked coldly, "Is it that you don't want me to live in the same house as your wife and children?"

The question was direct. It was the first time that Hagop mentioned Albano's family, and Albano caught himself trying to remember just how much he had told him in the letter. Had he said that his house was in Cannes and not in Nice? Had he told him his address? "It's just that, my family is in transition," he said. "My wife … well, she has not acclimated to the Côte d'Azur yet. She feels I have uprooted her from Paris, and now to impose a permanent houseguest would not be the right time." But Hagop was drinking the last of his wine and not paying attention.

That day, Hagop continued to order wine and to drink until he was sick. Albano did not have the heart to slow him down, but he worried. If Hagop had gotten used to drinking to numb his pain, the road to good health and a good life would be far harder to climb.

The rest of the week, Hagop continued to be interested in nothing outside his own physical comfort. He wanted cigarettes. He wanted food. He wanted a whore or two brought in. Albano conceded him all his requests but remained vague about possible prostitutes. Hagop still did not ask Albano about his family aside from brief, incoherent questions about "the palace." That entire week, he made little progress aside from learning to sleep in the bed. Each day, he woke up drunk, and that's how he went to sleep. Neither of them mentioned Xandra again.

This went on for an entire very expensive month, and the progress was slow. Each day, Albano would leave La Bastide early in the morning, and he would return late at night. In all his time with Hagop, he had not been able to coax him into taking another bath, but Hagop began to wash on his own, one body part at a time, over the sink, which felt to Albano like progress. For unknown reasons, he refused to leave the hotel room. He did not act fearful of the exterior world, only disinterested. He accepted for a doctor to come to the room to look at him and the doctor, a self-important man who acted disgusted during the entire visit, prescribed ointments and potions as well as an experimental drug that showed great promise in treating syphilis.

By the end of the month, there were at last signs of progress: the vermin was gone and his skin looked better. A barber came to the room to cut his hair and trim his beard. He and Albano had their first meal in the hotel restaurant rather than inside the room. During that meal, Albano was deeply uncomfortable. Hagop did not know French table manners. He burped, ate with his mouth open, wiped his lips with his sleeves. He spoke so loudly and drank so much that people asked not to be seated next to them. Soon, there was a circle of empty tables around theirs. Albano decided it was best for everyone not to repeat the experience until he could teach Hagop the ways of the French.

The second month, Hagop appeared to drink less, and Albano felt encouraged. They ventured on short outings around the hotel. They visited an excellent dentist, and Hagop was fitted for a denture, which would take some time to build. Together, they shopped for clothing. Albano said he would take Hagop to a proper tailor once he had regained some of his bulk. It was more difficult to find shoes that fit his distorted feet, and so Albano bought him several pairs of espadrilles. As he did all this, Hagop was passive. He silently observed things, and it was difficult to know if he was pleased, dissatisfied, or emotionally absent. All through that time, he acted like a demanding child that tolerated no lapse of attention and found it perfectly natural that Albano spent his days doing nothing else than care for him, order things for him, translate the newspaper for him, play endless card games with him, shop with him, take walks with him, and then return to his family at night.

To Albano's relief, Hagop no longer asked to move into his palace. He was capricious, mercurial, at times ebullient and playful like a child, and at other times, for long stretches of the day, sometimes for the entire day, he became sullen and antagonistic. By the end of the second month, Albano felt no closer to introducing him to his family. Every evening he would tell Xandra what Hagop had said and done, and they agreed that his behavior was too unpredictable. Early on, Albano had admitted to Xandra that Hagop had known all along that she was alive in Smyrna, burned and destitute, but that he had been indifferent to her fate. He had received her letters, had known that she was looking for him. He had not cared. This was as sad as it was peculiar. They decided that Hagop could not be told that she lived in Cannes. Hagop was in no shape to be reasonable.

In early January 1940, the phony war was still going on, without much combat. Whatever this war was supposed to look like, it didn't feel like one. There was in the air a sense of suspended animation, part anticipation, part dread. In Cannes, the temperature dropped, the sky was gray, and the sea turned nervous and black. They felt the sting of the first food and oil restrictions. Albano rented, in Nice, a small but handsomely furnished apartment with plenty of light. "The apartment is close enough from the center of town that you can be independent. You can walk to shops and restaurants and to the market. See, in this kitchen, you can make your meals," Albano said as Hagop followed him wordlessly from room to room. "There is running water, hot and cold, in both the kitchen and the bathroom. See, there is a radio for music."

Hagop looked around morosely. "How will I buy all this food and wine you promised?" he asked. "I have nothing." Albano handed Hagop several hundred-francs notes. Hagop pocketed the money and continued to brood.

"I'm afraid he is angry with me," Albano told Xandra that evening. "He is hurt that I don't introduce him to my family, and he has every right to be. He is bored; he is depressed; he drinks a frightening amount. He wants to live like a hermit. He hasn't a taste for much."

"Up until now, he had to keep moving to survive," Xandra suggested, "and now that he has a roof over his head, he is left to think, and thinking is painful."

"You and I know what it's like to live in a kind of fog when the only times of clarity bring unendurable mental pain. To be idle is a dangerous thing. The mind is left to roam and lick every corner and interstice of one's pain. And I understand all this. Only he always seems on the verge of saying something irreparably hostile. Hagop has moments of energy between stretches of lethargy when his anger flares up. But rage is the lone emotion that seems to make him feel good."

"You never took to the bottle or to anger," Xandra noted.

"It is a strange thing, Xandra. He is the Hagop we love, and at the same time he is not."

"You loved him more than I did. He is my brother, but he was never my friend."

"Maybe my expectations were selfish. I wanted to have him returned to us intact. But that would have been impossible; I realize this now."

"What will you do?"

"I'm sure he will get back on his feet soon."

"Perhaps the solution is to introduce your family to him by bringing them to him rather than the other way around. You could meet at a restaurant. He doesn't need to come to La Bastide. That way, he will not feel rejected, and neither will he see me."

"You might be right. Also, I want him to begin to change his mind about me and stop seeing me as a rich "Jewish Prince" as he calls me now."

"My brother never seemed the kind of person whose mind could be changed," Xandra said.

Over the following months, and through February, March, and April, those plans were abandoned as Hagop's behavior did not improve. After he moved into the apartment, which lacked the luxurious amenities of Le Negresco, letting him win at cards was the only means to briefly lift his spirit. He still would not take care of himself the way Albano had hoped. In fact, it was worse now that there was no maid to straighten the place or room service to feed him. He often didn't bathe or shave. The apartment was a disaster of dirty dishes, clothes, and cigarette butts in every empty dish. The only food Hagop consumed was bread from the bakery that stood at the street corner, and ever-increasing quantities of wine. Daily, for a month, Hagop asked to move back to the hotel and pouted when Albano explained that it was too expensive, that there were the war and restrictions, and they were all living on his savings. Although Hagop complained of boredom, he did nothing to entertain himself. He waited all day for Albano to arrive so that they could walk by the sea, go on an automobile ride, or shop for groceries. Despite Albano's encouragement, he refused to visit the Apostolic Church, where he was sure to meet members of the Armenian community, people that spoke his language. Hagop always came up with new excuses. "People look at me with disgust," he would say.

"It will take time, but if you try, you will succeed."

"I am not like you with languages. I never learned to speak French more than the few words it took to sell newspapers in Smyrna."

Albano hired a tutor to come daily, but the tutor complained that on most days Hagop refused to open his door. "Do you not want to learn the language?" Albano asked him.

"France was never the country where I wanted to live," Hagop moaned. "This is your idea of where I should be, and what can I do but comply?"

"I am only making suggestions so that you can live better in France. Is there a country where you would rather be? I thought you might like Nice. It's a beautiful city."

"It's too cold."

"Spring is coming. I will buy you warmer clothes until you get accustomed."

Hagop burst into laughter. "Buy me warmer clothes! Listen to yourself speak as though I am a woman for whom you want to buy fur."

"July and June will get warmer."

"I am alone here. I know no one, and no one speaks my language. At least in Aleppo, I had friends."

"Friends who would have murdered you in your sleep for a loaf of bread," Albano pointed out. "Why have you not tried to meet other Armenians, as I urged you to do?"

Hagop spoke bitterly. "You come, you go, in your fancy automobile. I don't even know where you live. A friend would not cast me aside. He would welcome me into his life. Not keep me hidden away like a leper."

"You aren't quite your old self yet. I thought that a few more weeks—"

"What is the harm in me meeting your family?"

"When you meet them, would you not want to be at your very best? And besides, would you not want those new teeth that will come soon?"

"So, do I scare you? Do you think I would scare them?"

"Nothing of the sort."

Hagop looked at him with drunken malevolence. "Come on, Albano. You must be just a little scared of me."

Even though it did not feel right to leave Hagop by himself, Albano made a conscious effort to spend less time with him and more time with his family. He had been neglecting them for months, and they were too isolated. He thought that it would do Lucienne good to meet other people, so they joined the synagogue in Nice. The pretext was that Gustave was fourteen, the age when he ought to be bar mitzvahed. But in reality, Albano thought that it would be good for the whole family to have a reason to get dressed up and get out of La Bastide. For some weeks, they took the automobile down to Nice to attend the Shabbat services on Fridays and stayed afterward to share the wine and bread and mingle a bit. But it did not seem to cheer Lucienne much.

One Friday night, as they walked down the stone steps after service, stopping to offer a few francs to the ever-growing sea of downtrodden men and women that awaited their help, Lucienne removed her hat, and Albano saw what he had not noticed before: her hair was turning gray. Lucienne was forty-one years old, so that was not so strange in itself. What bothered him was that she did not use hair coloring the way she always would have before. And she smoked too much. What did this all mean? Lucienne, usually so proud, was letting herself go.

To ask about this might offend her, so it would be best to say nothing and ask Xandra what she thought of it. On the steps, he paused long enough to observe his children. Marceline, in sharp contrast with her mother, was resplendent. Boys looked at her, and so did men. She was only sixteen years old, but the way she stood and moved, he realized now, and the kind of clothes she wore, made her appear to be a woman. The years, the worries, leaving Paris, all the time he spent with Hagop had blinded him to the fact that his family was changing. Gustave too was in between states. He sometimes looked like a child, sometimes like a man, but at still other times, he appeared to be a wounded creature that needed rescuing. The thought of Gustave getting older gripped Albano with anguish. The war had better come and go before Gustave was of age.

Lucienne, in the end, said that she did not like the synagogue. She felt that the Jews of Nice kept to themselves and that they did not like Parisians, which might or might not be the truth because, as Albano saw it, Lucienne was the one with the tight lips and the absent gaze.

No one mentioned the bar mitzvah after that.

It was a joyful thing, the following week, to watch Hagop be fitted for his new denture and to see him emerge out of the dentist chair an entirely different man. He smiled in front of the mirror again and again, trying on his hat, straightening his necktie, trying out this new face of his. It was as though his new smile brought forth the transformation that had been slowly happening to the rest of his body, and now it all came together splendidly. He had put on a good twenty pounds. His face was fuller, he looked healthier, and in the clothes Albano had him fitted for, Hagop looked almost distinguished.

The two of them went for a walk in Nice. Hagop stopped in front of every mirror and every glass-paned window to admire himself. He had learned how to behave in restaurants. They ate at Acchiardo in old Nice, and Hagop tipped his hat to women, and the women smiled. Albano was sure they had turned a corner. He was so encouraged that he nearly told him about Xandra. But as lunch went on and Hagop ordered a second bottle of wine for himself, Albano decided to say nothing.

The next few weeks were difficult at home. The war, phony or not, was putting everyone on edge, Lucienne especially. She endlessly confronted Albano for spending time away from La Bastide and the family. She had convinced herself that he was having an affair with a woman in town. He decided that the best approach would be the truth. He explained to Lucienne that he had been helping a friend who was a refugee from Syria.

Also, Lucienne's ways clashed with the financial constraints of war. She gave Xandra hell whenever she wasn't able to procure an item she wanted. She accused Albano of avarice when he asked her to be more circumspect with money. She did not go a day without demanding to return to Paris. And so, Albano decided to spread out his visits to Hagop. Between Hagop and Lucienne, Albano did not know which one was more difficult to handle. Both of them made demands and were angry with him, but at least with Lucienne, the complaints were something he could address. Lucienne ranted, but Hagop sulked. Both of them continuously asked for money and nice things despite his protest that money could soon be devalued or that his funds could run out entirely. Neither took the threat of a German invasion seriously, Lucienne because of the long hours she spent on the telephone with Parisian friends who told her that Albano was acting foolishly and urged her to return to Paris, and Hagop because he felt this war had nothing to do with him since he was neither German, French, or Jewish.

Albano was disappointed in Hagop and disappointed in himself. He felt every day less willing to bring him in contact with Lucienne and the children, less ready to tell him about Xandra. His own naiveté had brought on an inextricable situation. Hagop was devoured by demons Albano could not begin to understand and emotional wounds he was powerless to heal.

Xandra asked of him too. She told him to pay closer attention to Marceline.

"I am torn between Hagop and Lucienne. There is not a moment of peace. And besides, Marceline and Gustave behave less like children than the adults."

"Still, they are children. Marceline needs fatherly guidance."

"Why? Is there something I should worry about?"

"She is defiant with Lucienne, and Lucienne doesn't know what to do. And Gustave is confused. You were spending all kinds of time with him, but now that Hagop is here, you aren't available the way you were before."

"What I want most of all is be alone with *you*. I want to take *you* away for the day as we did months ago. Do you remember that beautiful time we had in Agay? Please meet me at the orchard tonight. The evenings are warmers. It will be a moonless night, perfect for romance."

Xandra hesitated. "The children go there at night."

"It's not as though you let me do anything they could witness," Albano said. Realizing he sounded bitter, he said, "I only want to talk to you in peace." He smiled and admitted, "And kiss you some." He thought about it. "Why would Marceline or Gustave go to the orchard at night?"

Xandra lowered her gaze. "They are teenagers, and I cannot control them."

"And I cannot control Hagop. But he is showing a few positive signs. Do you know that he is finding interest in bird watching? He wanted me to buy him binoculars the other day when we walked into town, and now he never leaves without a small notebook in which he records his findings."

"That is unlike my brother," Xandra said.

"Soon I am hopeful Hagop will re-enter the world of the living. He will accept employment, find a woman to marry, and hopefully put aside his rancor."

"May God hear you," Xandra said.

Because of all the time he spent with Hagop, Albano's affairs were being dangerously neglected. There was the matter of his work with Moshe. There was Lucienne, who was becoming more strident and upset. There was poor Gustave, who found himself without the closeness of the relationship they had when they arrived in Cannes, and Marceline, who in the blink of an eye had metamorphosed from a precocious girl into a headstrong young woman. On top of all this, he could find no time to replenish himself with his Sundays with Xandra. Also, if he was honest with himself, being around Hagop was a drain to his spirit. "It is time you find things to do for yourself," he found the courage to tell him one day in late April. "I need to tend to other things. You need to look for work, look for friends. Maybe meet a woman and fall in love. The truth is, I spend too much time with you and not enough time doing everything else."

They were inside his apartment playing cards. Hagop, who had been in a fine mood, whistling between his teeth and joking around, walked away from the table. He went to the window and lit a cigarette, sulking in silence. Finally, he said, "The money you give me is not enough."

Albano, who still sat at the card table, took out his wallet. "How much would you like?"

Hagop took a deep inhale of his cigarette and let the ashes fall to the rug. "When I was in Aleppo, I was a poor man. A man without even a house to call his own, a man dressed in shreds, a man full of lice and vermin. I was the lowest of the low. And yet I had more dignity than I have now, waiting for your visits, your money, and your whim."

Albano put his cards down and breathed through the hurt he felt. He had given Hagop every waking minute he had, neglecting his family, neglecting Xandra the most. "Let me find you work," he said. "That is the only way you will get your life back."

"Why, brother, can I not meet your children and wife?" Hagop said resentfully. "Is it that you find me unfit to breathe the same air as them?"

Albano had nothing to respond to this. Again and again, Hagop was returning to this complaint, and no matter what Albano tried to do for him, Hagop turned it around, mistaking everything for a slight. He wanted to tell Hagop that he needed to take responsibility for his life. Instead, he said, "We will find good work that suits you, and so you'll earn your own living."

"What is it that you'll have me do?"

Albano had tried to broach the subject of work many times, but this was the first time Hagop seemed receptive. Now he told him his plan excitedly. "You should learn the way I learned, from the bottom up. I worked in Moshe's warehouse at first, learning all about manufacturing and shipping, and then I took accounting classes and went into the finances, the marketing. And you must take French lessons. Once your French is good, you can enter management and sales." What Albano had in mind for Hagop was something different, something to do with resistance work, if and when he was sure that Hagop could be trusted. There was no rug business anymore. There was an office in Algiers; there were employees, invoices, and orders but no inventory. It was a front.

Hagop pursed his lips. "That is not the way family works in my world. You do not start your own relative at the very bottom of the ladder but at the top."

Albano thought of all the shelling of nuts Hagop's father had put him through. "This is the same way Moshe taught me," he said.

"I can see how that pachyderm would delight in watching a pretty boy sweat and carry heavy loads. But you know I am an intellectual. I am as smart as ten French men. It would be better for them to learn to respect me from the start by having me manage them."

"If it was my own company, things might be different. I would have more leeway. But I have sold my business to come here."

"How sweet it must be to be retired at such a young age."

"I am involved in a different kind of work," Albano said. "It's something to do with the war, but I do not make any money."

"What is it you do that makes no money?" Hagop said with contempt.

Albano was surprised that it had taken so long for Hagop to wonder about this, and even more surprised he had never prepared for an answer. He had no time to ask himself how much was safe to reveal, especially when Hagop took so poorly to vagueness and secrecy. "Many of us believe France unprepared to face Hitler," Albano said. "In the eventuality of a German invasion, and in case the enemy takes control of France, we are putting in place channels so that underground groups will be able to receive funds."

Hagop placed a new cigarette between his lips and lit it. He came back to sit at the card table, blew smoke in Albano's face and said, "You look tired my friend."

Albano looked up at Hagop and admitted, "I am tired, indeed."

"It takes energy to maintain all those secrets." Hagop smiled and took an inhale of his cigarettes and added, "and all those lies."

There was an expression on Hagop's face Albano didn't like. The same expression he'd had years ago before confronting him about Xandra when he had found the embroidered handkerchief she had made for him as a memento of her love for him. "What lies?" Albano asked, sounding unconvincing even to himself.

Hagop looked at him with satisfaction. "Your dirty secrets. Oh, do not bother with the charade; I know them all."

"My secrets?"

"I have secrets of my own," Hagop said.

"You do?"

"I have lied to you, I confess. Please do not hate me, my dear friend. I told you I didn't go to the Apostolic Church, but it was a lie. I have been there many times."

"You have?" Albano said happily.

"You were correct in one regard: the Armenian community is a close-knit one." He looked at Albano intently and smiled his Hagop smile. "People were eager to tell me who they knew from Smyrna who has ended up here." Albano felt a chill sweep through his body as Hagop went on. "Lo and behold, they told me of a woman who had survived the Smyrna fire, disfigured the poor soul, and who now lives here, in the next town, as a maid to a Jewish family. You can imagine my surprise when I learned her name was Xandra." He paused for dramatic effect and said, "And you can imagine how even more surprised I was when I learned that the family she worked for was *yours.*"

Albano looked at his feet, shook his head. He was sweating. Had Hagop screamed at him he would have preferred it. "This was not the way I wanted you to learn this," he said. "I was trying to find the right time to——"

"Is this why you never wanted me to see your house? Because you did not want me to see that she was there?"

"It is complicated," Albano said. His face was hot, his hands unsteady. "I must explain everything from the beginning for you to understand how this came about. I had started a family in Paris. I believed Xandra dead! And then——"

Hagop interrupted, "You are married to a French woman, that much is true. And so, my sister, she is *what* to you, exactly?"

"Moshe was the one who discovered her and brought her to France. She had nothing, and so I offered her to...." He hesitated, all the words that came out of his mouth, all his reasoning, all his justifications, now sounding trite and wrong. "Live with us," he added.

"So, I am forgotten in an apartment, and Xandra gets to live with you and your wife." He looked at Albano and smiled meanly. "A harem of sorts?"

"She is the caretaker of my children who love her very much, and she loves them back."

"Your wife knows that she was your whore, back in Smyrna?"

"It has nothing to do with——"

"Is she, still?"

"Hagop, how can you say such things after all this time? I have always had deep feelings for Xandra. She and I have a deep ... bond ... as well as ... a friendship."

"Does your wife know about your little arrangement?"

"I did not want to tell her that Xandra and I knew each other in the past," Albano admitted.

"What would be the harm in telling her if you are doing nothing wrong?"

"It was simpler not to say … It didn't matter … and we … I did not want my wife to be upset. And so, my wife thinks of Xandra as our children's nanny. Which she is. And that is all."

Hagop pondered this for a moment. "But you do fuck her, don't you?"

"I do not. We—"

"If you did not, you would have no reason to hide the past from your wife. Or your present from me."

"It's not like this. Not at all!"

Hagop burst into laughter. "And so, you expect me to believe that you fuck that ugly wife of yours, but not my sister?"

A new chill swept through Albano's body. He had trouble finding his voice. "How … how do you know what Lucienne looks like?"

"Do you think that I would hear the news that my sister is here and not go look for myself? I saw your ugly wife. And I saw those children of yours." He laughed triumphantly. "The binoculars you bought me? Those birds I was speaking of? It was them! That daughter you have? Now, that is a beautiful girl." He added, shaking his head, "But the wife?" He shook his head and clicked his tongue disapprovingly.

Albano felt a pulsing energy shoot through his arms and fists. "When was this?"

"Where do good Jews go on the Shabbath? Not to be closer to God, but to be seen and admired by other Jews. There isn't a grand enough synagogue in Cannes, is there? The good one is right here in Nice. All I needed to do is wait by the temple. I recognized your car. I saw you with them. You didn't see me. That is my genius, you see? I can make myself invisible. All those good Jews walk right past a hobo sitting on the steps of their temple." He took an inhale of his cigarette, waved his hand agreeably. "Oh, do not feel bad, it is the same with Christians and Muslims. If you want to hide in plain sight, dress in the way that ensures that no one will want to look your way." To demonstrate, he took the denture out of his mouth, hunched his back, made a terrible face, and laughed.

Albano put his elbows on the table and took his face in his hands, looking contrite but thinking fast. "I feel terrible Hagop. I did not know how to tell you any of this."

Hagop plopped his teeth back in his mouth and sucked them back into place. The act would have been comical had he not added, "Here is what I want to know: why bring me to France if it was to make me feel like a pariah?"

"I wanted to help you. I still do."

"Another thing I don't understand is how your wife lets you have a mistress right under your roof. Is it because the mistress is even uglier than the wife? Your wife could never believe you'd want to fuck her."

"Please stop using those vile words. Xandra and I don't have that—"

"Why concern yourself with vile words just as you are committing the vile deed, dear friend? I am told that Xandra is so ugly now no one can look at her. But you're trying to keep us apart, aren't you?"

Albano finally erupted. "How could I not? I had every intention to welcome you into our lives. Every intention! But you knew Xandra was alive all these years, and you didn't even bother to answer her letters. I am trying to help you, Hagop, you know I am, and yet you keep refusing to be helped. And you are refusing to help yourself!"

Hagop was nonplussed by Albano's anger. "Do you know what this looks like?" he asked sweetly. "Not to me, but to a stranger that might enter this conversation? It looks like my sister, whom you left to die in Smyrna, my sister who is so deformed that she will never find a husband, has become your slave."

"She is no one's slave!"

"She is unless she can leave if she wishes."

"Of course, she can."

"Even with the way her face looks? And war happening on every continent? Is she left with any other choice than to be at your mercy? It would seem to a stranger's eye that she is, in fact, your prisoner."

"I pay her a wage. I only took her from Paris and to the South of France to protect her!"

"The Russian nobles paid their serfs too; only they had the right of life and death over them. What would happen to an Armenian girl, the most hated and persecuted race in the world, if she was left on her own without protection from a rich Jew?"

"I wish you could understand. Xandra wants to be here."

"But you legally have no right over her."

"None whatsoever."

"So, she is mine," Hagop said.

Albano was astounded. "Yours?"

Hagop pursed his lips. "She is my blood. When I leave France, she will come with me."

Albano crossed his arms to control the shaking of his body. "This is not how the world works. Not this part of the world."

Hagop chuckled. "Which is why I must take her to a part of the world where it does." He slapped Albano on the shoulder, "You are so pale. You know I am having fun at your expense, don't you?" Albano looked at Hagop, relieved at first, but then he saw that the angry light in Hagop's eyes was intact. "Is it why you won't show me your family, dear brother? Why you cannot let me see the nice little Jewish family full of lies and deceit you have crafted for yourself? You are afraid I will tell your wife the truth."

Albano felt a profound sadness fall over him. "What is it you want from me?"

"I will tell you one thing that could be of comfort to me. I, exhausted as I am, must do everything myself. I must shop and cook for myself like a woman, and clean after myself when I am so tired. I am a beast of labor, no better off here than in the refugee camp."

"Do you want me to hire you a servant?"

"Never, Albano. No charity, please. You are already doing so much for me I am starting to feel insulted." Hagop sat down in an armchair, crossed his legs and tilted his back against the padding of the chair, observing him. "No," Hagop continued. "I will only take what is mine. My sister. She can tend to me." And with this, he smiled his new bright white smile, and his eyes shone with cold calculation.

Albano's mind raced. Hagop did not seem like a victim of anything, at this moment. He did not seem miserable. He was dominant, very much in control; perhaps he had been in control the entire time. Had it all been an act? The man Albano faced was not the Hagop of his youth, but neither was he the helpless immigrant, the traumatized victim of genocide he had appeared to be ever since he arrived in Nice. Had the absence of a response to his letters, had Hagop's every move since the boat brought him to Nice been nothing but manipulation and brewing resentment? No, it could not have been. You must be a little scared of me, Hagop had said weeks ago. And Albano had denied it. But now he realized that he had been wary of Hagop all along.

Albano felt the overwhelming urge to leave now, dart to the house, take the family and Xandra and drive off toward a different city. Where, he didn't know. Away from Hagop was all that mattered. It would be days until Hagop discovered where they lived if he didn't know already. No, no. He was overreacting. Hagop was his friend. A friend in need who had just learned news he disapproved of and was justifiably angry. Albano made sure to speak in a steady voice. He needed to gain time. "Xandra is busy with my children who cannot be without her."

Hagop flew his fingers impatiently. "Then at night. After they have gone to sleep she can come to my place, mend and clean my things, make me supper."

"I will ask her," Albano lied.

"What ask her?" Hagop said. "She doesn't get a choice. You *tell* her."

And so, that night Albano went to Xandra and told her the terrible thing that was happening. "And so, his anger is placed on you, wanting you, as though you're his property."

In Xandra's expression, Albano could read that she was not surprised. A part of her had expected this kind of thing from Hagop all along. "He is a traditional man from my culture. From his standpoint, this is a natural thing," she said.

"Do you really think it is about being served? No, it is about claiming you as property. It is about challenging me. I am worried, Xandra. Those things Hagop says … one minute he is laughing, the other he praises me, the next he threatens. I see it now. From the first moment, he resented me. For being rich, for having avoided the terrible things he endured. Now your brother sees that while he was in deep misery, I went on to do precisely what he had forbidden me to do, which was to be with you."

"But we are not together in that way."

"He doesn't believe it or doesn't care."

"What brother is he to me who would rather know me dead or trapped in poverty and servitude than happy with you?"

"I am deceiving Lucienne and the children, and now Hagop. Also, I am not giving you the life you deserve. I am asking you to make all the concessions."

"We are both making concessions."

"What if Hagop is right? My life is nothing but lies."

"The deceptions are the only way to keep all those you love close by and protected, and that includes Hagop."

"I thought that finding him would be one of the greatest joys of my life. I thought that at last, I would be complete. Instead, I am afraid it will be my family's demise."

"You think he is about to tell Lucienne?"

"I don't know what he wants to do. I cannot understand his motives or his designs."

"Do you think he will blackmail you?"

"I'm not sure," Albano said, although he had to admit to himself that he was already being blackmailed.

Xandra breathed in and looked resolute. "I can go to his apartment and work for him if this will appease him."

Albano shook his head forcefully. "Never. I will not let you near him. Tomorrow I will tell him I can hire someone to serve him or nothing at all."

"And then what do you think will happen?"

"I am afraid he will want to punish us for being together."

"Do you think he wants to physically harm us?" Xandra asked.

"Of course not,"

"He has done that before."

"He was young then."

"He has it in him," Xandra said.

"He will not harm anyone," Albano said with as much conviction as he could put into his voice. "But he might tell my family about us, and this I cannot have. I will make a telephone call to Moshe in Algeria."

"You will ask for his counsel?"

"His counsel, and once again for his help."

The following day, Albano came to Hagop's prepared, but to his great surprise, Hagop refused to let him enter the apartment. He was waiting for him at the foot of the building and coldly asked for Albano's set of keys back. Albano handed them to him, not understanding. "Let's go to the park," Hagop said.

For someone claiming not to know the city, Hagop now seemed perfectly at ease in the streets. Also, he walked straight now. The limping, that hesitant gate, was gone. Albano had the sinking understanding that Hagop had been pretending to be worse than he was.

The park was deserted but for three French sailors on leave. It was early May. Trees were in bloom, as were the tulips planted in well-groomed beds at the foot of the trees. He and Hagop sat on a stone bench facing a water feature where a dozen sparrows cleaned their feathers, sending sprays of water around them. The ground of crushed stone was covered in the pink petals of ornamental cherries. Hagop scooped a handful of pebbles and flung them at the birds with surprising accuracy. "You ask what I do in my days since you have refused me the dignity of employment?" he said. "I have been very busy. I take my bus to Cannes in the morning, and I wait. Many days I am able to catch a glimpse of those rare birds that are so fascinating to me with my pretty spyglass you bought me yourself." Hagop let the sentence float, his silence heavy with meaning. Albano knew exactly what it meant, and what it meant iced his blood. He said nothing so Hagop went on. "That nice, polite boy of yours. And that daughter, such a gorgeous girl. I do not think much of the ugly wife."

What to say now? What to ask? Albano sensed that he had entered a dreadful game of chess with an opponent far more advanced than he. "Why do you spy on my family?" he finally asked.

"For me to survive this long required a superior mind, a crafty mind," Hagop said. "You and I are the same in that way, cunning and clever. The question remains, who is the cleverer one between us. You brought me here and thought I would become one of your admirers. Someone whose life and thoughts you can control. But I am not that crippled man I appeared to be. I am in fact powerful."

"I don't want you around them," Albano said icily.

Hagop guffawed. "Oh, now it comes: the truth!"

"You need to take control of your thoughts. Until you do, I cannot let you into my life."

"Let me into your life? Why would I want to be in your life of lies? I despise everything about it. You brought me to France for your own vanity. You thought I would become indebted to you, forever speechless with admiration, forever humbled by my own shortcomings, forever blessing the ground on which you walk."

"You're speaking nonsense."

"You underestimated me. Just as you did when you thought you could trap me in the cave so that you could steal my money."

"Can't you remember?" Albano exclaimed, outraged. "You were robbed! This, after leaving Xandra and me in the cave with nothing!"

"You trampled the values I held dearest by desecrating my own sister—"

"Only I hadn't touched her."

"Leaving me no choice that day but to either kill you both or exile myself. I had twenty years to think of this, Albano. I loved you like a brother, and so I could not kill you that day at the cave. Instead, I chose to leave, and my life was a nightmare thereafter. And to this day I have nothing. Whereas you have everything, and all this because I sacrificed myself for you."

"Had you stayed put in the cave as I begged you to do, you would not have been taken by the police!" Albano exclaimed, furious. "Your demise was your own doing."

"And your vanity will be your undoing! You wanted me to witness your superiority; only you cannot control me. You should never have brought me to France, Albano. I will never stop short of gaining justice."

"What are you saying?"

"I have not yet decided what would please me. One word from me and your children and wife will find out who you really are and who their dear nanny is. Do I want to destroy your family? Or do I demand that you sign over to me all your money? It would only be fair. Or should I not be so merciful and repay myself for my sister's honor."

"I don't know what you mean?"

Hagop casually said, "You have a virgin."

Albano jumped to his feet and faced Hagop. "You are insane! If you touch a single strand of hair on my daughter's head, I will kill you indeed. I will!"

"Then do not fail, Albano," Hagop said with icy calm. "As each time you have damaged me, I have come back stronger. As you told me that day on Mount Pagus, one of us will die. And so, we shall see who it is."

Albano was seized with panic. He steadied himself. He thought of nothing to say, and so he turned away and left.

As he moved toward the exit of the park, past the row of ornamental cherry trees, he heard more pebbles being thrown into the water and birds scattering away. Once he turned back to look at Hagop, but the bench was empty.

On the drive back home, Albano stopped on the side of the road. He squeezed the wheel with his fists until they turned white. What would he do now? The madman Hagop had become had left nothing of the Hagop he loved. No matter what Albano and Xandra had dreamed up, that man, that friendship, no longer existed. The rage and contempt Hagop had expressed that day at the cave had taken root over the years, nurtured in the fertile terrain of his psyche by the terrible persecutions he had suffered and witnessed. In his few months in France, Hagop had gained in strength, but not the kind of strength Albano had imagined. His strength, bred of agony, had transformed into a sinister force. A force that could not be reasoned with. A dangerous force. Now Hagop was threatening his family, threatening to harm his daughter. How could this be?

Xandra would not be surprised. She alone had been able to see Hagop for who he was. She had witnessed his temper and harshness before. Even as she had prayed for the safety of her brother, she had been wary of him. Albano had been blinded by a ridiculous idea of how things could be that had no basis in facts. And now, to think that this crazy man knew his family's whereabouts, that he possibly even knew his address!

He thought of the conversation he and Moshe had had just a few days before. Moshe believed that Hitler would not relent. He was certain that this phony war was only giving Hitler time to prepare. The time to leave France was immediately Moshe had said.

Albano got to La Bastide transported by a new form of urgency. He stopped the car in front of the door, stormed into the house, walked past Lucienne and went straight to the kitchen to speak to Xandra. In Armenian he told her everything Hagop had said as Lucienne stood in the kitchen, her arms limp along her body, a look of complete confusion on her face.

"What will we do?" Xandra answered in Armenian, trying not to show her own panic or to look at Lucienne.

"This is what Moshe and I prepared for. We are ready. A few telephone calls are all it will take."

"When?"

"In the next few days."

"How?"

"We'll take our boat at night. We will meet another boat Moshe arranged once we're at sea. Once in North Africa, we will get new identities. No one here or elsewhere will know where we have gone."

"What about Hagop?"

"I will pay for his rent for two years in advance. I'll open a bank account in his name with enough money to live reasonably. I will leave that information for him, which he will receive once we are gone."

"This will enrage him," Xandra said.

"There is no better solution."

Albano then turned to Lucienne who was still standing near the kitchen door. "We are leaving," he said.

"What? Where? Why?"

"The plan you and I discussed, our departure for Africa. We're putting it in motion."

"What I want to know is –?" Lucienne began to say.

Albano interrupted her. "If the Nazis invade, the frontiers will close. Then they'll be no one to protect the Jews of France and no way to escape."

"What I don't understand is—"

Albano raised his palm to stop her from speaking. "Lucienne, I know that you think I am overreacting, and I know that you fear that I might be wrong. But whether I am or not, the result is the same. We are leaving France."

Lucienne said in a small voice, "What I don't understand is ... why did you rush to tell Sandra all this? Why tell *her* before telling *me*?"

Albano could not respond. After all these years of keeping his secret, in his anguish and his hast, he had been careless. Lucienne was looking at him interrogatively, and then a cloud passed over her face, a terrible realization. She stood very still, trembling and pale. But what could he tell Lucienne at this point? The menace came from everywhere, and they needed to run away, to go as far as possible. He did not expect Lucienne to understand. But in time, she would come to appreciate that he had wanted to save her life even if she was, as he could read on her face, suddenly finding out that he loved someone else, and that the person he loved might well be Sandra.

CHAPTER 8

The Naked Man

Three in the morning. Cassie kept her head firmly grounded on her pillow, her arms alongside her, afraid to move a muscle. Her skin tingled. Her palms tingled. She just needed to wait this out. Breathe.

Beside her, Hervé was sleeping peacefully, his bare back rising gently with each breath. What would this man whose name she did not know twenty hours ago think of her if she woke him up at three in the morning because she was having an anxiety attack?

Breathe.

The pain in her chest grew sharp. Her erratic little inhalations did not fill her lungs. The pain was not real, she told herself. It was an illusion. She had enough of those episodes under her belt to know that she was *probably* not dying. No actual physical danger came from feeling heartbroken.

How many of her memories were real? And even if they were, the offenses were subtle. Nothing that would allow her to point a decisive finger. And like the pain in her chest, nothing real had happened, no sexual abuse, no physical violence, not even shouting, threats, or insults, nothing that could justify her existing in a semi-permanent state of heartache. Her childhood was not exactly Oliver Twist material. Her father didn't drink. He didn't take drugs. He provided. Cassie had only suffered from benign neglect, small meannesses, cruelties that could be just as easily dismissed, even by herself, as a figment of her imagination. The pain came in weird waves, like this, and after what had transpired in the last two days, she should have expected a relapse, especially at night, when she felt most helpless. With her dad, there had been nothing overt. Nothing she could quite point to that would be considered a proof. No, he didn't drink. No, he didn't take drugs. Yes, he provided. But he did not love her.

The worse part of it was not the objective part: being treated with indifference, the micro injustices. The bad part was the sense of unreality. As Cassie massaged the memories in her mind, those gripes, as she called them, those recriminations, she could not, to this day, trust her suspicions. She could not even trust her memories. She was an unreliable narrator of her own life story. Was she one of those people who functioned in the world by believing themselves victimized? That's what her mother and sisters thought, which was sufficient to invalidate her experience. As for her dad, what did *he* believe? Was her dad aware that he had played with her mind? *If* he had played with her mind. But if he had, and now that she had met Marceline, could she dare think that he had done so on purpose? Was it, possibly, a form of retaliation twice removed?

Peter had played a role in all of this. His brief affair soon after the twins were born was something he had denied at first, he had said that it was *all in her imagination.* She was paranoid and insecure, he said, knowing full well that she did not always know how she felt, that she had a hard time trusting her intuition. After owning up to it – but only *after* she found the emails – Peter had called the affair a wake-up call, a chance for their relationship to evolve. In their sessions with the couples' therapist, he had been sincerely remorseful but also had expressed his loneliness in the marriage. Cassie was not always emotionally or sexually available. And she was angry. The general therapeutic consensus seemed to be that if Cassie chose to stay, she needed to forgive Peter. To stay but forever hold a grudge would be to punish him, but also herself. She forgave. With two babies, what other choice did she have? And besides, she loved him.

It was in one of their sessions that the therapist asked about Cassie's childhood, and, after listening gravely, coined the phrase "benign neglect." The benign neglect Cassie suffered as a child, the therapist explained, had possibly engendered a certain sense of anger and insecurity on her part. That neediness in her, that sense of longing, the suspicion that she was not all that lovable were always dangerously near the surface and could be the product of unrequited love for her father. And what might be happening, the therapist had explained, was that she could be emotionally unavailable at times, just like her father had been. Could Peter be blamed for feeling lonely with a distracted and distrusting person such as herself?

Cassie's pulse slowed. The sense of terror subsided. She inhaled fully at last. The anxiety attack ran its course in about twenty minutes, as it usually did.

Hervé's back, lit by the soft glow of the moonlight, was strong and smooth. When she returned to Los Angeles, she would have to add an item to her bucket list, a new, surprising item, one she did not know she wanted. One Night Stand: Check. But wasn't it the gentlemanly thing to do *not* to spend the night? It was unfortunate enough to be in the throes of an anxiety attack in a hotel room far from home. This one was happening while in bed with a stranger with nowhere to hide.

Hervé's light snoring stopped. He stirred. Cassie froze up. He turned on his side toward her and wrapped an arm around her waist. This was so unexpected, the weight of this warm man's arm on her, someone holding her for the first time in years, that she could have burst into tears with relief. His voice came in the dark, whispering. "You're up?"

"No, no," she said.

"Can I stay the night?" he asked sleepily.

"Now you ask?"

"I would love to make love to you again, but I don't have the ardor of my youth."

"Oh, no. By all means. Please go back to sleep."

"What are you thinking about?"

"I'm not thinking."

"I can hear you think from here."

"Just old gripes; please go back to sleep."

"About me being here?"

"Not about you. Nothing you want to hear about at three in the morning. Go back to sleep."

Hervé propped himself on one elbow. She saw him rub his eyes in the semi-darkness. "I want to hear."

She took in a breath. "My dad. He is kind of an asshole to me. That's all."

"Tell me about it," Hervé whispered.

"It's all petty stuff."

"Then be petty."

"I've had this feeling forever that my father favored my sister. Not even favored. Loved her, while he actively disliked me." Cassie stopped herself.

"Tell me," he said. He put his arm tighter around her waist and squeezed her arm gently.

Cassie sighed. "When I was a kid, he used to do and say small, mean things."

"What kind of mean things?"

"Small ones. When no one was watching. I have no witness, no proof, and my sisters and my mother think I'm paranoid."

"What kind of mean things?" Hervé insisted.

"No hitting, no verbal abuse. Nothing like that. All right, this is going to sound stupid. There were traps. Or things that felt like traps. Just little things, from him looking away when I spoke to not laughing when I was trying to be funny to showing no interest in my schoolwork, my friends, my boyfriends, and even my kids later on. Although none of that would have been a big deal had he not been so charmed by everything my sister said and did."

"Did you confront him about it?"

"Not at all. Part of me was sure I deserved it."

As she spoke, Hervé rubbed her arm, warmly, reassuringly. All Cassie had to go on were her feelings, of hurt, of pain, of jealousy toward Odile, of injustice. But every time she tried to explain what had happened to someone, it fell flat. It made her sound vindictive. By insisting, she dug herself into a bigger hole and still proved nothing.

"You think he was gaslighting you?" Hervé asked.

"A father gaslighting his daughter?"

"Why not? It's a form of control like any other."

"But what would have been his motives? Why me? If he were a controlling, mean guy, would he not be that way with my sisters too? So, in all logic, the problem was with me. Either I was unlikable, unlovable, and annoying, or I imagined things. The whole craziness of this affected my choices, how I looked at people, how I looked at myself, how I behaved."

"You seem fine now," he said, still caressing her arm comfortingly.

"It was a pretty deep hole to climb out of," she said.

"Why are you thinking about all this now, at three in the morning?"

"All these thoughts are coming back to the surface because of his sister. It's that aunt I told you about. You see, now there is a whole new piece to the puzzle. He hated his sister, and I now think it's possible that I reminded him of her."

"Now there is a motive for the crime."

Crime, yes. There was something hard lodged deep inside Cassie's heart that released its poison slowly, and her dad had put it there. "That's what I need to get to the bottom of," she said. "My life has never quite felt like my own. It feels like a collection of broken parts. And I carry the burden of making them all fit together. And suddenly, it's like I can see an outline for the whole. I don't know what it is yet, but I don't think it's just me being crazy in the head. Not anymore."

Cassie sighed deeply. The anxiety attack had passed, and she felt flooded with relief and also hope. Her relationship to her father might have been broken long before she got there. Her marriage to Peter had never been salvageable, and her current relationship to him might not be worth hanging on to. Her connection to her sisters could only be repaired if they wanted it to be. Her computer and phone were broken, and she was doing just fine without them. Her house, which barely held together, did not anchor her; it jailed her. And it was filled with discarded items no one wanted or needed but that she nonetheless felt obligated to keep. But being here, meeting Marceline, meeting Hervé, she felt herself on the cusp of something new, the discovery that she did not need to hold on to those things, that they were not her responsibility to fix.

Hervé had sensed the relaxation of her body. He was caressing her differently now, gently up and down her body, lightly, following the contours of her breasts, her waist, her hip, her thigh. "The ardor of my youth seems to have suddenly returned," he announced. With this, he began to kiss her.

****

Cassie awakened to the coos of a pair of pigeons on the balcony. Hervé was again sound asleep next to her. Had she dreamt their discussion in the middle of the night? Had she dreamt the sex? She slipped out of bed and into the bathroom, careful not to make a sound. She stared at herself in the mirror. Yowzer! She mouthed to her reflection. Yowzer, yowzer, yowzer. The mirror was too small to reflect anything below her shoulders, so the inner critic could only lament the bed hair, the smudged eye makeup, and what might very well be a love bite on her neck. Down below, where the mirror did not spread its accusatory reach, she was definitely naked. And there was one gorgeous male specimen sound asleep in her bed. Yow-Zer! How did she, of all people, let her guard down long enough for a man to charm her into going to bed with him?

She looked at the bathtub. She always wondered how in the movies people had sex, hopped into the previous day's clothes, and walked right out, or worse, had more sex without so much as the contact of a toothbrush on a stale tongue. This was no movie, she thought, spreading toothpaste on her toothbrush. She brushed her teeth energetically and removed her eye makeup thinking as fast as her comatose brain would let her. If she ran a bath, she would wake him up, accelerating the inevitable, the humiliating morning after when the man can't wait to leave, the woman feels guilty, and both parties avoid eye contact. She decided that she needed a bath and she needed it now. Perhaps, hearing the water, he would gather his things and run away. A bath was the perfect solution to all her problems, simultaneously cleaning her and allowing him a quick, wordless escape.

The old pipes whined and moaned as the water hit the tub with a thunderous splash. She dropped some shampoo into the water and the tub filled with foam. She got in and submerged her head completely and floated there with only her nose and feet out of the water. Bursts of panicky thoughts mixed in with flashes of recollection about her nighttime behavior. What in the world had she just done? This was thrilling in the way tightrope walking is thrilling. She, the poster girl for middle-age righteousness and modesty, had just had casual sex with a stranger on their first date. How could she have done that? Of course, she could. Anyone with a pulse would have, wouldn't they? The real question now was how she had managed all these years without a man's touch. It was all so wonderful. Better than wonderful. Her craving frightened her. It had been like going from a restricted calorie diet to binging on a giant plate of brownies. Forbidden. Desperate. Delicious. Wrong. But why should this be wrong? Her conscience was clear. She was a grown, unattached woman. And yet, she knew this was dangerous in ways that she hadn't begun to contemplate.

She pushed her head out of the water and found a naked Hervé standing in front of the mirror, looking critically at his tongue. "You don't have a second toothbrush, do you?" Hervé said.

"A second toothbrush? I don't even have enough panties to last me a week," she said, pointing at the half dozen bras and underwear in various stage of dryness hanging over the cast iron radiator.

He shrugged, squinted at the toothpaste, unscrewed its top, pressed a bit of paste on his finger, and proceeded to use his finger as a brush. "Why yo too-pash an ininch?" He asked, his mouth filled with foam.

"What?"

He bent over the sink, rinsed his mouth, and stood up again, looking as natural naked as if he were Adam himself. "Your toothpaste," he said, presenting her with the tube. "Why is it in English?"

She stared at the toothpaste in shock. "Hmm ... yes ... yes, indeed. I guess I never noticed."

He looked at her face, which rested above a mountain of foam. "I hope you're naked in there."

"Ahem ... yes—"

She had not finished responding before Hervé stepped over the tub and lowered himself into the water and sank in to his shoulders opposite her. "But...."

"What?" he asked.

"There is a naked man in my bathtub."

"And a naked woman," he said, tilting his head back and groaning with pleasure. "Nice tub."

"Can I ask you a question?"

"Usually not before coffee, but all right."

"Why did you go to bed with me?"

"You're surprised?"

"I am."

"Why would you be surprised?"

Cassie shrugged.

He blew on the mound of bubbles between them, making a hole in it. "I don't know why. I wanted to. Do I need to know? Is it important to know why? I mean, why did *you*?"

"Because you're charming and you asked nicely," she said.

"All right," he said. "I went to bed with you because you're desirable. And also, because you're interesting."

"Interesting?"

"Very much so. You do all kinds of interesting things."

"That's your reason?"

"And you're strange."

"Oh, that can't be good."

"No, no ... it's good. It's excellent. Sex is not everything, you know. Well, it is everything, but not if the next morning you can't stand the person you wake up next to. I like to wake up next to a person who's interesting."

"And strange."

"Strange is the icing on the cake."

They dressed and went down to the Jument for breakfast. They sat at their table, giggling like school children because the patronne had peered at them with suspicion. After their First Date (considering how unlikely all this was, Cassie giddily capitalized the event in her head), and their First Sex, and their Second Sex, all in under twelve hours, followed by their First Bath, they were sitting down together for their First Breakfast. Why Hervé had not darted out of the room after First Sex was no longer a question she asked herself. Why ask why about anything in this new bizarro world? In the recesses of her memory, she was a woman with grown children, an antagonistic family here in Paris, and a pressing life that awaited her in Los Angeles. But for the moment, all was right with the universe. "Our matchmaker is looking particularly disagreeable this morning," she told Hervé.

Hervé got up from his chair and moved to sit right next to her. He put his arm around her waist. "That's better."

"People are going to see …," she whispered.

"Oh, they have not seen anything yet," he assured her, lowering his arm and caressing the small of her back under her sweatshirt.

"You don't know this about me," she said, "but I'm a bit of a prude."

"Against all evidence to the contrary," he said, moving his hand away when the waiter approached. "What would you like to order?"

"Everything!" she said.

Hervé ordered two cafés au lait, two glasses of orange juice, buttered baguette, and confiture. They ate ravenously, whispering to each other, and laughed about everything. There could have been a hundred people around them, or none at all; she felt swallowed into this moment, this man, his eyes, his two-day-old beard, every pore of her body still reverberating from his touch.

"This is the best breakfast I ever ate," she said.

"Let's go back up to your room."

"Don't you have to go to work?"

"I'll call in sick."

"You will?"

"My absence won't make a bit of difference. You can't imagine the number of non-emergencies thrown at me in a single day. Grown people having tantrums like two-year-olds. I've had people break things, hurl insults at me over situations I can do nothing about. The other day, there was this angry old woman who barged into my office with her small purse and her thick glasses, clutching a bottle of mineral water. I see her, and I think, what can a frail old woman do? Well, she poured the contents of her water bottle on my keyboard! Just like that, the entire bottle, in front of my nose. There was nothing I could do."

Cassandra laughed. "That is something I can picture myself doing."

"What do you say? I'll call the office and let someone else handle things however they want. We could go out and play all day."

"Your coworkers won't resent having to pick up the slack?"

"They'll have my back today, and another time I'll return the favor."

"That's nice."

"They're idiots, the lot of them, but we show a united front against the people who come and go. Bureaucracy is first and foremost about self-interest." He pondered this. "It is quite awful when you think about it."

"This job might not be good for the soul."

"I'd say this is a correct assessment." He put his hands behind her neck and caressed it. "So? What do you think?"

They kissed, and at that moment she felt her life happen in real time, rather than in slow motion or rushed. How rare it was to be caught in a delicious moment and be aware of how delicious it was. "I can't. I'm supposed to meet my aunt at eight a.m. What time is it?"

Hervé looked at his watch: "half past seven."

She widened her eyes. "I'm supposed to be in the Jardin du Luxembourg in thirty minutes!"

"You'll be late."

"She is almost ninety years old, and she's going to be standing there waiting for me in the middle of a park!"

"Be careful she is not holding a water bottle."

"I have to leave right this minute."

"I'll take you there. It's on my way."

"You work in this neighborhood. How could the Jardin du Luxembourg be on your way?"

"It is now. Let's hurry. If I take the périphérique and go down the Champs Elysées, as long as there isn't a grève or a manif, we'll get there in time." He set cash on the table and, taking her hand, helped her out of her chair. Once she was standing, he enveloped her in his arms. "How about tonight?"

"Tonight?"

"Why do you seem so surprised?"

"Aren't we supposed to play it cool? Isn't that what people do? You know, keep the other person wanting and worrying?"

"Maybe in lousy movies."

"All right," she said. "Tonight."

Outside, the sky was clear and blue, and the temperature surprised them both. "Ha, is it possible that spring has returned?" Hervé said. "Wasn't that incredible? Summer, then back to winter overnight, and now spring?"

They drove through the city. The streets were packed with cars and buses. As Hervé swerved his motorcycle gracefully in and out of lanes, the cars honking in blocked traffic were of no concern to them. Cassie, her body glued against Hervé's, sunk into the moment, the speed, the city, the warmth of him. If this was all so dangerous, why did she feel so safe?

Thirty minutes later, they arrived at Place Edmond Rostand. "I'll park and walk with you to the fountain," he said.

"No, too much of a hassle. You go to work. How's my helmet hair today?"

"Creative," he said, looking at her appreciatively from his sitting position on the Bonneville. He extended a gloved hand and attempted to smooth out her hair. "There is an interesting spring to it."

"I have to run!"

"Seven at your hotel?" he asked taking her hand and bringing her toward him and kissing her.

"Okay. What time is it now?"

"Eight a.m."

"I'm toast!" She ran toward the park's entrance and sprinted toward the fountain as Hervé's motorcycle roared away. No time to contemplate what had happened to her in the last twelve hours; already she could spot Marceline standing by the fountain. She looked regal in a long, green wool cape, a black fringed shawl around her shoulders, a masculine black hat perched on her head, and small-heeled buttoned boots firmly planted in the dirt path. Maurice was standing by, five feet away, ready to pounce should she waver.

CHAPTER 9

Algiers

Marceline stood by the Medici Fountain. The day was going to be beautiful. She loved how the public parks of Paris seemed untouched by time, and she was pleased not to see too many tourists for a change. Without tourists dressed in their garish shirts and flip-flops, she could imagine this was 1930 before World War II, and she and Gustave were children in a game of hide and seek on a Sunday afternoon. And her beloved father was about to spring from behind a bush surprising them both.

She thought of that spring of 1958 when she had waited here, her heart racing, for Khaled to come, knowing that he was risking his life to do so. It was a messy time in history and in her life. The Algerian War was raging. The Fourth Republic was on the cusp of falling. De Gaulle was about to return to power. Fernand was with the OAS then, and she worked for the French secret services. There was a price put on Khaled's head, and he could only have been in Paris to carry out FLN activities. And yet they had both risked everything for a few minutes together by this very fountain.

She was interrupted in her thoughts by Cassandra, who was running toward her.

"I'm sorry! I ran … but still … I'm late," Cassandra said, panting. She was rosy-cheeked, her hair was a mess, and there was an expression of glee on her face.

"You look different," Marceline announced.

"A friend gave me a ride on his motorcycle. I must look awful."

"To the contrary. You look…." Marceline studied her before declaring, "Happy."

Cassandra blushed. "Do I?"

They began by walking around the Medici Fountain. The canopy of plane trees, filled with nascent buds, reflected in the water. Around the rectangular basin, stone vases connected by a rough iron fence were filled with tulips about to bloom. "How pretty," Cassandra said.

Something had changed, Marceline could tell. Her niece looked alive in a way she had not the day before. A man, Marceline decided. She knew that look. Above the basin, an enormous bronze cyclops watched over a white marble couple in a languorous embrace. "This is Polyphemus," Marceline said. "In the act of discovering Galatea, the nymph he madly loves, in the arms of Acis."

"That can't be good."

"Not for Acis," Marceline mused. "Polyphemus ends up crushing his skull to death with a boulder of sorts,"

"No one likes being cuckolded. Or betrayed," Cassandra said.

"How is my brother this morning? The correct thing to do would be to visit him in the hospital, but you understand that my presence would only inflame things."

"There wasn't much of a change last I heard," Cassandra answered in a tone of confusion.

"What are you not telling me?"

Her niece rubbed her forehead, as though she was massaging a difficult thought. "It's difficult to admit, but my mother and sister are not letting me into his room."

"I'm perhaps the best person you could admit this to."

"I guess we're in the same boat."

"Pariahs," Marceline agreed.

She gripped Cassandra's arm. "I hope you don't mind if I hang on to you. I'm in no mood for a broken hip."

"Absolutely."

As they walked around the Jardin du Luxembourg under the warming sun, Marceline told Cassie about Algeria.

On May 13, 1940, our family docked at Algiers's fishing mole as dozens of boats of all sizes unloaded their catch. It was early morning, but already the air was soft and warm. In our rumpled clothes and teetering on our sea legs, we got off the boat and stepped between piles of glistening sardines and mackerels.

Like the men from our boats, the fishermen and workers on the dock had tanned skins, dark eyes, and black hair. Some wore loose-fitting pants and no shirt. Other wore long tunics. Many wore turbans or felt caps. There were women, although in smaller numbers. They wore billowy white fabric garments that covered them from head to ankle. Many had a handkerchief-size piece of fabric covering the lower portion of their face. Some older women wore the same outfit but in black. My heart raced as I walked. It was all so exotic. The smells, the quality of the air, the city above, vast and white and foreign.

I looked back to speak to Sandra, who, to my surprise, had covered her head with a shawl that she held tight under her chin with one clasped hand. But it was my mother who suddenly seemed absurdly out of place in her precious skirt and blazer and her little veiled hat.

For a few minutes, the four of us waited on the dock while my father spoke to men a few feet away.

Next to us, a group of crouching men repaired a mountain of fishnets, their bodies sinuous and muscular. Others moved crates and buckets filled with fish, shrimp, and black urchins, or laid larger fish on tables or directly on straw mats on the ground. The market was being set up in muffled silence, but I had the sense that the quietness had been brought on by our arrival. The men made a point not to look at us directly, but it felt as though they were tracking our every move. Only a group of elderly, toothless men sitting on crates and smoking their pipes, examined us frankly until one cleared his throat and spat noisily on the ground, as though pronouncing judgment. Mother turned pale and uncertain on her feet.

Baba was still speaking to one of the groups of men crouched over the nets. We heard him speak in that guttural language that we now knew was Arabic. Finally, four of the younger men he had spoken to wiped their hands and walked to the boat to fetch our luggage. Mother, Sandra, and I huddled together, while Gustave crossed his arms and stood aside. It was though in this world we knew nothing about, we instinctively knew to adopt the expected behavior of our genders.

One of our porters, a boy about my age, tall and wiry with a striking face and smooth, beautiful skin, returned from the boat carrying our largest suitcase with one arm. In his other hand dangled my dainty, turquoise hatbox, incongruously precious in his rough hand.

"Thank you," I said and held out a gloved hand to take it from him. He ignored my outstretched hand and just peered into my eyes dauntlessly for a brief, disconcerting moment, challenging me. I removed my hand, and he walked passed me, carrying the cases.

We followed our porters and our luggage, walking away from the water and across the deserted wharf. The light of dawn was soft, and we could have been at any of the piers in the South of France. But there was a different taste and texture to the air, something rough and tempestuous. I had the sensation that rules were different here, and that perhaps there were no rules at all.

Ahead of us and up above was a long row of European-style buildings anchored by a series of massive arches. In the sky, seabirds screeched and flew in circles by the hundreds. Two automobiles were parked a short distance away. From one of them emerged a familiar silhouette.

"Uncle Moshe!" Gustave shouted. He and I ran and jumped into our uncle's arms. If Uncle Moshe was here, it meant that things would be alright!

Moshe, dressed as dashing as always despite his formidable girth, kissed us and laughed out loud. He and Baba hugged tearfully, and my mother and he exchanged their customary glacial hellos.

Moshe appeared as much at ease with himself in this Algerian port as he was in Parisian salons. He did not fit in one bit, yet it was everyone else that seemed awkward in comparison. With Uncle Moshe, others could be as stiff or disapproving as they wished to be; it did not seem to trouble him in the least.

The four young fishermen loaded up both automobiles, and Moshe gave them money, a generous amount judging from their pleased expression.

Each automobile had a driver, both menacing-looking men with fedoras planted deep on their heads. This time again, Sandra climbed into the automobile that contained our things, and we piled into the other.

As we drove up a ramp along the row of stone arches, Moshe asked. "Did you hear?" My father, who sat in the passenger seat, looked at him questioningly. Moshe shook his head, "I have bad news. The Germans have made it past Sedan. They are advancing toward Paris."

The next few seconds felt like a plunge into a new dimension. Moshe's words crept inside us, stealing beats from our hearts, turning our palms into pools of sweat. We held our breath in stunned silence. Outside, a white mosque stood, serene. Palm trees swayed in the morning light. My mother broke the silence. "But what about the Maginot Line? Surely they could not have broken through the Maginot Line in three days!"

"They went around it," Moshe said.

In the back seat, my mother placed her face in her hands. "Oh mon Dieu!" she murmured. My father turned, patted her shoulder, and looked at us with great sadness. My mother remained with her face in her hands for a long time. The one thing we had held on to, the one thing we had put all our hopes in, now had disintegrated as though it had no more substance than fog. The Nazis, unlike us, had been able to see the Maginot Line for precisely what it was: an illusion.

"No one believes Paris is safe," Moshe said. "People are expecting bombings. A mass exodus is underway. People from Belgium, Luxembourg, Holland, and France are moving away from the north. There are people on every road; they're in freight trains, automobiles, bicycles, pushing wheelbarrows, even on foot. It is mayhem. Many are running out of provisions and gas already. Millions of people are fleeing."

"What about the people we know in Paris," Baba asked. "Have you news of any of them?"

"Everyone is trying to go South."

"Oh, but this is terrible!" my mother exclaimed. "Our friends are probably trying to reach us, hoping to get shelter in the Cannes house, expecting to find us there!"

"They probably are," Baba said. "The house will be open to them. I gave instructions to Monsieur Malou to let in any of our friends who want to stay there."

"See, Alban?" my mother said, "Our friends are trying to get to the Côte d'Azur. That is where everyone wants to be, and you just made us come here, to this lawless place."

My father looked at her with discouragement. "Lucienne, Dear, if Germany has gone past the Maginot Line with such ease, how long do you think it will be before they invade the rest of France?"

My mother clutched her purse and opened her mouth, but she made no sound. So I asked, "You think it's possible, Baba?"

Moshe is the one who answered. "I want to tell you it isn't. But the truth is, this Maginot Line debacle makes it clear that our generals aren't prepared."

"But we have a great army, and our soldiers are brave!" Gustave said.

"It doesn't matter how brave our soldiers are if the generals aren't using their heads," Moshe answered.

Moshe explained that the Nazis had taken Czechoslovakia, Poland, Norway, and Denmark in just days. What made France any different? What would prevent us from being swallowed in a single gulp? My mind was full of the terrible news of the German offensive, and I took in the scenery with confusion as we drove through the streets. The city was starting its day as our automobile drove past rows of tall apartment buildings. On this block we could believe ourselves back in Cannes or Nice: there were tree-lined streets, Haussmann-style apartment buildings, bakeries and butcher shops, hairdressers and tailors, cinemas, shoe stores, cafés, palm trees, and laundry drying on windowsills. And then on the next block, the sights were unmistakably foreign. There were men in loose, white breeches and turbans that led camels and donkeys and their heavy loads. Veiled women carried woven baskets on their heads. Children no more than six years old did the work of men, sweeping sidewalks and throwing buckets of soapy water on the pavement in front of the entrance of buildings. The air smelled of unknown spices, and many of the trees might as well have been from a different planet. But in the middle of all this exoticism, there were familiar sights: French housewives carrying groceries and baguettes and men in suits and hats hurrying through the streets, briefcases in hand. Everywhere we could see the kepis of French policemen on patrol.

We reeked of fish and sweat, and I desperately wanted a bath, but to anticipate the next minute, hour, day, or lifetime was pointless. The Maginot Line was no more. Countries were capitulating in a matter of hours. The German army was advancing toward Paris. We were in Africa.

Moshe pointed out the window to the strange terraced construction on the flank of the hill: hundreds of low buildings with white façades and tiny windows, all perched on top of each other. "The old city," he said. "The Kasbah. It is the reason Algiers is called La Blanche, the White One. For the most part, Muslims live there. It's a veritable maze of streets. All walks of life coexist inside the Kasbah. There are respectable people but also prostitutes, pickpockets, deserters, and fugitives of the law. If you find yourself lost there, keep going down, and it ultimately leads to the sea."

"You will never set foot there, of course," my mother said in a horrified tone.

"Baba, how did you know?" I asked.

"How did I know what?"

"How did you know to leave France?"

"I did not know, sweet one. I only feared."

I sank into my seat, letting the vibrations of the automobile rock me. Gustave, Mother, Father and Sandra everyone important to me, was right here, safe for the moment in this vast new country. The French generals might not have been using their heads, but my father was. My faith in him was all that I had, and I clung ferociously to that.

As we drove, my father explained that we would be living under the name printed on the false identity papers Moshe had handed each of us in the car. Our last name was now the Dupont, one of France's most common names.

"I'm not sure who this name is supposed to fool, with your accent," my mother told my father.

"It's a good idea to be named like a hundred other families in Algiers alone," he answered.

We were to have a common name and live amongst common people in a nondescript apartment. We were to blend in rather than be noteworthy. It was the opposite of the way Mother had always told us we ought to be. She had always demanded that we distinguish ourselves, that our name be known, our standing noted.

We arrived on rue Mogador in front of a mastodon of an apartment building. It was imposing enough but by no means fancy. Past the front door and the lobby, there was an elevator, a dark spiral staircase, and the faint smell of bleach, soup, and trash. I smiled to myself thinking that to our mother this was the smell of 'everyone else.' The smell of common lives, of common people. A row of chipped mailboxes displayed French last names: Miramont, Pellerin, Perrier. And there was ours, ludicrous on that mailbox: Dupont. We had never lived in an apartment building before, so it was all very exciting to Gustave and me. What a new concept it was for people to live atop one another, without a garden, without a driveway, without many separate rooms for each function. I had always wondered about the strangeness of sharing an elevator or climbing stairs with strangers.

My mother and Baba squeezed inside the tiny elevator that could only accommodate two. "Let's go next," Gustave told Sandra when the elevator came back down. Sandra shook her head stubbornly, "It's like a coffin," she said, made the sign of the cross, and headed up the stairs.

"She'll come around," Moshe said. "It's a long way up."

Moshe squeezed into the elevator with us and showed us how to fold the metal gate and then the door. "We're on the fourth floor!" Gustave said with excitement as he pushed the button. He looked at me, cockeyed. "It smells like cod in here something awful." He sniffed me, "Oh, wait, it comes from you."

"This will be the best bath of our lives," I said as the elevator made its slow, creaking ascent in the center of the spiral staircase.

My parents were already inside the apartment. Mother was standing in the center of the foyer as though afraid to take another step. The high ceilings, tall windows, and a fresh coat of paint did not mask the obvious fact that this had nothing to do with the luxury she considered her birthright.

"What is this?" my mother asked, pointing to the living room furniture with an accusing finger. The décor of the main room reminded me of illustrations in an *A Thousand and One Nights* picture book. The Persian rugs were not only spread on the floor but hanging on walls as well. The dining table was at knee level and surrounded by low benches covered in embroidered cushions.

"That is nice," my father said, smiling. "It is the Algerian way."

"Alban, please have a proper table and chairs brought in."

"No, let's keep it this way," I said. "Dining will be like having a picnic."

"Marceline, no one has inquired about your opinion quite yet," my mother said. "Moshe! It's you, isn't it?" She said, turning to him. "You did this on purpose."

"Me? Never!" Moshe said in protest, looking falsely contrite.

My mother's discomfiture was such that I began to laugh. "Enough, Marceline," she said. "Your lack of empathy astounds me!"

I pointed to Gustave whose shoulders were shaking. "He's laughing too!"

Our mother was livid, and our contained laughter was making things worse. "It's not because we are in Africa that we shall turn to savages!" she said.

Gustave and I exploded into laughter.

She was angry and tired and under a lot of strain. Perhaps it would have been better for me to say nothing, but I, too, was under stress. I unconsciously knew that this new phase of our lives would require being open to new ways of being. I sensed this as clearly as I doubted my mother's capacity to adapt.

The apartment had three bedrooms, a single bathroom, and a kitchen. Sandra would be living in a maid's room under the rooftop.

My mother gasped at the kitchen, "Is food supposed to be prepared only steps away from the bedrooms?"

"We must make do," my father said apologetically.

"I just don't think that's possible, Alban. Do you realize that the smell of food cooking will be wafting through the entire place?"

There was no piano in the apartment, and no one suggested that we should rent one. My father explained that in the spirit of blending in, and until we were sure whom to trust, we would not be hiring any staff.

"Who will cook and clean?" my mother asked in a clipped tone.

"Sandra can," my father said.

"How perfect," my mother said icily.

"Perhaps we'll all learn how," Father said.

"How can you do this to me?" my mother said, her voice quivering.

I thought her drama entirely inappropriate when we were lucky to be safe and hundreds of miles away of the closest German soldier. "Mother," I said with impatience. "Baba is doing the best he can."

My mother spun toward me. "Young lady, I shall not tolerate your disrespect another minute!"

"Why be so narrow-minded?" I mumbled under my breath.

My mother took two steps toward me and without warning slapped me hard across the face.

I stood in shock. She had never slapped me before. My cheek stung. But I was not about to give her the satisfaction of showing it. I stared at her defiantly. Moshe, Gustave, and my father, embarrassed by the whole thing, avoided looking at me. My cheek hurt and my pride was wounded, but my anger demanded that I show none of it. My revenge would start by my acting indestructible.

"Bring your eyes down and apologize right this instant!" she shouted.

I just turned on my heels and walked away from her. Moshe jumped in and changed the subject to explaining how the kitchen worked.

Seething with anger but determined to appear unbothered, I accompanied Gustave and Sandra on an exploration of the apartment.

There were so many amazing new things that I soon forgot my anger. We were greatly entertained by a system whereby the trash went down from a small opening in the wall of the kitchen and fell into the apartment building's underbelly, four floors below, never to be seen again. We walked out on the narrow balcony from where we could see the hundreds of other balconies of buildings across the street. Gustave and I stood aghast, realizing that we could easily peer into the living rooms and bedrooms of the neighbors who lived right across from us and, with a lack of modesty that to us bordered on obscene, did not bother to draw their curtains. Beyond the rooftops was the Bay of Algiers. To our right, minarets stood against the azure sky. Invisible in the distance, an entire sea away, was France, and on the other side, past the mountain range, the mysterious rest of the African continent.

I took in the hectic street below, the balconies of countless apartments, the mingling sounds of French songs over the radio and of the melody of unknown instruments. The smell of the Mediterranean air, which had a different texture here, weaved itself together with the arid winds from the Sahara Desert that began right behind the city at the Atlas Mountains. In instants, I had fallen in love with Algeria.

The following day, my father took us for a stroll around the European quarter where most of the French and local Jews lived. "The French influence started in the 1880s when Algeria became a French overseas territory, through no choice of its own," he said.

The French, he explained, had built the city on the flank of the mountains in an architecture reminiscent of Paris, in a succession of terraces around the Kasbah, the old Algerian fortress. Two civilizations mingled in a patchwork of architectural styles. There were tree-lined streets and rows of Haussmann-style buildings. There were wrought iron lampposts at every street corner. Automobiles crisscrossed the city. An elaborate system of climbing and turning trolleys served as public transportation. We walked past stores of the kind we were used to, from the simplest boulangerie to the fanciest department store. But the soul of the city came from the Neo-Moorish architecture of the older buildings, the horseshoe arches, the rounded windows, the columns, the ornate mosaic motifs, the fountains, the shaded arcades over the sidewalk to shield pedestrians from the hot African sun.

The vegetation in Algiers went mostly unchecked, sprawling, wild. Foliage we considered houseplants in Paris climbed trees like monkeys. The palm trees we had discovered in the South of France here were indigenous. There were churches and temples, but it was the domes and minarets of a hundred mosques that dominated, shining like jewels in the skyline. Algiers smelled of the sea, of tagines cooking in stone ovens. It smelled of camel dung, and trash, and rose flower essence. As we took in the city, the smells, sights, and sounds moved through my senses like a shockwave. It was as though I had been asleep my entire life and were awakening at long last.

"There are three distinct cultures in Algiers," my father explained. "There are the North African Muslims, the North African Jews, and the French colonizers. Algeria is run by the descendants of Europeans who settled here about one hundred years ago after winning their war, and by the North African Jews because they were given French citizenship soon after, and so their children were able to have a French education and do well."

"What about the Muslims?" Gustave asked. "Weren't they given French citizenship and education?"

"No," my father said.

"Why not?"

"This is the kind of injustice that happens after wars," he said.

Father, Mother, Gustave, and I walked in the shade of trees along rue d'Isly. The cinema house still showed *Le Jour Se Lève* with Jean Gabin and Arletti, a movie that had come out in Paris months ago. We entered the librairie-papeterie. Gustave bought a comic book, but those, too, were a month behind. The many boulangeries were filled with the familiar aroma of brioche and baking baguettes, and we relished that small normalcy. We walked inside a beautiful building built in the Neo-Moorish style, the famed Galeries de France, where we would be able to buy everything nice we liked, from Mother's Guerlain face powder to the Schiaparelli scarves I coveted.

We had lunch on the terrace of a brasserie, and, sitting on the outdoor chairs, we could have believed ourselves back on the Riviera: same obsequious service, same spotless silverware and starched white tablecloth, same escargots à l'ail and choucroute garnie on our plates, same customers in dark suits with thin mustaches, same wives in blooming hats and tailleurs, with the same spoiled poodles below the table licking foie gras off their fingers. Mother relaxed. For a moment it seemed possible she might acclimate. But as soon as we stepped out of the restaurant, the smell alone reminded us of how far from France we were. It was the smell of kebabs and spicy merguez sausages grilling on impromptu cast iron grills set up by a street vendor right on the sidewalk outside the restaurant. To my mother's dismay, the Algerian way of life, its foods, its colors, its scents, could not be contained as it spilled out of the restaurants and markets onto proper-looking European streets. "They are cooking out on the street? Just like that?" my mother exclaimed. 'They' would become her code name for everything Algerian and anything that frightened her, which was one and the same.

We walked toward the sea. On the waterfront, the local French people, who were known as colons, were easy to distinguish from the fresh arrivals from France such as ourselves. The men wore suits, and the women dressed in Paris fashion. Yet there was a certain languor and self-assurance to them that could only come from several generations of feeling both entitled and superior to the indigenous people. The attitude of the colonizer, I presumed. My father said that although they were French, many had never seen France, nor had their parents.

I wasn't sure how to tell the Jews from the non-Jews because they all dressed in the European style, but the Muslims looked, moved, and dressed in their own ways. Some of the Muslim men dressed in European pants and shirts and even suits, but most dressed like the fishermen we had seen at the dock. They had fezzes, caps, or turbans on their heads, loose pants gathered at the ankles under long tunics called djellaba. Some wore woolen capes wrapped around their bodies. The Muslim men spoke in Arabic interspersed with French as they sat at the terraces of cafés, or had their beards trimmed in outdoor barber shops, or played cards on flimsy tables. There were men guiding donkeys loaded with belongings, men pulling camels, men carrying goats. We saw an autobus go by with a dozen men perched atop its roof. We saw a group of Bedouin from the desert sitting on the sidewalk, smoking and conversing with animation. The Muslim men had a disconcerting way of never looking at us. We walked among them, and they acted as though we were invisible. The Muslim women moved through the streets in small groups. Most women, but not all, covered their hair and faces according to Islamic law, and all you could see of them were their ankles and sandaled feet, the tip of their hennaed fingers, and the eyes, lined with black Khol, they averted when we looked at them. I was flustered to see that the women of European descent got to dress like French women, speak like French women, behave like French women, and not cover their heads. I wondered how offensive this might be to the Muslim population. But no one else seemed to be asking themselves that question.

"This town is a veritable Tower of Babel," my mother said. "Are you sure it is safe for us to walk like this?"

"The French police are everywhere," Gustave said. "I see more kepis than turbans."

"Just as in Paris, or any other city, there are areas of town to avoid," my father said, taking Mother reassuringly by the elbow. "Remain in the European areas and you'll be perfectly safe."

"Still, They are everywhere," she said. "We don't know what They are like."

I too wanted to know what the Algerian Muslims were like and how and where they lived. How different were they from us? How did the women feel about their veils? What did they discuss when they were amongst themselves? What did they care about? In Algiers, we would be living side by side, yet our worlds seemed hermetically shut off from one another.

Not all Muslims ignored us. To many who sold goods or begged, we represented their livelihood. We walked down one block, and a man in djellaba with a shaved head waved for us to get closer to the small table he had set out on the sidewalk, which was covered in a bright heap of mandarins and lemons. A boy in rags pursued us to offer, for a few francs, fried sardines rolled in newspapers. Further down the street, an old woman shoved in front of us a mound of sweets that resembled the kind that Sandra made. Because we were raised on the stuff, Gustave and I had a particular taste for fried dough drenched in honey. The woman pointed to her pastry and said in broken French, "Fruits déguisés, Cornes de Gazelles."

"Mother, can we buy some?" we asked.

"Out of the question! It isn't hygienic."

My mother never did allow us to eat street food. So we learned, along with many other infractions to her rules, to do it behind her back. Life was about to change for Gustave and for me. We were about to get a taste of something new: freedom, the kind achieved through sneaking, and lying, and doing things the moment our preoccupied parents had their backs turned.

We did not have far to go; down the steps from the apartment were new tastes and sensations just at our fingertips. I was seventeen and Gustave was fifteen, and the lure of a culture that charmed us, that intimidated us, and that we wanted to understand was too compelling to resist.

We ended our first stroll through Algiers by shopping at Le Bon Marché, the French department store. My father bought Gustave a miniature replica of a super heavy FCM F1 tank and for Mother a bottle of Soir de Paris. "And you my Princess, what will make you happy?" he asked.

I jumped at my chance. "Baba, I'm positively dying for a bottle of Chanel Number Five. Oh, pretty please, say yes!"

"She's far too young for that," my mother said.

"Isn't this a woman's perfume?" my father asked.

I put my arms around his neck. "That is what I will be in just a few months, Baba. I'll be eighteen, like it or not."

"Well, I do not like it at all," he said, kissing me on top of my head.

I went through that bottle so fast. I would have bathed in it had I been able to. I might have been more parsimonious had I known that it was the last bottle of perfume I would get my hands on for the next five years.

That first week, my mother made an effort. Baba went to work with Moshe, and so she tried to be brave and take Gustave and me to the department store. Afterward, we sat in front of grenadine syrup and madeleines on the terrace of the Le Bon Marché's restaurant. My mother struck up a conversation with a French woman in pearls. Her daughter, a bosomy girl about my age in white gloves, white ankle socks, and a smock dress, pouted and seemed set on not making eye contact. The girl's name was Béatrice. The family was Jewish. She did not tell this to us, but we could sense it, and she probably could tell we were Jewish as well. They were from Le Vésinet, a suburb of Paris. The father worked at the préfecture, and they had lived in Algiers for a year. The conversation, pregnant with euphemisms, started.

"Are you here on holiday?" the woman asked.

My mother scoffed. "Some holiday this would be, if you know what I mean!"

The woman laughed, displaying an impressive row of buck teeth. "François and I were biding our time until we'd be able to return," the woman said. "But with the situation, he wonders if we would not be better off staying here for a while."

"Indeed, perhaps it is best to stay put until things quiet down in France," my mother said, acknowledging in our presence for the first time that she approved of our coming here.

"Who would want to be here, if not compelled to be? I suppose you have to be born here. But if you ask me, the local French are much more like the Muslims than they care to admit."

"They are very local indeed," my mother said.

"What brings you here? I hope it doesn't have to do with the unfortunate affairs in Europe?"

"Oh, not at all," my mother lied. "Only my husband's business venture."

"François says that the German forces should never have attacked us."

"Why could they not content themselves with Denmark and Belgium?" my mother said.

"It is a delusion of grandeur for Monsieur Hitler to think that he can face our generals," the woman added with genuine conviction. "This war shall be over before it has begun."

My mother brightened, "Is this a fact?"

"My husband's colleagues at the Préfecture assure us of it."

"What a relief!" my mother exclaimed.

"And so what is your husband's business?"

"He's in the fine rug trade."

"Why we must exchange addresses! The girls are the same age. They absolutely must become friends."

Béatrice gave me a bored look.

We bid them goodbye and agreed to meet a few days later. Mother said that we did not yet have a telephone number. The lie showed that no matter what she said about not being worried, she regardless took the secrecy part seriously.

When we left the restaurant, my mother had a spring in her step. We chatted as we walked on one street and then the next. We discovered that Algiers went from the sea and climbed the hillside following the curves of the canyon and that the various levels of the city connected through an intricate assortment of ramps, stairs, terraces and gardens, most of them built on an incline. We went up and down stairs that connected parallel streets we did not recognize. We went up and down, and down and up, right and left, argued, attempted to retrace our steps, and before long, we were lost.

The realization came to us as a shock when we came face to face with a crouching camel next to which sat a turbaned man. My mother clung to her purse. "Oh my," she said with a shrill. "Gustave, do you know the way back?"

Gustave shook his head. "I don't know this city any more than you do."

"But aren't you good at maps and such?"

"I can read a map," he said impatiently. "Only as you can see, I don't have one at the moment, or else we would not be lost."

"Lost? Oh, but we must, must find our way home! Oh goodness!"

We turned into a small street bustling with brown men in djellaba. Where were we? My mother kept muttering "Oh goodness!" in a panicked voice. We walked into a street that was dark, odorous, and littered with trash. We turned around, and at the end of it seemed to sprout three narrower streets. "Which one have we come from?" my mother wailed.

We tried the largest of the three and found ourselves at the foot of stairwells which led to an animated public square were, bursting out from every door, street merchants sold grilled meat, baskets, rugs, piles of dates and dried apricots, fabric, live chickens, baby goats, and small dead animals. Women draped in veils sat on mats made of woven dried fibers with flat baskets filled with pastries in front of them. Feral-looking children, dogs, and cats ran amok. There were taverns outside of which Berber men smoked pipes and drank unknown beverages.

I gazed upward. We were at the foot of a series of lime-washed structures built on the side of a hill, with meandering stairs, haphazardly placed windows, and flat roofs.

"It's the Kasbah!" Gustave exclaimed.

"Oh my God," my mother whimpered. "They will murder us!"

The place was dense with Muslim men and women, but they ignored us completely and went about their lives in the jumble of cafés, workshops, and fruit stands. "No one will murder us," I told her. "Look, they're just regular folks." Despite my reassuring words, I remembered what Moshe and my father had said: this was not a place for French children or French mothers. And it was certainly not a good place in which to get lost.

My mother must had a similar thought. She froze in place, white, trembling. She grabbed me with clammy hands. "I … can't go on. I can't … can't move," she said, supplicant, her eyes glazed with panic. She went limp. Gustave and I supported her and led her to steps away from the crowd. She sat heavily on the stone stairs. My mother sitting on the bare ground of a city, was an almost incomprehensible sight.

"Are you ill?" I asked. "Let's ask for help."

"Not *Them*!" Mother shrieked. She added below her breath. "We need to find someone like *us*."

"We ought to find a policeman or someone," Gustave said. "But where?"

Indeed, wherever we were now, there was not a kepi in sight.

"You stay here with Mother," I told Gustave. "I'll go find a policeman." My mother did not object to this. She, who usually took charge of the minutest details of my life, was looking at me imploringly. "Neither of you move away from here," I ordered. "Or I'll never be able to find you again."

"What if you get lost too?" Gustave said.

"I'll try my best not to."

"Goodness," my mother whimpered.

I decided that the best course of action was to head up. At least the stairs weren't crowded, and perhaps from above, I would be able to see where the streets below led and thus regain a sense of direction. The instruction from Moshe had been to go down toward the sea, but it did not make sense to me. We might find dangerous streets on the way down. I left Gustave and Mother and started up the nearest staircase.

If anyone paid attention to me, I did not bother thinking about it.

I did not have to venture far inside the Kasbah to be stunned at the world before my eyes. I passed buildings with deep arches and wooden doors that opened to private courtyards. An entire civilization existed here, just meters away from the European area, one with its rules, its rhythms, its timelessness. Had I gone back in time a hundred years, I felt certain that very little would look different. Away from the bustle of the lower streets, people lived and breathed, children played in the dirt, mothers called them, grabbed them, and pulled them inside the many doors. Men disappeared behind doors. Through a window, there was the sound of two men speaking to each other. A little girl stepped in front of me and laughed. An old man sat on a rug against a wall and watched me as he drew on his pipe. Somewhere, someone pinched the cord of a sort of guitar, and a strange melody rose, echoing through the alley. I had the sense that people could be born, marry, have children, and die without leaving these walls. If you never wanted to be found, this is where you could hide. If you wanted to slit a throat and disappear into a crowd, this would be the place to go. There would be no one to rescue you if you were an outsider and they wanted you dead. The stairs I had gone up led to more stairs and more dark alleys. The names of streets were marked in both French and Arabic. As I climbed, I had taken a mental note of guideposts and street names, but soon they all began to sound and look the same. I had wandered inside the Kasbah for less than ten minutes, and already I was losing confidence that I would be able to find my way back, when at last I saw a respectable-looking Frenchman dressed in a suit and fedora descending the steps. The man looked perfectly at ease and unworried. I threw myself at him and asked for his help. I described the place where I had left Gustave and my mother. In less than two minutes, we found them. He followed me back to Mother, who was huddled against Gustave. Both looked wretched, Mother because she was still in the midst of her episode, and Gustave because he had been forced to endure her.

The French man offered to guide us back to the apartment, and we accepted eagerly. My mother eventually got up and walked. Her face returned to its normal hue, but she did not say a word. Upon our return home, Mother forgot any good manners, and it was left up to me to thank our rescuer. The man just tilted his hat at us and left without giving his name. Mother ran up the stairs of the apartment building and locked herself in her room. An hour later, we could still hear her sobbing behind her door, and she did not acknowledge our knocks.

"What's the matter with Mum?" Gustave asked me.

"I haven't the slightest clue," I told him.

Our indomitable mother had just suffered the first of many attack of nerves, as it was called at the time, the dynamics of which no one in the family, and no one at the time, understood.

It was May 1940 when our family arrived in Algiers. It was in Algeria that I transformed from a spoiled adolescent girl to an idealistic young woman with a delusion of invulnerability. It was in Algeria that Gustave went from a timid boy to having something to prove, at the risk of endangering us all. It was in Algeria that the Allied forces had their first breakthrough in 1942, with a direct impact on the outcome of the Second World War. The Jews of Algeria were instrumental in making the Allied landing in Algeria possible, and our family was at the heart of that day and the days that lead up to it.

It was also in Algeria that Gustave and I turned on each other. And it was in Algeria that our family collapsed, with our beloved father attempting one last time to do what he had done since we were born, his single objective, the reason for his existence: to keep Gustave and me safe.

****

We were arriving in Algeria at a time of unprecedented turmoil. Everyone's fate was up in the air. In the days after our arrival, the news from France went from bad to worse. On June 10th, a *Le Figaro* newspaper headline declared, "The German rush continues to face admirable resistance by our troops." On June 11th, it said: "The enemy has reached the lower Seine River but is being contained by our attacks."

And then nothing. It was as though, overnight, *Le Figaro* had stopped publication.

Paris fell on June 14th. On June 16th, a new government was shaped, led by the beloved Maréchal Pétain, who, to most everyone's dismay, promptly signed an armistice.

The week following Pétain's armistice, all of Algiers had their ears glued to the radio, hoping to decipher the facts through the rhetoric. Many tuned into the BBC in the hope of hearing more from General de Gaulle and his talk of worldwide war and his vow of armed resistance. Rumors spread faster than facts, and then, with the propaganda machine taking hold, there soon was no longer such a thing as a fact. In Algiers, we were spared the pain of seeing Nazi boots under the Arc de Triomphe, but we felt guilty for not sharing in the suffering. Didn't our luck, or cleverness, not imply a certain selfishness? We imagined our friends and neighbors reeling; we pictured the exodus out of Paris, our fellow Parisians powerlessness before the occupiers. The fact that we were far from all this gave us a secret sense of guilt, a shame that, perhaps, was the reason we all wanted to appear heroic in our own ways.

How to describe Algiers of the 1940s? How to separate this place and time in the context of the maelstrom the world had become? We were on French soil, following French rules, enforced by French police within the boundaries of the zone libre, the armistice's agreed-upon French territory unoccupied by the Germans. But the free zone was controlled by the Vichy government, which in turn was controlled by Hitler. And so, this was France under German control, and we were the vanquished. But to Gustave and me, there was a sense of disconnect between the way we were supposed to feel and the reality of our new life. In Algiers, the sky was spotless, the sea and air were warm, the vegetation luxuriant, the people alive and vibrant. Restaurants and cafés brimmed with people; the streets were bustling. By early June, just a month after our arrival, the air became hot. The local architecture was designed to harvest cool air and permit it to flow through houses. The city was a web of arcades, porticos, and courtyards. A briefly opened door would allow for a glimpse of the quiet private gardens that existed in the middle of the city. In those indoor courtyards and breezeways, mosaic fountains trickled water and gave the impression of an oasis. There, people napped, met, talked, had dinner, and lived their lives.

We wished Monsieur Baron Haussmann had been made aware of techniques known by generations of North African builders. In our apartment, the air was as stifling as a woolen blanket. Soon we saw how other people organized around the hot and cool hours of the day. French families that had settled in Algiers for generations, ruling the city and making every effort to shape it, had learned a thing or two over the last hundred years. Whether they admitted it or not, when it pleased them, they hardly resisted the Arabic influences of a culture developed over thousands of years. Concessions had been made. Even those who lived in buildings like ours ended up spending their evening hours on their apartments' terraces and balconies.

We began closing the windows during the hot hours and reopening them at sundown the way the locals did. In Paris, you would have no idea how people lived behind closed doors. Here, people lived their lives in the open for all to see. In the evenings, balconies came to life one by one and entire families flocked outside looking for a breeze, relinquishing inhibition and privacy in exchange for a breath of fresh air. There they watered their potted geraniums, played with their children, kissed, argued, dried their laundry, ate, and drank their aperitifs in plain sight. As the war progressed, people would often end up keeping livestock on their balconies: chickens for eggs, sometimes even a goat for milk. The balconies soon became vegetable gardens where people planted tomatoes, zucchini, eggplants, peppers, and herbs.

It wasn't long before our family started spending evenings around the small table on the balcony, tentatively at first, and then with relish. The first few weeks, my mother wanted to have nothing to do with it. She didn't want to appear common. But as spring made way for summer and the torpor gained on all of us, the clouds of her cigarette smoke joined the smells of the food that rose from a hundred apartment kitchens below. From up on the fourth floor, we watched the lives of our neighbors unfold, and they watched us. Sandra, who feared heights, refused to put a toe on the balcony and would hand us plates of food with her eyes shut.

Almost as soon as we arrived, my father got involved in activities that took him away from the apartment. He and Uncle Moshe opened an office in town, although it was unclear what kind of business they did. I had the sense there was a lot he and Uncle Moshe were not telling us, and an even stronger sense that it was better not to ask. Baba was an ardent anti-Vichyist from the start. To him, the armistice was a disgrace, a betrayal, and he believed that nothing good could come out of an alliance with the Nazis. He was the first to openly and prophetically declare Pétain a puppet. It took the rest of France and Algeria several more weeks, if not months to come to a similar conclusion.

I had to adjust to a new understanding of my father. In France, he had been a mild-mannered businessman, a hapless foreigner who appeared dominated by his wife. In Algiers, he was a man comfortable living under a false identity, who thought nothing of secretly moving his family to another country overnight, a man who conversed in French, Hebrew, Arabic, and Greek, a man who told people what to do. Now Mother, Gustave, and I were the foreigners. We were the ones who did not know the customs, the language, or the conventions. And now it was Mother, not he, who embarrassed me.

Mother did not appear to overcome her anguish of the day when we had gotten lost. She scarcely wanted to go out of the apartment. As summer went on, she closed all the shutters, allegedly to keep the heat at bay, but it might have been her way of tuning out the war. The balcony became her sanctuary. As soon as the sun began to set, she positioned herself on a chair, smoking cigarettes, her body leaning against the balustrade to better scan the street below for Baba's return. She seemed in a constant state of alert. What we all came to call her 'nerves' dictated her life. She ventured into the city only if my father accompanied her, and even then, she was jumpy, angry, and suspicious of all. She developed a panicky distrust for food and would not eat anything unless it had been prepared by Sandra, which was ironic since Mother insisted that Sandra was, in fact, crafty, lazy, and not mindful enough of how things needed to be properly washed and cooked. Once we managed to convince her to have dinner at a local restaurant that served Algerian specialties. My mother scanned the place. "Is this place hygienic?" she asked worriedly.

"This place is perfectly fine," Gustave reassured her.

She laid a napkin on her chair to protect her clothes before sitting, as the Algerian waiter looked at her with puzzlement.

I rolled my eyes. "I wonder what good you think that will do, which is none at all."

"Mind your mother, Marceline," my father said.

"She is acting rude," I said. "It's embarrassing."

"Quit speaking about me as though I am not right here," my mother said.

"Well, are you?"

"Marceline, don't be cruel," my father commanded.

"I think you're looking for reasons to complain about this country. Why can't you adapt as we do?"

"Marceline!" my father said.

"Why can't you make an effort! Your obsession with decorum, the name-dropping, all that might have been the basis of your existence, but now that has become outdated and senseless."

Mother's lips quivered. She stood up. "Take me home, will you Alban?"

We left the restaurant. I was furious at my mother for her inflexibility, and at my father for catering to her whims. It did not occur to me that she might be struggling with a psychological ailment, or that she needed empathy and care.

Soon after that, she got worse. She behaved like a hermit and spent most of her days complaining about her stomach, her teeth, her sleep, the lack of comfort, the heat. Without a staff to manage, a house to run, functions to attend, or friends to visit, she began to lack the will to get up or get dressed. She stopped reading newspapers because she found them too depressing and said she did not have the concentration to read books. She slept a lot or sat on the balcony and smoked.

Sandra was left with the responsibility of the apartment, the cooking, all the errands, and, now that my mother displayed a new, astounding disinterest for our education, the supervision of our lessons and homework. It is not that my mother asked her to do any of this, but Sandra just took it on. We thought we had saved Sandra by bringing her along, but the truth was, I'm not sure how we would have coped without her. Unlike my mother, she quickly adjusted to the ways of a Muslim country. Like Father, she was in her element here. She was Armenian and Christian but seemed more at ease with the humble folks of Algiers than she had ever been in Paris. She spoke Arabic well. Here, she was free to wear a shawl over her hair, which better masked her scar. In Paris, wearing a headscarf made her stand out as too foreign. She said she felt more comfortable that way. People stared at her less. The heat did not affect her. She was confident walking in the streets of Algiers, and was a natural at haggling and navigating the markets. She never got over her fear of the elevator and climbed and descended four flights of stairs several times a day carrying heavy food baskets or, if such was my mother's whim, just to fetch a pack of Gitanes or a special type of tea to settle her stomach or her nerves. My mother, for all her resentment toward Sandra, was the one who depended on her the most. As my mother fell apart, Sandra continued to do anything and everything for us children: the kinds of things usually done by mothers, I suppose.

****

From that time onward, the apartment, dark and overheated, without a whiff of air except at night, began to feel like a mausoleum. I could not bear it. And how could I when everything outside was so new and exciting? North Africa was as messy and uncharted as Paris was proper and familiar. To Gustave and me, the limitations imposed by our upbringing could hardly compete with the vastness of the Sahel, and of the Sahara Desert, immense and dangerous, that began just behind the city. I was a young woman who craved freedom. War was raging in Europe, killing men, bringing nothing but uncertainty into our lives, and redefining the role of women. And here, the sky was blue, the sea emerald-green, and a vast, mysterious city lay at my feet.

As a French demoiselle, I was penned within the boundaries of the European quarter. Sandra was my chaperone everywhere I went, even if that meant picking up a baguette one block away from our apartment. Sandra, unfortunately, took her role seriously. No matter my pleading, she refused to take me to lively areas such as Bab-El-Oued or let me enter one of the mosques or get a closer look at the market at the foot of the Kasbah. I could go on Boulevard Foch, rue Michelet, rue d'Isly. I shopped at the various pâtisseries and bookstores, spent hours trying every dress and every shoe at Le Bon Marché and the Galeries de France. I went to the library and the nearby parks, feigned interest in the local museums, pretended to be pious at temple. All of that with Sandra as my shadow. Meanwhile, Gustave, because he was a boy, roamed freely. Gustave would set out on his bicycle to explore the city in ways I could only dream of. The infuriating double standard accentuated the growing tension between Gustave and me. With Baba in the midst of a vanishing act and Mother acting so strangely, we were left to our own devices, and everything was cause for discord between us.

I soon paired up by default with Béatrice, the daughter of the woman we had met early on. Béatrice pleased Mother because her father was a prominent local bureaucrat who worked at the préfecture and because the family was Jewish, which inspired blind trust in my parents. It turned out that Béatrice pleased me too. She was neither attractive nor unattractive, neither smart nor stupid, and she accepted my dominance completely. She lacked imagination but was game for everything and would follow me, no questions asked, into whatever mischief popped into my mind. However, what pleased me most about her was that her passivity masked a cunning nature. She was entirely devoid of scruples when it came to parental disobedience.

At first, Béatrice and I spent most of our time at each other's homes, leafing through magazines and dreaming of actors we liked. But soon, we were bored. Bored with our little girl clothes, bored with our braids and ponytails, bored with the war, bored with the utter absence of boys in our lives, bored by our parents' sudden obsession with saving money. Rationing had been ordered from the moment France declared war. At first, it was a symbolic gesture to give us a sense of participation in the war effort. It was seen as uncouth to be wasteful, and sacrifices were expected of everyone.

"Nowadays, countries wage war, sending young men to be killed while life at home can remain precisely the same. But back in 1940, the war involved our entire nation. Before we could personally feel the dire privations and wounds of war, and before Germany began bleeding France of its riches, everyone did his and her bit. We acted patriotic, dressed and behaved in a way that was appropriate to the time, and were made acutely aware of the sacrifices of our men."

Well, Béatrice and I, or rather our bratty, seventeen-year-old incarnations, did not quite have rationing on the mind. We were consumed by the desire to get our hands on silk stockings or, better yet, some of those American nylons everyone talked about. But already they were impossible to find, even on the black market. Béatrice and I learned to do each other's hair to be more fashionable in smooth curls and victory rolls, and those immediately added five years to our features. We wore what we called, 'hosiery in a bottle.' Elizabeth Arden had issued a lotion to color the legs. We then enrolled Sandra's help to paint a thin line of henna to the back of our legs, which gave the illusion of nylons' back seam. With the exception of taking elevators or stepping on a balcony, there was nothing that Sandra could not do. When asked to attempt something she had never done before, Sandra had a funny way of mulling it over quietly in her head. Then she would tilt her head and say, "All right." The tricky bit was to hide our painted legs from our parents, but we managed by avoiding angles where they could see them.

Béatrice and I soon ran out of things to do or say. I was supposed to reveal nothing of our family's identity, and Béatrice had nothing to say of interest, or else she had secrets of her own. I grew restless. "We need to meet boys," I told her one day.

"But how?"

"Where are the boys? In cafés, in the streets, I guess. But our mothers will never let us talk to them."

"Well, there is the one place," Béatrice said.

"What place?"

She smiled a wry smile, "A place that crawls with all sorts of boys."

Béatrice had lived here for a year and knew the city well enough. She asked her mother to convince mine to let us go with Sandra to the University of Algiers, allegedly for its extensive library and gardens filled with rare plants. Mother agreed, and we set off. We picked up books at the library and strolled in the gardens. We sat on a bench in the dappled shade of a giant Strelitzia, refreshed by the mist of a water feature, and opened our books. Sandra sat at a short distance from us and took her mending out of her basket. Béatrice and I read and read, but it was hot even in the shade of the fountain. I lasted about an hour without a single boy in sight before saying, "Let's go back."

"Not quite yet," Béatrice whispered, eyeing Sandra. There was the loud ringing of the university bell. Béatrice perked up. She sat straighter and lifted her chest, and within minutes the appeal of the university revealed itself. Boys. Hundreds of boys, our ages and older, began filling the garden. Needless to say, we had to return to get new books the next day. And the day after that.

As we sat on the bench near the fountain, open books on our lap, we set out to reconnoiter so as to discern who was who. Many of the boys moved in groups, carrying textbooks. Some, a few, were here to study or eat their lunch.

Most were clearly no more interested in the garden's botanical wonders than we were. A few of the boys began to walk in increasingly closer ellipses around us.

One group of boys appeared to be more audacious than the others. They always seemed to be loitering in the gardens at the same time we were there. We knew that they were law students because they carried textbooks and made sure to sit on a bench not so far from ours and loudly debate law principles. We knew that they were Jewish because of the Star of David pendants they wore around their necks. The best-looking of the three, a confident boy with pomaded hair and expensive clothes, looked at me with insistence and was not shy about his interest.

One day, in a rare show of initiative, Béatrice took it upon herself to wear her Star of David around her neck too, a rallying cry of sorts. It was ironic to think that the symbol we wore with pride would within a short time be used to brand us as society's lepers.

We did not quite know what we wanted with those boys, but the blood in our veins ran hot, and so did theirs. We observed them, and they inspected us, but the activity was discreet because of Sandra, who sat there, pretending not to notice our shenanigans. As long as she was there, they would not dare approach us.

After a few days of this dance, it became clear that we needed to ditch Sandra. This would be a grave offense, and both of us would have a lot of answering to do, but Béatrice embraced the idea right away.

The following day, we put our plan into action. In the afternoon, Sandra and I picked up Béatrice at her apartment and headed for the university, as we had done daily for a week. But once we were deep into the streets, I turned to Sandra. "We want to be on our own now," I told her.

Sandra blinked, not understanding. "On your own?"

"Without a chaperone," I said.

She shook her head violently. "Your parents—"

"Will never know about this," I insisted.

"I cannot let you," she implored, still shaking her head. But we both knew that Sandra's resolve was no match for my willpower.

"Listen, I am doing this either way," I said. "I'm only telling you so that you won't worry."

"Is it to see those boys?" Sandra asked miserably.

"You can sit here and relax for a couple of hours, or run your errands. We won't do anything bad. Don't worry," I whispered to her, "no funny business. I'm never drinking that horrible concoction again."

"Funny business?" she repeated, confusion painted all over her face.

"We'll just walk around, talk to people our age. You know, be free for an hour or so."

"Marceline, it is war time. No one is free to do as they wish."

"It's the opposite; we're all free, Sandra. Including you." I kissed her, knowing it always softened her to mush. "Two hours. I promise! We'll meet you right here." With that, Béatrice and I scampered off and left her standing at the corner of rue Michelet and rue Richelieu. We ran into the crowd and hopped on a trolley as we had done many times with Sandra. We arrived at the University of Algiers's gardens just as the bell rang and walked the stairs casually, conspicuously without a chaperone, and pretended to take an interest in the bamboo forest. The boys pounced. Where did they even come from? Did they wait in the garden day after day hoping for us to stop by? They followed us for a while. We played coy for a respectable amount of time, and then the boys introduced themselves.

"Aren't you supposed to be in class?" Béatrice asked. "The bell just rang again."

"Mens sana in corpore sano," said one of the boys, his standing as an intellectual of the group made evident by the small round glasses I later found out he did not need. "It's not healthy to exclusively fill up your brain. One needs to enjoy the fresh air as well."

"I am Fernand," said the handsomest of the group. Fernand oozed shrewd charm and sported a Clark Gable mustache. Parted hair combed with shiny, scented pomade accentuated the resemblance. "This is André," he said, pointing to the intellectual. "And this is Émile," he said, introducing the biggest of the three, a boy tall and wide, an impressive specimen of a man. They were about our age. All three boys had black eyes and hair and skin tanned to a golden brown. They were an exotic kind of Jewish, more Sephardic than Ashkenazi. They were also, in my impression at the time, more self-assured, more virile-looking, more audacious than the boys, Jewish or gentile, one could find in Paris or the South of France.

"Our classes are in the building that looks down on the garden," big Émile said, pointing to one of the windows of the university above us. "When we see you, we come down."

I immediately liked his honesty. "What are you studying?" I asked.

"The law," André said, examining a leaf he held between his fingers rather than makinge eye contact. "First year."

"We've been friends since childhood," Émile explained.

"And you all want to be lawyers?" Béatrice giggled.

"one for all, and all for one. We do everything together," Émile said.

Fernand looked at me and smiled. "Not quite everything," he said.

"Where is the woman who is usually with you?" André asked.

"Oh, her? We lost her," Béatrice said, unconcerned.

I didn't think it too smart to let strangers know we might be vulnerable. "She's nearby," I lied.

"What happened to her face?" André asked.

Béatrice made a nauseated grimace. "I know, isn't it awful? I can't bear to look at her."

"She was burned in a fire," I said. The boys nodded gravely. Their respect told me something about the type of people they were.

They were Algerian-born Jews. As such they were different from the French colonizers, different from the local Muslims, and different from the Jews I knew in Paris. They were the descendants of Jews who had lived in North Africa for many generations but were given French citizenship with the Crémieux Decree of 1870. They were part of Algeria's human landscape, and this citizenship had been issued to a population caught between two worlds, with two sets of resentments and prejudices.

"To the Arabs, we're the French colonizer," Fernand explained. "Even though our families were in Algeria long before it was colonized by the French. Our families have been here for centuries."

"But to the French," Émile said, "we're Arabs."

"But we're a stupider type of Arab in that case," André said. "The kind that insist on being Jewish and doesn't even have the sense of being Muslim in a Muslim country."

As my father had explained to us, the Crémieux Decree had come with a priceless advantage not bestowed upon the local Muslim population: a free French education. The boys' grandparents had been the first generation to benefit from the law and thus were able to raise their income and social level. The boys' parents had integrated and slowly shaped Algerian society. In a generation, these Jewish families spoke only French, enrolled in universities, and became doctors, lawyers, politicians, and businessmen. Fernand, André, and Émile were born into a life of privilege. All were sure to inherit their family's businesses. And so, they moved with assurance and carefree exuberance and none of the restraint of self-conscious Parisian boys. Their life of amusements and privilege had afforded them a freedom they took for granted. They were passionate, political, and determined to live life to the fullest. I could not have known at the time that this group of boys would change my life.

"Are you allowed to leave the university gardens?" Émile asked.

I smiled. "We're not allowed to be here in the first place."

"Where are you supposed to be?"

"Shopping for hats on rue Michelet."

Fernand locked eyes with me., "Would you like to taste the best ice cream in town?"

"Where?"

"In Bab-El-Oued."

"I'm not sure we're allowed to go to that quartier," Béatrice said with widening eyes.

We knew the implication of following boys we did not know without our parents' knowledge. It might not seem like such a feat nowadays, but at the time, this decision put us at a crossroad. Refuse, and we would continue our dull existence with our reputations intact. Accept, and at last we would get to taste life, but it might be with our reputations forever soiled. It did not matter what we did with those boys. Being seen with them would put us squarely in the category of girls of ill repute.

I had already made up my mind. Béatrice only needed a slight push on my part. "Aren't we already well outside the rules?" I suggested to her.

"A bit of ice cream has never led anyone to jail," big Émile offered, flirting with Béatrice.

"I could be tempted," said Béatrice, who had never met a boy she didn't like.

Together, we took the trolley back across town to Place du Gouvernement. We arrived at a café with striped red-and-white awnings and rattan chairs set out on a terrace cooled by the mottled shade of sycamores. Above the door, a sign read "Café Djurdjura." Fernand helped me to my chair, and Émile helped Béatrice, thus implicitly laying claim to each of us. The five of us gathered around a small table. Around us, older men drank anisette. André crossed one leg over the other, his body away from the table, and took out a Nietzsche book, which he read ostensibly while not missing a bit of conversation. His father was part owner of Galeries de France. He was serious, conscientious about facts, and had an unsettling way of looking away as he spoke, so it was unclear what he thought of you and if he even wanted you there. Émile's father worked at the préfecture and could 'pull strings,' or so the story was. Émile's shirts were never large enough for his frame, and when he laughed, which was all the time, it seemed his clothes might burst. He was without anger but often got into fistfights, perhaps because hoodlums considered his mere appearance a challenge.

And Fernand. Women were quite into him. He was cool and self-assured, and his overuse of cologne and reputation as a womanizer made him easy to discount. But he was the leader of the group. It was he who, much like an army officer, could recruit, motivate, and organize his troops and later did.

Émile and Fernand lavished us with attention. I sat straight, folded my legs to one side, and lifted my bust as I had practiced so many times in front of the mirror. "This terrace reminds me of the South of France," I said.

"We've never been to France," Émile said. "I've always wanted to see Paris."

"I hear we're not missing anything. Paris is filled with stuck-ups." André said, not looking up from his copy of *Beyond Good and Evil.*

"At the moment it's crawling with Nazis," I said.

"The weather is dreadful in Paris. Gray, gray, and more wretched gray," Béatrice said. "You would positively loathe it."

As we chatted, the waiter, an Algerian boy about our age, moved through the tables. He was tall and thin and wore his white shirt, black pants, and black bow tie with surprising elegance. His body was chiseled, hard. His hair was cut very short, practically shaved, a style that was in contrast with the well-coiffed hair, glossy with pomade, of our new friends. For a brief moment, something about the Algerian waiter felt familiar. Had I seen him before? But the next moment, the illusion dissolved.

The waiter arrived at our table. "What is it you want?" he said abruptly.

Fernand looked at him angrily. "I hardly think that's a proper way to take an order," he said.

"You don't want anything?" the boy asked. Was it sarcasm in his tone? I could not be sure. He spoke French with a slight accent.

He and Fernand looked at each other in a way that made it clear that the two had a history. Was this boy the reason Fernand had brought us to this place? Perhaps to display us?

"Let it go, Fernand," Émile said. "He's not worth it." He turned to the waiter. "We'll share a coupe géante."

The boy looked above our head, as he asked, "Flavors?"

Émile declared with panache, "For these beautiful ladies, only the very best. Chocolate, mint, Grand Marnier, vanilla, raspberry, rose water, and coffee. And double whipped cream."

"Oh, please," Béatrice pleaded, her eyelashes fluttering, "what is it about Algiers that you have to add rose water to eve-ry-thing; tea, pastries, perfume? If I have to ingest anything that tastes of rose water again, I will positively die!"

"But what a beautifully-scented death this would be," André said.

"No rose water!" Émile clamored. "Please replace that scoop with ... more chocolate!"

"Bring us six spoons," Fernand ordered.

The waiter walked away, feline, his forearm muscles taught under his caramel-color skin. "Do you know this boy?" Béatrice asked.

"He's not one of us," Fernand said.

"What do you mean?"

"Muslim." André only said, as though no further explanation was needed.

"His people don't respect women," Émile explained to me.

"Whereas you do?" I asked. I might have sounded terser than intended, so I compensated with a smile.

"Not only that," Fernand said lyrically. "Women are our muses, our inspiration, our raison d'être."

The boy returned a few minutes later and set at the center of our table a bowl the size of half a soccer ball overflowing with colorful ice cream scoops, and topped with whipped cream and toasted almond slivers. He set a single spoon on a napkin next to the ice cream bowl. His fingers were rough and covered with scratches. I glimpsed up at him. His eyes pierced through mine.

"I asked for six spoons; can't you count? And bring us all water!" Fernand said.

The boy left our table wordlessly and came back to set five additional spoons and napkins on the table. He then put on the table a single glass of iced water and produced six straws, which he plopped one by one into the glass. Before Fernand could register the affront, the boy had turned away, feline and unhurried.

"I'll kick his teeth in for this disrespect," Fernand said under his breath.

Unlike Fernand, André and Émile seemed to find the whole episode very amusing. "Compare his day to yours," Émile said conciliatorily. "Fisherman by night, lowly waiter by day, the closest he'll ever get to beautiful Parisiennes is to serve them ice cream."

Fernand changed the subject and turned to me. "Do tell. What is life like in Paris?"

"Curfew at nine in the evening. Limited rations. Clocks set to Berlin time," I answered.

Fernand played along, "I meant to ask, what are people wearing? What kind of music are the clubs playing?"

"I guess we'll need to wait until after the war to find out," André said.

"Are you ladies students?" Émile asked.

"Or are you looking for husbands?" André added.

Émile grabbed André's Nietzsche and whacked him on the head with it. "Ruffian!"

Béatrice threw her head back and laughed.

"Some fancy law students you all are," I said.

Everything for the boys, as Béatrice and I would come to call them, was an opportunity to have fun. They loved to joust verbally and to challenge each other. They loved to play games and tell stories. As soon as the ice cream was consumed, they started a contest where Béatrice and I had to throw olives into their mouths to see how many they could catch. They wanted to make us laugh. We wanted to laugh, so we did. I was well aware of the reproachful eyes of European women who sat at nearby tables. We were trollops, as far as they were concerned. It bothered me, but it did not bother me enough. Sitting on the terrace of Café Djurdjura on this hot June day, I felt more optimistic. In the company of these boys who competed in wit and goofiness, away from my mother and the apartment, it seemed possible to breathe at last.

As the five of us chatted, I made a conscious effort not to look at the Muslim boy who stood at the door that separated the café and its terrace, his arms crossed over his apron, his eyes half closed like those of a cat. From that distance, I had the sensation that he was watching me but I could not be sure.

Fernand, Émile, and André gallantly walked us back to rue Michelet. We found Sandra standing in the exact spot where we had parted over three hours before. Her hands were clasped over her basket, which was still empty. When she spotted me, her whole body relaxed, but she did not look at me or speak to me. The boys, determined to make an impression, introduced themselves with utmost politeness. Sandra only narrowed her eyes at them.

When they were gone, and we had walked Béatrice back to her apartment, Sandra turned to me and said, "You cannot do this again."

"Sandra," I implored, "you need to understand: Mother is acting crazy. There is war. We don't know what the future will bring. I only want to live before it's too late." I had meant to sound dramatic, but suddenly it rang true.

She shook her head. "What if something had happened to you? What would I tell Albano?"

"You and Baba are on a first-name basis now?" I said to tease her. She blushed, embarrassed. "Tell Mother and Baba that you're not up to the task of watching me," I said. "And in the end, you'd get into more trouble than I would."

Was it a manipulating thing to say? Without a doubt. The poor thing must have known that her presence in Algiers was on a precarious footing with Mother being so upset that she was here at all. But I knew what I wanted, and I could not let Sandra get in my way.

The following days, we repeated the same scheme, and soon it became routine. Sandra went along with it, letting us ditch her and meeting us hours later. I came to wonder if she did not tacitly agree that I should be able to experience a bit of freedom. As always, she never told a soul. If Sandra was good at one thing, it was at keeping a secret.

The war, which had begun as surreal words printed in newspapers or heard on the radio, soon started to color everything and became palpable. Paris, our symbol for all of France, had been subjugated, trampled, and humiliated in defeat. When the Vichy government was first created, we put our faith in it. But in July 1940, less than a month after the Germans invaded Paris, Pétain's government abruptly revised naturalizations obtained after 1927. In doing so, it denaturalized my father, stripping him of his French nationality overnight and without the possibility of appeal.

"No one will come all the way to North Africa to take away my citizenship," my father told us at dinnertime. "That is because no one knows where any of us are. As long as we keep who we are a secret, we will be safe."

My mother clenched her fork. Her face was panic-stricken. "But if you are to take back your original nationality, what will it be? You left the Ottoman Empire before it became Turkey. Does that make you a Turkish citizen?"

My father thought about it with his usual equanimity. "I think, yes. And Turkey is neutral."

"For now!" she exclaimed. "But what if it chooses a side? What if it takes the side of the Axis? Then you could become an enemy alien!"

"Lucienne, I am a French-Algerian citizen, born and raised here as far as anyone is concerned, and so are you, and so are the children. That is all you need to remember. We are Alban, Lucienne, Marceline, and Gustave Dupont, and we are French."

"But who gave you these papers? Moshe? How can you be sure they will continue to work? Can you even trust that man?"

"The identity is fake, but the papers are real, not counterfeit. Moshe has friends, Jewish friends, in high places here in Algiers."

"Oh, Alban!" she wailed. "How can you put us in this situation?"

Gustave, who had been looking at our mother with disgust, exploded. "Baba is saving us! Can't you understand *anything*?" He stood up from the table and left the room, slamming the door.

Mother dissolved into tears "Everyone hates me!"

Now it was my turn to be disgusted. I too took refuge in my room, leaving it up to my father to console her.

We settled into this new life, with the Vichy regime and Nazi Germany as a background. We had to continue our education while keeping a low profile, so it was determined that we would study at home. Our mothers having decided this was the most economical way to educate us, Béatrice, Gustave, and I took tedious lessons from uninspired tutors. The lessons were a special kind of torture for Gustave, who was flustered by Béatrice's presence. She paid him no more attention than if he had been one of the stray dogs that roamed the streets of Algiers. After our lessons, Sandra would feed us lunch, and Béatrice and I would disappear into my bedroom, do our hair, and pool our clothes and accessories, coming up with endless combinations. Once we were dressed and our hair was nicely coiffed, we went into town with Sandra, ostensibly tagging along as she did her errands, but ditching her as soon as we got to the trolley station.

We did not have to worry about Baba finding out since he spent his day with Uncle Moshe in his Algiers office. My mother was usually asleep in her room or taken ill with one of her migraines. But Gustave was suspicious. One day, we did not dart out of the apartment fast enough. He was at the door to the elevator. "Why are you getting all dolled up?" he asked.

Sandra hurried down the stairwell to keep above the fray.

"Mind your own business," Béatrice told him.

Gustave was too shy to address Béatrice. He turned to me. "Does Mother know that you paint your faces like this?"

The question was tricky. Makeup was not acceptable for girls our age, so before our parents saw it, we removed it as carefully as we had applied it. The only option was to take the offensive. "Would you be more comfortable if Béatrice and I stayed home?" I asked Gustave. "Would you prefer us to be like the Muslim women, veiled, and unseen?"

"That's not the point!"

"If you want to make a fuss about a little rouge, you can," I said.

"Are you going to tell?" Béatrice asked him.

"There's nothing to tell," I said. "Unless you want to upset Mother even more. Or you can burden Baba with it, who is so tense as it is. Do as you wish."

Gustave considered this. "You better not do anything bad," he said. "And you better not cause Sandra to get in trouble."

"Attaboy," Béatrice said, tapping him on the head. Gustave's face turned crimson.

Day after day, Béatrice and I left Sandra behind, hopped on a trolley, and for a few hours met up with Fernand, André, and Émile at favorite cafés around Algiers where we had "la kremia", the local display of appetizers, and drank Perrier-grenadines and smoked untold quantities of Gauloises. By August, Béatrice and Émile were going steady. They kissed, hidden in public parks in the bushes behind shade trees, while we kept watch. Fernand courted me, and I found him attractive, but my experience in the south of France had made me wary of sweet-talking, confident young men. He and I played a game of cat and mouse that pleased me. I was getting the attention without committing to something I was not ready for.

Despite the war and the strange mood at home, my life was starting at long last. Béatrice and I wanted to ignore our worries. We wanted to spend time with boys and feel young and free. Our new friends were not parent-approved. With them, we did not feel shackled by propriety or decorum. For the first time, I experienced what it was like to be in the company of young men that did not involve strategizing or analyzing lineage. I loved the boys' directness, their passion, and as the year progressed and Hitler's path of destruction broadened, their outrage and desire to act. The boys knew the city; they were smart, educated, quick to laughter, carefree by birth. When the time came, they would also prove themselves to be courageous men.

Café Djurdjura became our favorite place to meet, although we soon had to forget the ice cream. One by one, the flavors were discontinued until there wasn't even milk or refrigeration.

****

The Muslim waiter's name was Khaled. He worked at Café Djurdjura most afternoons. He spoke French with a soft North African accent. From what I garnered through observation, Khaled worked two jobs. Like most of the native Muslims of Algiers, he was probably extremely poor. The cuts on his hands, those gashes and blisters that never healed, were from working at the fishing mole. Unlike the other waiters or my blabbermouth friends, he hardly said a word and made no effort to be sociable. If Khaled was capable of smiling, I never saw it. His somberness made us all seem shallow, or him very deep. He and Fernand had disliked each other at first sight, each representing one side of Algiers that resented the other, but Fernand's creative ways to mock and humiliate him were no match for Khaled's silent contempt.

Some days, I thought I felt Khaled's gaze on me, but I did not want to look up for fear that my friends would notice. His presence unnerved me. I thought about him too much and my continuously thinking about him unnerved me. His attitude angered me: his arrogance, his lack of apparent interest for me, his contempt for our group, the pride he displayed by not touching our tips were just all so infuriating. It was months before I could admit to myself that he was the reason why I was drawn to Café Djurdjura. That in the morning, I dressed thinking about him. That when I did my hair or put on lipstick, it was he who was on my mind. I was clear on two points: that I should not let my feelings be known and that I should not have them in the first place. I trusted no one with my growing fascination with Khaled. Not the boys, not Béatrice, not even myself.

The summer went on like this, my pretending not to pay Khaled any attention, and his ignoring us. Every day, our group, with affected lightheartedness that masked our fear, sat around the same small café table on the terrace of Café Djurdjura, as we waited to hear about the fate of France.

In late August, we were sipping watered-down orangeade when André arrived, brandishing *L'Écho d'Alger*. "The Marchandeau Law was abrogated," he said, flopping down on a chair. A terrible silence fell on us as we digested the news. We all knew the Marchandeau Law. It was a new law, barely a year old, that had declared anti-Semitic propaganda in the press illegal. The importance of this law had been deemed a vital necessity by the Troisième République, and now they wanted it gone? The abrogation of the law was an open invitation to hatred. "Soon there will be no one and nothing protecting Jews," I said, voicing what we all thought.

"The Maréchal's hands are tied," Émile offered. "His focus is on getting our prisoners of war back from Germany, and to make sure our cities aren't bombed. This doesn't have to mean anything."

"The Maréchal Pétain can do no wrong in Émile's eyes," André said.

"After all, if it weren't for him there still would be a French army," Émile argued. "He's the reason we are not on our way to a battlefield."

None of us answered. We wanted to believe in Pétain. We wanted to ignore our nagging doubts.

The temperature had not yet dropped by late September. The only signs that summer was gone were the shortening days and the softer sun. With September came the chilling news of a first official census of Jews in the occupied zone.

"Pétain's regime wants free reign to implement the racial policies it has been drooling after," Fernand said.

"A census doesn't have to signify they mean us harm," Béatrice said.

Fernand, André, Émile, and I did not even bother to respond.

Vallat and other notorious anti-Semites were given prominent roles in Vichy, and thus began the government-sponsored anti-Jew witch hunt. Every day, it seemed, the newspaper reported on measures reducing the rights of Jews and making their living situation more precarious. In early October, things got worse. A French official "Statute on Jews" was announced that mirrored Nazi policies in Germany. It was just as my father had predicted. It closed French Jews to a number of professions. One signature on a decree and French Jews could no longer be teachers, lawyers, or journalists.

Overnight, André, Fernand, and Émile were seeing their education become worthless, their future canceled.

We met at Café Djurdjura the day following that news. When Béatrice and I arrived, we found the boys slumped despondently on their chairs in front of a full ashtray. They had spent the night talking about the situation and drinking. Seeing them in such a pitiful state, unshaven, unwashed – even Fernand, who took so much pride in his appearance – morphed my worry and empathy into a feeling of anger I could not explain. It was not anger at the injustice, but anger at them.

Béatrice began to cry the minute we sat down. "My father said he might be fired from the préfecture. What are we going to do?"

"Will they let us pass the bar exam?" André repeated to himself, stunned.

"Will they even let us graduate?" Émile said.

I thought of my father, of our fake papers, of the money he had put away. Were we the only family who did not worry about employment or money? I noticed that the boys no longer wore their Stars of David pendants. I wondered if this was a conscious act.

"Can't the rest of France see how terribly unjust this is and rebel?" Béatrice said.

Fernand shrugged. "The French aren't going to rebel because they're all too glad this is happening to us."

"Everyone has their problems. Uncertainty, lost work, the long lines, the rationing, and the price of butter if there is butter at all," Émile said.

André rebelled. "How can you wax poetic about the suffering of gentiles at a moment like this?"

Fernand asked of no one in particular, "We can't join the army, we can't study and we can't find work; what is left for us to do?"

"There is no disgrace in working with your hands," I said. "You can become a fisherman or a merchant."

"Sweetheart, don't be rude," Fernand said with a thin smile.

"Whatever you decide to do, don't spend too much time feeling sorry for yourselves," I said.

They collectively stared at me with an expression of dismay. André, who had been holding his chin in his hands as he sipped his drink morosely from a straw, said, "Don't you realize what is going on?"

"They are trying to break our spirit," I said. "Don't tell me they've already succeeded."

My comment seemed to jolt the boys out of their melancholy and into anger at me. But their anger was reassuring. Anger meant action. "Easy for you to give us advice, Marceline," André said. "The situation changes nothing for women."

"How so?" I asked.

"Women can continue to care for their men, feed their families, make babies: what they've always done." Fernand said.

"Sweetheart, don't *you* be rude now," I said.

"In Russia, I hear they let women get equal pay as they do equal work," Fernand said. "Women are actually given guns to fight, and they can be soldiers. They even have female airline pilots."

"You better keep your mouth shut about your Bolshevik sentiments," André told him. "It will land you in jail faster than you can say Rasputin."

"I'm only stating a fact," Fernand said. "I'm not saying I am for equal pay or the vote for women or anything like that."

"America has given women the right to vote," I said. "Britain has too. Even Germany has since 1918. They're not the worse for wear."

"Oh, so women, that's who elected Hitler?" André said.

Émile, all too happy to move away from the topic of Communism asked, "Do you think that the women's right to vote would magically make them equal to men?"

"Being equal to men would be a demotion," I said. "Women are already superior. Especially to André."

Béatrice giggled nervously. André raised his palms, "What did I say?"

"The only injustices you perceive are those happening to you," I said, quite loudly. "We speak of the rights of men, and the rights of Jews, and the rights of Arabs. But in each group, there is a subgroup with no rights at all. No one ever speaks of the rights of women." Khaled, who was setting plates of appetizers on a nearby table looked up at me.

Fernand took my hand and patted it. "What's eating you, baby doll?" he asked.

Something was eating at me indeed, but I was not going to share that information with them. It was about another law that struck my family directly. My friends did not know my father or the fact that he was a foreigner. The new law concerning the *ressortissants étrangers de race juive* authorized the internment of foreign Jews on the sole basis of them being foreigners. That morning, we had learned through Moshe, who had eyes and ears in Paris, that there was a protectoral order tracking my father. He and Moshe were wanted for anti-French activities, namely the timely liquidation of their holdings, the closing of a profitable business, and the disappearance of capital. The police had looked for ways to expropriate us and confiscate our assets and had found them missing. The police had come to the Paris house and had learned that we had left for the South of France a year before. Another police team had knocked at our door in Cannes and had been told that we had taken all our belongings and vanished overnight. The Cannes commissariat de police confirmed that burned pieces of our boat had been found off the coast of Corsica when we had attempted to leave the country and that we were presumed dead. From there, they had not been able to trail us. If it hadn't been for our fake identity, the French police in Algiers would have easily found us. The strange exit out of Cannes, leaving the boat behind in the middle of the Mediterranean, all the precautions my father had taken, and that frankly had seemed overly dramatic then, were saving us.

And now Baba and Moshe were fugitives, and by extension, so were we.

In the weeks that followed, Jewish businesses in both occupied and unoccupied France were put under Aryan leadership or, to put it plainly, were stolen. All bank accounts changed hands. Jewish assets were frozen and controlled by the Vichy-run administration. One day, my father gathered Mother, Gustave and me in the salon. His face was grave, but he was calm. "This is how we are affected," he began. "Our assets are safe in Swiss accounts, but we will not be able to access that money. We will have to make what we have here last."

"What do we have?" Gustave asked.

"We have diamonds."

"How many? How much?" I asked.

"Enough. We are going to sell some. Not all of it, in case money gets devalued. I am hoping we can make it last a couple of years if we are thrifty."

My mother straightened and said with earnest bravery, "If things have come to that, I shall sell the Cité des Fleurs house."

"Are we going to sell our house, Baba?" Gustave said.

My father shook his head. "Lucienne, children, I am afraid I need to tell you the truth about our house. I've known of this since June, but I did not have the heart to say anything."

My mother blanched., "For goodness' sake, Alban, what is it?"

"The house has been appropriated by the Nazis as a habitation for their upper echelon operatives."

"I don't understand?" my mother cried out.

"Nazis have been living in our house," Gustave said with a degree of spite she did not deserve. "Sleeping in your bed. Eating out of your china, with your silverware. Sitting on your toilets."

"Gustave, please," my father said.

"For three months?" my mother murmured. "They've been in our house for three months?" She paused and stared into space.

"I am so sorry, Dear," my father said.

Without warning, she shot up from her chair and screamed at my father. "How could you let them? How could you give our house to the Nazis?"

The accusation was entirely absurd. "Lucienne, that is not how this happened," my father said in a soothing voice.

My mother was wailing now, "First, this woman! And now, my house!" She ran to her room and slammed the door yelling, "You take everything from me!"

We stood in the dining room in awkward silence.

"This time, she's really flipped her wig," Gustave said.

"What woman is Maman talking about?" I asked.

"She's overly exhausted," my father said.

"From what?" Gustave said. "She does nothing but sleep."

"We must all help your mother. This is a very hard time for her."

"It's a hard time for everyone!" Gustave shouted. He turned to me, yelling, "Except for Marceline."

"Stop concerning yourself with me!" I yelled back.

My mother had always given us the notion that she was the dominant force in our home. It was clear to us now that her intransigence, her domineering ways had masked her fragility. Taken out of her country, downgraded from her status, stripped of her money, the pillars on which she had rested all of her life crumbled. She fell into the deep state of despondency that had been threatening to engulf her. Now she refused to leave the apartment. Some days, she never dressed or got out of bed. She barely ate; her face was gaunt. She hardly paid attention to any of us and refused to come to the table at mealtimes. Sandra had to bring her trays with the few foods she would tolerate, bizarre things such as jasmine tea, hearts of palm, and canned sardines and toast. Whatever energy my mother still had, she used it to berate Sandra. Sandra, whom she relied on for everything; Sandra, who did the best she could to make what little money we had last longer. Sandra understood bartering and haggling very well indeed. She could make a lot out of very little and worked relentlessly while Mother cried and spent her time in the suffocating heat of the apartment, all curtains drawn.

The biggest blow for Fernand, Émile, and André, and for all the Algerian Jews, came a few days later. With a single signature on a document abrogating the Crémieux Decree, the Jews of Algeria were stripped of their French nationality. This was unbelievable news. Overnight, by virtue of being Jews born in North Africa, my friends and their families were no longer French.

"How could this be?" Émile repeated, dozens of times a day. "How could this be?"

"This is the excuse they've been waiting for!" André said. "They can say that Hitler made them do it and not bother themselves with public opinion."

"Do you not think that the Maréchal has to do something to appease the Germans?" Émile said limply.

André's face turned red. "Shut your mouth with your Maréchal, or I will punch you square in the jaw."

"I don't blame Émile for clutching to the hope that the Maréchal has the answers since no one else does," Fernand said. "The Vichy propaganda is efficient. They have you believe that he is Jesus reincarnate."

"And this Jesus hates the Jews," Béatrice said.

"This is Maréchal Pétain, Verdun Hero, Savior of France," André said. That's why he can't possibly blame his military for our defeat. He wants to convince us that France's defeat is a moral one. How else can we justify our terrible debacle? He wants people to believe that the Nazi occupation is only a symptom of the problem, and that the problem is us.'"

"Us the Jews?" Béatrice asked.

"Us the French, and the alleged slow rotting of society," André answered.

"Admit it," Émile said, "ever since the Great War, people have wanted to do nothing but have a ball, dance, and drink themselves into a stupor. Maybe a return to sound values would not be such a bad thing. Maybe it's true that the German's over took us in a matter of weeks because we were lazy and complacent."

"And let me guess," Fernand sneered, "And the only way France can regain pride in itself is through some sort of purification process, a strengthening of patriotism through wholesome outdoor physical activity and renewed patriarchy?

"And do not forget an invigorated form of bigotry," André said.

"Family values and outdoor life have never done people any harm," Émile suggested.

"Here we go," André exclaimed. "The glorification of physical strength in a frantic effort to cure ourselves of imaginary complacency!"

Whether in response to the frustration of being forbidden to fight, or because testosterone combined with the deep urge to act made men restless, or whether it was in admiration of those Germans' strong military bodies, every man in the city suddenly wanted to exercise, do manual labor, work in the fields, strengthen their bodies.

"It is all propaganda, Émile," Fernand said between his teeth, quietly enough so that people at the next table could not hear. "Our nation is ripe for it. Like drowning people latching to remnants of a sinking ship, we're looking for reasons for our terrible failure. We saw how Germany reinvented itself after the Great War. Whether we admit it or not, Goebbels' speeches and the Nazis' propaganda about race and strength are having an insidious effect on us. We hate the Nazis, and we hate Hitler, but how can we not admire the way Germany rose from the ashes? And here is Pétain suggesting that the French need some of that beautiful discipline, outdoor work, calisthenics! We're ashamed; we're blindsided; we're *conquered* for god's sake! We're not lazy or complacent: we're defeated! And we're defeated because Pétain capitulated on our behalf like the coward that he is. Pétain is making us think it is unpatriotic to point fingers at our incompetent army. *His* army. He wants us to blame ourselves. He wants our self-loathing."

"Pétain is exploiting our shame," André added, "and then points the finger at the obvious scapegoats, in line with the German propaganda; Communists, Freemasons, homosexuals, foreigners, and Jews. When in fact it is Pétain and his minions who are at the beck and call of the Fuehrer, not the Jews, or whatever foreigners they can find to hate. The first thing to purify is this damn government filled with an incompetent bunch of old fuddy-duddies." André was getting too loud. At the tables around us, people stared. From the other side of the terrace, Khaled made eye contact with me and slowly shook his head.

I put my hand on André's sleeve. "André, shhh…"

"Is the notion that our beloved leader has betrayed us too painful to contemplate?" André raged, not even noticing my hand. "The Nazis aren't even the greatest enemy of France. No," he shouted, "The greatest enemy of France is the Vichy Government!"

"My friend here has had too much sun and anisette," Fernand said with a bright smile to everyone on the terrace.

Khaled approached our table, he picked up empty glasses, and gazing above our heads said, "If you want to spend the rest of the war in jail, this is the way to do it." He picked up the rest of the glasses and walked away without another word.

We looked at each other in bewilderment. "I am amazed," Émile bellowed," "he does speak!"

Fernand was livid. "It is not his place to. He's not supposed to eavesdrop on us, or for that matter, to have an opinion."

"Although he is right. I am drunk," André said.

"You're missing the point," Fernand snapped. "He should not be allowed to speak to us at all."

"Can't you learn anything?" I said angrily.

Fernand frowned. "What is there to learn, sweetheart?"

"Your superiority is only in your imagination, Fernand. It is that attitude of the colonizer I presume. Can you not see that we are all one law away from having no standing in society at all?"

"What a nasty thing to say, young lady," Fernand said, smiling to soften the mood.

"It applies to me as well," I said. "Arabs, Parisians, Algerians, Jews, we're all in the same boat now."

The following week, Khaled began to work on the other side of the café's terrace. I suspected that Fernand had something to do with Khaled being given an area away from us, but to ask him would be to give the issue too much attention. Fernand knew the owner, who was Jewish. Perhaps he needed to feel that he still had some measure of influence over his environment. Now it was easier to watch Khaled come and go from a distance as he moved through the tables. On the one hand, I could observe him inconspicuously. But on the other hand, I had felt his presence and, his overhearing our conversation as a sort of closeness between us, if not a friendship. It bothered me that he could no longer hear us. Or at least not hear me.

As fall progressed, the weather changed. Temperatures dropped, café terraces closed. We met the boys inside cafés rather than on terraces, and so we had to keep our conversations even quieter. We weren't the only ones. An atmosphere of mistrust, more acute with every week that passed, was sweeping through the city. We learned to look around us for indiscreet ears. There were words and names we avoided.

Week by week, Jewish teachers in France and North Africa were fired from schools, Jewish bankers replaced, Jewish businessmen dispossessed, if not thrown into jail, without an explanation. André, whose father was part owner of Galeries de France, saw his assets confiscated. Émile's father and grandfather, who had worked at the préfecture all their adult lives, found themselves without any means of supporting their family. André, Fernand, Émile, and their families, in the space of a few months, had lost their nationality and their livelihood. Béatrice's family's fared even worse. Her father was fired, and they had no idea what to do. They considered returning to occupied Paris. German occupation or not, at least they had family there. It was my father who convinced Béatrice's father to stay put for the time being and even lent him money to do so.

Apathy seemed to fall upon Fernand, Émile, and André. They lost all desire to open a class book. What for, when most professions would be denied to them? There was little to do but sit for hours at Café Djurdjura and pore over the Vichy-controlled *L'Écho d'Alger* and *Gazette d'Alger* for hints of truth and sparks of hope for the Jews of France. But reading the newspapers was painful. Now sanctioned by the press, anti-Semitism was rampant. Every day in the news and plastered on billboards, Jews were depicted as dangerous, treacherous, and physically repulsive. I couldn't bear going to the movie theater where the official news channel, France Actualité, blasted carefully crafted propaganda disguised as news bulletins regarding our religion, which was now considered a race. Posters depicted us with noses like slices of Brie cheese, evil smirks, and clawed fingers. It would have been laughable if it had not made us physically ill to see how the madness was appealing to everyone and how powerless we were to stop it.

Meanwhile, the Vichy regime's deceptions were not yet so obvious that they might cause the French population to rebel. The French were lulled into torpor by the cult of Pétain's personality, which seemed to be turning into a bona fide religion. The Maréchal's portrait was everywhere. As the Germans began to plunder all of France's riches, and French people could no longer feed themselves or keep their homes warm, any thought one might harbor against Pétain was deemed unpatriotic, or worse, actively anti-French. What André had felt free to express just a month before was now akin to treason.

Outside, in the shade of entrances of buildings, little girls played hopscotch and jumped ropes. Little boys ran through the city, played marbles, and chased after cats and pigeons, but mostly they played war with increasing violence.

Winter 1941 was a trying one. To make ends meet, Jewish doctors became pedicurists, Jewish lawyers drove taxis, Jewish teachers shined shoes, and Jewish bankers sold in the streets the lemons and oranges from their gardens. For all my friends, money became scarce, and so did food. The boys grew thin; we all did. No one was getting appropriate nourishment for our growing bodies. But pangs of hunger were nothing compared to the terrible knot of anxiety ever present in our bellies.

In January, I turned eighteen.

When they are too old to play in the streets and forbidden to work or enlist, what is left for energetic young men to do? Disgusted, angry, terrified, stripped of a future, denied higher education and work, but relatively free to come and go, the Jewish men of Algiers young and old began to congregate. In no time, our favorite cafés served as outposts and rallying places. But Vichy spies were everywhere. We had to be discreet. Other French colonies in Africa, the Ivory Coast, Tchad, Cameroun, and the Congo had rallied to the call of General de Gaulle and France Libre. Why not Algeria? We received the news of colonies joining France Libre like cool water on a parched throat. Hope was a beautiful thing, and it was the only thing we had. There were rumors that the United States would soon end its neutrality. Most of it was little more than wishful thinking and jumbled signals on the radio. We did not know whom to turn to. We could trust no one. In Algeria, even more than the rest of France, there was deep distrust for the British ever since Churchill's decision to sink our ships right here in Mers-El- Kébir when he anticipated that the French fleet posted there would fall under German's control. This had resulted in the death of over a thousand French sailors.

"And what of America, who does nothing?" Émile said. "Will they ever enter the war? Show some courage?"

"They're not doing nothing," André sneered. "They're providing the Brits with weapons to use against us."

"That's propaganda," Fernand said. "Whoever our allies are, when they reach out to us we need to be ready."

"Ready how, without weapons or an army? And how would they reach out to us?" I asked.

"Think about it," Fernand said. "The police in Algiers are in Pétain's pocket. Who are the only people the Allied forces can absolutely count on being against the Germans? Who would have absolutely nothing to gain and everything to lose with France remaining under German control?"

"The Jews!" Béatrice said.

"That's right, sweetie."

I had my doubts about the Jews of North Africa being able to make a dent in this war but I understood the boys' need for hope. Still, I began to worry when it became apparent that the boys too seemed contaminated by the exercise mania bug that must have been in the air. Could it be that my friends were being lured by Vichy's lies? Every day, young, old, crippled or not, the Jewish men of Algiers made their way to the Gymnase Géo Gras, one of Algiers' gymnasiums, to partake in vigorous calisthenics. Fernand, André, and Émile stopped bothering to go to school and, joining other mustachioed men in tight clothes and pomaded hair, spent most of their time at the gym.

One afternoon, the boys arrived after one of their workouts and flopped down on their café chairs.

"Must you really work so hard?" Béatrice asked.

"Order of the Maréchal," Fernand said with a wink.

Béatrice turned to me. "Really?"

"Your brother was at the gymnasium's door today," André said.

"My brother?" I asked, surprised.

"That skinny fellow, Gustave."

"How do you even know who my brother is?"

"It is a small town," Émile said.

"He's been showing up on his bicycle every day, trying to get in."

"So, he wants to exercise like all of you fools?" I shrugged. "Let him in."

"He's too young," André said. "You should tell him to stay home."

"What harm is there in him exercising?"

"He's a nuisance, asking questions," Fernand said. "You have to tell him not to come anymore."

"I have no control over my brother," I said. "And by the way, if you know who Gustave is, does this mean he knows who you are?"

"Is that a problem?"

"I don't need him knowing my business," I said.

"He can't be trusted?"

"I don't know," I said. "He can be slippery."

"I'll tell him not to go to Géo Gras," Béatrice said giggling. "I think he's stuck on me."

"Stay out of this, Béatrice," I said. "I'll deal with my own brother."

In truth, I did not know what Gustave was doing with his days. Did he have friends? Was he still smitten with Béatrice, or had he found some girl his age to care about? He seemed to be home quite a lot, stuck between Mother and Sandra, perhaps ensuring the former didn't kill the latter. When I came home, he usually was in his room reading his comics, drawing, or melting his ear to the radio. He continued to be obsessed with war: armaments, tanks, navy equipment, deployment, and maneuvers. He read everything he could on the subject. Drawings of tanks and weapons and helmets and flags were all over the apartment. He was an excellent artist; too bad his talent was being used for something so pointless. At dinner, he incessantly mentioned that if it were possible for Jews, he would enlist as soon as he was old enough. But I think it was only to drive Father mad. This gymnasium thing would be good for him. He could use a physical outlet. "I see no reason why you boys have a problem with him," I told Fernand, Émile, and André. "Why do you even care?"

But the boys did not answer my question.

I came home that same afternoon, dreading the sight of my mother's uncombed hair, Father's tense jaw, the suffocating family silence. Lately, we had to change our lifestyle, and this didn't help. No more visits from private tutors, no more French restaurants or shopping excursions to the Galeries de France. Everyone in town was struggling one way or another, so it was something you resigned yourself to. And so, my mother lost her last few reasons to get dressed in the morning.

After leaving the boys, I met up with Sandra on rue d'Isly, and we walked back to the apartment together. "I finished this today," she said, opening her basket as we walked to show me what was inside. With rationing, it was hard to find the clothes I wanted. Sandra, after many pleas on my part, had hand sewn a girdle and porte-jarretelles – my first – with fabric she had bought on the black market.

I threw my arms around her. "You're a life-saver," I said.

She grumbled. "Tell your mother nothing."

"My lips are sealed," I said.

Before we got to the apartment, I asked Sandra, "What is Gustave up to these days?"

She shrugged, "This and that."

"But where does he go?"

"Here and there."

I laughed. "I know when you are trying not to answer my questions. It looks exactly like that right now." I took her arm and leaned against her. "Of course, you must know where Gustave is. He's your little favorite. I bet you know just where he is and what he does minute by minute. He is working with Moshe and Baba, isn't he? People say they saw him in town. By the way, what kind of business is this they're doing? Baba won't tell."

We arrived at the door of the apartment building, and Sandra pushed it open. "Everyone wants to do their own things," she said evasively.

"Yes," I said soothingly. "And what are those things exactly?"

"I do not ask."

"Oh, but you know."

She pinched her lips. "I don't tell what you do, and I don't tell what they do," she said, and she started up the stairs to our apartment.

"Oh, come on Sandra, come up the elevator! You're killing yourself."

"I like stairs."

"No one likes stairs."

"Everyone is stubborn," Sandra said. "I am stubborn, too."

"That you are," I said, shutting the metal gate of the lift behind me.

Later, in my room, I tried on the girdle Sandra had sewn. I liked how it shrank my waist and accentuated my hourglass figure. It was the fashion, and I always loved fashion. I also wanted the attention of men. In our group of friends, Fernand stuck out as the desirable one. He was an attractive fellow to be sure. Always well dressed and suave as well as educated and intelligent. He had a confidence and authority that I found very appealing. But I was clear on one thing as I looked at myself in the mirror: Fernand was not the man I was dressing for. All I could think about was Kahled, and this needed to stop.

The instant I got out of my bedroom, my mother pounced on me. She pinched my side and lifted my skirt in an uncharacteristic fit of crudeness and rage. "What is this!" she shouted.

"Don't you touch me," I said, staring her down.

My mother pushed me out of the way and stormed into the kitchen where Sandra was peeling onions for dinner. "I know what you're up to!" she screamed at Sandra. Gustave peeked his head out of his bedroom, and we followed our mother into the kitchen just in time to see her grab two onions from the countertop, and throw them at Sandra. Mother missed, and the onions rolled to the floor. "You're turning Marceline and Béatrice into whores!" she hollered. Sandra stared at us, at my mother, then at the onions on the floor. I stepped in, took my mother's arm and tried to move her out of the kitchen. "Don't be ridiculous, Mother. You're being mean for no reason."

"She stole everything from me!" My mother screamed. What she was talking about, I had no idea. Sandra bent down to pick up the onions with shaking hands.

"You're not making any sense!" I said. "You're mad at me, not at Sandra."

Before I could stop her, my mother had grabbed another onion from the countertop and thrown it at Sandra. Her arms were too weak to inflict much damage, but her rage was painful to witness. "You ruined everything!" she shouted at her.

Sandra backed against the kitchen's wall, put her face in her hands and began to cry silently. "Don't listen to Mother," I told her. "She has lost her mind."

My mother turned to me and hissed, "You think I'm crazy, but I know! I know what she does, and I know what you do!"

"That's it, Mother. I shall not listen to your mad rambles for another moment. I'm leaving!"

This shook my mother out of her fog, "Leaving? Where will you go?"

"Out. I'm going out."

"You can't go into the streets by yourself!"

"Well, I'm going to do it anyhow."

"Who will you see?" she shrieked.

"You answer that question yourself, since you think you know everything."

"You have to have a chaperon!"

"I do not."

"I'll tell your father!" my mother wailed.

"Tell him. Why should I care?"

"You can't! You – you can't – go with men. If you do, you'll be – *spoiled.*"

"Spoiled for what?"

"You will never marry well," my mother said pitifully.

"Again, this?" I scoffed. I went through the front door and slammed it behind me, and ran down the stairwell.

Once in the street, quite officially without a chaperone for the first time, and feeling very feminine in my girdle and high heels, I inhaled deeply and felt free. But as I walked in the street, all the streets seemed to lead to Café Djurdjura, and all my thoughts returned to Khaled.

When I returned to the apartment an hour later, Mother was eerily calm. My father was not home yet. I braced myself for his return. My mother was about to drag me through the mud, but I was resolute to tell him all the insults she had hurled at Sandra. To my astonishment, when my father came back, my mother did not tell him a thing. It was as though nothing had happened. From that day forward, my mother, perhaps realizing that by not telling Baba about my disobeying her that day, she had been complicit in my misconduct, chose to look the other way. All her fortitude and principles were washed away in this strange land. She withdrew even more. A kinder soul would have stayed by her side and taken care of her needs, but I hated her for not pulling herself together, and I would not spend a minute more than necessary inside the apartment. What little communication we had at home, what little openness was left between my mother and me, disappeared. And when these kinds of things take hold, it is difficult to find a way back.

Perhaps what was happening at home was an expression of the strain of the time, the secretiveness, the mistrust, the anger, the anguish. At home, no one dared mention our fears, the war, politics, or the Vichy government and what could be done about it. With my friends, that was all we talked about. At home, we considered my mother's nerves too fragile, and so we avoided the subjects. But even when my mother was asleep, my father did not discuss it. All he seemed to care to do was go to the office and carry on with business as usual with Uncle Moshe.

A few weeks later, in one of our rare dinners as a family, I tried to awaken my family out of its torpor. "What we need is a system to combat anti-Semitism at its roots," I said. "We've let it creep up on us. We thought it would pass, and look at us now."

"It's too late for that, Dearest," my father said. "In another century, perhaps."

"How come we Jews don't fight? We let people make up stories about us. We let them trample on whatever rights we have left. We need to rise, collectively."

"Now is not the time to rise," my father said. "Now is the time to survive."

This infuriated me. "All this beautiful pragmatism is precisely what brought us to where we stand now. Make no waves, behave, and wait it out until it goes away. Only it doesn't."

"Hitler is unstoppable for now," my father said, "The willingness of men to follow him is bottomless. But he will make mistakes. His army will exhaust itself."

"What will you do in the meanwhile? Nothing?" I said in a tone that was more condescending than I intended.

My father sighed. "We are not doing nothing," he said. "We came here."

"But if Hitler gets closer, what will you do? Will you put us in another car, on another boat? And to go where?"

"Jews have been persecuted for thousands of years. That is the way the world is. And then, wars are lost and won, governments change, countries are reshaped, new policies are made."

"And so?"

"If we are patient, if we don't get killed, if we think ahead and know when to flee and where to go, then we can endure. Then when people forget their hatred, or direct it at some other group, we can be free again. For a generation or two."

"What kind of life is that? A life of injustices and persecution?"

"We can survive injustices."

"What's to say that this current wave of hatred is not going to last another hundred years?"

"For Jews to be free again, first they have to stay alive. That is all I'm asking of you children. Be prudent. Be smart. Be discreet."

"To cower is not enough of a life for some of us," I said haughtily.

My father scowled. "And yet you and Gustave are going to stay put and hope everyone forgets about us," he said.

And then, out of nowhere, my mother pointed a finger at me, "This one," she screeched. "This one is a wild one! She goes with men!"

We stood, stunned by her outburst. My father's face reddened and he turned to me. "Do you, Marceline?"

I shrugged, "Absolutely not."

"Ha! my mother said." Mother spat.

Father turned to Gustave. "Does she?"

Gustave made an unconvincing gesture to signify his ignorance, his eyes locked on his plate.

My father turned to me with sorrow on his face, "Marceline," he said. "Please tell me this is not true."

"You would rather believe Mother, who's completely irrational, or Gustave who would do anything for attention?" I asked.

My mother did not like the bit about her being irrational. "She's at the café all day long," she shrieked. "With the riff raff of this town."

I turned to her "Who told you this?" And then said, "so, I go to cafés with friends. So what?"

Mother, again, pointed an accusatory finger at me. "She is promiscuous!"

"Are you being promiscuous Marceline?" my father said in an icy tone.

"I am not. But so what if I were?" I said.

My father refused to look at me, and this was more painful than shouts and screams. He turned to Gustave, "I want you to keep an eye on your sister," he said.

"What?" I yelled. "I don't need my baby brother as a shadow!"

"I'm sixteen!" Gustave said.

"Oh, but let's not forget, he is *a boy*! Boys have all the rights, all the freedom, and all the fun. And now I must have a little boy spy following my every move?"

"I don't know how else to safeguard you," my father said in an exhausted tone. Was he disappointed in me, or was he tired? "If you do not have the good sense to care about your honor, at least you should care about your safety. I do not need to remind you how dangerous a time this is."

"Your daughter is out of control, Alban!" my mother raged, "and you're going to let her do as she pleases?"

"You're the one who's out of control, Mother!" I screamed, throwing my napkin on my untouched plate. "Get out of your bed and pick yourself up. Do something. Stop thinking you're the only one who suffers. Besides," I told my father, "Gustave has too much time on his hands. He's the one you better watch. I heard he keeps pestering the Géo Gras crowd, asking questions."

To my surprise, my father got up from his chair, livid, and raised his voice. "If anything happens to either of you it will be as though you have killed your mother and me. Ask yourself if this is what you want!" He stormed out of the room.

I turned to Gustave and said between clenched teeth: "You better not follow me, or I'll have my friends beat you up!"

The last thing I heard as I left the room was my mother mumbling to herself, "She must marry well!"

****

Despite all that was happening, in the world and at home, and as day after day as war raged throughout Europe, all I could think about was Khaled. Was this how I coped? Was that how I created a window of happiness for myself? I dreamt of him at night, and during endless, empty days spent at Café Djurdjura watched him move through the terrace's tables, nimble, tanned, the posture of a dancer, more grace in his little finger than in any parts of my mother's silly counts and bankers combined. My sense of power lay in my ability to appear as aloof as he was. At times, I was sure he looked at me. Other times, I doubted it. The emotional distance I put between others and myself was my strength, or so I believed. I was cool-headed. I was smart. When it came to Khaled, however, I was an imbecile. I spoke too loudly or made a show of throwing my head back in laughter at something profoundly unfunny that Béatrice had said. Every one of my movements when I was in Khaled's presence, every word, every smile, was an act. After leaving the café, I felt embarrassed by my behavior and resolved to be better the next day, only to behave like a foolish girl all over again. I only hoped I was not too transparent. I only hoped I did not seem pathetic or, worse, attracted to him.

The answer came, and Fernand was the one who gave it to me. We were all sitting out on the terrace of café Djurdjura. Fernand met my eyes just as I looked up at Khaled. He waited for Khaled to be out of earshot and whispered in my ear. "I can see the games you two are playing."

"What game is that," I said innocently.

"The seduction game. I watch you, you know. I see how you dress. How you make yourself pretty. You're a beautiful girl, Marceline. You can do much better than him." I was embarrassed and eager to deny everything, but to deny too much would be an admission of guilt. "Are you jealous?" I said.

"Should I be?" he asked.

"If you think I'm being seductive, why assume you know who I am hoping to seduce?"

"Well," Fernand said, "I don't think it's for André or Émile."

"I don't think it's them either," I said, staring at him flirtatiously.

Reassured, Fernand sat back in his chair and smiled. I had always sensed that Fernand was attracted to me, but the same could be said of Émile and André. This brief interaction changed the dynamics between us: from that moment on, Fernand saw me as willing to return his advances. Days went on.

Fernand now flirted with me openly. He was always touching my waist, giving me his seat, petting my hand. Khaled had noticed; of this I was certain. I let Fernand flirt with me openly. I even flirted back. I was sick of waiting, sick of not knowing, sick of wanting. I hoped that it would change something, that it would force Khaled to come out of hiding.

It did.

One afternoon, Béatrice and I got up from the table and, as we had so many times, headed for Café Djurdjura's bathroom. It was a hot day. For the last hour, I had flirted with Fernand and watched from the corner of my eyes as Khaled impassively went from table to table. My pulse throbbed. I felt under pressure, like the countdown of a doomsday clock.

Outside, the nearby church bell marked three in the afternoon.

Béatrice and I walked away from the terrace and went inside the café, past Khaled, past the tables and chairs, past the side looks of French men who drank red wine at the counter, and down the windowless corridor that led to the bathroom.

Béatrice went in first, leaving me alone in the corridor, which was lit by a single small fixture. I leaned against the wall and waited in an exacerbated state of alertness. It was as though I knew that something was about to happen. Suddenly, the light went off, and the corridor was flooded in darkness. I waited, breathless. I felt a move toward me in the dark. In a few steps, Khaled was facing me. I shivered. He placed his hands on either side of me, palms pressed on the wall against which I leaned, encircling me with his arms without touching me. He was taller than me by a head. I lifted my face. His lips were inches from mine. My entire body vibrated. I smelled him. I felt his body's warmth. He said nothing. I felt that I heard his heartbeat and his breathing. Or were those mine?

A moment later there was the sound of the bathroom lock opening, and Béatrice was in the corridor. "Marceline, what are you doing in the dark?" she asked. An invisible hand turned on the light again. In the narrow hallway, it was just Béatrice and I. Khaled was gone.

****

Marceline smiled to herself. Cassandra was smiling too. "Young love," Marceline sighed.

"Did Khaled become your boyfriend?" Cassandra asked. "Please tell me that he did."

Marceline realized that they had walked all around the park and now they stood by the Medici Fountain, were Acis and Galatea, locked in their embrace, awaited doom. Rain was falling again, barely a drizzle but enough that Cassandra's black hair was covered in minuscule glimmering drops, like a spider web blanketed in dew. "I believe I see my car by the gate," Marceline said. "Isn't that Maurice over there?"

"Yep. Double-parked, as usual."

"I guess this is as good a point to stop as any."

"Not without telling me about Khaled first!" Cassandra exclaimed.

"Is that a command?" Marceline asked wryly.

"Oh, no. I did not mean it that way. I'm sorry. I can be pushy," Cassandra said. "I've been told that before."

Marceline found it endlessly irritating the tendency women had to put themselves down for attributes that were considered qualities in men. "So, be pushy," she told Cassandra. "Don't apologize for it. Persistence is a strength, my dear. Not something to feel wishy-washy about."

Cassie shook her head. "My dad did not like that about me, I don't think," she admitted.

"Well, I guess not if you mean to get into Gustave's good graces. But as far as the rest of the world is concerned, passion, grit, and perseverance are perfectly wonderful traits."

They reached the Luxembourg Garden's gate. Maurice retrieved a large umbrella out of the trunk and helped Marceline into the car. "Meet me tomorrow at my house," she told Cassandra. "Eight o'clock in the morning. And this time, don't keep me waiting."

In the car, Marceline settled in her seat and looked out the window through the droplets. Decade after decade, people dressed differently, the cars changed, but Paris remained the same. She watched Cassandra cross Place Edmond Rostand and head inside the brasserie at the corner, then come out again and sit at the terrace. Marceline never again would have that kind of freedom, the ability to rely on her body to come and go as she pleased. That old carcass of hers had had a good run; she was in no position to complain. She had been blessed with exceptional health and vigor. How old was she when men stopped looking at her? Her sixties perhaps? Her niece was not even forty yet: young and free. But she did not seem the type of woman who could grab that freedom and enjoy it.

People had a way of creating barriers for themselves: politeness, convention, guilt, the opinions of others. It was a blessing not to care about those sorts of things at all. Although Marceline wasn't a stranger to guilt, she chose not to let it cripple her. Women like herself got things done and were chastised for it. It did not matter that she had spent her life – risked her life – in the service of France. She had not played nice, and she had more enemies than friends. Gustave was not her only enemy, only her earliest one.

The rain seemed to subside. Maurice turned off the windshield wipers and things went silent inside the car save for the groan of the engine. Marceline sank deeper into the leather of the seats as they raced through Paris. What a bother how certain events of one's life were mired in so many shades of gray. As she had recounted that family fight to Cassandra, Marceline had been clear on her own innocence. But now, after telling her story, she wasn't so sure it held ground. Was she truly blameless? She understood now, and with utter clarity, that she should never have threatened to have her friends beat up Gustave, her father should never have asked Gustave to surveil her, and Gustave should never have taken that challenge to heart. But all that had happened, and the seeds were planted. And there had been no going back from that point.

CHAPTER 10

Lingerie

The drizzle had stopped, and sunshine peeked through the scattered clouds. On the terrace, the tables and chairs, protected by the wide awning, were dry, so Cassie decided to have her lunch outside. A waiter came, first looking surprised to find her alone there. She ordered the plat du jour, poached eggs in wine sauce with extra ketchup. Her senses felt strangely heightened. The air felt crisper, as though cleansed, the colors brighter. She felt sexy for no reason at all. Was anyone noticing? The Paris of today felt very different from the Paris of the day before. Even as Marceline was speaking, Cassie had kept replaying in her mind how Hervé had taken charge of things, how he had touched her. None of it felt real or possible: not her response to his touch, not his touch, not the fact that he had wanted to touch her at all.

Her lunch arrived. The eggs were perfectly poached, the sauce so heavenly that she took the brave step of forgoing ketchup. She ate ravenously. When she was done, she ordered an espresso and took out Hervé's notebook.

She wrote quickly, in bullet points, trying to be as thorough as possible. At every turn of her story, Marceline came out as the star character, with her dad in a supporting role. She seemed to be making every effort to be honest, but Marceline could not help but see the world as filled with orbiting people, and with herself at the center, radiating her influence. Cassie wondered if her dad had had a hard time asserting his masculinity with such a commanding, confident sister. Maybe that's why he had chosen a wife eager to accommodate him and make excuses for everything he did.

She had trouble reconciling the father she knew with the man Marceline described. First, he had been a little Jewish boy navigating the lead up to World War II, and now he was a teenager. She felt her previous ideas of him slip away. Who was her father? What did he want in life? How did he feel about things? About her? She still had no idea why Marceline deserved his hatred. In fact, had he not tried to rescue his sister from her attacker in the South of France? Had he not kept her secrets? In Algeria, he had wanted to prevent her from getting into trouble. He must have cared for her. And in her own way, Marceline cared for him. There were signs of sibling rivalry, but nothing that would explain his eventual hatred. Cassie lifted her pen. What was Marceline trying to convey? She seemed intent on building a case.

Marceline had spent plenty of time explaining what it was like to live at a time when the information fed to you was propaganda, and you did not know what was true and what was not. Cassie wondered if she should question Marceline's story. After all, she still had not heard her father's.

Two hours, one lip-smacking île flottante, and two more espressos later, Cassie closed her notebook. Once again, she had been coaxed into writing for someone else. It must be life's karma to toil over what other people were too lazy or unfocused to do. What story was she going to write? Marceline's story, or her father's? After hearing the events from Marceline's standpoint, it would be more difficult to write a story that honored her father. And if she didn't do him justice, would her family hate her for it? Was she willing to take that risk? She stared at her hands. There was an indentation on her right index finger from the pressure of the pen. Already, her body was becoming accustomed to a life without electronic devices. Her hands did not feel like they belonged to the person she was four days ago. For some reason, they felt like more capable hands. Notions of a book fluttered in her mind. Marceline's memoir was not what she had in mind. She wanted to write a novel. Change the names and call it fiction. Fill in the blanks with her imagination.

****

After lunch, Cassie set out following the outer edge of the Luxembourg Garden, turning right on rue de Tournon until it became rue de Seine. Rather than take the métro, she decided to head to the hospital on foot and try not to think of what would happen once she got there.

Tonight, she would see Hervé.

See. Hervé? Since when was she "seeing" anyone?

The next portion of the street brimmed with shops, bakeries, and art galleries, and she wanted to enter every one of them. She could not help but see her surroundings through Hervé-tinted glasses. Even this butcher shop was quaint. And this patisserie. And how interesting people looked, how beautiful Paris was, and how vast and varied the city was from street to street!

She scanned the shop windows, realizing that she had been unconsciously looking for a lingerie store. How had she allowed for the garments closest to her skin to be so pitiable? What did it say about her? She had told herself she wasn't shallow enough to care, but wasn't it more likely a lack of self-worth?

She entered Monoprix and wandered through the clothing aisle until she stood in front of the bras and panties. She needed nothing as fancy as the designer lingerie at the Galeries Lafayette, but what about a little something lacy and cute? And why just cotton? Who made that rule? In the dressing room, she looked at her legs in the full-length mirror. Not bad at all. All those stairs at home had done her good. Her butt wasn't horrible for a woman her age. Her curves seemed positioned in right places. Whatever imperfections,

Hervé had not seemed to mind. She tried half a dozen bras and matching panties and quickly narrowed down her choice to two sets, one light pink, one dark gray.

She left Monoprix and walked ever so slowly toward the hospital, stopping in front of shop windows, delaying the inevitable: the idiotic bureaucrats at the hospital, Odile and her tears, her mother with all her secrets. Odile's tears were the trump card. The fact that her sister had no control over her lachrymal glands did not prove that her suffering was superior to everyone else's. As for Mademoiselle Pinçon, that horrible woman, she needed to come up with a way to bypass her. Cassie was outnumbered, and it made her do and say nutty things. Walking into the hospital was stepping into the unknown, which was not the staff, or her mother, or Odile, or even her father – she knew what to expect of them. No, the unknown was herself. There had been more than a few instances in her life when she saw red, and all modicum of self-control had gone out the window. Cases in point: the letter of gripes she should never have sent her parents and telling Peter she wanted a divorce when a good cry should have sufficed. She felt, at this juncture, dangerously ripe for an outburst of crazy.

She passed a craft shop window with boxes to build miniature airplanes and boats. Alex, like her father, loved building things. He was in the robotics club in high school and even won a prize for it. Engineering seemed to be his thing. Had they known each other, Alex and her dad could have bonded perhaps. Had her dad loved her children, she could have forgiven him everything. Her dad's incapacity to love her children was her fault because she had left the country – at least that was the narrative. But she had always felt as though his rejection of her country of adoption, of her children, of her marriage, and of herself was her dad's way to punish her for a crime she was unaware of having committed but of which she bore the weight.

She realized now that as Marceline was telling her about Gustave, it was Alex that Cassie pictured. The similarities between her son's and her father's personalities jumped at her for the first time. Both were sensitive, introverted, and shy, more comfortable working and functioning in solitude, and yet lonely. But whereas Alex was loved for being who he was, her father at the same age had been victimized. It was awful to think of the kind of damage this could do to a boy. Her father had never let anyone know his suffering, but in doing so, he had prevented everyone from truly knowing him. Cassie thought of her dad as a boy. She thought of Alex and of all the boys who grew up feeling that they fell short of society's expectations.

She took the Pont du Carrousel across the river. The Louvre was on one bank; on the other was the Musée d'Orsay. Above, blue sky and shapely white clouds. In the distance was the metallic Pont des Arts and the stone arches of the Pont Royal. And couples. Couples who walked hand in hand below on the quays made her long for something.

Love. How could she not want it now?

She put her elbows on the balustrade and looked down. Below, on the stone ledge of the Seine's bank, a young man and woman were nestled in each other's arms. When the man leaned forward to kiss her, and his lover tilted her neck back and lifted her arm around his neck, the two replicated the statue of Galatea and Acis.

Without being sure why, Cassie began to cry.

****

At the intensive care reception desk, there was a new woman with a warm smile that Cassie had never seen before. She looked like a decent person with proper human feelings and emotions, not like that nightmarish Mademoiselle Pinçon. Maybe if Cassie played it cool-headed and normal, in other words, if she acted the opposite of how she felt, this new woman might not ask for an ID and thus not discover that Cassie was banned from the room.

There were four people in line ahead of her, and quickly several more came after her. As she waited in line, Cassie rehearsed in her mind how she was going to put this new clerk in her pocket by killing her with kindness. But when her turn came, Pinçon was back at the desk, looking at her angrily from above her computer screen.

"I'm here for my appointment," Cassie said, improvising.

"What appointment?" Pinçon asked without as much as lifting her gaze.

"With the Chief of Services," Cassie snapped. "Docteur Juin told you to make it happen. We've gone over this how many times now?"

"Ah, yes," Pinçon said, pretending to remember suddenly. She looked down at her screen and said resentfully, "He will see you next Thursday at eight in the morning."

"Ha! I told you he would see me! Wait, what day is it today? Did you say next Thursday? But that's a week from now! I'll be back in California by then."

Pinçon shrugged, indifferent. "That's what's available."

"I'm sure he can squeeze me in for five minutes."

"I'm not a miracle worker, Madame."

"Look, he obviously accepted to see me, so what is it to you if it happens now or later?"

"He is extremely busy."

"Me too, and yet here I am, wasting my precious time with you."

"Madame, it is not necessary to be rude," Pinçon said with just the right amount of superiority.

"I flew across a continent to see my father."

"If you want a different time, I can give you the email address of the Chief of Services' secretary's assistant."

Cassie felt hot. "His assistant?"

"His secretary's assistant. The secretary's communication has to pass through her assistant first."

"But why?"

"That's the proper channel."

"Fine, okay. Could I see her now, rather than email, to expedite things?"

"Oh, that will be impossible."

"Why is that?"

"The Chief of Services' secretary's assistant is on maternity leave until January."

Cassie's face must have turned crimson. "You know what your problem is?" she began to say, with no plan on how to finish her sentence.

"Non, Madame, what is my problem?" Pinçon asked defiantly.

"You're part of a giant bureaucratic maze. Did you see the movie *Brazil?*" Behind her in line, people began to groan.

"Do you want that email address or not?" Pinçon asked.

Cassie did not even know what she was saying. She was trying to say something, make a point, but her sentences came out jumbled, nonsensical. "Red tape, glued everywhere. Employees on maternity leave clocking their nine to five and protecting each other's back."

"Madame, there are many people in line behind you."

"The result is, nobody cares! You're like mini-Hitlers, with your Fascist ways, and...." Cassie paused, searching for a powerful ending to her rant. "And an utmost disregard for human lives!" Audible snickers came out from the people in line behind her.

"Madame, that is absurd," Pinçon said. "The hospital saves dozens of lives every day."

"Give me the name of the Chief of Services!" Cassie said, much too loudly.

"Madame, as I have explained again and again to you, we do not give out names of employees."

"Oh, stop 'Madaming' me!" Cassie yelled. "It's my dad in there! My dad! I'm going to see him whether you like it or not." With this, she turned away from the desk. The people in line parted and watched with keen interest as she marched toward the patients' rooms.

Pinçon was up on her feet, calling after her. "Madame, please be reasonable."

"I've been reasonable my entire life!" Cassie shouted. She heard the shuffling of feet behind her, and she pressed forward. Now she had her hand on the knob to her father's room, expecting to be yanked out by the scruff of her neck, or tasered, but they were not stopping her.

Just as she opened the door to her dad's room, her mother came out of it.

Raymonde looked at Cassie and then at the two interns on her heel. Everyone stood around awkwardly. "Oh. Bonjour, Maman," Cassie said sweetly. "I was just coming to see you. Are Odile and Sabine in there?"

"Just me," Raymonde said distrustfully. She stood by the door, her arms crossed, a stubborn expression in her eyes. "Odile's boy has an ear infection," she said, eyeing the interns. "Sabine ... I don't know where she is, as usual."

"What did the doctor say?"

"He's not stopped by yet."

It was one thing to fight strangers; pushing her way past her mother was another. Cassie's fury and righteous indignation drained out of her to be replaced by the realization that she was, in fact, terrified to enter her dad's room, to risk being rejected by him once more. She sighed and asked her mom, "You want to have coffee?"

"I guess," Raymonde said.

Cassie took her arm and said, "Let's get out of here." The interns, embarrassed for her, took a step back, then another. No one was making eye contact. On the way out of the hospital, she avoided looking at Pinçon, the interns, the people in line, and those sitting in the waiting room.

They crossed the street and entered Bistro Saint-François. Inside, they found a table by the window with a view of the hospital. The café was filled with hospital personnel and a handful of people whose shell-shocked expression told her they too were here to visit a loved one. There was a huddled family of redheads, a solitary man looking fixedly out the window, a red-eyed Muslim woman and her small daughter, and a young Asian man in an elegant suit. Raymonde pointed to Cassie's Monoprix bags.

"You've been shopping?" she asked. It sounded like a reproach, as though she was accusing Cassie of frivolity.

"I ran out of things to wear."

"There are laundromats you know," her mother said.

Yes, and you could also offer for me to use your washing machine, Cassie thought. Instead, she said, "Are you hungry?"

"I don't eat at all hours." By this Raymonde meant that Americans ate "at all hours," whereas in France there were proper and improper times to eat. This was an infuriating theme: France good; America bad. But she had better act calm and composed if she was going to talk her mother into letting her back into her father's room.

"I'm glad we could have some time just the two of us," Cassie said conciliatorily, "and I'm sorry I messed up your rug." Raymonde grunted an unintelligible answer. "How is Papa feeling today?"

"His vitals are the same."

"Still sleeping?"

"Still sleeping."

"Don't they plan on waking him up? Doesn't he need to eat?"

Raymonde tensed up. "They are feeding him through tubes and whatnot."

"What about you? Are you sleeping all right?"

"A few hours here and there."

"I've meant to ask you about Sabine. She seems exhausted." The exact term she was trying to convey was "clinically depressed."

Raymonde sighed, relieved perhaps that they were talking about something safe. "We don't get to see too much of her. Apparently, she has better things to do than to come over and visit her parents."

"Not even for Sunday lunches?" Sunday lunch. That fraught, tension-filled family institution Cassie had been glad to elude for the last twenty years, although moving to another continent hardly exonerated her.

"She's never had us over either. Not even when she was with Paul. You know she still doesn't cook? Odile says that Sabine has yet to become an adult," Raymonde added, looking sideways to avoid Cassie's stare. "But you know me: I'm neutral."

"I'm not even sure what being an adult means," Cassie mumbled.

"I guess that's the women of this generation. They want a career so badly that they compete with men. Well, men don't like competitive women."

"They don't?"

"They want a woman who can take care of them. How can you be in a relationship if you won't cook for your man?"

"I managed."

Raymonde made a small, undecipherable grimace, which Cassie instantly interpreted as scorn. Her warming feeling toward her mother dropped down a few degrees. Raymonde's way of being judgmental was undisguised and made worse by the fact that she saw her bluntness as honesty, although in her relationship with her daughters, honesty was expected to be a one-way street. "What's the point of Sabine coming here if she's going to make this long face. The last thing we need is her negativity."

"Maybe she's struggling."

"It's better for her that Paul left her when he did. Better that than a divorce. That's what Odile says."

"Tell Odile that staying married is not a sign that your relationship is not a complete failure." She bit her lip. Too late. Her mother would give Odile a report of this before the day ended. "I'm a bit concerned about Sabine."

"You can't be all that concerned. Sabine said the two of you hardly speak."

This hurt Cassie. More of that wholesome honesty. "I think she is trying to manage her emotions on her own," she said defensively. "I didn't know anything about this. I would have been there for her."

"If she had needed you, she would have told you about it I think."

"She looks awful. Something is wrong with her," Cassie insisted.

"Sabine isn't the one in a coma, last I checked," Raymonde said. "She had two hands and two feet. She should be more helpful in this time of crisis, not just waltz in here when she has five minutes."

Maybe that's what becoming an adult meant. That moment when your parents cease to see you as vulnerable and in need of their care and start thinking you should take care of them. "You don't realize that your father has been a lot of work. And that's even before he got the surgery. And with Gustave, forget sleeping! He has to get up to pee four or five times a night. And the snoring. And to go up and down the métro with him is out of the question. And I can't very well leave him alone, so I'm sequestered at home. And I do all the shopping and cooking and cleaning and laundry. But you know me, I don't like to complain." The waiter arrived and set two espressos on the table. Raymonde downed hers like a shot of tequila before adding angrily, "You'd think Odile was the one taking care of him from seeing her here every day. But let me tell you, she is not. I am."

Cassie rolled her eyes. "I'm sure Papa is head over heels in appreciation of her regardless."

"Well, you know how her smile 'lights up the place,'" Raymonde said. Those were Gustave's words. Her mother's sarcasm wasn't lost on Cassie, who had often wondered how come her own smile never managed to light up anything. "She comes over once or twice a week," Raymonde continued. "So, of course, she has all this energy and patience. She does her two bits and then she's out the door looking like Mother Theresa. She doesn't know what it's like to take care, and take care, and take care some more. The minutiae of it and the exhaustion."

Cassie felt the urge to defend Odile. "She has young children. She must have a pretty clear idea of what exhaustion feels like."

Raymonde shrugged. "You know how Odile is. She likes everyone to walk like they're her little soldiers. She always says that you gave your twins too much freedom. She said that's what all their troubles sprang from."

"They're over it now. They made it into college," Cassie said defensively. She considered it an amazing feat to be the parent of modern-day teenagers. They were guinea pigs in a global human experiment with parents acting as the blind leading the blind in the age of sexting and cyberbullying. Modern-day kids did not only have to keep up with the Joneses, the way past generations did; they had to keep up with the superrich, the infamous, and the shameless. Alex and Jeanne had gone through this, plus a divorce, and miraculously come out in one piece. "I don't think that I have ruined their lives quite yet."

"To each their own," Raymonde said.

Did she really expect positive reinforcement from her mother? The temptation to provoke became irresistible. "I saw Marceline again," she said.

Raymonde was visibly shaken. "You did? When?"

"Right after I left your place this morning."

"But why?" Raymonde whimpered.

"For one, I had nothing better to do since you're not letting me see Papa."

"It's one thing to see her once, but it's another to have a relationship with her. Your father's not going to like that," Raymonde said. Her eyes darted around the café for a solution. "If he asks you, don't tell him that you saw her."

"Why not?"

"He's going to think I told you about her."

"Which you did."

"He's the one who mentioned her!" Raymonde said, indignant. "When he was unconscious."

"But you're the one who gave me her last name. I could not have found her without it."

"You and Odile were pressuring me!" She had raised her voice. They eyed each other like boxers in the ring.

So, this was what her mother feared? She was afraid that her husband would be mad at her? "What I still can't figure out," Cassie said, "is why Papa hid his last name from us? Was it so that we could not find Marceline, or so that we would not learn about his childhood?"

"In those days, it wasn't uncommon for people to drop a syllable or two from their names," Raymonde said, sounding unconvinced. "To sound more French."

"Or less Jewish?"

Raymonde shook her head in defeat. "Your father is *really* not going to like that."

"It doesn't surprise you that you know so little about his life before he met you?"

Raymonde was agitated, defensive. "When he married me, he wanted to start from scratch. He did not want his new family to be polluted by ... old stories."

"Was his Judaism part of the pollution?"

"I told you! It wasn't important to him!"

"But important enough to hide."

"He wasn't trying to hide anything," Raymonde snapped. "Why do you always have to make accusations? Your father made his choices, and it has nothing to do with you."

"Hiding his heritage from his daughters? It seems to have plenty to do with us."

"Your sisters would not care. They would respect his decision."

"But what was his decision? And why?"

"What is it to you?"

"For one, I'm curious about the idea that I'm half Jewish."

"You could not be Jewish if you tried. I'm not, and if your mother is not, you're not either. End of story."

Apparently, her mother had done her homework. "Is that why he married you, Maman? So that his daughters could never be suspected of being Jewish?"

"That's an awful accusation!"

"Is it?"

"Here you are, digging in the dirt and trying to drag us all into it?"

"If by digging you mean being this family's archeologist, I'll take it as a compliment. Unless being Jewish *is* the dirt you're talking about?"

"Stop it, Cassandra. Cut it out!"

"Is Papa hiding his Judaism from us or from himself? Is he ashamed of it?"

"Shame has nothing to do with any of this." Raymonde's expression had changed. She looked about to become hurtful. "Why do you keep disparaging your father, especially now."

If Cassie did not want to get demolished, she needed to back the hell off. She braced herself and pushed ahead instead. "If there is no shame, then why do you react like I'm accusing him of war crimes?"

"Why do you take so much enjoyment in hurting people?"

"Oh jeez, Maman!"

"And you make up stories. You always do that."

"What is there in his past that you are both trying so hard to hide from us?"

"There is nothing. Absolutely nothing!"

"How about a living aunt? Don't tell me you're not hiding stuff. She's more than eager to tell me the story if I can't hear it from you."

Raymonde's face turned crimson. "You know what your problem is? You're a pathological liar! You always were! Something is very wrong with your brain!" She sprang up. "I'm going to see Gustave."

This was a lost cause, but Cassie tried anyway. "How about letting me see him too?"

"Why? So that you can accuse him of being an anti-Semite?"

"You're twisting things around."

"No, you are!" Raymonde shot back. She was standing by the table, red and vibrating with fury. "You come in, spread your venom, spill your accusations, create a whole big mess of things with your lies. And you steal!" With this, she left the café. She would have slammed the door, had there been a door to slam.

Cassie sat, shaking. This was their M.O. Their kryptonite against her. They called her a liar when in fact it was they who were doing the lying. And it worked. Usually, she shut up. Or left the country. She wanted to leave the country now. She sat back in the pleather of the bench seat and controlled her breathing. This was what they did. This was what her parents' forty-year marriage could be summed up to: the wife covering for the husband, closing her eyes, taking his side blindly, no matter what. Even to the detriment of her daughters.

Cassie stayed in the café to regroup. Her tantrum at the hospital and this fight were not making things easier. She watched the rain fall in the street. At times, gusts of wind were so strong that all umbrellas overturned at once. When would the rain stop? How could people live like this, trapped in shitty weather, in drudge, in car exhaust, in lies, self-loathing, and loneliness? She ordered a chamomile tea to counteract the effect of an espresso with her mother. She wrote in her new journal details of Marceline's story she wanted to be sure to remember. About thirty minutes later she raised her head. Outside, Sabine was crossing the street and was heading toward the café. Her face was pale, drawn; the collar of her coat turned up. She entered and made her way toward Cassie and plopped down across from her. "Maman said you might still be here," she said. "She was livid. Her anger at you seems to be on a whole other level."

"What a shocker."

"You don't care?"

"I care, and at the same time, I don't. She's trying to shut me up. The usual intimidation."

Sabine nodded in understanding. "We just saw the doctor," she said. "They think they'll have to start giving Papa dialysis. He's severely anemic. They'll give him a blood transfusion too."

"What about the infection?"

"They're trying something stronger."

"Shit."

"You think I look terrible?" Sabine asked with a forced smile.

"I do? What? No!"

"That's what Maman just told me."

"She what? No! I did not mean it that way. You look beautiful. I guess I was just asking about you. You're right. I should have asked you directly."

"Asked me what?"

"It's just that you seem sad. I was wondering if I could help."

"She made it sound like I was somehow failing in your eyes."

"I care about you. I'm not judging you. I don't know how Maman does it: pitting us against each other, creating this environment of suspicion."

"Maman said that you think I need to grow up."

"What? No! That's complete bullshit! *Odile* was the one who said that," Cassie yelped. "It wasn't me!"

"Oh, great," Sabine said.

"See, she did it again! Now I'm throwing Odile under the bus. I'm sorry. No one thinks you need to grow up." Cassie shook her head in admiration. "How does Maman do it? She's a genius at this, like a criminal mastermind."

"As long as we hate each other we might not turn against her," Sabine said.

"You think it's deliberate?"

"I don't think she has any idea she's doing it. It's more like a hyper-developed instinct of self-preservation."

"I'm beginning to think that she resents Odile the most."

"Why?"

"Because Odile's perfect. At least we're the official fuckups."

Sabine laughed softly. "Well, I certainly am."

Cassie looked at her beautiful, sad-looking sister. "Tell me, how are you doing?"

Sabine sat deep in her seat, brought her hands to her coat's collar like she was trying to disappear into it. "I would have given birth this week," she said. "The due date was supposed to be right now. I would have two babies. Two car seats, you know, double stroller, that kind of thing."

"I'm so sorry."

"You know what's weird?" Sabine said. "I never knew them, but I miss them. Or maybe I only miss the life I had imagined. I made that choice. It was my choice to end the pregnancy. I tell myself that it's for the best, that I could not have given them a good life. I tell myself I'll have other babies; life goes on. But it doesn't feel as though life is going on. It feels like life kind of stopped."

"Do you have friends who can support you?"

"I'm avoiding everyone. I can't keep up the effort of being witty or pleasant."

They were quiet for a long time. The waiter came and Sabine ordered a hot chocolate and Cassie a second espresso. There were new people inside. People came and went, never for long, here to have a cup of coffee, or a bite to eat, before resuming their workday, facing their problems: the café as a respite from the mini-traumas of life, the minutiae, the stress, the loneliness.

"Maybe you could take a break, go elsewhere," Cassie said. "Travel. Pretend to be someone else; I don't know. That or maybe have the space to think. Time to just digest this, instead of having to go on keeping on while you're feeling like this."

Sabine shook her head. "I don't think running away is the solution."

"It worked for me. At least temporarily."

Sabine looked at her watch. "I have to go back to work. Do you want to have dinner together?"

"Okay … I want to but I can't. Keep this to yourself, but I have sort of a date."

Sabine sat back in her seat and smiled. "A sort of a date or a date-date?"

"This man. I met him yesterday."

"Met him?"

"And what a meeting this was," Cassie said significantly, emphasizing the word meeting.

Sabine laughed. "How is that possible? You've only been here for two days!"

"He wants to see me tonight again. That's the incredible part. And, well, I need to run back to the hotel to make myself pretty with this." Cassie dug into her Monoprix bag and dangled below the table a demi-cup bra and matching panties, pearl grey with baby pink lace trims. "See? This is me pretending to be someone else."

"Put it on right now so that I can judge the full effect," Sabine said. "I cannot believe that you already have a lover!"

"Believe me, neither can I."

****

At seven-thirty in the evening, Cassie heard Hervé's Bonneville roar in the street below. She looked down from the balcony, and he looked up and waved to her. She rushed down the stairs to meet him. He was still sitting on the motorcycle. "What are we doing?" she asked.

"It should be a dry evening. Do you know where you'd like to eat?"

"Anywhere there is food. I'm starving."

"What? I could not hear," he said. "Come closer."

She stepped closer to him. "I was telling you—"

He interrupted her by extending his arm to bring her next to him. They kissed a fantastic kiss. "I could wait to eat," she said, already breathless.

"Is the Eiffel Tower still up there?" he asked lifting his chin toward her balcony.

"There is no way to know for sure. Unless we check."

He parked the motorcycle and fastened it quicker than she had ever seen him do it. Within minutes they were up in her room, and he was undressing her.

****

Two hours later they were on the motorcycle, zooming through Paris. Her body against Hervé's, she felt like mush as they drove past the Opera, down Boulevard des Capucines and rue Cambon, and around Place de la Concorde, then on rue de Rivoli and along the Parc des Tuileries toward Bastille. Paris was a swirl of lights.

He took her to dinner in a small wine bar, cozy and dark. They sat across a tiny table, their legs entangled. Dusty rows of bottles and a couple of locals were their only witnesses. Over oysters and Bordeaux, she told him about her time with Marceline at the Jardin du Luxembourg. She described the interaction with her mother, how the cross-examination had culminated in spitefulness on both sides. He listened to her, interrupting only for clarifications. She could not help but compare him to Peter. Peter never asked her how her day was; he told her how his went.

"So, this is how my father made it in one piece through World War II," she said. "He was in North Africa the whole time under a new identity. I am still waiting to find out why he chose to discard the Jewish part of his name, married a non-Jew, and broke off all relations with his mother, father, and sister."

"His mother and father made it out alive too?"

"Sadly, my grandfather died there."

"Of old age?"

"Probably. No, wait. He was born in 1902 and died in 1942. So, he must have been forty when he died."

"He died in 1942. In Algiers?"

"Yes."

"How?"

"I don't know yet."

"Wasn't there some military coup there? Ah, yes. That's it. The Allied forces liberated Algeria, Tunisia, and Morocco in 1942. It was a whole landing operation. The Germans never saw it coming. In retaliation they broke the agreement with Vichy and invaded the rest of France."

"How do you know this?"

"Bah, I read stuff."

"You're a good listener, you know."

"The quality of my listening skills depends entirely on the order of the evening. Had we had dinner first, I might have been distracted."

"I would not have lasted through dinner," she admitted.

He took her hand and kissed the inside of her wrist. "You and I are very compatible."

"I have noticed that."

"I like where this is going."

She cocked her head. "Where *is* this going?"

"I'm hoping for more of the same," he said. "Seeing you. I like you a lot."

She laughed. "Can we maintain this pace? When would we ever sleep?" Her mother's words rang in her ears. You're a liar. You've always been a liar. In her account of what had happened during the day, Cassie had been careful to leave out the humiliating time at the hospital. When Hervé asked her if she was planning on confronting her father, she had remained evasive. When he asked her what her kids were studying, she had left out the fact that they attended schools in New York and Miami. What had started as a harmless white lie by omission was beginning to look a lot like an elaborate scheme of deception. If there was a moment to come forward with the truth, it was now. "I … I want to tell you that I'm not … as available as…."

He pulled his hand away and frowned at her. "Is this the moment when you tell me that you are involved with someone else? Because let me tell you right now, I am not the kind of guy who has an affair behind someone's back." The interruption of the contact of his hand felt jarring, awful, an abrupt withholding of tenderness.

"No," she said, wounded. "I'm not involved with anyone." Hervé took her hand back, and she could breathe again.

"What are you afraid of then?"

She only had another five days in Paris according to her return ticket. That's what she was afraid of. If she told him this, the moment would be ruined. "Maybe it's just that this is all so very unlike me. I'm the mother of teenagers. This seems like something they should be doing. Not me."

"Aha, I see. A case of too much fun? Where does that come from?"

The truth. Any delay in telling the truth would make things worse and turn her into a deceitful person if she wasn't already one. And the truth was that there was no room for Hervé in her life. It was materially and logistically impossible, and he needed to know this. "It's just that, the way my life is at the moment, you and me…. It … complicates things."

"Cassandra," he interrupted, "I'm attracted to you. You appear to be attracted to me. It doesn't need to be a complicated thing."

"It's just that I don't think I will be in Paris … forever."

"Neither will I! Who's speaking of forever? There are a lot of places I'd rather be. Any place without desks, preferably somewhere without internet reception. A place where people know what matters. Somewhere closer to the essence of things. Anywhere would be better than Paris."

"The countryside?"

"I was thinking more in the vein of Southeast Asia, the Middle East. That's where I'm headed first chance I get."

She felt a hurt she had no right to feel. Here she was, afraid to push Hervé away by revealing that she lived in the United States when his future so clearly did not include her. "I hear India is incredible," she said.

But Hervé was telling her that there was one thing she could have right now, and that was lust. And golly, did lust sound good. And she was single. And he was single. And they were both adults. She'd be an idiot to mess this up, this little bit of magic that had just come into her life unannounced. Her sense of self had always been an unsolvable puzzle, with every layer of experience adding to the confusion. Was she French or American? Was she Christian or was she Jewish? Was she brave or afraid? Was she strong or weak? Was she talented or destined to remain in someone's shadow? Was she lovable or not? Should she not be able to know who she was by now?

But maybe because of her family's secrets and lies, pieces of the truth had been lost. And without them, the puzzle of who she was could never be solved. And as in a puzzle, everything was interconnected. Each piece recovered brought meaning to the next one: her father hiding his Judaism; Odile as the favorite daughter; her mother's silence; Sabine's hopelessness. What did this all mean when put together? And strange things were bubbling up to the surface. Intuitions about her marriage she had been reluctant to examine: Peter's rearranging of the truth; the increasingly suspect Jessica narrative. Disparate things now appeared as part of a cohesive whole. There had been rules and regulations in her life. There had been a system, a rigid one, put in place by herself for her own safety. But walls were crumbling. Control was escaping her. Revelations about how she should understand the world and herself were on the tip of her consciousness. And now there was Hervé, like a major upset in the order of things. She felt like a color-blind person allowed to see the blue of the sky and the green of forests for the very first time. She sensed tectonic shifts about to take place.

Cassie looked at Hervé and smiled. She had only a few more days in Paris, and she would need to fit another lifetime into those few days, carpe diem for all it was worth, because this was her shot at experiencing, for the first time, really, what it felt like to be a teenager. She raised her wine glass. "To an uncomplicated thing, then." Hervé reached across the table, took her hand, and kissed it, and she felt as though she was falling.

The End of *The Curator of Broken Things, Book 2.*

Book 3 of *THE CURATOR OF BROKEN THINGS* trilogy is available now as ebook and paperbacks.

Thank you for reading this book. If you enjoyed it, I hope you will consider reviewing it online.

I write for my readers and it is always a wonderful thing for me to receive emails and feedback, so don't be shy. Also, to receive bonus material such as historical details, prequels, characters' back stories, side stories, fun extended dialogues, and other insight into the Curator of Broken Things world, head over to my website www.corinegantz.com and sign up for the newsletter. I love to keep in touch and have a lot of material that didn't make it into the books.

Take care,
Corine.

ACKNOWLEDGEMENTS

Thank you to my first readers, Joanna Kamburoff, Katherine Kohler, Catie Jarvis, Peggy Schmouder, and Betsey Parlatore, for kindly and carefully sifting through versions of the books when they were still a mess. I am incredibly thankful to Donald Berman, a man with the soul of a writer, for his precision in English *and* French, and for his support for the novels. A great thank you to Lisa Yoo for her creative talent and expertise in design. Most of all, thank you to my husband Joe for his tireless editing, his honesty, his intuition, his kindness, his ebullient optimism, and for not wavering in his belief in me in the past 30 years.

ABOUT THE AUTHOR

Corine Gantz was born in France where she spent the first twenty years of her life. She studied Contemporary Art at the Sorbonne and worked in advertising and marketing in Paris, San Francisco, and Los Angeles. Her first novel, *Hidden in Paris*, was published in 2011 and has been translated in nine languages. She is the mother of two sons and lives near Los Angeles with her husband.

Email her:
corinegantz@live.com

Visit her website:
www.corinegantz.com

For information, email:
corinegantz@live.com
www.corinegantz.com

All rights reserved
Copyright © 2018 by Corine Gantz
The Curator of Broken Things Trilogy

Carpenter Hill Publishing

ISBN-13: 978-0-9834366-6-9
ISBN-10: 0-9834366-6-5

Proofreading and copyediting by Donald Berman
donaldberman@hotmail.com

COVER ART

Cover illustration by David Navas
www.davidnavas.com

Cover design by Lisa Yoo
www.yisaloo.info